George James Atkinson Coulson

The Clifton Picture

A novel

George James Atkinson Coulson

The Clifton Picture
A novel

ISBN/EAN: 9783337065034

Printed in Europe, USA, Canada, Australia, Japan

Cover: Foto ©Andreas Hilbeck / pixelio.de

More available books at **www.hansebooks.com**

THE CLIFTON PICTURE

A NOVEL.

BY THE AUTHOR OF "THE ODD TRUMP," "HARWOOD," "THE LACY DIAMONDS," "FLESH AND SPIRIT," ETC.

PHILADELPHIA:
J. B. LIPPINCOTT & CO.
1878.

PREFACE.

Some memories of personal adventure, some rude outlines of real character, and some fragments of Oriental superstition are here brought together to form The Clifton Picture. The colours have been applied at odd times, during brief pauses in a busy life, whose chief energies are employed in a far different field from the flowery domain of literature. No artistic arrangement of contrasts and harmonies, of lights and shadows, has been attempted. The recital of actual experiences, in former books, has once and again been attributed to the vagaries of fancy, and it is probable a similar criticism awaits the present volume. But the cases are rare in which an unknown writer has received such gentle treatment from readers and critics; and no one can be more profoundly sensible of this kind reception, nor more heartily grateful for it, than the author of the Odd Trump novels.

New York, *May* 13, 1878.

CONTENTS.

		PAGE
CHAPTER I.	The Photograph	7
II.	The Rayncfords	12
III.	Mr. Daltman	18
IV.	Mr. Glendare	23
V.	Miles	29
VI.	Mildred	35
VII.	The "Nellie"	40
VIII.	Knighthood	44
IX.	A Departure	49
X.	Haidee	54
XI.	The Soldiers	59
XII.	Annot	63
XIII.	Some Letters	69
XIV.	On the Sea	75
XV.	The Battle	82
XVI.	Robbery	88
XVII.	Annie Laurie	94
XVIII.	Insurmountable Obstacles	100
XIX.	At Hawkley	106
XX.	The Search Begun	112
XXI.	A New Enterprise	119
XXII.	The Mordaunts	125
XXIII.	Courting	131
XXIV.	Hardy's Story	137
XXV.	Fixing the Day	144
XXVI.	Fixed	150
XXVII.	Mr. Boston	156
XXVIII.	The Chase	163
XXIX.	Across Channel	170
XXX.	Fishing	177

PAGE

CHAPTER XXXI. At Bath.. 183
XXXII. The Picture.. 189
XXXIII. Sista.. 196
XXXIV. Disinterested Affections................................ 202
XXXV. The Start.. 209
XXXVI. A Proposal.. 215
XXXVII. The Abduction.. 221
XXXVIII. The Rescue.. 227
XXXIX. The Arrest.. 232
XL. Cross-Examined.. 239
XLI. Mr. Plimpton.. 245
XLII. The Meeting.. 251
XLIII. A Challenge.. 257
XLIV. Reunion.. 263
XLV. The Picture.. 269
XLVI. Mr. Dancer.. 275
XLVII. Hyland's Perplexities................................ 281
XLVIII. To Brentam Mills................................ 287
XLIX. The Will and Letters................................ 293
L. The Overcoat.. 299
LI. Tulwar and Picture................................ 305
LII. L'Envoi.. 311

THE CLIFTON PICTURE.

CHAPTER I.

THE PHOTOGRAPH.

WHEN the tide fills the bed of the Avon, Clifton Downs is one of the most pleasant localities in pleasant England. Twice in the day the channel is full, and from Bristol to St. Vincent's Rocks, you may find numbers of sea-going steamers passing up and down, and always attracting the attention of the loungers on the Downs and the Suspension bridge. There is a railway on each bank of the river, one of them connecting Clifton with a port at the head of Bristol Channel, passing through several miniature tunnels. From the high rocks on the north bank the trains slipping along the rails look like toy-carriages, and when passengers alight at the station they look like Liliputians, and the loungers above mentioned wonder how they will ever climb the rocks and so reach the level of the Downs.

Coming across the Suspension bridge in a pony-carriage, one of these loungers stops to watch the train, two hundred and fifty feet below him. A veritable lounger. Too indolent to drive, the reins are wrapped around the whip, and he manages the pony orally. He is twenty-five at least. A brown beard covers the lower part of his face, hiding his mouth, except at the corner, where a cigar parts his thick moustache. The train slides under the tunnel, emerges again, and stops at the station, while a dozen passengers alight.

" If those fellows would only stand still a moment," he mutters, " I'd take them. They look like a colony of ants swarming about down there. No use! Get along, Tommy!"

Tommy wagged his ears, and proceeded soberly onward. He knew the legal pace across the bridge. When he passed through the great portal on the Clifton side, he struck a trot, turned up towards the Observatory, and halted when he reached its base.

The gentleman alighted. You would not hesitate to give him

7

this title, as he stood there idly, under the August sun, in a vel-
veteen coat and felt hat.   He took a tripod from the carriage, then
a photographer's camera, placed it upon the tripod, and, peering
through, got the Observatory into focus.   He was quite deliberate
in his movements, and when he had arranged his apparatus, the
passengers had surmounted the two hundred and fifty feet, and some
of them were strolling over the Downs.   As he withdrew his head
from under the cloth that excluded the light from his instrument,
he noticed an obstruction between him and the Observatory.

A feminine obstruction, of course.

It was a girl who had just climbed the Zigzag.   Instead of going
to the hotel with her escort, she had left him to attend to the bestowal of luggage, and raced out to the Downs.   She had seen that
duck of a bridge three or four times while in the train, and life was
a burden until she stood upon it.   But she came to the Observatory
first, and paused to examine that structure.   How should she know
that the photographer was waiting?

He waited with exemplary patience, while she flitted across his
line and back again.   She wore a lilac-coloured dress, with delicate
little sprigs running over it, a straw hat, pushed backward, and a
shower of brown curls falling below it.   Rather a pretty child, he
thought.   So did Tommy, as she stopped her restless flitting a transient instant to pat his neck.   The photographer lighted a fresh
cigar, and was about to withdraw the slide of the camera, when she
suddenly darted into his "field" again.

There was a post standing near the Observatory, with a printed
placard upon it.   It was a gala-day in Clifton, and there were to be
fireworks at the gardens.   She was apparently absorbed in the
announcement of the festivities, as she stood with upturned face,
directly in the artist's way.

"Three-quarter face!" said he, "and still as a mouse.   I'll take
her!"   He withdrew the slide, and watching her narrowly, dropped
the cloth over the instrument before she moved.   That August sun
had settled her destiny in less than a minute.

He gathered up his implements and replaced them in his vehicle,
passing her with a grave bow.   She looked eagerly at him out of
startled gray eyes, bowed in return, and then walked sedately around
the Observatory.   When Tommy recrossed the bridge a few minutes
later, she was standing at the rail, looking down into Nightingale
Valley.   There are few lovelier views upon the surface of this planet.

"Not so young as I thought!" said the artist, as Tommy took

him past the graceful figure. "Eighteen, I fancy. I wonder how she took?" If he had known how intently she was watching him, he would have been less composed as he receded from her view.

Across the bridge and skirting the Valley. Up the hillside Tommy walking soberly. There was no law against trotting there, but the law of the summer sun. Arrived at last at the pretty little cottage where the photographer had rooms, Tommy stopped. He wanted some provender.

The artist had constructed a dark closet with boards and curtains, and this seriously reduced the area of his sitting-room. Into this den he entered, and performed all those mysterious operations by which photographic pictures are made presentable. Assuring himself that his picture was a success, there were some hours of necessary delay to be passed before the "negative" could be made positive. So, taking hat and cane, he started out for a walk before dinner.

Should he go back to the Downs, and try to get another sight of the girl? No! Bother the girl! Most likely he would never see her again. By-the-bye, he had her picture though! Now there were probably half a dozen fellows who would give any price he might please to ask for that picture. But he would not sell it. The Observatory was beautifully taken in the background. He would take it full size first, then he would take a small carte. Then he would obliterate the background, and take her in miniature for a locket.

With these thoughts in his mind, he strolled down the river bank. Two hours to spare. Pipe in his pocket. He would walk down to Hasper Head, three miles off, and smoke one pipe there. Then he would climb the hill and go back to dinner. Nothing attractive about the walk, but the view from Hasper Head was fine. A long stretch of the river, the cliffs on the other side, and probably a lot of vessels going up or down, as the tide was in.

There goes a schooner now, down stream! Fair wind and plain sailing. She will be in the channel in two hours. Now, it would be jolly to take a short cruise in such a trim-looking craft. And that reminded him of Frank Daltman again.

Frank had a yacht somewhere. He had invited him to join him in sundry cruises. That is, some time ago, before he took to vagabond-life. What would Frank think of him, if he knew he was photographing all creation and selling pictures? Bother Frank! He was a bad lot anyhow. Why did he think about him so much to-day?

Schooner abreast now. Hillo! she is tacking. There she goes—straight for the Clifton side. Tacking again! And now she lies head up stream. Surely, she is not going back! Anchored! by this light!

A boat lowered. Two men only, rowing ashore. Ah! the mystery is explained. There is a lady on the bank. And two men. They are carrying a large parcel between them. In the boat and back to the schooner. But the lady is not with them. Now the boat is hidden by the hull of the schooner. Ah! there they come, over the rail, still carrying the parcel. Anchor up. Now she swings round and off again.

Pipe out. There goes the lady up the cliff. She is a stunner to climb!

Spread out on the grass, peering over the face of the cliff, he can see the deck of the schooner as she passes below. That parcel is laid out on some shawls, and it seems to be vital! Schooner slipping away, but the parcel moves, and then a little white hand comes out and fumbles at the end of it. Hillo! what is up now?

The two men run up, wrap the parcel in the shawls, and, raising it from the deck, carry it to the companion-way. It is positively kicking now, for he can see the boots. But they blunder along, and at last get down the stairs. Then the stern of the schooner comes into view and he sees the name: "Ariadne, of Glasgow."

The climbing lady is atop of the opposite bank, and she is looking at him. Half a mile distant. He cannot distinguish her features, so, of course, she cannot distinguish his. He has a great mind to bow to her, but concludes he will not. He lies motionless. She stands like a statue. He might as well be asleep or dead, lying there in the sun. The schooner is turning the point below, and the man at the helm is waving a handkerchief. Shall he return the salutation? Never mind. The lady is doing it. And she slowly retires from the edge of the bank as the vessel disappears.

Now suppose he should get up and run down to the point for another glimpse of the schooner? Wait a moment. Perhaps that sharp-eyed lady will reappear. Sure enough! There she is. My lady, you came too soon. He does not move a muscle. For ten minutes she stands there watching him. There is a field-glass hanging on a peg in his cottage room. He would give ten pounds, now, for one look through it. He would like to know that lady, if he should ever meet her again.

She wore a little round straw hat, with a scarlet flower on one side. He could see the brilliant colour across the stream, as she stood motionless on the hill-top. How they glared at each other, each deploring the defects in human vision, and each wishing for the sharp eyes of the sea-gulls, that were flapping their leathern wings far above the surface of the Avon, yet ever and anon darting down after some floating waif on the river. By-the-bye, there must be a storm brewing, as the sea-birds were so far inland. The lady was a statue. The man was a log. And by some occult mental process he knew, when she finally retired, that she was coming to investigate him. She would walk up the north bank, cross the bridge, and walk down again on his side of the water.

As soon as the lady was hidden by the bank he arose and, throwing off his habitual indolence, walked swiftly back, reaching Nightingale Valley before the lady could possibly reach the bridge. Could he reach the cottage before she crossed? Risky! So he plunged into the covert and waited.

Here she comes, by this light! The round hat with the scarlet flower. Walking rapidly, yet with stately grace. Glancing around her as she passed, he got a good view of her face, not ten yards distant. Her full lips, slightly compressed, her soft blue eyes, full of placid watchfulness and suggesting the idea of unyielding determination, and over all her exterior that unmistakable high-bred appearance that cannot be simulated and cannot be hidden. You would not think of calling her pretty, but you would think of Cleopatra, Zenobia, and other historic names of warlike women. When the turn of the road hid her, the photographer emerged from his hiding-place and resumed his walk. Reaching the cottage, he sat down to meditate while he smoked. And when the sun disappeared and the nightingale in the valley began his evening song he called his landlady.

"Mrs. Noils," he said, "please take care of Tommy for a few days. I am called, or rather sent, somewhat suddenly to—to another part of the country."

CHAPTER II.

The Raynefords.

HAWKLEY had belonged to the Raynefords for twenty generations. It is an old stone house in good repair, and the wall
on the eastern side has two or three dents in it, made by Cromwell's
cannon-balls. These are historic marks, and are carefully preserved,
to illustrate the story of Miles Rayneford, who was besieged there
by Roundheads in the olden time. He was the last warrior of the
race, and died, sword in hand, just within his own threshold. His
son was stricken down by his side, sorely wounded, but was well
nursed by Mistress Hildah Martin, whose father, a grim old Puritan,
was left in charge of Hawkley after the battle. The war drifted
away from the county, and young Miles Rayneford was forgotten
by everybody except pretty Mistress Hildah. And when peace
came, under the Commonwealth, and old Martin died, Miles married his gentle nurse and the next generation were Presbyterians.
Father Martin left enough worldly wealth to cover all defects in
his genealogy, and the Restoration found Miles Rayneford a portly
gentleman with two sons, who affected agricultural occupations, and
scorned the frivolities of the court. And as England grew more
and more corrupt in morals and manners, the Raynefords became
more and more unfashionable, inheriting an honoured name, maintaining a spotless reputation, but losing caste among the gentry of
the neighbourhood, who came to talk of the Raynefords of Hawkley
as an old race that had died out or been supplanted by a succession
of humdrum country 'squires, that were more than half Dissenters
at heart.

But the Raynefords regained caste two generations ago. There
came a certain Miles Rayneford (for they kept up the name of the
last cavalier, whose sword hung over the mantel in the great dining-
room), and he was learned in the law, and won high honours in Parliament, and finally died Lord Rayneford of Hawkley. His son,
the second Baron, married the daughter of the Earl of Hyland,
with a good fortune in her own right, a large part of which he
managed to spend, leaving her a widow with two sons, Miles and
Hyland, an encumbered estate to be inherited by Miles, third Lord
Rayneford, and about a thousand pounds a year of her original
dower, which went to her second son, Hyland Rayneford, when she
took her place by the side of her lord in Hawkley churchyard.

And as the early manhood of these two gentlemen was attained in the proximate past, the present history is concerned with them and their fortunes.

The brothers had spent their early lives together. They were at Eton together, and chewed the same Greek roots side by side. But two years after he reached his majority, Hyland, impulsive, restless, and obstinate, took service with the East India Company, and sailed for Calcutta to "lose his liver or gain a lac," as he expressed it. It was a sore trial to Miles, who was fond of the wayward boy; but his affectionate remonstrance availed nothing, and Hyland left his native land brimful of pluck and energy, and confident of success in rupee-hunting. His thousand pounds a year he thought was only modified penury, but he wisely resolved to leave his capital in three per cents, and live within his income. His modest ambition—for he was only twenty-three—was to secure a revenue of twenty thousand a year, and then rest from his labours.

"You know, Miles," he said, as they stood apart on the deck of the big ship, slowly following the snorting little tug down the Thames—"you know a fellow cannot dawdle through life with no object before him. I must make a little money out of John Company before I get too old."

"You have money enough now, Hyland," replied his brother. "You are richer than I, although I am lord of Hawkley."

"Lord Rayneford, Miles," said Hyland, "your name is better than money. And if you will take it, I will give you half of mine. I shall be no poorer, for I don't count my thousand a year as anything. I am going to live on my salary out yonder."

"Well, come back with me, Hyland," replied Lord Rayneford, "and I will live economically, and you and I together will work to clear the old place. I will promise not to marry, so you will be Lord Rayneford when I die."

"'England expects every man to do his duty,' brother," said Hyland. "You will be obliged to marry. Young noblemen are not allowed to lie about loose in this country. I know six mammas this moment who have designs upon you. Ah! old Miles, I think if I were Lord Rayneford I would die when I assumed the title! Nobody in the wide world but you, Miles!" and he turned aside a moment to hide his emotion; "and if you were to die, all the wide world would be dead to me!"

"And yet you leave me, Hyland."

"Tut! What is a journey to Calcutta in these days? Why, we

shall hear from each other every week. Let me go, Miles, just to look at the country, and kill a tiger, and ride on an elephant, and learn to swear in Hindoostanee. If the field is not promising I'll come back to you. Hillo! there's the last bell. Good-bye, brother!"

Now these young gentlemen, so open and truthful, had each been carefully concealing from the other certain sentiments which modified the distress of their first separation.

Two miles from Hawkley a retired manufacturer had erected a villa. It was not gorgeous, but was large and well appointed. Mr. Brentam had made his fortune by twenty years of diligent work in iron founderies and forges, and while he withdrew from all active participation in commercial affairs, he still retained shares in various works, and was a director in two or three that were near Hawkley. He was a busy man, always foremost in charitable enterprises, and always prompt to join in schemes for the promotion of workingmen's interests. At Brentam Mills, he had a village of model cottages, all constructed under his personal supervision, and all inhabited by thriving families. For a wonder, he was totally indifferent about his status in the neighbourhood, and for a second wonder, the "good families" did not turn up their noses at him. He was a widower and childless, but he had a nephew, Frank Daltman, and a niece, Mildred Carey. These were orphan children of his sisters, and they were more troublesome to him than all his wealth.

Place aux dames. Mildred Carey was two years younger than her cousin, and at the date of Hyland's departure was the acknowledged belle of the county. Her father was a member of one of the "county" families, who had married Miss Brentam because she was a shareholder in Brentam Mills, a corporation which paid good dividends. Mr. Carey was constitutionally impecunious, but his brother-in-law secured the inheritance of Mildred in the marriage settlement, and when she was orphaned, and removed to her uncle's house, it was vaguely understood in the neighbourhood that she was an heiress of respectable dimensions. The girl was educated at expensive schools, was very much of a lady, a little haughty, a trifle self-willed, but a very general favourite. Of course, all the young gentlemen of the neighbourhood, eligible and otherwise, adored Miss Carey. But the most ardent of her admirers was Lord Rayneford, who was living a life of agony under the conviction that Mildred manifested a decided preference for his younger brother, Hyland.

Hyland, who was not the least bit of a coxcomb, had gradually reached the same conclusion. And the most curious feature in this triangular involvement was the fact that Hyland was the solitary youth in the charmed circle of which Mildred was the centre who did not surrender to her attractions. He knew that Miles was a silent worshipper of this goddess, though no words ever passed between the brothers to reveal the true state of their feelings. Miles was jealous because he was madly in love, and he constantly suspected his brother of hypocrisy, when Hyland's indifference to Mildred's charms was most manifest. And Hyland, generous and considerate, forbore to utter his sentiments touching Mildred's haughtiness and obstinacy, lest he should pain his brother. Somehow, these three were continually playing at cross-purposes. Mildred was incensed, while Hyland stood aloof, she thinking he had detected her liking for him, and therefore becoming more haughty and distant to Lord Rayneford, because she imagined that the brothers discussed her, and their relative chances of winning her. Miles would not believe that any man could be in the society of his idol without yielding homage, and therefore concluded his brother's coolness a pretense, which was the more galling because he suspected Hyland of sacrificing his own inclinations for his sake. And Hyland, slow to discover his own attractiveness of mind and person, was in a state of chronic instability, under the impression that Miss Carey had resolved to bring him to her feet for the mere purpose of "throwing him over" as soon as he should essay serious courtship. No such purpose was in his thought. The youth was a motive-hunter. He spent his life in investigating the springs of human action, and at twenty-two he thought he had mastered many of the most inscrutable problems of mental and moral philosophy. The philosophy that was fashionable in his day was a queer mixture of the theories of Zeno, Epicurus, Chrysippus, and their modern disciples, Hobbes, Mill, and Auguste Comte. It was compact and portable, and it could all be summed up in one or two postulates: First. Nothing is good except that which gives pleasure. Second. No motive can influence humanity except the desire for pleasure, or, its converse, the repugnance to pain. Consequently all those sentiments that presuppose disinterested beneficence are a delusion or a sham. And if the reader will extract anything more or greater from the separate or united teachings of the worthies above enumerated, he or she is in a fair way to square the circle.

With this budding philosophy filling his mind, and charming

him by constantly recurring proofs of the innate selfishness of humanity, Hyland was not fitted to play the lover. And if he had been, Mildred was not the woman to awaken tender emotions in his soul. Her accomplishments amused and entertained him, and he enjoyed her society until he discovered in her a pronounced preference for his, and then, seeking her motives with no better light than Positivism could furnish, he coolly decided that she wanted a new conquest to gratify her vanity. The youth had not learned that the vast chambers of a woman's mind could not be explored by so feeble a glimmer!

So Hyland promptly caught at the opportunity for escape when the Calcutta appointment was offered. He had been conscious of the subdued jealousy of Miles, and as he knew no more eligible admirer than Lord Rayneford was seeking her favour, he was the more eager to give his brother a clear field by retiring himself. All this he kept secret when they were parting and afterwards.

And Lord Rayneford also, who did not wear his heart upon his sleeve, drew some comfort from similar reflections, as he watched the ship that bore Hyland away passing down the river. He was not afflicted with Hyland's philosophy, and concluded that his brother would never entertain matrimonial plans while his revenue was so limited. And therefore, he was going to India, to burn out the tender emotions under her tropical skies. So, being a quiet man and sensitive to a degree, he had not spoken of Mildred at all in his later colloquies with Hyland.

The Raynefords had been two weeks in London before Hyland's departure. The appointment was offered by a friend of Hyland's father, at whose house they were dining, and accepted on the instant. The duties would be easy enough—chiefly literary work, some civil engineering, and a good deal of drawing, which was specially attractive to Hyland, who had a *penchant* for art.

"The salary is not large," observed Mr. Plimpton; "but three hundred pounds will pay your expenses, Hyland. And if you take to India life, there are numerous chances of promotion out there."

"It is more than I am worth," said Hyland, in reply; "and my conscience will compel me to serve John Company diligently to earn the three hundred. I'll stick at it until I master the lingo, anyhow."

When Lord Rayneford returned to Hawkley, he found the news of his brother's departure had preceded him. Hyland was a general favourite, and Miles received many congratulations upon his brother's good fortune, and was entertained with many predictions of his success. Miss Carey, who was too self-possessed to manifest any emotion, received Hyland's parting messages with great politeness and composure. But she was a good deal chagrined to find nothing in these last words, faithfully repeated by Miles, beyond the ordinary farewells of an ordinary acquaintance.

"How long will Mr. Rayneford be absent?" she enquired.

"He says," replied Lord Rayneford, "that he will stay until he makes a lac of rupees. I thought, at the time, he meant silver rupees, but it just occurs to me that he may have intended to say *gold* rupees. If he did——"

"Well?"

"If he meant gold rupees," continued Miles, slowly, "I don't think he will ever return! Money don't grow in the jungles! And Hyland is such a determined fellow when he makes up his mind, that he will not relinquish his purpose on account of difficulties."

"He will meet Frank there," observed Miss Carey; "I mean my cousin, Frank Daltman. When you write you might send him a letter from Uncle Brentam. I will write to Frank also."

"Thanks! You are very kind. I thought Mr. Daltman was at the Cape?"

"His regiment was ordered to Calcutta, recently," replied Miss Carey. "By-the-bye, your brother never met him. I remember he told me so, a few weeks ago. Did you go to the Crystal Palace? Of course! you were two weeks in London. How beautiful the Victoria Regia is! Ah! that reminds me. You have not seen our rhododendrons! They are in full bloom. Will you walk in the garden?"

When Lord Rayneford rode home that evening, he thought Mildred had been so remarkably kind that he must be growing in favour. Since he had received his inheritance he had been diligently economizing, as he had resolved to remove the encumbrances that burdened it and reduced his revenues. Like Hyland, he was "a determined fellow," and he resisted all temptation to spend, and had already made some decided reduction in the indebtedness of the estate. And that evening he pondered over rent-rolls and mortgages, and calculated how much longer he must wait before he could ask Miss Carey to become Lady Rayneford.

And Mildred, at the same hour, was saying to herself that she would unbend to my lord more graciously than was customary, as he would be sure to have the earliest news of Hyland, in whose career she felt a decided interest.

2

CHAPTER III.

Mr. Daltman.

MR. HYLAND RAYNEFORD, who affected utter scorn of the theory that gave special privileges to men of gentle birth, was, nevertheless, received with favour into the best society in Calcutta, as the scion of a noble house and heir-apparent to a title. The only brother of the bachelor Lord Rayneford was a welcome visitor in all the English families resident in the Indian city. His official duties, in the service of the Honourable East India Company, had a semi-political character, and the young army-officers received him with open arms. It therefore happened that he had established very intimate relations with Lieutenant Frank Daltman long before the tardy mails brought the credentials referred to in the previous chapter.

There was not much in common between these young gentlemen either. Hyland did not scruple to avow his purpose to earn and save money to add to his scanty patrimony. Mr. Daltman, on the contrary, who was passably affluent, was chiefly interested in devising methods whereby he could get rid of his superfluous cash. There were sundry amicable contests between them, growing out of this difference. Rayneford constantly declined joining in expensive amusements, refusing urgent and cordial invitations to parties in which no outlay was required of him, upon the ground that he did not intend reciprocal entertainments, and was uncomfortable under a sense of obligation.

"The truth is, Frank," he said one day, at the close of such a debate, "I am set upon a single purpose, and I must have a good lot of money if I accomplish it. If I had not this purpose in view, I should be as reckless a spendthrift as yourself. I want twenty thousand pounds, and when I get that much, and spend it—for I mean to spend it—I shall give up my miserly habits."

"You must be after a regular estate," said Daltman. "What do you intend to buy with twenty thousand pounds?"

"Ah!" said Hyland, "that is a secret. It would not interest you. Don't you know every fellow has a separate object?"

"Except when two fellows want the same charming angel."

"And even then there is a difference. One fellow will want her money, and the other will admire her beauty, or her wit, or her rank."

"But I mean," said Daltman, "when two fellows are really in love, you know. Regular spoony. No sham, but genuine, heart-breaking love."

"Well," rejoined the philosopher, after a pause, "love has all the elements I have mentioned. Some fellows will love a pretty face, and others a good rent-roll. You are not silly enough to believe in any such stuff as 'disinterested affection,' or the kind of humbug you read in novels?"

"I don't know," answered Daltman, doubtfully. "I thought there might be something of the sort in nature. But I have had no experience in the spoony line. Now, holding your sentiments, I don't see why you can't take your twenty thousand with an incumbrance."

"What sort of incumbrance?"

"A wife! You can get a wife with the requisite quantity of tin——"

"But that would be *her* tin," replied Hyland. "Many thanks for the suggestion, but it will not do. I want twenty thousand of my own."

"Yes," said Daltman, "the settlements would be a bore. But you might find an angel with a liberal father, who would not tie the tin up too tightly. Now, I am not going into the matrimonial business until I find a damsel with ten thousand a year; and I intend to direct the expenditures too. And in order to do this I must find a damsel who has property in her own right, and who will not come to my loving arms encumbered with a burglar-proof and husband-proof lot of settlements. You need not look so shocked! The only difference between me and all those other fellows is that I don't mind telling the truth."

"Well," said Hyland, after a pause, "there is nothing in your sentiments that contradicts true philosophy. But I must reflect upon it before I can commend your plans. I suppose there must be a difference between marrying a wife and buying a horse, or I could not recoil so promptly from the mere statement of your scheme. I will investigate, and give you my conclusion to-morrow. I must consult some authorities."

Hyland kept a diary. This was not so much a record of events as a record of his wise conclusions. After the conversation above written he made the following entry:

"Had a discussion with Frank Daltman to-day that has set me to thinking. He openly avows his purpose to marry a woman with money, for the sake of the money. And I am perplexed to account for my instinctive contempt for such a scheme, and for the man who can construct it. Because I see so many examples of just such meanness, if I may so term it, that Frank differs from other men only in his bold avowal. I thought I had reduced motive to its last analysis, and had demonstrated that pure selfishness was pure philosophy. And now I must objectivise the subjective, and analyse my prompt recoil.

"First, by way of introduction: Can I marry for money?

"No! a thousand times no! Tentatively: maxim first.—One can never safely distrust one's instincts. Because instincts are either moral or sentimental, and therefore cannot be subjected to the tests applied to material phenomena. I refer, of course, to human instincts, which are (perhaps) the faculties that cognise prerequisites.

"I instinctively recoil from Frank's principle. That is to say: some inexorable law dominates my mental organism that does not hamper Frank. It must be a law. For I cannot debate the proposition any more than I could debate a proposition that involved falsehood or dishonesty. I simply refuse to entertain the idea. Things that equal the same thing equal each other.

"Analysis: Marrying for money involves both falsehood and dishonesty. No man tells the heiress that he wants her money. No such case of courting is on record. The suitor addresses personal charms, mental endowments, moral beauties. If Frank told the truth he would say: 'You have twenty thousand pounds, and I desire to possess it, therefore marry me.' It is not probable that he will make his approaches in this fashion. And if he does not he will lie. No English gentleman can lie.

"Conclusion: No English gentleman can marry for money."

Hyland left his diary at this point. He was satisfied that he had mastered the difficulties of the case, and when he dropped in at Daltman's bungalow the next day, he was prepared to show his friend the nature of the obstacles to his scheme.

He found Daltman spluttering defective Hindostanee to two native servants, who were busily employed in packing some valises, strapping up a gun-case, and making other preparations for a move.

"Good news, Rayneford!" said Frank; "my company is going into the hill country—to Nuttagur station, in fact."

"Nuttagur?" answered Hyland; "that is the new Sanitarium."

"Exactly. The major says you are to go also. Have you received your orders?"

" No."

" Well, it's all right. Civil engineering, sketching, and all that sort of thing. The major goes also. You will have a jolly time. No military rules or duties, and plenty of girls to flirt with. The Mordaunts are there, you know."

" The Mordaunts?"

" Yes. Two charming ladies. Heiresses expectant. You and I will toss up for the choice. Their chances are equal, and the old gentleman is on his last legs."

" You may take them both," replied Hyland; " I have thought over the matter, and reached a conclusion."

Daltman drew up a camp-stool, which he handed to his visitor, coolly kicked over a native, who was squatting on a refractory valise that refused to be locked, turned it up endwise, and sat on it. He then produced two cheroots, lighting one and handing the other to Rayneford.

" Now, then," he said, " fire away! What is your conclusion?"

" An English gentleman cannot marry for money," said Hyland.

" Why do you restrict the prohibition to Englishmen?"

" Because French gentlemen seem to marry in no other way," replied Hyland; " I have not clearly decided whether or not their marriages are proper. I may investigate that point another time. But it is a clear case that an Englishman of good breed cannot honourably court a girl English fashion for the sake of her money."

" I understand!" ejaculated Daltman, after puffing at his cheroot in silent meditation a few minutes; " you object to the love-making and all that sort of thing. Why, my dear fellow, it is just like ' my dear sir,' and ' yours truly,' in epistolary communications. They don't mean anything. They don't deceive anybody. Now, these French beggars go through a lot of ceremony just like ours, with the difference in idiom. The suitor visits the lady with the most elaborate formality and solicits the honour of an interview. The lady tells him to give himself the pain of sitting down. The gentleman bows twice, takes a seat, and informs the object of his affections that he is desolated until he can bestow himself, his box at the opera, his chateau, and his Paris house upon her. The lady expresses herself as charmed with the prospect, and begs to refer him to monsieur, her papa. But we English don't go through all that humbug exactly, though we do a different sort of humbug. We get spoony, and read up poetry to quote, and scorn all mercenary considerations. But in both cases, all the parties interested weigh the matter in business fashion. The mammas or papas settle the business, and the rest is all ceremony."

"But what do you offer in exchange for the money?" persisted Hyland; "I cannot see an equivalent."

"Equivalent! Come, now, that's cool! Don't a fellow give up his liberty? A respectable Englishman is obliged to become a galley slave when he marries. He must take his wife to balls and operas. He must dine and sleep at home. He must go to church. He must subscribe to all sorts of charities——"

"And pay his subscriptions with his wife's money," interrupted Hyland.

"Of course! That is the worst part of the business. The revenues are diverted from their natural channels. It is matrimony that entails expense. Matrimony means an establishment, and all sorts of outlays unknown to bachelors. In fact, the married man is only his wife's banker."

"With a liberal percentage allowed for his disbursements," said Hyland. "You have not made out your case, Daltman. You cannot marry a woman for money. You cannot sell a spavined horse as sound."

"I've known some very respectable people to do that same," muttered Daltman.

"Doubtless!" responded Hyland; "but *you* cannot gain your own consent to follow in their respectable footsteps. You may sell any portable property you possess, except your self-respect. If I were to marry a rich woman," he continued, growing more earnest as he proceeded, "it would be under the pressure of most extraordinary circumstances, and I would never rest until I had settled her entire estate upon herself!"

"I should like to hear some rational argument in support of your theory," said Daltman; "all you have said might point a moral or adorn a tale—I mean a novel, you know—but none of that sort of bosh will go down in real life. I challenge you to produce a solitary case in English society that will illustrate such unmitigated humbug! Usually, you have some philosophical formula wherewith to enforce your conclusions. Propound one here. Formulate!"

Hyland recalled to mind his recorded philosophy of the previous day, and was about to present his major proposition, when the door opened and a strange gentleman entered. He was a tall, slender man, about thirty, pale and emaciated, and looked more feeble as he supported himself with a stout cane, while he shuffled into the room.

Hyland arose, and offered his camp-stool to the new-comer, who accepted the seat with a courteous gesture.

He was apparently exhausted by the effort at locomotion, and sat quietly fanning himself with his hat, while Hyland stood by, furtively studying his placid countenance. Daltman arose and took the stranger's hat, substituting a palm-leaf fan.

"Rayneford," said Daltman, "I am delighted to introduce my friend, Mr. Glendare. You fellows should know each other, as you are both afflicted with very similar forms of lunacy. You are insane on the marriage question, and Glendare has nearly killed himself in the effort to convert a lot of these rascally Hindoos, under the auspices of the Missionary Society. I believe he is regular, though, representing the Church of England in this heathen land. Mr. Hyland Rayneford, Glendare, a brother of Lord Rayneford of Hawkley."

The gentlemen shook hands. Hyland noted the firm grip of the slender fingers, and the glance of intelligent appreciation, as the missionary's eyes met his. They were clear, blue eyes, full of expression, in spite of his physical feebleness, and in spite of the spectacles that covered them. He wore a full beard, black and silky, and the most prominent thought in Hyland's mind was the memory of an old proverb, which he had heard in his boyish days:

> "Black beard and blue eyes,
> Very weak or very wise."

"In this instance," said Hyland to himself, "I will wager a trifle that the weakness is physical only. The philosophy that might stun Daltman will make no impression on Mr. Glendare!"

CHAPTER IV.

MR. GLENDARE.

"I INTERRUPTED a discussion by my entrance," said Mr. Glendare. "I overheard Frank's bold challenge as I stood at the door. Pray go on with it, while I recover my breath. This is my first walk, Mr. Rayneford, after a compulsory rest of six weeks." There was a crisp accuracy of accent and intonation observable in his short speech that gave Hyland some other pieces of information.

"Scottish!" he thought, "because no other nationality can produce such crisp sentences. The great gentleness in his tones is due to the piety. These missionary gentlemen must have an extraordinary quantity of piety to fit them for their work, and keep them at it, especially in India."

"You do not look very vigourous," Hyland answered. "I suppose your six weeks of 'rest,' as you call it, was enjoined by the doctor?"

"Yes," said Daltman; "regular fever—jungle fever, no doubt, as Mr. Glendare took no end of pains to catch it. It would have killed any other than a Caledonian. But he is not through yet. He is ordered to the hill country, and will follow us—how soon, Hamish?"

"I hope to accompany you," answered Mr. Glendare.

"We start to-morrow," said Daltman, "an hour before sunrise. I should say you could not possibly go with us if I had not known you to undertake and accomplish greater impossibilities."

"The undertaking is not so formidable. Colonel Mordaunt says we shall go by easy stages. There are two companies of infantry to go."

"Well," answered Daltman, "you can travel 'en prince' in a palanquin——"

"Not I," replied the invalid. "I am going on horseback until I gather strength to walk. The doctor says two or three days will set me up. But I desire to hear your debate. When you say 'formulate' I know there is a debate on the tapis. Recommence, I beg you."

"I shall need your aid, Mr. Glendare," observed Hyland; "Frank has enunciated certain heretical doctrines relating to matrimony, and, as I hold opposite views, he challenges me to a controversy."

"Formulate!" reiterated Daltman; "fire away, both of you! I engage to defeat your antiquated notions with a little common sense, and an appeal to universal experience. Open the ball, Rayneford!"

"An English gentleman cannot marry for money," said Hyland.

"That sounds like a quotation from the tables in the Prayer-book —'a man cannot marry his grandmother.' But I beg pardon. Hamish, do you endorse Rayneford's postulate?"

"Allow me to moderate the session," said Mr. Glendare; "perhaps I will give the casting vote. You have the floor. Answer Mr. Rayneford."

"The answer is easy," replied Daltman, contemptuously: "Englishmen *do* marry for money every week in the year, excepting the Lenten season, perhaps."

"I do not contradict you," said Hyland. "I meant to say, an English gentleman who marries for money violates his honour. He obtains a wife under false pretences. He professes certain sentiments which he does not really entertain. He asserts a preference for one woman over all other women in the world, when in reality his attachment is to her bank-book. He therefore violates the truth."

"You have a very bald way of stating things," said Daltman. "This marrying business is not like ordinary affairs. Sentiments! Pooh! Of course a fellow is expected to profess a lot of sentiments, but they do not deceive, and are not intended to deceive, anybody. Under strict analysis they all fall into the same category of conventional usage, which requires politeness from a gentleman, even when he is about to cut another fellow's throat. Now, when you marry a woman you give her the worth of her money. You give her your name, your protection, a certain place in society which she could not reach as a spinster. Mrs. Frank Daltman would be a welcome guest in a score of houses which she could never enter as Miss Snooks, if she had forty thousand pounds at her back. Bless you! she knows what she gets for her money. Sentiments! Of course! You are miserable except when in her society. You think of her all day, and dream of her all night. All that humbug is part of the game. It is just like 'your obedient servant' at the end of a letter."

"Do you keep up the delusion after marriage?" said Hyland.

"Yes! that is, to a certain extent. You are not expected to be spoony beyond the honeymoon, but you must keep up the ordinary civilities of life. The money is now in joint ownership. The style in which it enables you to live is a part of Madame's life, as well as yours. Mrs. Daltman expects Mr. Daltman to frequent expensive clubs, and to indulge in many little elegancies which were denied in his bachelorhood. Mr. Daltman takes Madame to the opera, to the Continent, to the Nile——"

"And provides a maid to wait upon her, paying her wages from Madame's revenues. It is a sorry sort of business, Frank. I shall argue with you no longer. You sneer at sentiments, and your prematrimonial profession of them is hypocrisy. I cannot conceive how a man that ever had a mother can hold such utterly selfish theories regarding women. And I tell you, frankly, that I am sorry for Mrs. Daltman in advance."

Mr. Daltman laughed.

"If Mr. Rayneford relinquishes the cudgel," said Mr. Glendare, in soft accents, "I think I shall take it up."

"Formulate!" responded Daltman, defiantly.

"Mr. Rayneford's proposition was too broad," continued the missionary, "or he would have made a stronger argument."

"State it in your own fashion," replied Daltman; "only don't draw your arguments from the Prayer-book. I want a philosophical statement."

"Well," said Mr. Glendare, gently, "there are two sorts of philosophy. One is the sort taught by Zeno, Epicurus, and other worthies of antiquity, and this has recently come into fashion again, with some slight modifications. The other is the philosophy of Christian nations, and is more or less in accordance with the doctrines of Revelation. The main difference between the two, as I apprehend, is in the acceptance or rejection of the doctrine of a personal Deity, who has created, and therefore governs."

"Ah!" said Daltman, "let us confine ourselves to civilized society. You cannot inveigle me into the misty regions of Epicurian philosophy! There you would be at home, no doubt, while I only remember with a shudder my youthful explorations in that direction when they were compulsory. I only meant to object to 'goody' talk. It is all right in church, you know, but Rayneford has not made his fight on moral grounds."

"I think he has," replied Mr. Glendare. "His main point, indeed his only point, relates to the obligation to tell the truth. You cannot get along very well, Frank, without dipping a little into moral philosophy."

"Sail on, then," said Daltman, discontentedly. "I promise to listen politely anyhow."

Mr. Glendare laughed. "I am not going to preach, so do not look so woebegone. The doctor has forbidden preaching for three months. If I had only to draw my arguments from Holy Writ, you would be utterly demolished by a few quotations."

"Go on with your moral philosophy," replied Daltman; "I am curious to see how you will mix it up with matrimony."

"Well, then, give heed," said the missionary. "All obligations that affect intelligent creatures are founded upon Relations. Because of the Relations subsisting between God and man, as Creator and crea-

ture, man is bound to serve and honour God. Because of the brotherhood of the race, man is bound to conserve the interests of his
brother man. This is the foundation postulate. These obligations
are modified and augmented by the variations in the Relations. If
God is recognized not only as a Maker, but also as a Father, you
see how much more urgently the obligation to obedience and reverence presses upon the child. And if the mere brotherhood of race
is elevated into blood-kinship, you see how much more emphatic the
obligation to kindness between the children of one household."

" All that is rational!" quoth Daltman, as Mr. Glendare paused.

" These are natural obligations," continued the missionary; " they
are not confined to Christendom or to civilized society. The authority of the Father is recognised among savage tribes. The Carib
jealously guards the decaying bones of his ancestry, which is a proof
of the universality of the law, because the Carib manifests scarcely
any other glimmer of moral sense. And it is the indestructible fragment of the original Law written upon the Nature of Man at creation. Because the Fatherhood of Man is but the shadow of the
universal Fatherhood of God.

" Concerning the obligations that affect human society merely,
you will not deny the superior claims of brotherhood over mere
neighbourhood. The sons of one father are more to each other than
mere acquaintances and friends."

" Certainly!" responded Frank. " All that you have said is on
my side of the argument. A fellow is justified in marrying a rich
woman, because he will be more able to help his family out of her
revenues."

" I have not quite concluded," said Mr. Glendare, gently; " there
are other relations, involving other obligations."

" Ah, well," replied Daltman, " I did not intend to interrupt you.
Pray excuse me and proceed."

" Somehow it has come to pass," said Glendare, after a brief pause,
" that the marriage relation is understood to involve more intimacy
—a greater identity of interest, than any other. The current idea
in civilized society affixes to this relation such closeness of union
as does not attach, for instance, to the relation subsisting between
mother and child. Whenever this identity of interest is lacking,
somehow the common idea of humanity regards the union of husband
and wife as a sham or a fraud."

" Plenty of such cases," ejaculated Frank, "among my personal
acquaintances."

"No doubt!" replied Mr. Glendare, "and I dare say you have thought in your lucid intervals that these cases were a mere caricature of marriage?"

"Well, yes!" said Daltman; "a fellow would be a jolly fool to get into a mess of that sort. My loose notions of matrimony, as Rayneford calls them, do not include anything indecorous. I only object to putting spoons in the place of money. Spoons are not objectionable, of course, provided the revenues are all right; but spoons are poor substitutes for pounds, shillings, and pence."

"You bring me to the culmination," replied the missionary; "I instanced the current judgment of society, because such judgment is usually founded upon truth. There must be in all true marriages such an identity as can only exist between one man and one woman. That is: they must both be fully persuaded that no other being in the wide universe is so dear as the life partner. It has never seemed to me that the exhortations to mutual forbearance, to mutual self-denial, to mutual patience were decorous. Because the interests are identical, and it has always seemed like exhorting a man to make his eyes direct his hands. If man and wife are not one in such a measure of unity as attaches to no other relation—then they are two separate monsters."

"That is all very fine," said Daltman, "but what has it all to do with the argument?"

"Only this. Mr. Rayneford's postulate stated that an English gentleman could not marry for money. My conclusion is: that no man can marry for *anything* except the inexorable demand of his soul, that craves the companionship of one elect woman out of all the women on earth. He cannot choose between two women, if he is a true man; indeed, it is not a matter of choice at all. It is only the cognition of the fact that he has found the predestined partner of his life. It is a cognition through the God-given faculty of intuition, irrespective of argument, motive, or appeal. He *loves* her. It is not the sort of stuff that you call 'spoons.' It is the earnest conviction of his soul that she must be his wife, or his entire life must be a blank. In so far as the purpose of God in his creation terminates upon sublunary things—he feels that he was created for the solitary purpose of protecting, defending, comforting this one woman. All other human obligations are subsidiary. And finally, in Holy Writ, this relation is invested with such awful sanctity, that it is the one relation constantly selected to illustrate the union of the Redeemer and the redeemed. And the sins of Apostasy and

Idolatry are constantly represented as violations of the marriage covenant. So the common sentiment of men among the wisest and the best, and the revealed decree of God, unite in placing the marriage relation in the front rank among all the relations of earth. It would be more rational for you to say you would not accept a mother unless she were rich, than to say you would not accept a wife until you knew the extent of her rent-roll. You may make a legal contract, binding you to give your name to a woman, and to live with her as husband and wife—but except upon the conditions I have stated, you will not only dishonour yourself as an English gentleman, but you will deny and degrade your manhood! There is the noon gun! Mr. Rayneford, you are going my way. May I take your arm?"

CHAPTER V.

MILES.

THERE came a letter from Hyland to Lord Rayneford a few months after the events last narrated. It was an odd mixture of youthful philosophy with more or less graphic accounts of Hyland's adventures in the hill country. There were also whimsical descriptions of his new acquaintances among the military men and civilians, and specially a florid description of a Mr. Glendare, whose excellent traits were once and again eulogised as being the more remarkable because of Mr. Glendare's concurrent piety. " How a missionary," wrote Hyland, "and a Scottish missionary, and a Presbyterian Episcopalian to boot, can be so wise and philosophical staggers me! It overturns many of my pet theories. Probably Mr. Glendare is the exception that proves the universality of the contrary rule."

Then there were some cautious allusions to Mr. Daltman. Hyland was too thoroughbred to write uncomplimentary things about his associates. So he confined his references to Frank's exploits in field and jungle, his elegant dancing, or his easy mastery of Hindostanee. This led to some slight talk about the ladies, as Frank was paying devoted court to Miss Mordaunt, the reigning belle of the Sanitarium. An invalid of great beauty, and of considerable prospective wealth. Daughter of Colonel Mordaunt, commanding the station.

" When we came up here," said the letter, " Frank told me there were two Miss Mordaunts, and kindly offered one of them to me. I did not clearly see how he obtained the right of transfer, but he is one of your *veni, vidi, vici* fellows. I found on my arrival that the other was a shy, angular girl, ten years younger than her sister, and totally ineligible, of course. The sly rascal gave me a choice of names: Haidee and Juliet. I selected Haidee, because I inwardly shudder at the bare idea of a Juliet. Well, Juliet is the elder, the belle and the heiress. Poor little Haidee is a nonentity. I positively do not know what she is like, and I am thinking of alimony.

"Talking of alimony, old Miles, I have reached a definite conclusion. I shall never marry—I dare not! I have talked with Glendare about it scores of times, and between us we have exhausted the topic. There are two reasons that make my conclusion : first, I have never seen a woman that I would be willing to marry. I have never met the woman who could awaken within me the emotions a gentleman *must* experience before he dares encounter matrimony; second, I honestly believe there is no such woman on the surface of this planet, and if there were I could not ask her to marry me, because I could offer no equivalent. Glendare quotes sometimes :

   ' I bear i' my belt a gude braidsword,
    And I'll tak' dunts frae naebody !'

and I give the quotation because it expresses my feeling in some measure. That is : I will marry none but the very best of her sex, and I will not place myself under the life-long obligation to the peerless woman who might throw herself away upon me. Don't you see, Miles, that I am hedged in on two sides ? Frank insists that the obligation is reciprocal ; that the husband merits the wife's devotion because he gives her protection, counsel, status as a matron, and a multitude of self-abnegations. But he does not count the transfers on the other side. A wife yields her very identity. She is no longer a personality. In a few years shy little Haidee will be a woman—Miss Mordaunt. But if I confirm Frank's plan, and marry her, she will only be Mrs. Hyland Rayneford. And if I get my lac (which has actually begun to grow), and some more lacs, even enough to outweigh as many lacs as her sire leaves her—still, I cannot outweigh the tremendous enunciations through which she must pass to wifehood.

" I'll none of it !"

Lord Rayneford laid down the letter at this point, and meditated.

"The boy is in dead earnest," he thought, "and he is telling me the exact shade of thought that possesses him. What an odd mixture of whim and nobleness he is! I can hardly believe him entirely insensible to Mildred's attractions, yet I have never heard one word from him about her. He says he has never met the woman whose attractions were sufficient to kindle his affections. Then he has none to kindle!" Reaching this conclusion, he took up his brother's letter and proceeded.

"Now you are ready to ask why I do not relinquish the lac and return to England? If I have forsworn matrimony, my thousand pounds may be considered affluence. What can a single fellow want that a thousand a year will not purchase? This is a very sensible question, Miles. And I will be frank with you, brother, and tell you my exact thought upon this topic also.

"This money came to me by inheritance. I have earned none of it, and therefore I cannot enjoy it! I must get another thousand a year with my own hands, and then I will give away the old one. Do you know that I got my fortune through the operation of a will made by our maternal grandfather? No doubt you know this. But do you know that this special thousand was set apart by Lord Hyland, because *his* father had so devised it, when our mother was in infant days? Now I am not going to take money that was thus saddled upon me two generations ago. Two generations before I was born!

"I'll none of it!

"For you see, Miles, it is really *your* money. If there had not been this tyrannical old will in the way, the beneficent law of primogeniture would have secured it to you. It belongs to the estate. It would pay off those abominable mortgages! Take it, Miles!"

"The boy is distracted," said Lord Rayneford, pausing once more. "The Indian sun has turned his brain; I must write him another letter." And he seized writing materials and dashed in *medias res.*

"My dear Hyland," he began, "I have already mailed you an eight-page letter to-day; but your last missive, just received, demands a prompt reply. You were always more or less demented, my boy, but this last exhibition of lunacy alarms me. My money, indeed! Now heed me, Master Hyland! If you take any steps to dispossess yourself, or if I am so unhappy as to outlive you, and so inherit your thirty thousand pounds, I vow that I will give the money to some lunatic asylum. This would be an appropriate monument to

your memory, you dear old goose! Do not trouble yourself about
the mortgages. One is paid, and I am accumulating funds to pay
the other. When you bring that lac home, I think it very probable
that I shall be as rich as you. I have a scheme in mind that has
grown into definite shape since your letter arrived. I think of paying
off all my encumbrances by one *coup*. I cannot trust it to the mail,
but a sentence in your letter has given coherence to certain vague
purposes, and I think I shall begin my experiment at once.

"The sentence I refer to is your unequivocal declaration that you
have never met the woman you would marry. Then you do not
love Mildred, and I do! There, brother! you have the only secret
I have ever kept from you. I have admired Miss Carey all my life,
and would have told her so long ago, only I thought you, Hyland,
were also smitten. And now your letter assures me that you are
heart-whole. I could never play rival to you, but if you do not
yield homage to her charms, I am free to court her on my own
account.

"And I'll do it!"

When Hyland received the letter, his comment upon this tender
passage was—"Poor old Miles!"

However, Lord Rayneford drove over to Brentam Villa that same
afternoon. Hyland's letter would be entertaining to Miss Carey.
He would read some passages to her, especially his remarks about
Frank, and if opportunity served, he would read what Hyland said
about matrimony, also.

He met Mr. Brentam as he passed through the gates of Hawkley.
The old gentleman was astride his black cob, his groom trotting
soberly behind him.

"Ah!" said Mr. Brentam, "this is a fortunate meeting. You are
going to the Villa?"

"Yes," answered Rayneford. "I have a letter from Hyland, and
I thought you would like to hear what he says of Mr. Daltman."

"Certainly! And if you will take me up in your drag, I will
send my horse home. Ah! this is superb weather; never saw hops
so promising. Here, Tom! take Sultan home. And, Rayneford,
let us drive down by the mills. It is a little longer, but I want you
to see my hops. How is Frank? How is Hyland?"

"Both well. They are at a Sanitarium in the hill country."

"Yes. Wish they were here. At least, I wish Hyland—no use
though, it would take too long to get him home, even if he would
come! I have a scheme, better than anything in India."

"Why, I have a scheme as well," said Lord Rayneford, laughing, "and I intended consulting you about it this very day."

"Ah, but mine is a money-making scheme; a commercial scheme, and Hyland would make an excellent partner. Let me hear your scheme, and I will reveal mine."

"In confidence then," said Lord Rayneford, "I have thought I might better my fortunes by incurring a little risk, personal and monetary."

"Well?" said Mr. Brentam.

"I thought I could take a cargo to America, and bring back a cargo of cotton——"

"Running the blockade!"

"Exactly! Do not look so astonished. The risks are not nearly so great as one might suppose. I only require a navigator who knows the coast—a cargo that will be certain of ready sale—say in Charleston or Savannah, and a ship that can outsail the cruisers that blockade the port; a steamer, in fact."

"And a supercargo," added Mr. Brentam. "Where will you find a trustworthy supercargo?"

"Here," replied Rayneford, laying his hand on his own breast.

They rode along in silence a mile or more. Miles, who was greatly discouraged by his companion's grave face, began to discover a hundred objections to his scheme that had not occurred to him before. It was the more humiliating to have his folly revealed to him, by the few crisp sentences he expected, from the keen business man, who was also Mildred's uncle.

"This is most extraordinary!" ejaculated Mr. Brentam, at length; "where did you pick up this scheme of yours?"

"Hawkley is encumbered, Mr. Brentam," replied Miles, "and I am most eager to free the estate from debt. One or two ventures like that I have named would, if successful, do all I hope for."

"And if not successful?"

"Then I should be obliged to practice economy so long, that another purpose I entertain would have to be relinquished. I may as well tell you at once. I would ask Miss Carey to be my wife if my estate were free. But I cannot ask her to marry me while my revenue is so slender."

"Mildred has—some money of her own," said Mr. Brentam, cautiously; "as her guardian, I should be very glad to give her and her fortune into your custody, Rayneford. Have you spoken to her?"

"Certainly not! It would not be decorous to do so without your

consent. It is true that I expected to have your sympathy and
your approval. You have been so kind and have encouraged me so
constantly. But my poverty is an insurmountable barrier."

"Suppose you ask her?"

"If my scheme is feasible—if you, with your experience, can endorse it—if you think it wise to risk as many thousand pounds as I
can raise upon this venture—I will endeavour to learn Miss Carey's
sentiments. But you evidently think otherwise."

"Young men are always rash!" quoth Mr. Brentam, "always!
When I was twenty-five, I was rash as you are now. And I gained
conservatism through dismal experiences of failure. But I learned
something else. I learned that obstacles and unfavourable criti-
cisms should never divert one from the accomplishment of a set
purpose."

"I do not understand you," said the other.

"I mean to say you cannot have formed a plan of this magnitude
without considerable thought. And yet you appear ready to relinquish your purpose at the appearance of the first obstacle. And
that exists only in your fancy!"

"You mystify me still more," said Lord Rayneford.

"Do I?" replied his companion, with a chuckle; "then know
that your scheme is mine! I have the vessel in my mind. She is
in the port of Glasgow this minute, and is for sale. I know the
navigator. I know what cargo will prove most certainly profitable,
and I regretted Hyland's absence, because I wanted him for supercargo. You are an excellent substitute, only——"

"Only what?" said Miles, eagerly.

"Only English noblemen don't usually go prowling on the seas
hunting money."

"But I shall become plain Mr. Rayneford—or Mr. Miles, until I
get the money. I have spoken to no one but you, and we can keep
the secret."

"There's my hand!" said Mr. Brentam, "and now—mum!"

CHAPTER VI.

MILDRED.

"MUM" was a very good word at this juncture, as an equestrian party surrounded the dog-cart at the close of the dialogue just recounted. Miss Mildred Carey led the cavalcade, consisting of half a dozen ladies and gentlemen, all laughing and talking at once.

" We thought you were asleep!" she said, as she reined her horse alongside the vehicle. " Good-afternoon, Lord Rayneford! We have followed you a mile, and you have never once looked back! What in the world were you discussing so earnestly ?"

" Mr. Brentam selected this route to exhibit his hop-field," answered Miles, deceitfully. " It is beautiful."

" Did you see it ?" enquired Miss Carey.

" Yes—no—that is, I only glanced at it."

" A very cursory view, I imagine," retorted the lady. " You have just passed the field, and you did not turn your head."

" His head was already turned, Mildred," said her uncle. " I have been giving him a lecture on the rashness of youth."

" Thrown away on Rayneford!" ejaculated Mr. Sedley, a spruce cavalier who rode on Miss Carey's right. " He never was rash since I have known him."

" But I am growing reckless," replied Lord Rayneford, looking into the sparkling eyes of Mildred; " and am now meditating a desperate deed."

" Going to stand for the borough ?" said Mr. Sedley.

" Not I."

" Going over to Cork to join the steeple-chase for gentlemen riders ?"

" No, indeed."

" You are certainly not going to bet on the new horse ?"

" No. I shall not bet on anything."

" Well!" said Mr. Sedley, " I can think of no other desperate game—that is—except matrimony! By Jove! I have guessed it !"

Miles reddened a little, then laughed. The ladies—there were three of them—exchanged glances, and stole furtive looks at Mildred, all unconscious. It was totally in vain that Rayneford sought for some encouraging token in her countenance. Every one else in the party was certain that Miss Carey was the object of the young nobleman's attachment, if he really entertained serious intentions, but she gave no sign to him or to any one else.

"Speaking of matrimony," she said, quietly, "I received a letter from Frank to-day, in which he informs me that your brother is preparing to enter that honoured state."

"Hyland?" answered Miles. "Why, I have a letter from him to-day, which I brought over to show you."

"Let us ride on, then," said Mildred, shaking her rein. "We will meet you at the Villa and compare notes. If Mr. Rayneford has not revealed his intentions to you, it looks very suspicious. Come on, Mr. Sedley! We will ride round by the mills. *Au revoir!*"

"I think," said Mr. Brentam, as the gay party disappeared down the lane leading to the mills—"I think we will be wise if we drive back and get to the Villa before them. We shall have the advantage of a mile if we take the village road. I have all the details of the blockade-running scheme in my library, and we should decide and act promptly if we act at all."

"You surprise and charm me, Mr. Brentam," said Rayneford; "I am more than ever in love with the adventure, and feel more confident of success since you approve."

"Do not be too sanguine, Rayneford," replied his more sober companion; "there are difficulties to be surmounted, and many things to be considered. There is always the risk of a total loss. Do not forget that. Wait until you see my paper."

The conference in the library was prolonged until the visitors had all departed. Mr. Brentam had fairly set down all the arguments for and against the scheme. Blockade-running was still in its infancy. Miles stipulated for absolute secrecy, to which proposition Mr. Brentam heartily agreed. Rayneford was to become Mr. Miles to-morrow, and to sail within ten days, for "Nassau and a market." Mr. Brentam was to undertake all the details, furnish all the capital, and give the supercargo a third of the net profits.

"Now, Miles," said the elder, as they concluded their interview, "you have an excellent chance. The 'Nellie' is a good ship—a fast sailor, and is now in the Clyde. Your ignorance of commercial matters is in your favour. There is nothing to do but get the best prices for what you sell, and pay the least for what you buy. You have nothing to buy except cotton. Your brokers in Charleston will arrange all minor details. You are prudent and brave, and I am sure caution and pluck will bring you out. I will add that you are the only young man I know, except Hyland, that I would trust. Now go see Mildred."

"As to the matter of secrecy," said Miles, pausing at the door, "I suppose Miss Carey must be the exception?"

"I think there should be no exception," replied Mr. Brentam.

"I hope to occupy such a position as to——"

"Humbug!" interrupted the other; "you would not tell your wife everything?"

"Yes."

"Well, you would not be wise. There are many things that a man should not tell his wife. Such as other people's secrets, for example. Now, I am specially anxious to keep my share of this adventure secret."

"But your niece?——"

"Specially secret from her! Do as you please, however. Only have a clear understanding before you tell."

Lord Rayneford found Mildred alone in the drawing-room. She was reading Daltman's letter. Miles took Hyland's letter from his pocket and sat down beside her.

"Now, Miss Carey," said he, "we will compare notes as you suggested. What does your cousin say about Hyland?"

"I thought I would show you the letter," she replied, "but I find Frank has written 'private and confidential' at the top of the page."

"Indeed!" said Rayneford, with a pang of jealousy.

"Yes. But I may tell you that he and your brother have found two charming sisters in India. Frank has made satisfactory progress with the elder, and Mr. Rayneford—but that is the part I should consider confidential."

"Ah! Well, I am not under so stringent an obligation," said Lord Rayneford. "Hyland declares himself heart-whole. The younger sister is a mere child——"

"Indeed!" replied Miss Carey. "Well, this is what Frank says." And she read from the letter: "We had a kind of toss-up before we arrived, and Rayneford won Miss Haidee. He is always lucky. She is rather young, but a lady of great promise and prospects. The old colonel will cut up well. Of course, I think Miss Juliet beyond compare. Still, Rayneford is in luck, as his prize is just in his style, dreamy and romantic. She has no end of queer notions, and believes in chivalry, and all that sort of humbug. And my friend Rayneford is just full of the same kind of stuff. You should hear him talk about reciprocal obligations. He is in the same style as Hamish. By-the-bye, Hamish is developing wonderfully——"

"Hamish?" said Miles. "Hyland does not mention him."

"Mr. Glendare," explained Mildred; "he is a missionary who was asked up to the hill country for his health."

"Oh, Mr. Glendare! My letter is filled with his praises. I imagine he must be a very superior man, as Hyland is not usually lavish of his commendations."

"He is related to us, and has always been a good friend to Frank."

There was something in Miss Carey's tones that aroused the jealousy of her companion. He was a man of direct honesty, and after a few minutes' reflection, he plunged.

"You did not ask what desperate venture I had in my mind?"

She looked at him steadily, without reply.

"I thought you might have seen it in my eyes," he continued, "or that you had long ago discovered my admiration of you. I do not know what are the proper words to employ—except to ask you to be my wife. If professions of ardent attachment should be made, I fear I cannot put my thoughts into appropriate words. I——"

"Lord Rayneford," said Mildred, interrupting him, "I beg you will say no more. You distress me greatly."

"I would not willingly do that," said Miles; "am I to understand you as rejecting my suit——"

"Do not say that, I beg you," said Mildred; "you are so truthful and honest, that I know you are serious. But let us agree to consider your proposal a jest. I beg you!" she continued, as he was about to speak—"you do not know how it pains me."

"Have you never suspected my sentiments, Mildred?"

"I have feared you had some—some liking for me, my lord, but I hoped it would pass away. I entertain so high a regard for you that I could not refuse your attentions. Besides, I could not know certainly that your feelings were more than friendly."

"I am such a novice," said Lord Rayneford, after a short pause, "that I do not know whether to accept this answer as final or not. I should have spoken years ago but for two reasons."

She looked at him enquiringly, and he continued:

"I thought Hyland loved you until to-day, and I did not dare to think of you while he was in the way. But this letter assures me of my mistake. And when I read his assurance, which I know to be true, that he had never met the woman he would marry, I came directly to you. The other reason was my poverty. And even now my estate is sadly encumbered, but I hope for entire deliverance from debt in the near future. And indeed I meant my proposal to contain this condition—that your acceptance should be contingent upon my success——"

" My lord, you insult me !" said Mildred, haughtily. Then, seeing the pained expression upon his handsome visage, she arose and held out her hand to him. " Forgive me, Miles ! We have been friends from childhood, and your preference for me is the most flattering tribute I have ever received. Let us be friends still. If I could love you as you deserve, and as I *must* love the man I marry, I would be proud to be your wife, and no gifts of fortune could affect my regard for you. And it is only because I know this to be impossible, that I decline the great honour you offer me so peremptorily. It can never be, Miles ! Nay, my friend, do not say another word. I have no heart to give you !" And she put her slender fingers over her eyes to repress the sudden tears that trickled through them.

Lord Rayneford kissed the hand she had placed in his, and, drawing it upon his arm, took up his hat.

"Come," he said, with courteous kindness—"come out on the lawn. We will not renew this subject. We have known each other too long to be other than friends. And I think I can labour for your happiness—after a while—even if some other fellow should succeed when I have failed. Dry your eyes and come out. Your uncle is there. We will not annoy him with our—our quarrel ! And, good-bye, Mildred. I am going away for a time. Not on account of this—quarrel of ours, I assure you. Mr. Brentam, I must say adieu. I am going to take a short journey to-night."

Five minutes later, as Miles climbed into his dog-cart, Mr. Brentam sidled up to him.

" Did you tell Mildred about your adventure ?" he asked.

" Not a word. If you keep the secret, no one except ourselves will know of Mr. Miles' departure. I shall wait at Glasgow for your letter."

CHAPTER VII.

The " Nellie."

ON the first day of September, just as the sun touched the edge of the western horizon, the sharp-eyed skipper of the "Nellie," screw steamer, saw the topmasts of four war-ships, two of them rising and falling on the restless tide, at the entrance to Charleston harbour. The other two were evidently standing out to sea, and the last glimpse the captain caught of them, by the fading light, showed their masts in line on both bows of the "Nellie," indicating their approach to the exact spot his vessel occupied. What wind there was came directly from the coast, and the "Nellie" did not show a rag of canvas. But the two war-ships spread their topsails to the gentle breeze, while the black smoke from their funnels stained the golden sky above the low line of the South Carolina coast.

Captain Sparks was in the foretop, and the supercargo stood near him holding on by the shrouds. They had each taken a steady look through the glass, in the last minutes of daylight, and when the approaching ships had disappeared in the gathering gloom, the two men descended to the deck and walked aft without exchanging a word. Seating themselves on the edge of the after-hatch, the captain comforted himself with a large slice of plug tobacco, while the other waited with exemplary patience for an expression of his opinion.

"Wa-al, Mr. Miles," said the skipper, at last, "them's the same two fellers as give us a chase off Nassau."

"Do you recognise them, captain?"

"Ya-as! And you may just bet your bottom dollar that they recognise us, too. Now we've got to move along purty lively, one way or t'other. Mr. Brown!"

The mate came aft at the call.

"Mr. Brown, just go 'round to every man on board and give strict orders: Fust. No lights of any kind; no pipes or cigars. Second. No jawin' after the next half-hour. If anybody has got any gab in his locker that won't keep, let him get it off at oncet. At half-past seven I'll muzzle every mother's son of 'em, if they speak above a whisper."

"Aye, aye, sir!" responded the mate.

"Git along, then, and give your orders. Now, Mr. Miles, yonder's Charleston, off the starboard bow. There is two blazers layin' off and on, a mile this side the bar. There's two more blazers bearin' right down on us. I crave to know what you propose to do?"

"I intend to obey your orders, captain," responded the supercargo.

"But I'm under yourn! Will you risk the run to-night, or shall we turn tail and skeet out to sea, or run down the coast and try for Savanny?"

"I leave all to your judgment, captain," replied the supercargo. "I do not wish to incur any needless risk, but should like to land."

"Risk!" responded the captain. "It's a risky business all through! If them fellers overhaul us, good-bye to ship and cargo! Confistication is the word. I s'pose you knowed that when you started on this cruise?"

"Certainly. But I relied upon Captain Sparks so entirely, and have seen so many evidences of his skill and acuteness on the voyage, that I feel tolerably confident still."

"Wa-al," said the captain, with a grin of satisfaction, "I'll do my level best. This is my guess. Them cruisers have sighted us, of course. We could not see them without their seein' us. They are bearin' straight down on us this minnit."

"That seems very probable."

"Well, now to dodge 'em ag'in. Off Nassau, I concluded they would spread out, so I run right between 'em. Now, you can't fool 'em twicet with the same trick, so I propose to put the helm hard-a-port, to run an hour due noath, then head for the coast ag'in, and run in. We'll git round that feller on the starboard bow, and while he is runnin' east, we'll be goin' west. Not likely to run afoul of each other this week!"

"But the two steamers at the mouth of the harbor?"

"They'll be watchin' out for signals. And while they're gapin' out to seaward, I propose to run in between 'em."

"I am content, Captain Sparks. What shall I do?"

"I would say, git down in the cabin and turn in."

"Many thanks, captain. I prefer the deck."

"There may be some old iron flyin' round here, promiscuous-like," said the captain, in a hoarse whisper. "It is most likely they'll catch sight of the 'Nellie,' and if they do, you may bet your last stamp that they'll want a closer acquaintance. Now, I don't propose to stop when they tell me. In fact, I'm pressed for time! So they'll be thunderin' apt to shoot at us a few!"

"All right, captain," replied the other. "I am more determined than ever to stand by you. One of those bits of old iron might hit you, and in that event, I should like to see your plan carried out."

"Thought so!" muttered the captain, as he rose. "Too much derned grit to keep his head out of a mess. Well, Mr. Miles, I've done harder things than this more than oncet. I guess we'll git through. Brown! have you gi'n your orders?"

"Aye, aye, sir!"

"Hard-a-port!" said the captain. "Steady so! Silence in the ship for the next two hours. I want to do all the jawin' that's done, till we're in smooth water. Mr. Miles, I'm goin' forward to the wheel-house. Will you come along? I want to give my orders without howlin'."

The "Nellie" was painted a dull lead colour all over. Even the funnel was freshly painted every day, and in the night she was totally invisible at a short distance. The only light on board was a feeble glimmer in the binnacle, and this was so completely shadowed by the sliding shutters and by a tarpaulin screen in addition, that the vessel might be considered in total darkness.

No sound was heard but the wash of the sea and the thump of the machinery as the "Nellie" plunged ahead on her new tack. The supercargo counted the slowly-creeping minutes, and almost expected to see the dawn appear, while the skipper masticated his quid in apparent unconcern. The hour passed, however, and as the captain approached the steersman, a faint streak of light shot up in the sky to seaward. A minute later another gleam, a little south of the first, also marked the eastern sky.

"All right!" whispered Captain Sparks. "Hard a starboard, Tom! So! Steady now. Can you see the compass, Tom?"

"Aye, aye, sir!" said the helmsman.

"Keep her west-sou'west to a hair."

"Aye, aye, sir!"

"Them was rockets," said the captain to Mr. Miles; "they signalled one another. S'pose they was sayin' they couldn't see us."

"What next, captain?" whispered the supercargo.

"I guess there won't be nothin' startlin' for an hour or two. I'm goin' to git a mouthful of grub. Look right over the davit amidships. Do you see that star?"

"Yes."

"That's the north star. I calkilate we shall see the lights on them blockaders inside of two hours. I'm steerin' for 'em, straight.

While you see that star on the starboard quarter we are going right. My notion is this: them two fellers shootin' rockets out yonder have left the other two to watch the harbour. Nat'rally they're layin' off the bar. So if I steer for them, I am steerin' for the harbour."

The "Nellie" kept steadily on her course, while Mr. Miles paced the deck between the wheel-house and forward hatch. Nothing visible but the stars and the delicate tracery of the rigging against the dark vault, as the vessel rolled from side to side. While the supercargo was watching the little Dipper, the captain and mate approached with noiseless steps; they had on rubber overshoes.

"Ease her up a point, Tom!" said Captain Sparks. "So! steady, now! And don't you mind any orders from me spoke out loud. When I want you to change your course I'll whisper. D'ye understand?"

"Aye, aye, sir!"

"No matter how much I cuss or cut up rough, keep her nose pointin' just as you've got her till I whisper. Keep your ears open and keep your wits about you. Don't git skeart! I know every inch of this harbour, and once past them blazers we're all right. All hands below, Mr. Brown?"

"Yes, sir. No one on deck but us four."

"All right. Mr. Miles, one of them blockaders is right off our port bow. In ten minutes we shall see her. I caught a flash o' light just now, and I expect to pass her only forty rods off. All quiet now!"

Mr. Miles peered eagerly into the gloom. Twenty times in the ten minutes he thought he descried the dark hull and tapering masts of the cruiser, but each time he was mistaken. Suddenly the captain touched his shoulder, and pointed his bony finger over the bulwark. At the same instant there was a flash of blue light abreast the "Nellie," and the supercargo saw the outlines of the war-ship with her side bristling with guns.

"Ship ahoy!" came across the water. "What ship is that?"

"The United States supply-ship 'Union'!" promptly answered Captain Sparks.

"Heave to!" There was an unmistakable menace in the tone of this order.

"Aye, aye, sir!" replied the cheerful Sparks. "Hard a starboard, mate! Hard down, you booby! Stop the ingine! Cuss your clumsy skin! D'ye hear? Stop the engine!" And then in a whisper, " Port, Tom! Port! two points. So! steady!" And the " Nellie" glided past the row of guns.

" Heave to! you scoundrel!" shouted the officer, now plainly visible as he stood in the shrouds of the frigate; " heave to, instantly, or I'll sink you!"

" Sink and be blowed!" answered Captain Sparks. " Starboard, Tom! We are pooty well out'en this mess! Duck your heads down! He's goin' to shoot!"

A vivid flash, the whistle of a ball just over their heads, and the roar of the gun all came together.

" Leetle more starboard, Tom!" whispered the captain.

Another flash and roar, and another, and Mr. Miles felt the " Nellie" shudder with the shock that nearly brought him to his knees. There was a pang of disappointment, but he braced himself up to meet the inevitable, and was surprised to see Captain Sparks and the mate shaking hands and laughing uproariously.

" Needn't be skeart, Mr. Miles! That bump was the bar! No harm done, and that blazer is clean licked! Hang out your lights, Brown! Everywhere! Don't want to get a shot from Sumter! Slow her down, Tom! all plain sailin' now. Say, Brown, don't you think them four fellers are doin' some fancy cussin' this blessed minit? I s'pose they've let forty thousand dollars slip through their fingers. Tumble up, boys, and hang out your lights. Gimme a cigar, Mr. Miles! Thankee!"

CHAPTER VIII.

KNIGHTHOOD.

THE duties devolving upon Mr. Hyland Rayneford at Nuttagur station were not very onerous, but he did not lead an idle life, by any means. There were surveys to be made, day after day, as the Honourable Company projected certain improvements in that locality. Mr. Rayneford was apt with his pencil, and Colonel Mordaunt, who was a capital civil engineer, illustrated his frequent reports with sketches made by Mr. Rayneford. There were occasional expeditions in all directions from Nuttagur—sometimes five miles and sometimes twenty miles distant. Some parts of the surrounding country were historical spots, deriving additional interest from the fact that hostile forces had traversed the ground in the dark days of the Sepoy mutiny. Nuttagur had been a missionary station only in the old time, but was now a military post as well, and the officers who were stationed there congratulated themselves upon their good fortune in being so many feet above the arid plain of Calcutta.

The Sanitarium, as it is called, is on a little range of hills east of Kushnugur, and the altitude was not very great. After the mutiny, the station had assumed increased importance as a military post, and the missionary buildings had been given over to John Company in exchange for more commodious ones a little more inland. Mr. Glendare, whose health seemed to improve by constant exercise and exposure, made frequent trips to the new station, always walking, and generally accompanied by Hyland and two or three natives, partly soldiers and partly servants. One of the latter, Zeba by name, considered himself Hyland's bodyguard, and was a splendid specimen of Hindoo humanity. He was very proud of his military status, and of his medal and clasps won during the time of the revolt, when his regiment had once and again passed through sanguinary battles with his rebellious countrymen.

Mr. Glendare was a skilful amateur photographer, and many of the more striking bits of scenery between the mission and the camp were transferred to his portfolio. Some of them were copied by Hyland, in hours of luxurious ease, on the verandah of the mission bungalow. The red tape of the instructions demanded *pencil* sketches at the date of this story, but the more accurate presentments of the sun-painting are now admissible in engineers' reports.

Zeba had been assigned to Hyland soon after the arrival of Colonel Mordaunt and his fragment of a regiment at Nuttagur. Some of the expeditions through the jungle were thought to be more or less risky, as the memory of the famous mutiny was still uppermost in the mind of the commanding officer, and armed attendants always accompanied the Europeans in their wanderings. Zeba, in his red jacket and turban, was a picturesque warrior, overflowing with politeness, and Hyland and Mr. Glendare were both attached to him. His English was remarkably good, and on many occasions their journeys were enlivened by argumentation upon knotty points in Theology. The native was a devout Mussulman, and consequently a profound fatalist. The verbal warfare was triangular, as Hyland resisted Mr. Glendare's Calvinism as stoutly as he opposed the errors of the Hindoos' creed. The missionary was very earnest in his efforts to make a convert of Zeba, who, in turn, took great delight in bringing the pithy quotations from the Koran against the Scripture texts hurled at him by the missionary.

"It seems to me, Mr. Glendare," said Hyland, on one occasion, when the trio were consuming cheroots under the shade of a great rock, a few miles from the station—"it seems to me that you and Zeba might reach a compromise. I can detect but little difference between you in this matter of fate. Of course, you have an advantage in quoting from Holy Writ; but considered philosophically, your postulates have a family resemblance."

"Man write Sahib Glendare's Book. Man write Koran," said Zeba, sententiously.

"There!" said Hyland. "You are driven to the proof of inspiration, you see."

"Yes," replied Mr. Glendare; "if the Koran could give evidence of its inspiration, Zeba would stand on very solid ground. But the book lacks any such proof. There is so much in it that is unclean, immoral, and unphilosophical, that its character is bad. Nothing good could come from so much evil."

"Lotus grow in the mud!" said Zeba.

"Bravo, Zeba!" said Mr. Glendare, with unaffected admiration. "I have never encountered a disputant more ready than you! Your answer is most acute, but the lotus is not the product of the mud. It owes its sweetness to the sun. It derives its beauty from the heavens. If it were not for these influences that give it life and character, you would not be attracted. The difference between your sacred book and mine is found in the internal evidence furnished by both. Mine inculcates beneficence as the one law of the race. Yours teaches no such lesson."

"Sahib teach too much!" responded the Hindoo. "Soft hand for friends; sharp tulwar for enemies!" And he tapped the hilt of his weapon with his slender fingers. "In Paradise the brave warrior pitches his tent near the tent of the Prophet. Your Book say, 'Love enemy!' No warrior love enemy. Sahib make laugh for Hindoo! When you fight Nena Sahib, you say, 'Kill, kill!' You not kill when you love!"

"It is strange," said Glendare, turning to Hyland, "to find the same traditional form of belief in opposite creeds. The Christian habitually looks forward to a future dwelling near the person of his Prophet. Here is the same anticipation declared by our heathen friend——"

" Mohammedan not heathen!" said Zeba; " there is one God, and Mohammed is His Prophet!"

The discussion was rudely interrupted at this point by a scream of terror. The two daughters of Colonel Mordaunt had walked out from Nuttagur, escorted by Mr. Daltman, to the present line of survey. A railway was projected, and the route followed the range of hills, terminating with the giant rock under whose shadow the trio were reclining. Hyland started to his feet and dashed round the base of the rock, followed by his two companions. He found the ladies, with Daltman, on the survey-side. Juliet, the elder, was pointing her trembling finger at the thick jungle fringing the hill-side, and Daltman, shading his eyes with his hand, was eagerly peering in the indicated direction. Haidee stood a little apart, her face bound up in snowy muslin. She was a victim of neuralgia, poor child!

" What has happened?" said Hyland, glancing from one to the other.

" A tiger!" said Juliet, catching his arm and clinging to it. " I saw it twice! Mr. Daltman laughed at me; but I saw it. There! there!"

The Hindoo passed the excited group, his gun cocked and his finger on the trigger. Twenty yards in advance he stopped, and, slowly turning his head from side to side, closely scrutinised the dense vegetation in front.

" What have you seen?" asked Hyland, as Daltman turned towards him.

" Nothing," replied Daltman, slowly, while his eyes contradicted his words. " Let us return by the railway survey."

" It is through jungle, a long mile," interposed Mr. Glendare; " it is wiser to retrace your steps."

" That is through jungle also," said Daltman. " Suppose we send the Hindoo back for reinforcements? He can leave his weapons with us, just to tranquillize the ladies, you know."

" And send him unarmed?" asked Hyland.

" Yes, certainly! There is nothing to dread. Besides——"

" Besides what?"

" He is only a native," whispered Daltman.

Hyland walked up to Zeba and touched his shoulder. The Hindoo turned with grave politeness and bent his head.

" Salaam, sahib."

" Have you seen anything?"

"Nothing, sahib. Yes. The tree yonder shook."

"Is the tiger there, Zeba?"

"Yes, sahib."

"Are you frightened, Zeba?" said Hyland, looking keenly into the black eyes of the soldier.

"No, sahib," responded the other, steadily.

"Then listen. We will go back to the bungalow. You and I will lead. Then the ladies. Then Mr. Daltman and Mr. Glendare. Lend me your sword."

Zeba turned his left side to his interlocutor, and Hyland drew the keen blade from the scabbard. The Hindoo, still facing the hillside, retreated step by step, walking backwards.

"Give me the tulwar, Rayneford," said Daltman.

"Not I!" replied Hyland. "Your hand is too large for the hilt."

"Give me the weapon!" said Daltman, impatiently. "You are only a civilian."

"And therefore not under military authority. I decline to part with this sharp——"

The report of Zeba's gun interrupted the sentence. Hyland turned around, and saw the native facing the huge rock beneath whose shade they had just been resting. The blue smoke was curling from the muzzle of his gun, still pointing to the summit of the rock. All eyes were directed to the same object, and took in the same appalling vision—a great tiger, crouching for the spring, and then the yellow body flying through the air, and then the shock of his enormous bulk against the Hindoo, facing him with unflinching pluck, and then a confused mass of struggling life, the white turban and red jacket of the man mingling with the black stripes on the lithe yellow body of the brute, as they whirled around on the earth.

With two bounds Hyland reached the group, and as the tiger crouched again, while his tail waved from side to side, he paused, with uplifted weapon. The two glared at each other an instant with burning eyes.

"Pooh!" whispered Rayneford to himself, while his heart beat under the strong excitement; "pooh! it is only an overgrown cat. Now if Frank has sense enough to take the women away. Ah!"

The tiger drew his body together, and, with an angry growl, once more leaped from the ground. Hyland took one step aside, and with a swift sweep of the tulwar struck the beast between the ears. One great paw, already dripping with blood, caught his shoulder, tearing away his garment, and leaving a long gash in his flesh, from neck to elbow. But the sword-cut had told, and a second blow, aimed with cool precision, bit deeply into the neck of the tiger, almost severing the head from the body. The spinal cord was cut, and the combat was over.

All this passed in a few, short minutes. Hyland stood erect and panting, wondering where the warm blood that trickled into his hand, still grasping the tulwar, came from. Miss Mordaunt was indulging in a fit of genuine hysterics, supported by Daltman, who was assuring her of present safety. Zeba lay prone upon the ground, torn and senseless, his white turban mottled with a dull crimson, and with streaming wounds in breast and arms. Mr. Glendare was bending over the Hindoo. The tiger was stretched out in hideous magnificence at Hyland's feet, and Haidee, who had not moved, gazed alternately at the various groups, but watching most intently the central figure, with the long, red stain on his right arm, the flush of battle on his cheek and brow, and the look of dauntless valour in his blazing eyes.

"Oh, how beautiful!" she whispered. "The knight! the gallant knight! Sir Hyland evermore!"

This was not the usual method of conferring knighthood; nevertheless, Haidee never withdrew the title. It was better than the accolade.

CHAPTER IX.

A DEPARTURE.

IT was not very remarkable that this romantic young lady should heartily admire the prowess of Hyland. She was deeply read in works of fiction, and finding very few living impersonations of her various heroes, she naturally yielded her admiration at the first example of pure manhood she had seen. She had overheard the brief colloquy between Rayneford and Daltman. The latter had earned her displeasure by sundry former exhibitions of non-romantic selfishness, and she felt her neuralgic cheek glow with sympathy at Hyland's prompt rejection of his proposal to sacrifice the native. She had been incredulous as to the proximity of the dangerous brute, until she saw his body in the air, and then his bulk, in her eyes, rivalled that of an elephant. Between his first leap and the last sweep of the tulwar there seemed to be only a transient instant of

time, and there stood the victor, weapon in hand, and more than a
match for a dozen tigers, in Haidee's estimation.

"Sir Hyland," she murmured to herself, "not of the couchant
leopard, but of the bounding tiger! Oh, how I should like to paint
his shield!"

But Haidee had a common-sense, practical side to her character,
and while the animal was still quivering in death-agony, she approached and touched Hyland's arm.

"Let me bind up your arm," she said.

"My arm?" said Hyland, startled. "Why, yes! it *is* scratched.
I did not know it. Thank you! That will do, I think. Your
handkerchief will be utterly ruined."

"No, that won't do, I think," responded Haidee, quietly. "I want
another handkerchief. I'll get Juliet's."

"No need. Here is mine. You are brave to come so near the
tiger. But he is no longer dangerous."

"*You* went nearer!" she answered, glancing at him, while she
drew the knots in the handkerchief; "besides, you have your sword!"

"What glorious eyes the little skinny creature has!" thought Hyland; and then aloud, "Miss Mordaunt, I am very grateful. My
arm is nearly cured already."

"It is a dreadful wound!" replied Haidee; "the doctor will have
to sew it up! See how the blood comes through! How could you
strike that terrible blow with this arm?"

"He must have scratched me when I gave him the first cut, but
I did not know it. Poor Zeba! Let us look after him. He taught
me the trick of the tulwar. A downright blow and a cut. Is Zeba
badly hurt, Mr. Glendare?"

"Very much torn in the breast and neck. The scalp is torn
from the side of his head. How shall we get him to the station?"

"Do you and Daltman take the ladies, and send a palanquin.
I will stay with him. Suppose we bind up some of these wounds
first? Tear strips from his turban. Thank you, Miss Mordaunt,
we can attend to him. How magnificent he looked as he stood here
facing that wild beast! Did you see him?"

"Yes," said Glendare. "I saw you as well."

Miss Mordaunt was sufficiently recovered to walk. Daltman
reloaded the Hindoo's gun and gave it to Mr. Glendare.

"We will send help to you within an hour," he said, as they prepared to separate. "As we have the ladies to protect, perhaps you
had better give me the sword."

"Certainly," said Hyland; "take it."

"And do you intend to leave Mr. Rayneford totally unarmed?" said Haidee, looking alternately at Daltman and the missionary.

"The only important matter is to get you to the bungalow," replied Daltman. "I apprehend no danger, but you ladies will feel more secure if we are both provided with weapons."

"No need for controversy," said Mr. Glendare. "The colonel has sent your dandies. There they come. If you can walk, Miss Haidee, we will get Zeba home in your dandy."

A dandy is simply a long pole with a strip of carpet or canvas in the middle, which is hooked up at the ends. The rider sits in the loop of the carpet, grasps the pole, which is lifted to the shoulders of the bearers, and they travel sideways, at his ease. Colonel Mordaunt had grown weary at the prolonged absence of his daughters, and had sent the dandies to meet them and hasten their return. Zeba was carefully lifted from the ground, and, supported by Mr. Glendare and Daltman, was strapped in the dandy. In a few minutes the party was passing the jungle on the homeward march.

"I had no thought of deserting you, Mr. Rayneford," observed Mr. Glendare, as they emerged from the shadow of the jungle. "My purpose was to escort the ladies to this point, and then return to you."

Haidee, who was walking by the side of Juliet's dandy, threw back an approving glance to the missionary. Mr. Glendare nodded in reply.

"What eloquent eyes the child has!" he said.

"She is a little heroine," whispered Hyland. "What in the world is her head tied up in that absurd fashion for?"

"She is a martyr to neuralgia," answered the missionary, in the same tone. "Doctor Leigh has been treating her ever since she left Calcutta. He does not allow her to remove her bandages upon any pretext."

"Her sister might walk a little, and let her ride," muttered Hyland. "She seems quite recovered."

Miss Juliet was chatting very gayly with Daltman, who walked by the side of her dandy.

"I suppose that does not occur to either of them," observed Mr. Glendare. "Certainly not to Haidee."

"They do not seem to resemble each other," said Hyland, after a pause in the conversation.

"No; I am not sure that I am only retailing camp gossip when I tell you, confidentially, they are not related."

"I do not understand," said Hyland.

"It is said that one of them is only the adopted daughter of the colonel. A brother officer was killed in the mutiny. Colonel Mordaunt adopted the child."

"The younger?"

"I am not sure. Nobody knows. Nobody ventures to ask. The colonel's whole family perished horribly, except one daughter. Frank says he has reason to know that Juliet is the colonel's own child. But——"

"But what?" said Hyland; "pardon me if I should not ask."

"I was going to say," continued the missionary, reluctantly, "that Frank is sometimes rash in his conclusions. Still, I have no reason to doubt him in this matter. The colonel makes no difference in his treatment of them. Hist! Zeba is speaking!"

At a sign from the missionary the bearers stopped, and the Europeans all gathered round the wounded Hindoo, who was muttering incoherently in his native tongue. Mr. Glendare bent his head down and listened.

"He is talking in one of the Punjaubic dialects," said Mr. Glendare; "and I cannot understand him."

Haidee plucked her voluminous bandage from one ear and listened a moment.

"He says give sword and scabbard to Sahib Hyland," she said. Zeba muttered a few more words, and relapsed into insensibility.

"He says there is one God, and Mohammed is his Prophet," continued Haidee, "and he has fainted again."

The march was resumed. Haidee adjusted her head-dress and rejoined her sister.

"I suppose Frank is right," observed Mr. Glendare; "she understands that lingo. The adopted daughter came from the western provinces, where the natives speak the purest Pracrit."

After the bungalow was reached and the Hindoo's wounds had been dressed, Dr. Leigh examined Hyland's arm. He was a peppery old army-surgeon, with about as much human sympathy as a hyena.

"Humph!" he said, after bathing the wounded limb; "it is quite possible, Mr. Rayneford, that you will have to draw your pretty pictures with your left hand hereafter!"

"What can you mean, doctor?" said Hyland, aghast.

"Fever. Inflammation. Nerves lacerated. Mortification. How the devil can I tell? You are cut to the bone."

"And Zeba?" said Hyland, repressing a groan.

"If he were white he would be dead already," replied the medico. "One can never tell about these natives. One eye is gone. That much is certain. And I think I'll take off one arm to-morrow."

The grisly anticipation put the doctor in a good humour.

"If you keep perfectly quiet—stay out of the sun—stay in the bungalow a week, and don't use your arm at all, I'll—I'll try to save it. There is some poison in the beast's claws. I have healed up far worse sword-cuts, but this is torn and ragged. Remember what I tell you! Every movement of your body irritates the wound. And the hot weather is against you."

"I will obey all your orders, doctor," replied Hyland, submissively.

"Very well. If you get feverish, I'll strap your other arm to your body, to keep you from clawing at the bandages. You had better go to bed at once."

"I have had nothing to eat," murmured Hyland.

"Eat!" said the doctor, in disgust. "Eat! Who ever heard of a man eating with one foot in the grave—one arm, at least! I suppose you would like a bottle of pale ale?"

"Indeed that is true, doctor."

"Plain tea morning and evening," replied the doctor, dogmatically; "a little boiled rice at noon. No meat and no beer for a week. Get away with you! I must get the native to his quarters."

Haidee had an ayah, a shrivelled, old, saffron-coloured woman, with an unlimited capacity for lying and sleeping. She indulged in cat-naps every hour of the twenty-four, but could start up, broad awake, on the instant. During the night she made hourly raids into Hyland's room, (acting under stringent orders,) and made rapid, cursory addresses in Hindoostanee to Hyland's native servant, squatted at the foot of his couch, and pretending to keep the punka in motion. The youth slept through it all. This pastime was continued several days and nights in succession, until at last the tyrannical doctor allowed him to walk out after nightfall for an hour at a time, and increased his rations. The arm healed rapidly, leaving a long, red seam, and in two weeks he was taken off the sick list and restored to liberty.

Before Zeba, minus one eye and one arm, crawled into the sunlight, Mr. Rayneford was ordered to the Himalaya Mountains. The government had sent a corps of botanists, geologists, and surveyors to this locality, and Hyland, following in the trail of a body of pilgrims, bound for the temple of Bhagaritha, set out from the shades of Nuttagur to prospect and report upon the cinchona plantations just begun under the auspices of John Company.

CHAPTER X.

HAIDEE.

A GREAT part of the magnificent country, where the Ganges issues from the Himalayan range, was totally unknown to Europeans at the date of this history. It had been discovered that the cinchona-tree, hitherto confined to the slopes of the Andes, would grow, at similar altitude, in Northern India, and the chief object of the expedition with which Hyland was connected was to explore these regions, report upon the fauna and flora, and make such topographical surveys as might be necessary. The belt of land upon which the cinchona was found to flourish varied in all particulars, except in its elevation above the sea level. It is said that trees above and below this narrow belt preserve the same exterior appearance, while their bark yields only a meagre percentage of quinine. But the experiments on the slopes of the Himalayas had been very encouraging, and the true bark, apparently identical with the Calisaya, had been successfully cultivated and tested by government agents, and found to be rich in the active principle of the Peruvian tree.

Among the new acquaintances that Hyland made there was a Doctor Connor, a native of New York, but a traveller of such enormous experience that all parts of the habitable globe seemed equally familiar to him. He had spent a series of years in South America in the employment of the English " monopoly," as it was called— a company of capitalists who had contracted for all the bark of the cinchona-trees in the countries that produced them. He was so true an expert, that he could distinguish at a glance between the real and the "bastard" bark, and could announce beforehand the percentage of quinine that would be given by any selected specimen. His faith in the medicinal virtue of the drug was nearly boundless, and he had a multitude of carefully attested examples of marvellous cases in which quinine had rescued the victims of various diseases from the very jaws of death. There was something irresistibly comic in his furious onslaughts upon "quackery" in all its forms, coupled with his enthusiastic faith in his favourite remedial agent.

Hyland was attracted to the doctor from the first. As he had wandered all over the face of the earth, having a smattering of all known languages, his *répertoire* was filled with bits of personal adventure, mingled with much valuable historical fact; and so long as the sovereign virtues of "quinia" were not contested, the doctor was an eminently pleasant companion. It happened that there were no other educated men in the party, and Doctor Connor and Mr. Rayneford naturally sought each other's society.

Before the party reached the mountains, the Bhagaritha pilgrims left them. The surveys were to be made at Bhootra, and here they found a populous station, where the various scientists above mentioned had preceded them. There was a vast extent of country between Nuttagur and Hyland's new field, and the adventures of the Nuttagur station were soon forgotten in the constant round of duties engrossing his attention at Bhootra. Nevertheless, there came a letter from Hyland to Mr. Glendare a few months after the separation.

" I wish you were up here in this grand climate !" he wrote. " We thought the hills at Nuttagur were a great improvement upon Calcutta. But what do you say to ten thousand feet above the sea level ? I have been to that altitude more than once. At present we are only a paltry two thousand feet high, and my surveys will not go much higher. The Bhagaritha pilgrims, who left us several days before we reached Bhootra, seek their shrine ten thousand feet up—somewhere in the course or near the source of their sacred river.

" I am very much interested in the cinchona plantations. They are undoubtedly flourishing, and Doctor Connor, our chief botanist, pronounces them genuine. By-the-bye, I must tell you more about my new friend. He is an American, but has lived everywhere, talks no end of lingos, and is a skilful physician. I have witnessed some remarkable cures under his treatment. He is sane upon all subjects, except the curative powers of quinia. I cannot tell you how much he claims for his favourite drug, but the other medicos up here assert the fact that its exhibition in several cases (where he has certainly been successful) is something new in medical lore. He does not call it a panacea, but he says this much with great confidence and emphasis : all diseases that are intermittent yield to it, properly administered. And he specially enumerated neuralgia among these ailments. This attracted my attention particularly, as the little lady with the big eyes is a martyr to that disease. Just think of it! I actually never saw Miss Haidee, during all my stay at Nuttagur, when her head was not swathed up in bandages! And my sympathy for the child made me specially attentive to Doctor Connor's remarks, and I made a memorandum of them, which I enclose.

"Perhaps it is indecorous in me to meddle, but I cannot help it if it is. I would incur more serious risks in such a cause. Pray see Doctor Leigh, and put the matter before him. And do it judiciously, my dear friend. These medical men do not cut each other's throats only because they slake their appetites on such fellows as you and me, but they are terribly jealous of each other! I wish you could read it to the doctor out of some medical book!

"Be judicious, I pray you. Do not arouse the latent antagonism. For if Doctor Leigh should say 'no,' all my high hopes and expectations would be dashed. The colonel would not allow any experiments, of course. Apropos of experiments! I spent two days at the snow-line, three weeks ago, and I had a dull headache at noon, three successive days, after we came down. Doctor Connor gave me the horrible stuff—only once—twenty-four grains! In three instalments, three hours apart, and I have, had no headache since. I cannot say a word in praise of the taste of quinia. Neither can I eulogise the sensations that follow its administration. My head felt too big to go into an ordinary barrel for three or four hours. But no headache came with the next noon, my friend! I was cured!

"I am so thorough a convert to Dr. Connor's theory, that I should not hesitate to administer his drug to my sister or daughter, if I had either, a victim to neuralgia. Especially, as the doctors, differing about every other point, agree in pronouncing quinia innocuous at least."

Mr. Glendare received this letter at high noon, when the chief personages introduced in a previous chapter were at tiffin in the colonel's bungalow.

"From Rayneford!" he exclaimed, when he had broken the seal.

"Read it aloud," said a chorus of voices.

Mr. Glendare glanced over the letter, and then read the quotation given above. The comments that followed were highly instructive.

"Humbug!" said Doctor Leigh. "There are no specifics. Yankee quack probably, maker of patent pills. How the deuce can he prescribe for a case he never saw?"

"Rayneford is sold!" said Daltman; "never saw such a fellow! Ready to run off with any new dodge that comes up."

" A tiger dodge, for instance," murmured Miss Haidee, who was sipping pale ale, and munching a biscuit with aching jaws. Nobody seemed to hear her remark.

" Very thoughtful in Rayneford," said Mr. Glendare, "and I think Frank's remark very unjust. Rayneford is the most conservative man I know."

" Not very conservative, to suggest wholesale poisoning of my patients! Sorry I did not take his arm off!" said Doctor Leigh.

Mr. Glendare folded his letter and put it in his pocket. This was clearly not the time to argue with Doctor Leigh. Haidee sat next the missionary, taking her ale, a gulp at a time. It was a part of Dr. Leigh's "treatment." When the rest left the table, and strolled out on the verandah, she remained at the table, meditating. At last the ale was finished, and as she arose she saw the slip of paper, which Mr. Glendare had dropped from the letter. She took it up and read as follows :

" If there is an intermission of pain from three to six hours, the patient should take from twelve to twenty-four grains of the sulphate of quinia within the interval. It is better to take enough at once, and the patient can tell when he has enough, which will be when he hears a thousand hornets buzzing in his head. Sometimes, and with some constitutions, twelve grains will do. I have no confidence in smaller quantities."

" Ah! this is Sir Hyland's memorandum!" said she, replacing the paper by Mr. Glendare's plate. " So he remembers the ' poor child' with her head swathed in muslin! And he has written that letter, and sent it five hundred miles, I suppose, at least, because he sympathises with the ' little lady with big eyes!' And Doctor Leigh says he is a humbug! Very well, then! I'll see if I cannot humbug him!"

Adjoining the colonel's bungalow Doctor Leigh had his laboratory. It was a small room, filled with villainous smells. But Haidee was familiar with all its nooks and crannies, for she was a volunteer nurse and hospital stewardess, chiefly because she could understand the natives, who always talked Hindoostance when afflicted with febrile diseases. Quinia was also a favourite remedy with Doctor Leigh, and he had privately made up his mind to try its efficacy upon Haidee while Glendare was reading Hyland's letter. He meant to give her two or three grains and watch the results.

But she—poor slip of a child—aged eighteen, and full of woman's wit, and woman's relentless determination, walked softly into the doctor's laboratory, while he was puffing at his cheroot on the broad verandah. She knew as well as he where he stored his treasures, and in less than eight minutes she had weighed three times eight grains of sulphate of quinia, and deftly folded the three powders and stowed them away in her pocket.

"I have no pain from eight o'clock to bedtime," she reflected, "and I intend to take these powders at nine, ten, and eleven. I suppose I cannot read 'The King's Secret' to-night, but I can wait until to-morrow. Besides, I have read it twice already. And I'll tell nobody about it. Does Sir Hyland suppose the poor little child would be snubbed by old Doctor Leigh? Child! I vow I think men are the greatest geese—not Sir Hyland though. Never mind!"

Haidee's ayah jerked fitfully at the punka cord between naps, at about nine o'clock that evening. Haidee emptied one powder in a cupful of ale and drank it. The facial contortions that followed would have made the fortune of a circus clown, but she bravely clenched her fist and refrained from expletives. When ten o'clock came, she repeated the dose. It is a wonder she did not swear in Hindoostanee, but she did not. Before eleven o'clock she distinctly heard sixty-five thousand hornets, and while their music was at its height, she quietly disrobed and sought her couch.

The next day Haidee informed Doctor Leigh that she was quite free from pain. Might she leave off her head-wraps? By no means! Another day passed, and still no neuralgia. She ate four mutton-chops, while the doctor stared at her speechless. That evening her pretty face appeared at the dinner-table uncovered. She was still carnivorous.

"Quinia be blowed!" said Dr. Leigh to Mr. Glendare, in a whisper; "notice the quantity of grub that child is consuming! When you write to Mr. Rayneford, tell him we have managed to cure the child without using his Yankee humbug! Haidee! Will you try the quinia?"

"I think I prefer another slice of mutton, doctor," she answered, "thank you!"

CHAPTER XI.

THE SOLDIERS.

AS a coincidence, it may be noted that Mr. Supercargo Miles was disposing of quinia at a huge profit in Charleston, at the very time Hyland was starting for the cinchona plantations. The cargo of the "Nellie" was well assorted, and, acting under the general instructions of the shipper, the supercargo sold his wares rapidly. The new crop of cotton was just appearing upon the market when the "Nellie's" hold was emptied. But there had been some cases of yellow fever, and the disease was spreading. By the urgent advice of his brokers and bankers, Mr. Miles took a trip into the interior, with the understanding that he would prolong his absence until a decided frost should have driven out the dreaded scourge of the coast. He yielded to this arrangement the more readily because the blockade was far more efficient than usual; and even if he could have completed his loading, he could not have ventured over the bar.

He spent a week at a pleasant village, less than a hundred miles inland. Here the talk was all of the army. Every voice was still for war. The larger part of the population belonged to the gentler sex, the men being all afield, excepting those whose age disqualified them for military service. The items of news were gathered from the city papers, and Miles was surprised to find the women, of all ages and conditions, as belligerent as the hero of the old ballad:

> " La guerre est ma patrie,
> Mon harnais ma maison,
> Et en tout saison,
> Combattre c'est ma vie."

With his limited knowledge of political questions, and with his inevitable English prejudice, Miles could not discover any satisfactory reason for this strange unanimity. But he learned very speedily to moderate his own expressions, and to withhold any hint that the "invader" could possibly have some show of right on his side. Curious to investigate the masculine modes of thought, he gradually extended his travels inland, always approaching the scenes of actual conflict, until he found himself within an easy day's ride of a prospective battle-field. "The fighting instinct" distinguishing all bipeds, from the cock-sparrow up to man, was too much for his prudence, and gathering all the information respecting routes that was attainable, he crossed the Tennessee border one morning, and started in search of a camp of ten thousand Confederate soldiers, somewhere between him and sunset.

The Charleston bankers had furnished him with letters—some were circulars addressed to various moneyed institutions in the interior towns, and some to prominent army-officers in Tennessee and Virginia. Late in the afternoon he was pacing soberly along the dusty highroad, when he was suddenly confronted by an armed man, who emerged from the bushes on the roadside.

He was a tall, raw-boned specimen of the genus homo, clad in grey trousers and grey flannel shirt, a cartridge-box strapped to his waist, a long knife in his belt, and a Minié rifle in his hands, the bright bayonet glittering at the end of the barrel, depressed to the line of Miles's body.

"Halt, there!" he said, passing his thumb to the gun-cock. Miles drew up his horse.

"Who air you? Where air you goin'?" said the soldier.

"I am an Englishman," answered Miles, "and I am looking for General Smith."

"Hum!" said the soldier, doubtfully. "Got any despatches?"

"I have a letter for General Smith."

"Got any we'pons?"

"None."

"Well," drawled the soldier, "I reckon you can ride on. Walk your horse. If you go too fast, a Minié ball will be derned apt to kitch up with you!" And he tapped the butt of his weapon as he raised it to a "shoulder arms," and straggled back to the bushes.

A few minutes later, Miles was again challenged by the apparent twin brother of the first soldier. A similar interchange of views took place, and while the second sentinel pondered, Miles concluded to propound some questions on his own account.

"It seems I am approaching the camp," he said. "Can you tell me, my friend, if I shall find General Smith?"

"Our old man is Gen'l Smith," answered the warrior.

"And are you a member of his corps?"

"I belong to the Forty-ninth North Kalliney Infantry," replied the soldier, with dignity; "and if you call me 'Tar-heel,' I'll be dogon'd if I don't mash your mouth!"

"Call you 'Tar-heel'?" said Miles. "Certainly not! I do not even know what it means."

"I forgot you was a Britisher," replied the other. "Say! do all Britishers wear plug-hats and gloves in hot weather?"

"Not all, I fancy," said Miles. "What road shall I take to reach the camp?"

"Better climb down outen your saddle, I reckon," said the soldier, coolly. "You can lead your cattle. Is Queen Victory a-goin' to jine us ag'in the Yanks?"

"I really cannot say," replied Miles, glancing at the sober face of his interlocutor, wondering if the question was seriously propounded. "So! I am afoot, you see. And now, which way?"

"Right down the road. It ain't no ways from here. You'll come to the school-house at the head of the road. Plenty of fellows thar to p'int your way out. Say, Britisher, you'd better come outen that hat afore you git into camp! You can mount ag'in, if you like!"

As Miles rode along he took off the objectionable headgear, and examined it narrowly to discover its special faultiness. It was a good hat, tolerably new, in a good state of preservation, and certainly in the latest London fashion. Utterly at a loss to account for the parting advice of the sentinel, he replaced his hat as he turned the bend of the road, when the "school-house" came into view. There were some twenty soldiers, the most of them spread out upon the grassy mound, some playing with soiled cards, some smoking pipes, their guns stacked near the building. Half a dozen horses, with military saddles and holsters, were fastened to the low boughs of the trees, and a small group of officers, seated on the rough bench on the school-house porch, rose as he approached. A negro boy, with glittering white teeth, took his bridle when he dismounted. The soldiers united in a chorus of murmurs, as he passed them—

"Come outen that hat!"

"Good afternoon, gentlemen," said the supercargo, removing his hat, as the officers courteously touched their caps; "will you pardon a stranger if I enquire what the deuce ails my hat?"

A roar of laughter from the officers was the immediate response, and then one of them, offering his hand to the new-comer, motioned him to a seat on the bench.

"You will excuse our merriment, sir," he said, "but your countenance showed such manifest perplexity, that we could not help it. It is nothing. The boys don't often see a dress hat, and they must have their joke. They have a vague idea that none but Yankees wear them."

" And they take me for a Yankee?" said Miles.

" Hardly. A gentleman of that nationality would not be likely to come to these headquarters—unattended. You passed a sentry or two?"

" Yes," replied Miles; " but they also criticised my hat. I told them I had a letter for General Smith, and they allowed me to pass."

" Ah! I am he, sir," said the officer.

Miles produced his credentials, and while the general perused the letter he glanced at the strange surroundings. The soldiers had already returned to their amusements, forgetting the stranger, and intent upon their cards and pipes. The boy had fastened his horse, removed the saddle, and was busily rubbing the animal down with a handful of straw. The officers were variously attired, none of them having a regular military costume, all wearing long boots with spurs, and distinguished from the rank and file chiefly by their red sashes and long sabres. Over all there was the indescribable appearance of reality, as contradistinguished from the trim equipments of holiday soldiers.

" You are welcome, Mr. Miles," said the general, as he finished the letter. " Let me present my friends: Major Hurd, Captains Stanly and Green. Mr. Miles, gentlemen, from England."

The officers arose and greeted the new-comer.

" My correspondent informs me," said the general, " that you are merely taking a holiday trip through the country. I suppose you know you are quite near our outer lines?"

" I heard to-day that a Federal force was near," replied Miles, " but I do not know how near."

" Our pickets have exchanged compliments this afternoon," said the general; " we shall all be better acquainted with our visitors to-morrow. May I offer you some whiskey? It is not very good, but the best we can get."

" I thank you, no. If you gentlemen will join me, I have some cigars in my wallet."

" It would be absolutely deceitful in us to refuse," observed Major Hurd, " as we have not seen a real cigar for a month."

While they smoked the two captains walked apart on the piazza engaged in earnest discourse. It was evident that the Englishman's arrival was the subject under discussion, as they glanced at him from time to time. When they threw away the stumps of their cigars, they approached and unfolded the topic of the colloquy.

"General," said Captain Stanly, "Green and I have been talking about Mr. Miles, and his accommodation for the night. With your permission I will ride over to Dale's, where he can get an eatable supper and a bed."

"Certainly," replied the general; "Mr. Miles, you will be welcome. Mr. Dale is a countryman of yours by birth. We cannot make you comfortable here, and hospitality is best shown by securing the comfort of your guest. We are on the eve of battle, and must stay with our men. It would be highly indecorous in any of us to sleep under the roof of a habitable house to-night."

"You are very kind," said Miles. "Does Mr. Dale keep a house of entertainment—an inn?"

"There are no inns within forty miles of us," replied Captain Stanly, smiling; "but in this country we do not need them. Do not hesitate on that account, however. I will ensure you a cordial welcome. Tom, saddle the gentleman's horse, and bring mine also. General, I will return within the hour. It is only a short distance, Mr. Miles."

Miles offered no further objection, but mounting his tired horse, dropped a silver half-crown into the black palm of Tom, whose eyes grew to the dimensions of the coin, as he looked alternately at its shining surface and at the retreating form of the donor. Silver was scarce in that latitude.

CHAPTER XII.

ANNOT.

THE level rays of the setting sun shone in the faces of the equestrians as they rode away from the school-house. They were challenged twice by sentinels within half a mile of the camp, but were allowed to proceed, after a whispered word from Captain Stanly. Turning from the main road, they rode a mile through the forest, and when they emerged from the shadow, they were on the edge of a vast cornfield, separated from the woodland by the ordinary worm fence, with which Miles had grown very familiar in his day's ride. At the end of the field they entered a lane, bordered by hedges of the Osage orange, the dwelling of Mr. Dale coming into view at the terminus of the lane.

"This hedge looks very home-like to me," observed Miles; "it is the first I have seen in America."

"Yes. Mr. Dale values his hedge more highly than his house. He has cultivated it six or seven years. I hope the track of the war will not mar this neighbourhood, but one can never tell."

"I have a great desire," said the Englishman, with some hesitation, "to see a battle. If it would be proper, I should like to ride back to-morrow, if you gentlemen anticipate——"

"It is tolerably certain," replied the soldier, laughing, "that we shall have a little debate to-morrow. But I cannot tell you just when or where. You cannot see much, however, without incurring some risk."

"I suppose not," said Miles, coolly. "The only question relates to the propriety in the case. As an Englishman and non-combatant——"

"Oh, there will be plenty of 'outsiders,' as we call them. Newspaper correspondents, embryo surgeons, and some chaplains. The latter somehow get mixed up with their charges though, and make first-class fighters."

"Fighters!" said Miles. "Surely you do not mean clergymen?"

"Certainly! Our parson is a long-legged Scotch-Irishman from North Carolina, and he has done a man's work in a dozen battles already. He never allows his boys to go into action without a prayer beforehand. Come over in the morning, and I will introduce you. Here is the gate. Allow me to pass you. I can open the latch with my sabre."

A good-sized wooden house, of two stories. A broad verandah along the whole front. An old gentleman shading his eyes with his hand, watching their approach, and a young lady at his side, at the top step of the verandah. Climbing plants entwined about the pillars, the Virginia creeper, the honeysuckle, the wistaria, and the jessamine. Instead of the trim lawn, there were numerous flower-beds, wherever the trees, which stood in clumps, would allow the sunlight to reach the earth.

"That is she!" said Captain Stanly, in a half-whisper; "Miss Dale. Ah! if I could only join your party to-night, instead of prowling about in the woods, catching a mouthful of sleep where I can, and smoking corn-cob pipes!—— Your servant, Mr. Dale! Miss Annot, it is very tantalizing to be allowed only this brief greeting! I have brought you a visitor, Mr. Dale; a countryman of yours, who brings letters from Charleston to the general. We have ventured to offer him the hospitalities of Dale Manor to-night, as our accommodations are not very inviting. Mr. Miles, sir. Mr. Dale and Miss Dale."

"You are welcome, gentlemen," replied Mr. Dale, descending the steps, with his hand extended. "Dismount. Here, Toby! take the horses."

"Alas!" said Stanly, "I am obliged to return to camp. I cannot even dismount. But I hope to return to-morrow night, if—nothing happens in the meantime to prevent. Good afternoon. Miss Annot, please do not sing 'Annie Laurie' until I come to hear it. Good night, Mr. Miles."

Mr. Miles mounted the verandah steps in a cold perspiration. A thousand thoughts rushed over his mind, and always uppermost, the painful sense of high indecorum of which he was guilty, in thrusting himself, an unbidden guest, upon this household. He looked back at Captain Stanly, cantering down the lane, and half resolved to ride after him. In the midst of his confusion, he met the dark eyes of the lady as she advanced and offered her hand.

"Father will be too exacting to allow much music to-night, Mr. Miles. It was very kind to come. Walk in."

"I do not know what apology to offer, Miss Dale," stammered Miles. "*You* know, and *I* know, this is an unwarrantable intrusion. Yet when the gentlemen over there proposed it, there seemed to be such an air of proprietorship about them all, that I was too stupid to see the matter in its true light. And now, if you will allow me to ride back, after a short visit, I will be very grateful. The moon——"

"Must have exerted an evil influence upon you!" said Mr. Dale. "What! Leave us to-night? Ho, ho! You will be lucky if you are allowed to go to bed. Come in, sir! The house is yours. You will have to talk incessantly until the short hours. I assure you, your visit is a real godsend to us, and you have a thousand welcomes. An Englishman, too! Mr. Miles, he said——"

"Yes," replied Miles, "that is the name I bear. But I cannot enter a countryman's house as a guest under false colours. Miles is my name, but not my patronymic. Will you admit me, with this much of an explanation? I brought a cargo from our country to Charleston, running the blockade, and I left the half of my name in England."

"The other half of your name is not Brentam?" said Mr. Dale, confidently.

"No," answered Miles, startled; "certainly not."

"Then own my house! Don't you know how those Spanish fellows do? In speaking of their houses they always add, 'which is also yours.' In their case it is only surface politeness. In my case it is a genuine welcome. Annot, my child, Mr. Miles will *dine* with us; none of your suppers! Toby! Take Mr. Miles to the octagon room and wait upon him. The more entirely you feel at home, sir, the more you honour me. Here is the staircase."

Miles, escorted by his black attendant, ascended the stairs. The octagon room was over the verandah, and he could see from the window the end of the hedge-bordered lane and the forest beyond. Toby danced around him, plying his brush and removing the travel-stains from his garments. When he descended to the lower story, he found his host and Miss Dale seated in the drawing-room. Dinner was announced when the candles were brought in, and the visitor did ample justice to the meal. He had been living upon cigar smoke since an early breakfast, and he relinquished his knife and fork with a sigh, after an hour's steady occupation.

"We are living upon our own resources," observed Mr. Dale, "and wine is not within reach. Milk in abundance, however."

"It should be called nectar," replied Miles. "Really, I am ashamed of my voracious appetite! It is due to your matchless climate, Mr. Dale. Nothing more, I thank you."

"Well, let us go on the verandah and smoke. How beautiful the night is! Do you notice the chirp of night-birds and insects, as different from those that we hear in dear old England?"

"Dear old England!" echoed his daughter. "Shall I ever see England?"

"Annot was born in Charleston," explained Mr. Dale. "She calls herself an English maiden, though. She heard a singer in New York, some celebrated tenor, singing 'The Maids of Merry England.' Go sing a verse, Annot. Let Mr. Miles be pleasantly reminded of his fair countrywomen."

She obediently passed into the drawing-room, and presently, after a short prelude, Miles heard her voice—a grand soprano—filling the room and floating out into the night. He sat entranced, trying to catch the meaning of the words, and then forgetting them for the melody. She sang two stanzas, and while he still dreamed she glided back to her seat by her father's side.

"A fine song," said Mr. Dale.

"It is most beautiful," said Miles, half to himself. "How does it happen that such a voice is buried in this Western wilderness? Excuse me, Miss Dale, I did not mean to say that in your hearing. Did I say wilderness? This is a veritable paradise! Since I landed I have not encountered many attractions to wean me from my native land. I have been living with traders and rough seamen, intent on money-making—longing for Somerset——"

"Somerset!" said Mr. Dale, interrupting him. "Do you come from Somerset?"

"Yes."

"You spoke of Glasgow so constantly at dinner that I concluded you a Scot."

"I sailed from Glasgow."

"Somerset! Do you happen to know Hawkley?"

"Yes."

There was a half-hour of silence. The gentlemen smoked. Miss Dale sat patiently waiting for the conversation to be resumed. Her father was apparently absorbed in his own thoughts. At last he turned abruptly to Miles.

"Will you pardon me if I ask a question or two? Do not answer me if they are improper. You spoke of traders just now. Are you a trader?"

"I am supercargo of a blockade-runner at present."

"And at other times?"

Miles hesitated.

"Do not answer, my friend. Let us go in, and Annot will give us some music."

"But I would rather answer if you will allow me. I inherited some little property. It is encumbered. I earnestly desire to be free from debt, and therefore I am blockade-running. A foolish pride, I suppose, made me desire to earn the money I need without the knowledge of my associates. If I can get out with my ship, and get back to England with a cargo of cotton, I will have enough for my purpose."

"Pray say no more, Mr. Miles," said his host. "It was not merely curiosity that prompted the question, however. Let us go in."

As they passed in, following Annot, Miles touched the arm of his host.

"I will ask permission to propound a question or two, also," he whispered.

"As many as you please," replied Mr. Dale.

"Not now. Miss Dale, if you will sing that song once more——"

"You will assist me?" she answered.

"Let me hear it first, please. If I capture the melody, I will try the bass."

Song followed song as the swift minutes sped away. In turning over the music, Miles selected a song and placed it before her. It was "Annie Laurie." She quietly substituted another and sang it. After some delay he uncovered it again, and set it up on the music-desk.

"You do not care particularly for that?" she asked.

"Not if you prefer anything else," he answered.

"I will sing anything else you would like," she said, with a troubled air. Miles suddenly remembered the parting words of Captain Stanly, and was astounded to feel a jealous pang shoot through his heart. While he still meditated, she continued: "Oh, this horrible, horrible war! Do you hear the guns?"

"I have heard something like shots occasionally," replied Miles, looking into her pale face with genuine sympathy. He had choked the jealousy.

"Only the pickets exchanging compliments," said Mr. Dale. "They are miles distant, Annot."

"Yes, father," she answered, vehemently, "but we *hear* them! Oh! if we could only fly from the dreadful sound! I really cannot sing any more to-night. What horrible discord those sharp reports make! Oh for the time when He shall make wars to cease!" And her gentle eyes were moist as she closed the piano.

"Poor child!" said Mr. Dale. "We will go to Charleston, Annot, in a week or two——"

"And hear the constant cannonade from the forts and ships!" said she. "Every time I hear the spiteful snap of the guns yonder, I think some poor woman may be a widow—some poor child an orphan. Oh, the wickedness of war!"

"You are the first woman I have met in America," said Miles, "who does not strenuously advocate war."

"Yes, and therefore the war continues. But my interests are not identical with theirs, because we are English, and have an English home. Oh, father, let us go home!"

"My dear," replied Mr. Dale, "there are certain obstacles in the way. I cannot sell this Dale's Manor, and I have not enough money to litigate for the other Dale's Manor. We have a little patrimony in Somerset, Mr. Miles, which we think is unjustly withheld from us.

If I could gain possession of that I would gladly return. But the present holder is a cold, hard man, and an enemy."

Miles had an indistinct memory of Dale's Manor as a portion of the estate of Mr. Brentam. It was an extensive tract of farm lands, south of the mills and the village. The name clung to it only in the traditions of the villagers, and he had scarcely heard it since his boyhood.

"I have a confused recollection of a spot sometimes called Dale's Manor," he said, after meditating some minutes; "I think it is near Brentam Mills."

"Yes."

"Anything you choose to tell me about it shall be held confidentially. I confess a burning curiosity, but I would not presume to ask any questions."

"You are an English gentleman," answered Mr. Dale, "and I will tell you the story without conditions. Sit here by me, Annot, and correct me if I go astray in my narrative. Take the arm-chair, Mr. Miles."

CHAPTER XIII.

SOME LETTERS.

THE monotony of Hyland's life in the north country was broken one day by the arrival of a mail from Calcutta. There were three letters for him: two from England and one from Calcutta. Recognising the hand of his brother in the address of one of the English letters, he opened that first. The reader has already had an extract from this letter, but there was a postscript added, that engrossed Hyland's attention.

"Since writing the foregoing, my dear brother," it ran, "I have proposed to Miss Carey and have been rejected. I cannot account for it, except upon the general ground of my unworthiness"—(Miles was too true a gentleman to tell even Hyland that Mildred had intimated her preference for another)—"or upon the supposition that she may like some other fellow better. It has discomposed me somewhat, yet I do not at all feel that life is a blank to me henceforth. Neither do I think of renewing the attack. They say a lion only jumps once for his prey. If he misses the first *coup*, he does not essay a second, but just marches off. I return to my original programme, namely : to live single, and leave the title to you and your heirs.

"However, I do not intend to leave you an incumbered estate, and am therefore about to engage in an enterprise that looks promising to me. It is a close secret, brother, and I will tell you about it when—it is accomplished. Meantime I am going to disappear—do not be alarmed—I am not going to incur any risk of bodily damage. I have been concocting the scheme ever since you left me, and I feel tolerably confident of success. But my partner enjoins strict secrecy upon me, and I have his pledge also to the same effect. If you do not hear from me for, say, six or eight months, just conclude that I am spending the summer and autumn in Siberia, making surveys for railway lines. You know I am an accomplished engineer, and do not be foolish enough to indulge in any apprehensions on my account. I think I can promise to communicate with you within six calendar months. Possess your soul in patience thus long, brother.

"I may confess that my recent disappointment makes me the more eager to engage in this new affair, as I desire the cares that will necessarily devolve upon me to banish the memory of this failure. But if I had been fortunate in my suit, I should still have undertaken this enterprise, as I am resolved to get Hawkley clear if possible. My rental is nearly four thousand pounds, and if I had no incumbrances I should feel rich enough.

"And now, Hyland, good-bye for a short time. I may not be able to write you, the mail facilities in Siberia are defective, you know. Keep writing to me as usual. I hope to find a good budget of letters waiting for me at Hawkley when I return.

"Your affectionate brother,

"MILES."

Poor Hyland was stunned. Somehow there had grown up between these two men a sense of proprietorship on one hand and of dependence on the other. Hyland was so much more prompt and aggressive in his character, that Miles had fallen under a sort of tutelage, and Hyland always felt a responsibility upon himself when thinking of the elder. At Eton, once and again, Hyland had thrashed a bull-headed "commoner," who was seeking a quarrel with his brother simply because he was a "nob," and on both occasions Hyland had adroitly managed to induce a previous quarrel with the bully, without the knowledge of Miles. The fight, by Eton law, was Hyland's right, and his brother did not dare to interfere.

And in later life Hyland had devised ways of egress from financial difficulties, utilizing Lord Rayneford's own resources, wisely and well. And now, he felt that Miles had suddenly snapped the leading-strings; and with the inevitable conceit of youth, he fancied that all would go wrong without his oversight. " New enterprise!" he muttered; "more likely some old humbug that I could have exploded if I had been there! Siberia! I have a great mind to start on an overland journey to that charming country and look the fellow up! But Siberia is not the objective-point. The letter is clear. He names Siberia as the most distant place from his real destination. Probably he has gone to the antipodes. I think I will explore Patagonia! I wish I could find him, and he could cease being my brother for ten minutes till I punched his head! Dear old Miles!"

Then Hyland opened the other English letter. This was written fully two weeks later, and was from Mr. Plimpton.

"My dear Rayneford," it began, "I am so heartily delighted with your assured success in India, that nothing short of very grave anxiety would impel me to interrupt your career or disturb you in your present occupations. Your brother, Lord Rayneford, has unaccountably disappeared. Do not be alarmed. There is not the slightest reason to suspect anything like foul play or to dread any personal danger. But he is gone, and positively *nobody* knows whither! He has gone of his own accord, and after the most deliberate preparation. And he has taken elaborate measures to conceal his purposes and destination from every one. I went down to Somerset, and spent some hours with Mr. Brentam, who received his last communication, and who could give me not the slightest clue as to his whereabouts. Mr. Brentam allowed me to copy the note, which was quite brief. I reproduce it for your benefit: 'My dear Mr. Brentam, I have decided to leave England to-morrow, and shall be absent some months, having certain matters in charge of considerable importance. The business that takes me away is one in which another person is deeply interested, and we are mutually bound to keep all its details secret. Although somewhat out of the beaten track, it still involves little risk of bodily harm, and I expect to return to Hawkley within six months or less. I will take measures to communicate with you, if necessary, and if any unforeseen calamity should overtake me, you will be notified as soon as possible thereafter. I enclose the legal authority for you to take charge of my interests, if any exigency should arise, in the matter of rental, etc. Very truly yours, Rayneford.' That is all. This note was dated in Liverpool, Monday, 8th instant. I went to Liverpool, and by searching the records found only one ship left that port on the 9th. It was the 'Asia,' for Melbourne. It happened that I met a detective—a Mr. Dancer, whom I have employed on one or two occasions with great success, and I told him the story. You see, I am the only near connexion of your family here, and I felt bound to leave no efforts untried to assure myself of his present safety. In two days Dancer brought me the assurance that Miles had not sailed in the 'Asia.' He had been at the Adelphi Hotel, and had taken his luggage on the morning of the 9th in a cab, without leaving any orders. Dancer, with his usual pertinacity, hunted up the cab, and after assuring himself by several proofs that he had the right one, he questioned the cabby, and learned that he had taken Miles to the Lime street station, and saw him on the train for Bristol. Here the trail was lost. But Dancer is still 'working the case.' I should say, he is a private detective, and no one knows of his employment except myself.

" Now, what do you think of the matter? Here is a young nobleman of spotless reputation, of sober habits, suddenly disappearing from the surface! There has never been any case of insanity in the family. There was nothing in his circumstances to induce him to withdraw from society. He was engaged to read a paper on the Poor Laws before the Humanitarian Society this week, and had half promised to spend three days with me in London, but he excused himself a week before he left from both engagements, upon the plea of ' urgent private business.' He has paid up some small obligations maturing six months hence, and methodically prepared for an absence of that duration.

" If you are in his confidence, pray enlighten me enough to relieve my anxiety about him. But I do not believe he has told even you of his intentions. It really seems to me, Rayneford, that I should cut India and hunt for him, if he were my brother.

" Your friend and kinsman,

" H. PLIMPTON."

" This is improving!" said Hyland; " Miles runs mad and absconds, and then Plimpton runs mad and sets a detective on him! And I shall run mad and complete the trio, unless I go back to England. Ah, this other letter is from Glendare. No mistaking his calligraphy. Let us see if he has gone mad also."

" My dear friend," said Mr. Glendare's letter, " Daltman tells me a mail will go to the plantations to-morrow, and I will avail myself of the opportunity to say a few words to you. It seems like a year since we parted, and I have had no chance to communicate with you since the arrival of your 'Quinia' letter. By-the-bye, that letter created a great stir in our camp at Nuttagur. Doctor Leigh scouted your American friend's theories, and to prove his errors he incontinently cured Miss Haidee without exhibiting your darling remedy. In a few days after your missive arrived, she discarded all her headgear, and has had no symptoms of neuralgia since. It is a pity you did not put Doctor Leigh upon his mettle earlier, as you would have been able to discover for yourself how attractive the child is. She is really very pretty, and if she would quit novel reading and take a course of substantial literature, she would soon rival her sister.

"Colonel Mordaunt seems to be failing, and Doctor Leigh tells me he will certainly be compelled to quit this climate very soon, to preserve his life. He was ordered back from Nuttagur a month ago, and Calcutta makes him worse. He is still reticent, as of old, and discloses none of his plans, but I have reason to think he is projecting a trip to England. Frank certainly is. And do you know that I am expecting to go with them? Certain family matters combine to call me home. Come with us, Rayneford."

"Here is the third madman," said Hyland.

"Colonel Mordaunt says," continued the letter, "you can easily get leave of absence. Indeed, he volunteered to hint that a word from him would secure *that*, and at my suggestion he has already taken the initial steps. You see, my friend, I would not have you take the long journey to Calcutta upon an uncertainty. We shall have an excellent ship, the 'Lord Clive' steamer, twelve hundred tons, sailing on the 22d. Frank is going to sell out when he reaches England; at least, he says so. He has inherited some money, and he does not think India furnishes a field for spending equal to his talents. To indicate his ability, I may mention his last purchase. Captain Morgan had a yacht, now at Cardiff, and at tiffin yesterday he happened to speak of the expense of keeping the vessel in repair. He had just paid some large amount for a complete overhauling. Master Frank asked why he did not sell out. Morgan replied, 'All the fools who have enough tin to buy a yacht already own one.' Frank asked the name of Morgan's vessel. The 'Juliet,' schooner, eighty-five tons. What did she cost? About two thousand pounds. 'I'll give you a thousand,' said Daltman. 'Done!' said Morgan, 'with the cheque.'"

"Frank bids me write you to join him in a cruise three months from the present date. He will sail out of Cardiff, steer north, and circumnavigate Great Britain."

"Here is one more madman than I needed," said Hyland. "Daltman professes to abominate salt water, yet he buys a vessel, arranges a cruise, and invites me to bob about on the short waves of the Channel for weeks! Declined, with thanks! Let us finish the letter though."

"Since writing the preceding page," concluded Mr. Glendare, "I have seen the colonel. The *application* is granted. Four months. You cannot accept Frank's invitation unless you get an extension of leave. Nevertheless, come quickly, and we will reorganise our Nuttagur party on board the 'Lord Clive.' Remember the 22d, and hasten.
                                   "Your friend,
                                        "HAMISH GLENDARE."

Hyland picked up the enclosure that fell out of his friend's letter. It was the regular announcement of leave on the printed form, requesting the Honourable Hyland Rayneford to report for duty at Calcutta "four months from the 22d of the current month."

There was a great deal of sound common sense in Hyland's composition, but there was also an instinctive antagonism to "management." Whenever his quick discernment detected another's purpose to lead him or drive him, there always arose the prompt determination to resist the influence. It is by no means certain that this trait was an indication of weakness, or a defect in his character. It may be the instinctive recoil of normal humanity from creature domination. Whether created or evolved, man is the lord of the earth. If created, he was made in an exalted image; if evolved, he was the fittest that survived, and the survival includes royalty. Within proper limits, the consciousness of high station does not involve self-conceit; but beyond those limits it degenerates into arrogance and insolence.

"Now," said he, as he meditated upon the letters, "a trip to England was just what I desired before I read Glendare's letter. But he did not know that. Neither did the colonel, or Mr. Daltman. They have arranged their plans, and my movements are a part of them. We shall see."

Four days after he re-read the letters. In the meantime he had concluded that his brother was safe, and had increased his resentment against Mr. Plimpton, because he had presumed to hunt for Miles "with hawk and hound, the fussy old granny!" But there had also grown up in him an irrepressible longing to see Miles. So on the fifth day he was on his way to Calcutta.

He arrived on the 22d, and found two notes, one from Colonel Mordaunt, giving his address in England, "14 George Crescent, Bath." The other was a scrawl from Daltman, the ink scarcely dry.

"DEAR RAYNEFORD—You have not arrived, and the ship sails in ten minutes. Mildred writes that your brother is off to the Continent or somewhere else, and asks if you have heard from him. Mr. Brentam does not know where he is. Better come on in the next steamer. Yacht will be all ready in sixty days. Morgan says she sails like a witch. Don't know how a witch sails. We shall have a jolly time on the 'Clive,' but we shall miss you. Why the deuce didn't you come?   "Yours,
                                        "DALTMAN."

The black smoke from the funnel of the "Clive," far down the Hoogly river, was all that Hyland ever saw of the steamer.

At nightfall a one-armed native presented himself, as Hyland sucked at his cheroot.

"Salaam, sahib! Another ship sails in two days. Will sahib go? Zeba will go also. Colonel Sahib gave Zeba ticket for other ship, but he waited."

"Did you wait for me, Zeba?" said Hyland, touched by the Hindoo's manner.

"Yes, sahib. Help find. Got tulwar." And he touched the hilt of his weapon. "And got one arm and one eye left."

"One more madman!" thought Hyland, looking into the sharp black eye of the native.

CHAPTER XIV.

ON THE SEA.

THE "Bengal" was a screw-steamer from Calcutta, bound for London, with an assorted cargo, and having limited accommodations for passengers. The previous steamer was the regular passenger vessel, and had taken out a goodly company, so that Hyland and Zeba were the only voyagers, excepting the officers and crew, that steamed away from the mouth of the Hoogly river into the bay of Bengal on one hot morning. Zeba, who had come aboard in the habiliments of European civilization, relapsed into Asiatic barbarism as the ship began to rise and fall upon the regular swell of the sea, and resumed his muslins.

The first days at sea are usually delicious, except to the sufferers from *mal de mer*. To a thinking man, if free from cumbering cares, the horizon presents an array of vast problems, which are not readily solved, but which demand attention throughout one entire day at least. And the after-monotony does not completely banish them from the mind. The effect of the expanse of waters upon Hyland was to arouse his philosophy, and the results of this awakening were sundry entries in his diary.

"Out here upon this hot sea," he wrote, "five feet eleven seems to dwindle down to modest dimensions. If I were to stick a pin in the dome of St. Paul's, it would make no appreciable addition to the weight, and would be invisible at the distance of a yard. But the proportion of the pin to the dome would be a thousand times greater than my proportion to this vast sea. Nay, the ship might slip under one of those big waves and go down, hardly adding a bubble to the restless ocean. But there are thirty men on board, and each one has some link binding him to the earth. And the ship and cargo represent pounds, shillings, and pence.

"There is that heathen Zeba, in scarlet jacket and white kilt; one sleeve pinned up, one eye darkened. He is hanging his tulwar, naked, to the rigging. And now he is walking around it, as it swings to and fro. And now he is spread out upon the deck watching it. Ah! he takes the weapon down, and slips it deftly into its scabbard with his single arm.

"Zeba has just passed me with his 'Salaam, sahib!' I asked him what he was doing with his sword. He said, 'Sahib's brother yonder! ship sail straight to him.' Then he walked aft, and has gone to sleep on his mat. I asked the mate how we were steering. He says, 'A bit noath of west.' Now, if my geography is not at fault, Miles must be at the Canary Islands or the 'still vexed Bermoothes.' What atrocious humbug!

"How shall I record a philosophical explanation of this mental phenomenon? To state the case first: The Hindoo, who is of Brahmin blood, practises some superstitious rite with his tulwar. When he finishes, he tells me, with superb confidence, that Miles is nearly due west from me. So great an impression does this make upon me that I cannot rest until I learn from the mate the exact direction. And this very minute I am cogitating a scheme to test the tulwar again, when we make our highest south latitude.

"Now, an educated Englishman, who has no more respect for Indian superstition than he has for the senseless chattering of monkeys, is seriously impressed by the incident. Zeba looked thoroughly in earnest, watching the sword swinging in the rigging with unwinking vigilance until it ceased rotating, and then, accepting the oracle's response, went to sleep. I suppose all the philosophers in the world could not shake his faith in the tulwar. While I, Hyland Rayneford, knowing Kant and Spinosa and Descartes, am under some degree of bondage to the solitary eye of this heathen. Because the gleam of his eye was the first thing that impressed me when he said, 'Salaam, sahib!' I was *compelled* to ask him what the tulwar said.

"Kant asserts that freedom is the postulate of the pure, practical reason. Causality, in the sense implied by freedom, belongs to man in so far as he is a thing-in-itself. But causality, in the sense implied in the mechanism of nature, belongs to him in so far as he is a subject of the realm of appearances. Here is the case then: on one side noumenon; on the other side, phenomenon.

"How, then, can my freedom, which is an essential attribute of my personality, be invaded by the sham phenomena of a heathen rite? In fact, I do not know that there were any phenomena. I know nothing, except the Hindoo's devotion to me, which, after all, I only infer. Can there be some secret law—dynamical—underlying the superstitions observances of the heathen? What is the genesis of superstition?"

While Hyland was weaving these metaphysical cobwebs, Zeba was quietly dreaming on his mat, the rays of the tropical sun beating on his prostrate body. The day before the "Lord Clive" sailed Zeba had overheard a discussion between Daltman and Mr. Glendare, in which the prominent fact was the disappearance of Lord Rayneford, and the missionary had asserted very emphatically that Hyland would certainly go to England to seek his brother. The devotion of the Hindoo to Hyland was not demonstrative, but it was real. It reached its climax at the tiger fight, though months of kindly intercourse while the two threaded the jungle in Hyland's surveys had generated respect and esteem on both sides. Rayneford was constantly reminded of the acute intelligence of the native, who learned everything and forgot nothing. Zeba studied with curious interest the character of this English sahib, who never swore at him, never manifested contempt by look or gesture, but provided for his comfort on all occasions with spontaneous kindness. But in the short colloquy preceding the combat Zeba recognised the warrior, and since the days of Tubal Cain the warrior has been acknowledged lord among all the tribes of earth. Haidee dubbed Hyland "Knight." Zeba called him "Sahib," and meant it.

Four hundred miles southwest of the "Bengal" a far more brilliant company was gathered under the awning covering the quarter-deck of the "Lord Clive." There was very little wind, and what there was came from the south, so that the motion of the ship increased the apparent force of the breeze. The colonel was lying in a grass hammock swinging between the mizzen-mast and the wheel-house. Miss Mordaunt, having conscientiously undergone the conventional forty-eight hours of agony in the dark recesses of the ladies' cabin, was propped up with pillows against the skylight, receiving the polite attentions of Mr. Daltman. Mr. Glendare and Dr. Leigh were pacing the deck and talking politics.

Haidee had waited upon Juliet through three or four hours of actual sickness, which began with the first tremulous roll of the ship off soundings. Then came the other hours of querulous discomfort, and Juliet dismissed her and demanded the ayah. The doctor prescribed a teaspoonful of brandy every two hours, which the ayah faithfully administered, and as faithfully stole a tablespoonful for herself at shorter intervals, which she took neat. So Haidee betook herself to the deck, with the "Chronicles of Sir John Froissart." Mr. Glendare had adroitly substituted this volume for the lighter literature in which Haidee was accustomed to revel. At present she was totally engrossed in the conflict between Sir Bertrand du Guesclin and the Captal De Buch. It was nearly as good as "Ivanhoe." Hot knights, broiling in hot armour, chopping each other with sword and battle-axe, while she sat on a pile of cushions in the shade.

"I wonder what detained Rayneford?" said Mr. Daltman. "Hamish gave him three or four days extra time."

"Probably he prefers India," replied Miss Mordaunt, languidly.

"But here was a free trip, and no abatement of pay!" said Daltman. "I suspect he desires to stand well with John Company, and expects his zeal to be remembered. He told me he was after the rupees."

"He is in a fair way to get them," observed the colonel. "Sir John told me that he was reluctant to spare Rayneford, who was the best man at the plantations."

"Is the pay large enough, colonel," asked Daltman, "to compensate a man for such a life?"

"It is a very pleasant life," said the colonel. "The climate is temperate as compared with Calcutta. The pay is about four times as great as that of an army lieutenant, and he has no mess expenses."

"It seems to me," muttered Daltman, "that the pay of civilians is too great, or the pay of army-officers is too small. Here I have been knocking about from the Cape to India three or four years, living among the African niggers at one place, and the rascally Hindoo niggers at the other, and coming out in debt at the end of each year! If my good old aunt had not remembered me in her will, I should have been in the *Gazette*. Now Mr. Rayneford just steps into a comfortable revenue without the slightest trouble or risk or exposure. It is all luck! There was that tiger business. Rayneford's luck put him in the exact spot to bag the game!"

"It seems to me," said Haidee, shutting Froissart up with a snap, "that Mr. Rayneford walked up to the exact spot, looking for the luck! There was nobody between him and the tiger except poor Zeba. Papa, why did Zeba not come with us?"

"He asked permission to wait for 'Sahib Hyland,'" replied the colonel. "He confidently expected him, and at his request I transferred his ticket from the 'Lord Clive' to the 'Bengal.'"

"How could the Hindoo expect Rayneford?" asked Mr. Glendare, pausing in his walk.

"Zeba is a necromancer," replied Colonel Mordaunt, reluctantly.

"Go on, papa, please," said Haidee.

"Your head is full enough of nonsense already, child," said the colonel, smiling, "but you know something of the superstitions of the western provinces. Many of their delusions are connected with their weapons. For example: if a man kills a tiger with a sword-stroke, in a fair encounter, the sword becomes an oracle thereafter. The responses are thought infallible if the warrior's blood is mingled with the blood of the beast on the blade. Zeba has been practising his black-art with his tulwar, and it told him Rayneford was coming to Calcutta."

"But Zeba did not fulfil the conditions," said Daltman. "He did not kill the tiger outright."

"No. But he says Rayneford is Lord of the tulwar."

"The conditions are still halting," replied Daltman; "Zeba had already shot the brute before Rayneford encountered him."

"No," said the colonel; "Zeba's bullet was flattened against the rock. He brought it to me a day or two after Leigh let him out of hospital. The tiger was in full vigour, and totally unharmed."

"I thought so," murmured Haidee.

"It is very curious," pursued the colonel, "but the conditions were very accurately met at all points. Rayneford demanded the weapon at the first appearance of danger. He refused to relinquish it, when you demanded it, in turn. Zeba missed his shot, and Rayneford conquered by his unaided prowess. And while he held the dripping tulwar in his wounded hand, his own blood ran down over hilt and blade."

"That is true," murmured Haidee; "I saw it!"

"How the—deuce does the tulwar reveal its secrets?" said Daltman; "can it talk?"

"Zeba translates its mysterious responses by his own methods," replied the colonel. "I do not understand them. His caste is the Chehteree, and he is an undoubted noble. I found him a dozen years ago at Lahore. He stands next to the Brahmins, and would die rather than occupy a servile position. I made him corporal, and have always had unlimited confidence in him. He talks all the dialects, but while he was delirious, he jabbered constantly in the Pracrit. Haidee understood him. Her ayah, Sista, is from Lahore also, and she has caught the lingo from her. During the mutiny, Zeba brought Haidee and Sista to me, out of the very jaws of death, travelling over forty miles through a country filled with enemies."

"His fighting days are over," said Dr. Leigh. "With one arm and one eye gone, he is only half a man."

"He would give a good account of himself," replied the colonel, "with an ordinary antagonist. I have seen him toss his tulwar whirling in the air, catch it by the hilt with his left hand as it fell, and slice off the top of a post four or five inches in diameter."

"The savage!" murmured Juliet.

"The warrior!" whispered Haidee. "Papa," she continued, aloud, "you do not explain what Zeba meant by 'Lord of the tulwar.'"

"Mr. Rayneford became Lord of the tulwar when he slew the tiger. And the oracle, according to Zeba's superstition, cannot withhold its response when he consults it, or when it is consulted in his behalf. It is all abominable nonsense, of course, but living so many years among these people, one is more or less influenced by their superstitious notions. A month's residence in England will brush away all these cobwebs."

Haidee went back to her own cushions with Froissart. She read a few pages, and then the monotonous shiver of the ship as the screw revolved and the monotonous wash of the sea induced somnolency. So she fell asleep, with the book on her lap. She dreamed that she had somehow exchanged places with the Captal De Buch, and that she was suddenly surrounded, captured, bound and carried off. She saw the long lances of her captors, and felt herself borne swiftly away, though she still recognised the rise and fall of the sea. She heard the clank of armour, steel scabbard rattling against steel boot. She heard the voice of Du Guesclin, ordering careful treatment of the captive, and all the while she felt the roll of the ship. This was very confusing, and opposed to the record in Froissart.

In spite of her romance she was a girl of extraordinary sense, so she began to ask herself what Du Guesclin had seized her for. Money? This was not at all chivalrous, but she had a dozen sovereigns in her pocket, and she had a vague idea that this sum was a small fortune in Du Guesclin's time.

Now suppose she offers what money she has for her liberty?

That would accomplish nothing. Because these strong men can take the money whenever they like. Better say nothing about it. Ransom? Of course, there must be a herald or something sent to her father. How can she get a herald? Suppose she sent Sista, her ayah? The old wretch would fall asleep forty times in a mile. If she could only get Zeba!

There is Zeba, coming across the plain, tossing his tulwar up in the air, and catching it as it descends, and then pausing to examine it closely, hilt and blade. He does not notice her. He is too intent upon his mummery to notice anything.

Ah! here comes a knight to her rescue! He pauses to confer with Zeba and takes his tulwar. It is Sir Hyland's tulwar. But this new-comer is grey-bearded and decrepit. See! He opens his visor and shows his wrinkled face. Nevertheless he is preparing for battle, while Zeba composedly seats himself on the ground to watch the conflict.

The knight has changed his mind! He dismounts, props his long lance against his saddle, while the steed stands motionless as a statue. The knight approaches Zeba, and sticks the tulwar in the ground.

6

Now he and Zeba are circling round the weapon in a kind of solemn dance.

Now he takes off his helmet, throws his shield upon the ground, and, with his grey locks and beard streaming in the wind, approaches her captors—and she awoke.

Zeba was taking his dream at the same hour on the sunny deck of the "Bengal." He got his arm back in his dream, and was doing some very valiant fighting in the Punjaub. Anon, he was threading the jungle under the starlight, carrying Haidee, while Sista crept along behind him. Then he was in a land of fogs and snows, as his imagination painted England, following Sahib Hyland in his search for his brother. This brother was under the control of some wicked Afreet, and Zeba was perpetually circumventing the bad spirit by consultations with the charmed tulwar.

Hyland was conversing with the second mate, an old sea-dog, who was going to England on his last voyage. Mr. Jones was a Welshman, and he was eloquent in describing the beauties of his native principality. He was hopelessly deaf, and carried a small slate swung to his neck, and Hyland conversed with the pencil. The old sailor liked grog, also, and could never have reached England as a ship's officer if the "Bengal" had not sailed out of the Hoogly at a time when navigators were exceedingly scarce, and his infirmity was forgiven for the sake of his undoubted seamanship.

CHAPTER XV.

The Battle.

THE grey dawn found Mr. Miles in the saddle. He had heard at intervals, through the previous night, the spiteful snapping of musquetry, but was not fully roused from his slumbers until the more prolonged roar of heavier metal ushered in the coming day. As he collected his faculties and took in his surroundings, which seemed gorgeous in comparison with the rude entertainment he had hitherto found, he recalled the vehement words of Annot on the previous evening, and hoped she slept well enough to escape the sounds of conflict, while his window-sashes rattled with each discharge of artillery. He could sympathise with her in her horror of the strife as he pictured the heaps of human bodies, torn and shattered, only a mile or two distant. Sleep was out of the question, so he dressed rapidly, while the eager desire to see the battle grew upon him. It was inevitable; the instinctive impulse of manhood, that drew him down-stairs and out upon the broad verandah. Here he found Toby, putting the final touches upon his horseman's boots.

"Ah, Toby!" he said, "you are astir early. Are those my boots?"

"Yes, massa," replied Toby, "jest finished. You hear dem shootin's? 'Spect dat what woked you up. Dey's flingin' dem bustin' balls over yonder!"

"Shells?" said Miles.

"Shells! Sho' as you born! Dat fight must be down in de Long Hollow."

"Where is it, Toby?" asked Miles, as he drew on his boots.

"Not fur from de school-house, sah."

"Can you get my horse, Toby?" Miles was getting excited.

"Sartain, sah! Walk in to breakfus'-room. You gwine over yonder? Take cup of coffee fust. Heah some cold chicken. Git some breakfus' while I saddle."

Instead of going to the school-house, Miles skirted the cornfield at the entrance-gate, and guided by the sounds of strife, growing more distinct every moment, he reached the crest of a little hill, and caught sight of veritable battle smoke. He was as brave as became a man of gentle breeding, yet the first glimpse of that sombre cloud seemed to check his pulsations. There was a slight elevation opposite his hill, less than a mile distant, the "Long Hollow" lying between. From this vantage-ground came the shells, now actually visible as they burst into flame over a strip of woodland on his left. He could see moving figures under the trees, and the incessant streaks of fire, preceding the sharp report of the rifles, on the edge of the covert. Notwithstanding his ignorance of warfare, it was apparent to him that the object on one side was to dislodge the infantry in the woods, while the return fire could do little damage to the distant battery. There were no signs to indicate which side was Confederate, and he debated whether he had better ride onward to the wood, or retrace his steps, and seek his friends of the previous evening at the school-house. While he sat irresolute, he heard the tramp of a galloping horse, and turned his head in the direction of the sound. A youth of eighteen or twenty swept by him on the instant, touching his cap as he passed, his long scabbard rattling against the side of the magnificent horse.

"Better move off the road, sir !" he shouted : " the cavalry will be here in a minute or two."

Miles turned from the road and cantered into a broad meadow, passing through a gap in the fence. The rails had been recently pulled down, and were thrown in a pile on the roadside. There was the track of horse-hoofs and of wheels, cutting the soft grass of the meadow, all recent, and he remembered passing the road on the previous day, when there were no such marks visible. Presently a horseman came through the gap, then another and another, and then a troop, trotting four abreast. Before they overtook him he had reached a narrow valley, the dry bed of a water-course, and the fortified hill and the wood were both hidden.

"Halt !" The order ran along the line and the officer in command rode up.

"Good morning, Mr. Miles." It was Captain Stanly. "Did the salutation of the gentlemen on the hill awaken you ?"

"I heard the reports of large guns," answered Miles, shaking the other's offered hand, "and could not resist the temptation to come out."

"Ah !" said the other. "We are about to silence them. If you will ride back to the gap, you can probably see—— Hillo ! That shell was intended for us ! There is another ! Attention ! Captain Green, take two companies and ride back to the road. Take the left hand and join me at the north gap, where those fellows passed through last night. They will think their shells are driving us back. The woods will hide you after you reach the road. If I reach the gap before you, you have only to follow. Forward !"

"The devil take the hindmost !" said Green, as he dashed away.

"May I go with you ?" asked Miles, as Stanly resumed his trot.

"It will be quite warm up there," answered Stanly.

"Well, the morning air is quite cool," said Miles.

"I cannot give you the permission," said Stanly, gravely, "neither can I forbid your presence. But I strongly advise you to go back."

"Many thanks," replied Miles, touching his horse with the spur. "Only tell me what I must do and what avoid. I desire to be as near you as I may, but would not violate proprieties."

"Your principal occupation will be to dodge shells. When we reach the north gap we shall be in full view, and then we shall ride over that battery. But the present owners will object, and we must ride a full half-mile in the face of the storm. They will exchange shells for grape, and if I bring two hundred men back with that battery, I shall be thankful. Hurd was badly wounded this morning, and I am senior captain."

Miles glanced backward, and tried to count. There were about five hundred men in the regiment, and Green had taken nearly two hundred of them. The rain of shells which had been falling in the low valley, before Green's departure, had now passed to the main road, and Stanly's party was in comparative safety.

They halted again at the edge of the meadow, waiting the arrival of Green with his command. Peering through the undergrowth, Miles was astonished to see the strip of wood suddenly yield up a long line of foot-soldiers, their bayonets gleaming in the sunlight as they dashed down the Hollow.

"Now, then," said Stanly, whirling his sabre from the scabbard; "gentlemen, the general wants yonder battery. Let us get it for him. Here comes Green at a gallop! Draw, boys, and follow!"

A roar of cheers burst from the troopers as they plunged through the gap in the fence, answered by a terrific yell from the infantry racing across the Hollow; answered by the rattle of musquetry from the base of the hill crowned by the battery; answered by the shower of grape-shot that tore through their ranks and emptied their saddles, until Miles, fascinated, saw Stanly leap his horse over the low earthworks, and heard the ringing steel, as a hundred sabres clashed with the bayonets of the footmen. In another moment the Confederate infantry rushed, panting, into the conflict, while the remnant of the cavalry urged their horses up the hill, into the very mouths of the cannon, which were belching out death at every step of their mad career.

Years afterwards Miles recalled that horrible scene, and the prominent picture engraved upon his memory was the copper-coloured gun, the blue smoke curling from its muzzle, the begrimed face of the gunner as he went down under the stroke of Stanly's sabre the instant before that gallant cavalier rolled out of his saddle, and while the hoarse shout of victory resounded on the hillside.

Miles knelt by the side of the fallen soldier and took his hand.

"Are you hurt, sir?" said Stanly.

"No. But you are."

"Yes. I caught a bayonet in my thigh as I crossed the ditch. And I think I have a bullet in my body. Something struck me just as I cut that poor fellow down. Could you get a drop of water?"

Miles looked around him. The dead artilleryman was lying prone upon his face by the wheel of his gun. There was a tin cup tied to his belt. Miles cut the strap, and went down the hill, at whose foot a little stream trickled through the grass. He dipped up a cupful of the water, and finding it mixed with red, he dashed it down in disgust. He thought of Annot's horror of battle and bloodshedding, and wondered what fiend had tempted him to look upon such ghastly scenes. He ran along the brook up-stream, and found a clear spot, filled the cup and reclimbed the hill. Stanly was propped up against the knee of a stranger, who was examining the wound in his breast. He looked up as Miles approached. A sturdy gentleman with great, kind eyes, now full of sympathy. A brown beard covering his face, and a thoughtful air all over him.

"Let me add a little to your cup," said the stranger, producing a flask; "your friend is hit hard."

"The doctor," thought Miles, giving the drink to Stanly. The frown was gone from his brow, and there was a pleasant smile on his lips.

"Many thanks, gentlemen," he said. "Mr. Miles, I have only a few minutes left. Please open my coat. Thank you! There is a ribbon—— Ah! you have it! The locket. Take it to her. Tell her I stole it. Good-bye!"

The stranger laid the body softly down upon the grass.

"He was a born warrior!" he said. "I saw him coming across the ditch, and saw him get his death-wound. I—I saw something like it once before. At Balaklava."

"You are a countryman!" said Miles.

"Yes. For you have the English speech."

"Is he dead, doctor?" said Miles, pitifully.

"Quite dead. The femoral artery is cut, and a bullet is in his right lung. By-the-bye, I saw you also, when you crossed the ditch, but you were unarmed. Was this gentleman your comrade?"

"I never saw him until last night. I hardly know how I got into this mad gallop. I suppose my horse bolted with me."

"Yes. And you drove your spurs into his sides as you leaped the breastwork," answered the stranger, dryly.

"I was riding by Stanly," muttered Miles, confusedly, "and somehow I felt that his enemies were mine. But I have enough of this. What a horrible sight, doctor! Here are a score of dead men, who were alive ten minutes ago. Poor Stanly! How can I tell her!"

"Her?" said the other. "Had he a wife?"

"No. I do not know certainly, but it is probable that a fair girl's life will be darkened by this sad event. Can I do anything?"

"Nothing, I fancy. Yonder is the surgeon. I am not a doctor, only a volunteer hospital steward. The fight is over. Did you ever hear of anything so mad as that charge upon the battery? If I had been in command on this hill, I should have swept those fellows from the face of the earth! It was the utter insanity of the attempt that gained the success."

"Were you on the hill?" asked Miles, feeling a little antagonism arising in his mind. Without knowing it, he had become decidedly partisan.

"About the same time you arrived," replied the other, coolly. "I came with the infantry from the wood yonder. How now, Tom?" he continued, as a foot-soldier limped up. "What is it?"

"The doctor wants you, Mister Boston," said the soldier. "Goin' to cut off Blake's leg! Say, mister!" addressing Miles, "hadn't you better come outen that hat?"

Miles started as he recognised the sentry who had given the same advice on the previous afternoon, and who had protested against the title of "Tar-heel."

"Ah, my friend!" replied Miles, "I am happy to see you again. You have had some rough work on hand since we parted."

"Yaas!" replied the soldier; "it was rayther lively comin' through that Hollow. Them woods ain't half a mile off, but I'll be dogon'd if it wa'n't six mile when we come through on the double-quick!"

"Was the gentleman—Mr. Boston, you called him—was he with you?"

"Reckon he was. No call to be thar, neither. The cap'n allowed he must stay in the woods. But he allowed some of the boys mout want him, so he just trotted along with us. Many a time when one of our fellers was just turnin' his toes up, Mr. Boston has knelt down by him to git a message or talk some religion. He can saw off a feller's leg as good as the doctor, and he can preach as good as the parson."

"He does not belong to your side," said Miles—"that is, he was not born in your country."

"No. I suppose he was borned a Yank, as his name is Boston. But he could not help that, could he? Anyway, he is true grit. Hello! who is this? Jim Stanly, and dead as a hammer! Oh, heavenly Marster!"

And the rough soldier fell on his knees by the body, covered his grim countenance with his hands, while the tears trickled between his fingers.

"Oh, Jim!" said the soldier, between the sobs that burst from him, "if I only knowed the man that done this, I'd have his life if I followed him to the gates of hell!"

"My friend," said Miles, deeply touched by the other's distress, "be comforted. Captain Stanly fell, sword in hand, at the head of his regiment. He did not suffer half an hour. And he lived long enough to send his last messages to those he loved."

"Did he mention me—Bill Hardy?" said the soldier.

"Not to me. Mr. Boston was with him, while I went to the rill for some water. He only lived a few minutes after I got back. What does the trumpet mean?"

"The recall. We've won this skrimmage, but we've paid an awful price for it. Here comes the old man."

And he arose, caught up his gun, and stood erect and stern, presenting arms as General Smith, followed by his staff, rode down the hill.

"Good-morning, Mr. Miles," said the general. "This is a sad blow. Poor Stanly! Hardy, get three more men and take his body to Dale's Manor."

CHAPTER XVI.

ROBBERY.

THE fight referred to in the previous chapter occurred on the border of East Tennessee. The forces engaged were very nearly equal, the Federal army having a battery of six guns and their adversaries a cavalry regiment. It was a small affair, not more than six or eight thousand men in both forces, and was important so far as it checked the Federal advance, and chiefly because of the capture of the artillery.

Miles rode back to Dale's Manor, while Hardy and his comrades were constructing the rude bier to convey Captain Stanly's body to the cemetery. It was a little church-yard on the border of the estate. When he reached the gate, and while he was debating the question as to how he should break the sad news, he was startled to hear a pistol-shot and a scream for help, evidently coming from the house. He dashed the gate open, and gallopped to the verandah. There were three horses, with fragments of harness hanging about them, fastened to posts near the door. Then he remembered seeing two or three artillerymen striving to carry off one of the guns on the hill, and when the impetuous charge of the cavalry made this impossible, they cut the traces and rode down the hill on the opposite side. He threw himself from the saddle and rushed into the drawing-room.

Mr. Dale was on the floor, a soldier stooping over him, with pistol in hand still smoking. Miss Dale was on the sofa, one soldier holding her down, while the third was tearing her watch from her neck. The look of horror, mingled with eager expectation on her face, brought him to her side at a bound. He caught up a water-pitcher from the table, and dashed it to fragments on the head of the nearest soldier. The other released Miss Dale and half drew his sabre, but Miles was upon him, throttling him before it left the scabbard. In the fierce struggle his spur caught in the carpet and he lost his balance, and as he fell there was another pistol-shot, and he rolled over unconscious.

When General Smith, followed by a dozen officers, rode into the grounds at Dale's Manor, he was surprised to see three blue-coated soldiers gallopping down towards the stables, somewhat encumbered with baggage. When these last-mentioned gentlemen reached the stables and found a high picket-fence between them and the woods, they dropped their baggage in the bushes, slipped from their saddles, and began to climb this formidable obstacle. And when each of them felt the points of three sabres penetrating his nether extremities, each one dropped on the ground, surrendering at discretion and howling with pain.

"Bring them to the house, Green," said the general; "tie them up securely, and let us see what they have done."

The scene in the drawing-room was appalling. Annot Dale apparently lifeless on the sofa, and two apparently dead men on the floor. Toby crept valiantly from under the verandah as soon as the marauders were securely bound, and summoned the servant-girl from the kitchen. Miss Dale was gradually restored to consciousness, and was able to give a coherent account of the matter. The three men had ridden up to the verandah, dismounted, and seeing her and Mr. Dale through the open window, had entered the drawing-room. They asked for whiskey, and her father replied saying there was none in the house. One of them then demanded money, and Mr. Dale asked him "if he was a soldier or a robber?" The soldier struck him, and her father seized a chair, and as he raised it the soldier drew his pistol and shot him. At the same moment the other two seized her. Then Mr. Miles rushed in and grappled one of the soldiers, and while struggling with him was shot also. This was all she knew until they aroused her from her swoon.

The measured tread of the soldiers bearing the body of Captain Stanly interrupted her recital, and while they paused upon the lawn, Mr. Boston entered the crowded apartments. He seemed to take in the situation at a glance, and, kneeling by the side of Mr. Dale, carefully examined his wound. Then crossing the room, he examined the prostrate body of Miles.

"General," he said, rising from the last investigation, "these gentlemen should have prompt medical attendance."

"Is there any hope?" whispered the general.

"Hope!" replied the other, aloud; "certainly! Neither is fatally injured. If you will send for the surgeon——"

"Mount my horse, Bascombe; he will take you over fences," said the general. "You will find Doctor Nicholls at the school-house. My compliments—and request him to come instantly. Miss Dale, we will carry your father up-stairs. Be hopeful."

She had caught the arm of the last comer, and was trying to see into his soul through his frank blue eyes.

"Be hopeful, madam," he repeated; "I would not say so if I doubted. It were hideous cruelty to deceive you with false hopes. Your father's case is not at all desperate."

"And Mr. Miles?" she said, pointing over her shoulder.

"His hurt is even less serious. The bullet has cut some locks of hair, but I think the bone is untouched. In an hour we shall have a professional opinion. I have seen many worse cases than these recover very rapidly. This gentleman is recovering consciousness even now."

Two or three men raised Miles from the carpet, and propped him up on the sofa. He gazed around the room with a perplexed countenance. The general, assisted by Captain Green, was carrying Mr. Dale into the hall, his daughter holding his nerveless hand in hers.

"It is Annie, bonny Annie Laurie!" said Miles, attempting to rise. "The brute is actually holding her! Kill! kill!"

"This is a favourable symptom," observed Mr. Boston, quitting her side. "So long as men desire to fight, the chances are on their side. Let us take Mr. Miles to his room also."

"Fust door at top of de sta'rs," said Toby. "Ef I had been heah when dem robbers come, I'd a made sure of a couple of 'em!

Door on de right, sah! And, Massa Doctor! you'd best come down sta'rs ag'in. De sogers done begun to search de pockets of dem robbers. Mebbe you'd best see what dey find! I seed Miss Annie's watch-chain. All dem sogers alike! Dey all steal chickens. 'Spec' dey all steal watches too!"

" Hardy," said General Smith, " give Mr. Boston whatever valuables you find. Will you please take charge, sir? I will come down in a minute or two."

Mr. Boston found the three prisoners on the grass, their arms tied behind their backs. The North Carolina warrior was kneeling by the side of one of them, and industriously emptying his pockets. Close by the prostrate robbers was the rude litter of boughs, upon which the body of Captain Stanly reposed in sombre silence. Three or four soldiers stood by the litter, waiting for orders to take up the burden and resume their march to the church-yard. There was a little heap of spoons and forks, three gold watches with chains on the green lawn. One chain of delicate workmanship was strung out like a golden thread, and upon this Toby pounced instanter.

"Dis Miss Annie's watch, sah!" he said, handing it to Mr. Boston. · "Dat b'long to Mass' Dale. Dis is Mister Mileses. I seed him windin' it dis mornin'. He jest screw de handle round. Don't hab no key. Dem spoons and forks all ourn. Dey done stole five times more. Sarch de boots, cap!"

"Seems to me you're running this business, Mister Nigger!" said Hardy, discontentedly. "Say! Yank! turn over! I want t'other pocket."

"Nauthin' in t'other pocket," growled the prisoner, "'cept my knife."

" Well, dogon your trifling picter, I want the knife! Turn over!"

The soldier groaned as he turned. The sabres of his captors had scarified his legs.

" What sort of meat do you cut with this knife?" said Hardy, drawing out a gold locket suspended by a blue ribbon. " This looks like another watch. Blood on the ribbon, too. Say, Cuffee! whose is this?"

"Dun'no!" answered Toby. " You may swar it was stole, anyhow. Sogers don't go ridin' round wid dem things in de pocket."

" Whose is it, Yank?" asked Hardy. " Dogon the thing! it won't open!"

"Give it me, Hardy," said Mr. Boston. " I think I know the owner. You took it from Mr. Miles, friend, did you not?"

"Don't know ary Mr. Miles," replied the prisoner.

"The gentleman who arrived while you were robbing the lady," said Mr. Boston, composedly; "the one you shot last."

"Didn't shoot nobody," retorted the soldier; "never drawed my pop at all. The man you mean smashed my head with a pitcher, dern him! I found the watch on the floor."

"Here's some more forks, Sambo!" said Hardy. "How many forks does your master own, anyway?"

"Nebber counted," replied Toby. "An' my name's not Sambo, nor Cuffee neither. Aint got no mars'r, neither."

"Hello!" said Hardy, turning the prostrate soldier's pocket inside-out; "look here! gold and silver! Say, Yank! have you been in the mining business?"

"Dat b'longs to Mr. Miles too," said Toby; "he done gib me one of dem silver pieces when he got his breakfus'. Dese cavaltry sogers beats de debble for stealin'! You see dey can tote more. No gold or silver in dis house for sartin. Mr. Dale done sent all he had to Charleston."

"It must be as he says," observed Mr. Boston; "these are all English coins, and Mr. Miles came from England."

"Guess he won't go back!" growled the prisoner. "Dern him! He can't walk around loose with a ball in his skull."

"These *were* his coins?" said Mr. Boston.

"I s'pose so," answered the other. "There, Johnny Reb! you've skun me out purty clean. Give me a chaw of that tobaccer, will you?"

"Can't waste tobaccer on you, Yank," replied Hardy, biting off a piece as he spoke. "Mighty scase in these parts."

"It's my own tobaccer, dern you!"

"Yes; and I reckon these spoons and forks was your own, too. But they are all confisticated, you see."

General Smith appeared upon the verandah, followed by the officers who had carried the wounded gentlemen to their rooms. The body of Stanly was once more raised from the ground, and the procession moved out the west gate. The spire of the little church was visible over the treetops, and the church-yard was soon reached. A squad of soldiers had been despatched to this spot immediately after the battle, and had already dug the grave, and had constructed a rude coffin, into which the body was placed. Mr. Boston read the burial service, and the sad ceremonies were soon over.

As they returned to **Dale's** Manor, General Smith walked **apart** with Mr. Boston.

" My friend," said the general, " is it your intention to return **to** England, as you said last night?"

" Yes. I must go to Charleston first, and then try for home."

" We shall miss you. I thought your heart was in our cause **at** first, but I have discovered that **all** your sacrifices of comfort have been made only in the general cause of humanity. You **have** stricken no blow on our side."

" Nor on the other. You **will join** the main **army in a few days,** general, and my services will be **less** needed. But **a voice is calling** me out yonder in the far East, and go I **must** !"

" A female voice?" asked the general, slyly.

" Ha !" said the other, with a whimsical face, " how can **one** distinguish at such a **distance** ! But it seems to say ' Come !' and, by the Three Kings, I would ride **over ten such batteries as that** you took so gallantly to-day to obey the mandate."

" What a shame it is," said the general, looking into the dauntless eyes of his interlocutor, " that a fellow of such stuff as you are made of should be a mere civilian !"

" Well," said the other, sheepishly, " I have done a little soldiering in my time."

" Not here, surely !"

" No. Over there. Beyond the sea. It is a very unsatisfactory occupation, and I'll none of it, unless, indeed, England should call me again. But I thought of staying a day or two here, until my countryman is better. Don't you think there is some soldier stuff in him, too? I mean Mr. Miles."

" He is a hero !" responded the **general** ; " **and this reminds** me. I think—or at least, Green says he thinks, that poor Stanly was pledged to Miss Dale. I passed through Dale's Manor with **his** body, because I fancied she might desire to be present at **his** burial. But it **is** possible that the shock of this murderous assault and the dangerous condition of her father would make the present an inopportune time **to tell her of** Stanly's **death.** Will you please break it to her ?"

" Perhaps. But Mr. Miles received his last words. Better wait until he **recovers.**"

" Well, take charge of **the matter.** And now, good-bye. Here comes Bascombe with Dr. Nicholls, and I can get my horse. To-night my command moves. I must ride **over** to my quarters and prepare for the march. Ah, Mr. Bascombe, you will have to walk back. My compliments to Captain Green, and request him to report at once at headquarters with his command and prisoners. Doctor, please leave your instructions with Mr. Boston."

The grounds of Dale's Manor were cleared before the sun disappeared behind the church spire. The doctor promised speedy recovery to Mr. Dale. Mr. Miles would be better to-morrow. Miss Dale had retired for the night, leaving Mr. Boston in charge of both patients, under Doctor Nicholls's orders.

Mr. Dale slept fitfully. Once in the night he called " Annot" in a dreamy voice. Mr. Boston leaned over him and listened.

" Annot!" said Mr. Dale.

" What will you have, sir?" whispered Mr. Boston.

" They have not found everything. I have the silver, but the picture is gone!"

" What picture?"

" Do you not know? Yours, mine, ours."

" Be patient. It will be found."

" In the locket, you know," said Mr. Dale, dozing again—" I mean the Clifton Picture."

CHAPTER XVII.

ANNIE LAURIE.

ON the day after the battle the sun arose upon the Long Hollow, where all was calm and peaceful. A long mound crossed the valley at the hill-foot. Yesterday it was the breastwork over which the cavalry had charged. To-day it was merely the same soil returned to the ditch, but covering the mortal remains of three hundred men. The war had spread out its crimson skirts to that remote corner, and drifted away again towards the sea-coast, leaving the mound as a memorial of its visit. Victors and vanquished had disappeared in the night, and bountiful nature soon spread her green mantle over the long ridge, the grass taking brighter hues and more vigourous growth from the festering mass beneath.

Mr. Dale recovered rapidly. On the second day he was well enough to hold long consultations with Mr. Boston, whom he entirely monopolized. Mr. Miles was feverish and required more nursing,

and Miss Dale divided her attentions between her father and their
guest, giving the latter the larger moiety as her father improved.
She was at Mr. Dale's bedside at nightfall, when Toby put his black
head in at the door and beckoned her out. Toby was major domo,
literally, since the day of the battle, and he felt the pressure of the
household cares. His hair curled more crisply. The "whites" of
his eyes dilated, and he moved about the mansion with a solemn
dignity that struck awe into the bosom of "'Manda," the cook and
housemaid, whom he dominated with stern authority.

"He done call for you, Miss Annie," whispered Toby, as she
passed into the hall, "and I reckon he's outen his head ag'in. If you
will please watch him a minute, I'll go down to de spring and git
some cool water."

"Better send Amanda, Toby," said Miss Dale; "I might need
you."

"Werry well, misse; only 'Manda sich a goose, she's afeared ob
her shadder."

"Well, go yourself, then, Toby, and tell Amanda to remain within
call."

Miles was lying with his face to the window. He put out his
hand as she approached, and she noted the brightness of his eyes
and the faint flush on his forehead.

"Forgive me for calling," he said, his face full of perplexity,
"but how am I ever to tell her?"

"Tell whom?" He lay quiet several minutes, meditating.

"Annie Laurie! Bonny Annie Laurie! 'I'd lay me down and
die.' And that is just what he did. She wouldn't sing it, you
know! Heavens! She'll never sing it again!"

"Shall I sing for you?" she said.

"Aye! But you cannot sing *that*, you know."

"I will sing anything you prefer——"

"England expects that every man, this day—certainly! England
is right! What is on my head?"

"Only a napkin. I will have some cold water presently."

"I swear to you," he broke out, earnestly, "I stuck by his side
through it all! It was a gallop into the very jaws of Tophet!
Great sheets of sulphurous flame and a hail of bullets! But
where he rode I rode. When he leaped into a forest of sharp
steel I leaped also, and I had not so much as a riding-whip in my
hand!"

She turned to see who entered the room. It was Mr. Boston.

"Tell her countryman," continued Miles, "I never drew back an inch. And he died with his hand in mine. But how the devil can I tell her!"

"No matter now," answered Mr. Boston, gently, "you shall tell her anon. I saw you ride. Here, let me moisten your napkin again and bind it on your head. Ah, this is cool! Toby, give me a glass. Drink a little, Mr. Miles."

"She cannot sing *that*, you know," observed Miles, confidently, after drinking. "She will never sing it again. I did not know how I loved her until I thought of that! I did not know how much agony I could endure until I undertook this task!"

The shadows grew deeper, and there was a long interval of silence. Mr. Boston stole out, leaving Annot. Toby, on velvet feet, brought a candle into the hall, and then dropping into a tangled bundle of legs and arms, fell asleep in the corner. Annot sat and mused upon the incoherent ravings of the patient, endeavoring to find some clue to his meaning, when he suddenly whispered—

"It is not her real name, you know. It is Annot Dale! And Miles is not my real name either. Everything is changed. Oh! why did not a bullet find me as I rode through that infernal storm? Me instead of him? Better for Bonny Annie Laurie; better for Hyland, and far better for me! She can never sing it again! And she would not sing it for me! Certainly not!"

A blaze of light broke upon the girl's mind. She had found the clue!

As she sat there in the darkness, recalling the events of the past few days, she remembered the scraps of conversation she had overheard between the young cavalry subalterns when they carried the wounded stranger up-stairs. They spoke of some one who rode unarmed at the head of the column as having a charmed life. She thought at the time they were speaking of Mr. Boston, as she had heard of his reckless exposure of himself on other occasions. She now recognised Miles as the "Mad Britisher."

Then she recalled the short colloquy at the date of his arrival, when Stanly requested her not to sing "Annie Laurie." And she remembered that the guest had asked for the song once and again during the evening, with a certain polite persistence. When she arose the next morning she had said, "I will sing 'Annie Laurie' for Mr. Miles to-day." There had been a long and interesting conversation the night before between him and her father, in which she occasionally took part, and she felt well acquainted with the new-comer, chiefly because he was a countryman, but also, because, with her quick perception, she had detected many traits of the man's character, enlisting her sympathy and awakening her admiration. She was greatly disappointed when Toby announced his departure " to see de scrimmage." She had no sympathy with "scrimmages," and could not account for the man's desire to look upon the revolting scenes of the battle-field. During the morning she had been stunned by the incessant roar of heavy guns, and was constantly oppressed with a vague dread of impending horrors. The arrival of the marauders, the injury to her father, the rude grasp of the men as they tore at her watch-chain, seemed like some horrible nightmare, until Miles burst into the room, with glowing eyes, and cast himself upon her captors. She saw the soldier who bestrode her father's body raise his pistol and shoot her defender, only a yard or two distant, and her quick eyes perceived that the accidental entanglement of his spur saved his life; for he was falling when the soldier fired, and the bullet shattered a mirror on the opposite side of the room. Then came oblivion, until General Smith stood over her.

After this she could only recall disconnected ravings. Miles eagerly assuring her that he had dared everything for " Bonny Annie Laurie." He had ridden by the side of some one for her sake through nameless perils. Who was it?

" Stanly!"

She remembered now that the officers spoke in whispers when they spoke of Stanly. He was not among them. There had been a burial service at the church. Mr. Boston had borrowed her Prayerbook! It was clear. Stanly was dead. And while she recalled the gay countenance of the gallant young soldier at their last parting, she covered her face with her hands and wept.

The tears were beneficent. Her mind worked more coherently after the "good cry."

Now there were subsequent perplexities. Somehow, Mr. Miles had confused her name with Annie Laurie's name. So when he spoke in his delirium of Annie Laurie, he meant Annot Dale. Indeed, he had said so. But why did he constantly refer to the song? Why did he assert so vehemently that some one—"she"—would never sing it again?

She heard the murmur of voices at the other end of the hall, as her father and Mr. Boston conversed. She heard the regular breathing of her patient, who had fallen into quiet slumber; and, underlying all other sounds, and sustaining them as a rich bass upholds the melody of the soprano, she heard Toby's diapason, as he awoke the echoes with his prodigious snore.

Ah! Is this the mode of egress from the labyrinth?

Stanly had requested her not to sing until his return. And he would never return! That explained the stranger's reiterated assurance. And he had inferred, or perhaps Captain Stanly had told him——

Told him what?

Only this: a week ago Stanly was at Dale's Manor, and had startled her by saying, "Miss Dale, when this cruel war is over, I am going to ask the dearest woman in the world to be my wife." They were standing on the verandah together, and Stanly had been very poetical. The dialogue was interrupted by her father's approach, and the captain had no opportunity for renewing it. At parting he pressed her hand very warmly, and with an indefinite air of proprietorship which she resented at the time.

So he had told all this to Mr. Miles, no doubt; and Mr. Miles recognised this proprietorship when she declined to sing Annie Laurie! And he had been with Stanly when he fell, and was charged with a message to her, which he shrank from delivering because—because——

Why, he said, "I did not know how I loved her." Whom did he mean?

The warm blood mounted to her cheek and forehead as she meditated. "Do not lay too much stress upon the mutterings of fever," she thought. It was hardly possible that this gentleman could have any serious admiration for her. The date of their first meeting was too recent. She would dismiss the whole subject from her thoughts until he became sane.

She stole out into the hall and caused Toby's bass to terminate in a "shake."

"Go sit by Mr. Miles, Toby," she whispered. "Don't go to sleep until I send Amanda."

"No, misse," answered Toby. "I kind o' forgot myself for a minute. You see I was flustered a' totin' de water. I run all de way to de spring and back."

Toby did not explain that he was horribly frightened, seeing armed robbers in every bush between the house and the spring. He did not run, he flew.

Mr. Boston, half surgeon and half nurse, looked in upon Mr.

Miles an hour later. The fever had departed, and he was sleeping profoundly. Mr. Dale was doing well.

"Miss Dale," he said, "your father and I have been arranging for a departure. We are all going to Charleston as soon as he can travel, which will be within the week. Mr. Miles will be up to-morrow, I think, and probably Mr. Dale also. In order to ensure success to our plan, you will please take due care of your own health, and to do that you will please retire now. I am going to sleep on this lounge, and should Mr. Dale or Mr. Miles require attention, I am a light sleeper, and can watch over both. May I say good night?"

"You speak with so much authority," she answered, smiling, "and you tell me such good news, that I will obey without a murmur. How kind you have been to us, Mr. Boston!"

"Tut! tut! I am the gainer in all. In our own dear land we shall know each other better. My home is in Devon."

"Do you mean to say father is going to England?"

"Yes. Before the forest-trees put on their gay attire we shall all be in England; that is," and he meditated a moment—"I must get some sugar first."

"Sugar!"

"Yes. I am hungry for pure sugar. I have been on the plantations in Louisiana, and watched the process from cane-cutting to crystallization. It is good, but I cannot get it out. I think I must go to Porto Rico."

Annot took her candle and went to her chamber, wondering if the whimsical stranger was insane, or if he was merely making game of her. There was an air of such direct sincerity about him that she instantly dismissed the latter proposition.

She had also dismissed the other Englishman from her thoughts for the night, so she extinguished her candle, and drew her chair to the open window. The night was delicious. No sound outside save the whisper of the pines. No frightful guns; no tramp of armed men, marching to death. England! Was it possible that she would at last get beyond the reach of murderous strife? How could they go? Ah! Mr. Boston had doubtless arranged that they should sail in Mr. Miles's ship. And so her thoughts went back to Mr. Miles again.

Annot did not like fighters. If Stanly had come to her in civilian's garb, deprecating war, and had courted her in gentle fashion, he might have won her. But he came at first with his sabre clanking against his boot—ferocious. She was more easily attracted to the blockade-runner, because he wore no military equipments, and seemed a man of peace. But he had deliberately gone to the battle, merely to gratify a blood-thirsty spirit. They were all alike. Could there be any circumstances that would justify men in inflicting mortal injury upon their fellows?

Then that awful minute after her father was shot came into view, and she saw again the whirling figures in the drawing-room, the two robbers who held her in their rough grasp, and the impetuous assault of the Englishman. Well, he was certainly excusable that time. It did not seem at all probable that a mild expostulation would have been appropriate there.

If they sailed in his ship, she would talk to him about it. And just then she heard his voice, as his window was next hers.

"If Miss Dale is well enough," he was saying, "I should like to see her just one minute. When I saw her last she was in the grasp of those scoundrels."

"But she has retired, my friend," replied Mr. Boston.

"Well, I must wait. You tell me she is entirely uninjured?"

"Entirely. Her excellent appetite at supper emboldened me to gratify my own. I had not eaten anything for twelve hours. I think she had probably fasted twenty-four."

"The wretch!" said Annot.

"If I could hear her sing——"

There was a pause. A hundred thoughts gallopped through her mind.

"Because," continued Miles, "if she would sing Annie Laurie just once for me, I would be willing to do like that other fellow, and 'lay me down and die.'"

CHAPTER XVIII.

INSURMOUNTABLE OBSTACLES.

IT was high noon when the invalids crept down-stairs the next day. Mr. Dale had been wounded in the breast; the bullet, deflected by unerring Providence, glancing at the articulation of a rib with the sternum, had torn its way out near the spinal column. Mr.

Miles had a scalp wound, not dissimilar from those inflicted at Celtic fairs with skilfully-wielded shillalahs. Coma was the first result in both cases, and fever the second. The supercargo had been slightly delirious, but at this bright noontide both were decidedly convalescent.

Mr. Boston was in consultation with Toby all the morning. The railroad was twenty miles distant, and the knotty problem to solve related to the transfer of Mr. and Miss Dale, with needful luggage, to the nearest station. The war had been driven back from the neighbourhood for the nonce, but there would surely be a return wave in the near future, and Charleston offered the most secure refuge at present.

A neighbour of Mr. Dale's, whose lands adjoined Dale's Manor, had long cast covetous eyes upon his possessions. This neighbour had fifty bales of cotton at the railway station, unsold. He was loyal, distrusted Confederate scrip, and was waiting for a "gold" purchaser. After a prolonged consultation with the supercargo, Mr. Dale sent for Mr. Brooks, and in the course of an hour titles were passed. Mr. Brooks had a clean deed to "Dale's Manor and furniture." Mr. Dale had an order for the delivery of the fifty bales of cotton, and Mr. Miles purchased this for the "Nellie" lading for ten thousand dollars, "deliverable alongside." The payment to be made in gold or its equivalent in Charleston.

It is noteworthy that all parties to this triple arrangement were entirely satisfied with their respective bargains. Two hundred dollars per bale was a moderate price for the staple, as Mr. Miles, who had recently canvassed the market, knew. Ten thousand dollars for Dale's Manor was moderate, in the estimation of Mr. Brooks, and was also a highly satisfactory price to Mr. Dale, although he had refused five hundred thousand dollars for the same property from the same purchaser. It is true the larger offer was made in a currency that did not circulate freely beyond the limits of the Confederacy. Mr. Brooks departed before dinner, with the understanding that the house would be vacated during the week. For the domestic animals, and such household supplies as might be left, Mr. Brooks engaged to convey the entire party to the station and to prepay the freight on the cotton.

They dined sumptuously. After dinner, the host and Mr. Boston went out under the pines with cigars alight. Annot and Mr. Miles remained in the drawing-room. The shattered mirror was still on the wall.

"Did you know," said Annot, pointing to the glass, "that the same bullet struck you first?"

"Is it possible?" said Miles.

"Yes," she replied, with a shudder. "You were there by the chair. The wretch fired from the corner of the table, and I saw the mirror crumble when you fell."

"How could you see all this?" asked he, looking admiringly at her. "I only remember clawing at the rascal's sword as I fell. I am not sure that I heard the shot."

"What did you think of doing?" said Annot.

"I intended to master his weapon and kill him, and then kill the man who stood by your father," answered Miles, tranquilly. "I thought I had finished the other with the pitcher."

"So did I. Oh! how can men be so cruel?"

"They had you in their grasp," said Miles, indignantly. "You!"

She was silenced. Some intonation in the other's voice stunned her. If her gentle and pious thought could be translated into masculine vernacular, it would probably run thus: "What a devil of a man this is!"

"I have a message to deliver," said he, presently, speaking slowly and deliberately. "It was entrusted to me under solemn circumstances." She made no reply, and there was another pause, while he collected his thoughts.

"Do you know anything about the battle on Saturday? Do you know any of those who were killed?" asked he, at length.

"I am not sure. I thought I heard the gentlemen mention one name when they were taking father up-stairs."

"And that was——"

"Captain Stanly."

He glanced furtively at her face. It was serious, but bore no traces of very violent agitation.

"I was quite near him," he continued, "when he was—hurt. And he gave me this." Here he produced the locket. "He told me to give it to Annie Laurie, and to say that he had stolen it. That is all. I thought he meant you. Did he?"

"It is mine," she answered, taking the locket with grave composure, "or rather, it belongs to father. He has been very much distressed, thinking the robbers had taken it."

She touched a spring and the case opened. Miles looked over her shoulder. It was the picture of a lady, like Annot and yet not Annot. His eyes saw a dozen discrepancies at the first glance.

"We have other pictures of my mother," said Annot; "but father has always liked this the best. He calls it the Clifton Picture. This building in the background is the Observatory on Clifton Downs. It was taken twenty-five years ago."

He was watching her keenly all this time. It was about time for her to burst into tears or faint. He had arranged all this in his mind; but she was totally oblivious. Not up to the exigencies of the occasion.

"May I ask if Captain Stanly knew whose picture it was?" he said, dubiously.

"Probably not. It was on the table there, I remember now, when he was here last," and here she blushed; "but he merely glanced at it." She closed the case with a snap.

"It is very like you," said Miles, "and perhaps he thought it was you?"

"Perhaps."

He arose and walked restlessly across the room and back again. He had screwed up his courage to discharge this awful obligation, had steeled his heart to endure the sight of her speechless sorrow or her hysterical outcry, and lo! she was cold as marble!

"Miss Dale," he said, taking a seat by her side again, "I am presuming terribly; but may I ask you to listen to a bit of personal history?"

"Presuming!"

"Before I left England," he went on, "I asked a lady to marry me. She refused me. I have known her from my boyhood, and I thought I loved her with unspeakable devotion. If she had accepted me, I think it very probable that no other woman in the world would have attracted me. Yet I know now that I never loved her at all."

She looked at him, astonished.

"Bear with me," he continued, "and pardon the egotism. But I *must* tell you. I cannot live another hour under the same roof with you otherwise.

"I cannot tell how the feeling began. She was away at some school on the Continent, and when she came home she was a woman. The intimacy that became us as children was not becoming in matured people. I thought I must have her, and then I thought Hy— I mean my only brother, wanted her also. After some years of doubt, my brother went away—far away, to India, in fact—and I was constantly humiliated by the conviction that he went merely to leave a clear field to me. At last there came a letter from him, in which he said in precise terms he had never seen the woman he would marry.

"Look you! This brother of mine is so constituted that a falsehood would blister his tongue. He would cut off his hand rather than write a lie. And when I read his letter, I knew he had never been a rival. And then I went and told her very much as I am now telling you.

"I am—that is—I have certain lands in England, and this lady is the probable heiress to other lands adjoining mine. She is an heiress now, indeed, but not too rich to make my suit indecorous. I thought I ought to marry, and I thought this lady was precisely the woman made for me.

"And now comes my confession! While my brother, whom I love dearly, seemed to stand between us——"

"Your elder brother?" said Annot, deeply interested.

"No; I am the elder. Why do you ask that?"

"I thought you had said—or I dreamed——" And she put her hand to her forehead, musing. "No matter. Excuse the interruption, and go on."

"When Hyland was gone——"

"Hyland?"

"Yes; my brother. When he was out of the race, it seemed to be more of a business for lawyers and settlements. Do you understand me? I had not then discovered my lack of every sentiment that should possess the man who seeks a wife. And therefore when I was rejected, with great gentleness, by-the-bye, I was more astounded than wounded."

"Yet you came to America on this dangerous expedition——"

"I had already arranged for that before I spoke to her. What! you think this was the exploit of a desperate man, rendered reckless by disappointed love? Ah, no! I did not know what love was then.

"I did not know that I could be so involved in passion that life is worthless—worse than worthless—unless it is spent in the society of another. That a gentle girl could so master me in a few short days that I am miserable out of her presence. I have learned all this at Dale's Manor.

"Do not answer me, please. Although my words betoken madness—for I have only known you four days—I am not mad. And I will not annoy you with any more professions. I discovered the other night, when you refused to sing one song, which he had prohibited—and the next day, when he sent the picture to you, with his last utterance—that a gallant gentleman had known you before I came. Will you not believe me when I say I would gladly have died in his stead the other day for *your* sake?

" I have said all this to you because I could not help it. If I had consulted proprieties, I should have waited until the shock of this bereavement——"

" Pray spare me these allusions," she said, resentfully ; "there is no need for such extensive condolence !"

He was stunned this time.

" You have been so candid," she continued, while a rosy glow overspread her face, "that I should relieve your mind of part of its distress. Captain Stanly was nothing to me beyond a mere acquaintance."

He was still speechless, but touched the locket in her hand.

" I did not sing Annie Laurie because—because he had some foolish thoughts about me. At least, I fancied he had. And he rode away looking sad, and perhaps I was oppressed with a presentiment. He took this without my knowledge. I am like your brother," and here she laughed with forced gayety, "in that I have failed to find my destined partner." She moved to the piano, and he followed her mechanically. He was in a stupor. Without a prelude she struck the keys and sang Annie Laurie.

She turned to him at the conclusion of the second stanza. He was kneeling on a stool at her side. He held his hand out for hers, but she busily turned over the leaves of the music-book, wondering if he could hear her heart beating.

" Miss Dale," he said, in low tones, the more earnest because subdued, "hear another word. You are Annie Laurie. You are all the world to me ! And I beg you to regard me as an earnest suitor for your hand. I am a gentleman of good name. In due time I will satisfy your father, and meanwhile I will say no word of love to you. The dread of losing you by foolish delay is my only excuse for speaking now."

She turned again, a perplexed expression on her glowing countenance. He had captured her hand by this time, kissed it, and released it.

" Please get up," she said, moving away. She looked out upon the lawn. Her father and the bearded Boston were enveloped in fine blue smoke. Miles stood submissively behind her. If she could only go to her room and have a good cry now !

"I have said nothing to you about your brave effort to rescue me," said she, as a tear or two slipped down on her dress. "But I appreciate it. I am honoured by all you have said——"

"Oh, Annot!"

"Don't interrupt me, please." The sound of her name and his blazing eyes frightened her. "You know, certainly, that this sudden fancy of yours will probably wear off as you get stronger."

"Oh, Annot, I love you!"

"Yes; so you have said. But you have been wounded, and are still feeble and cannot know your own mind. I will forget all you have said——"

"Oh, Annot! I have no mind where you do not reign. Feeble! I will undertake any task, encounter any danger, for one smile from you. If you could only say one word—if you could tell me I might hope to win your favour some years hence——"

"There are serious obstacles, sir." She spoke with grave dignity, albeit glancing shyly at his eager face. "I may say insurmountable obstacles."

"Tell me the worst of them. If you do not positively hate me——"

"Hate you!" He was kissing her hand again by this time. "Ah, no! How could I hate one who has been so kind? But I am only a poor country girl—oh, yes; insurmountable——"

"My queen! my darling!"

"And you—nobody knows it excepting me—you are Lord Rayneford!"

CHAPTER XIX.

AT HAWKLEY.

ONE hot morning the "Bengal" touched at Cape Town, and Hyland learned that the "Lord Clive" had sailed a week before. She had stopped only for coals and water and the mails.

"No shore leave, Mr. Jones," said the captain, as he stepped into the yawl. "Ah, I forgot the beggar was deaf! Pass his slate, one of you." And he scrawled down his order. "Will you come ashore, Mr. Rayneford? We have four hours."

Hyland was watching the mate's countenance as he deciphered the captain's hieroglyphics.

"But I want to go ashore myself," muttered Mr. Jones.

"When I return, then," answered the captain; "tell him so, Mr. Rayneford, please. Will you come?"

"I think I will wait for Mr. Jones," answered Hyland; "I want to see the process of coaling."

A barge was alongside, and the black diamonds were being transferred to the bowels of the "Bengal," half a ton at a time.

"Mr. Jones desires to visit the town," thought Hyland, "to get a supply of rum for his private use. If I go with him, the old rascal will find it difficult to smuggle it aboard."

Mr. Rayneford was restless in his habits. Once or twice he had strayed on deck during the night when it was the mate's watch, and he fancied that he detected the odour of rum about that excellent officer, as well as some thickness of speech. Latterly, these symptoms had disappeared, because the mate's private stock was exhausted, and the daily allowance was too moderate to make any sensible impression on Mr. Jones's seasoned carcase.

"Four bells!" said Mr. Jones, as the captain came aboard. "Mr. Rayneford, let us go ashore under canvas. We will take this shore boat and sail in. Here, blackie! put up your sail. Half a crown for your boat for an hour."

"You sail him yourself?" asked the negro. Hyland bawled the question in the mate's ear.

"Certainly. Squat down amidships. Drop aboard, sir. Push off her bows, blackie! Away we go!"

Hyland sat astern, watching the mate's management of the little vessel as it danced over the waves. One hand on the tiller, the other holding the main sheet, Mr. Jones seemed to guide the boat by instinct. The wind came in puffs, and each time that the sail filled and the boat careened to leeward the sailor, with ready hand, put the helm down and brought her head to wind.

"Do you see how easy it is?" said the mate; "you could sail back to Calcutta in this cockleshell if you only watched the wind. See! Here comes a strong puff! You can see the ripple on the water. Helms-a-lee! And now give way again. Would you like to try it? Well. Take a good grip of the sheet. Now, keep the tiller steady and watch for the puffs. Ah! Well done, sir!"

Hyland soon learned the secret of steering, and brought the boat alongside the quay in good fashion. Telling the negro to wait for them, the two walked up the quay.

"Only two things to remember in sailing these fore-and-aft

boats," observed Mr. Jones: "first, don't get skeered; second, don't be a fool!"

Hyland looked at him enquiringly.

"I mean there is not the danger that a lubber thinks there is. When she lays down, her head comes up to windward nat'rally,—so long as the sea don't wash aboard. Water aboard plays the devil! Then the other thing is to meet the wind. When it comes with a roar, draw in your sheet and put her head up. Put the wind's eye out! Let it whistle on both sides of your sail. A lubber will try to scud away from it. A sailor will keep his face to it the harder it blows."

Mr. Jones had privately decided to buy two quart bottles of rum. There were two pockets in his pea-jacket that would accommodate so much bulk, and the chances of smuggling that aboard were in his favour. As his companion stuck to him he walked boldly into a shop on the head of the quay, after they had traversed one or two streets in the hot town.

"Rum!" he said to the shopkeeper. "Two quarts."

"How much?" said the shopkeeper.

"My friend is deaf," said Hyland, taking the slate. "Wait a moment."

"If you will wait until we reach England," he wrote on the slate, "I will give you five gallons of rum. The captain would not allow you to take it aboard, if he knew it. And if I knew it and failed to tell him, I should be guilty of fraud."

Mr. Jones read the sentence, and then wiped it off with the bit of sponge attached to the slate.

"A tumblerful of rum!" growled Mr. Jones, laying a shilling on the counter. "I s'pose you won't try any, Mr. Rayneford?"

Hyland shook his head, and the mate emptied the tumbler into his gullet. Five minutes later Hyland was steering back to the "Bengal." He paid the half-crown to the boatman, and clambered aboard the steamer, followed by the mate, who was silent and grumpy.

"I was dubious about old Jones," whispered the captain, as the mate walked forward. "He wanted some private grog, I know, but I don't think he has brought any aboard."

"About a pint," said Hyland, "and that went down his throat."

"A pint!" said the captain, derisively. "That is no more to him than a spoonful. Up anchor!"

That night, when the "Bengal" was riding over the long swell of the open sea, Hyland lighted his cheroot and went on deck to admire the constellation of the Southern Cross. Mr. Jones, still moody, was pacing the narrow walk between the bulwark and the cabin-hatch. Hyland touched his arm, drew him to the binnacle light and took his slate.

"You are angry about the rum," he wrote; "but you will not remain angry if you reflect a little. No better seaman than yourself is on this ship. But all your seamanship is worthless if you get too much grog."

Mr. Jones read, nodded his head, and rubbed out the writing.

"I could go to sleep in any storm," wrote Hyland, "if I knew you were on deck and sober. But I could not sleep in a dead calm if I knew you were in charge and—*not* sober."

Mr. Jones read, obliterated the record, and nodded again.

"But this was not all. If I had not prevailed upon you to relinquish your purchase it would have been confiscated. The first word the captain said when we came aboard was a question. And I was very glad that I could answer it."

Mr. Jones read, applied the sponge, and held out his horny hand.

"All right, Mr. Rayneford. I was scudding away from the wind, and you faced it. I was a lubber, and you were able seaman."

When the "Bengal" passed Eddystone Light there was a fierce storm raging, and the captain decided to run into harbour at Plymouth. Hyland, watching the light-house as they swept by, catching blinks of light occasionally, was rejoicing at the prospect of setting his foot on English soil.

"Dull work over there," observed Mr. Jones, "sitting out on a bit of rock and keeping the light up."

Hyland nodded. Mr. Jones was loquacious.

"I have a son in that business," he continued. "He is light-house keeper at Linton Sands. Better nor Eddystone though! Going ashore at Plymouth? Well, I shall be at Milford in a week, I suppose. I shall come to an anchor there. I can see Tom once a week, or oftener, for that matter. I'll rig out a sloop for my own sailing, and I can go to Linton Sands when I like. Thomas Jones, at the Harp Inn, Milford."

Hyland wrote the address on his tablets.

"Mr. Jones remembers my promise of five gallons," thought Hyland, "and I must not forget it."

When he stepped on board the tug, far in the night, Zeba followed, taking Hyland's portmanteau from one of the sailors. The Indian's own wardrobe was in a knapsack, strapped to his back military fashion.

"Farewell, captain!" said Mr. Rayneford, as the tug cast off. "Please send my luggage to Charing Cross Hotel. If the storm abates you will be in the Thames to-morrow, will you not?"

"Aye! aye! storm or no storm. I only want a few hours of daylight. Good luck to you, Mr. Rayneford!"

There was some magnetic influence streaming from the earth and infusing new vigour into the soul of the young Englishman when he leaped ashore on that blustering coast. He stamped upon the ground exultant, while Zeba shivered behind him. Everything was nautical about the streets bordering the harbour. Hyland found a cab, after traversing one or two long streets, and he and the Indian were soon in the warm waiting-room at the railway station, hovering over the blazing grate.

"Train for Exeter, Taunton, and Bristol!" said an official, putting his head in at the door; "no intermediate stations!"

"Taunton!" said Hyland. "This is the ticket for us. Come, Zeba! In two hours you shall have a bedroom with the temperature of Calcutta."

A five-gallon demijohn, boxed, addressed "Mr. Thomas Jones, Harp Inn, Milford, Wales. To be left. Freight paid," was the first result of Mr. Rayneford's visit to Taunton. No other obligations detaining him, he spent the better part of the succeeding day in travelling across country to Hawkley. He had telegraphed from Taunton, addressing Nancy Hicks, care of Lord Rayneford, announcing his arrival, and the housekeeper, arrayed in her best gown, welcomed him at dusk. Master Hyland had been her special charge from babyhood, and he had nothing to do, after satisfying the demands of hunger, but listen to her account of the mysterious disappearance of my lord. The old woman was a miracle of discretion, and this was positively the first opportunity that had been presented to pour her story into an ear that was at once sympathising and discreet.

"He bade me good-bye, Master Hyland," so ran her story, "and he told me to heed his last instructions. Everything to be kept as usual. He would be absent six months. The safest thing to tell enquiring friends was just the truth, and that was that I did not know where he was going. Mr. Plimpton came first, and he brought a strange—gentleman with him. He called him 'Dancer.'

He is an ugly little man with red eyes. They asked me no end of questions between them, but I had only one answer. I was not frightened about Master Miles. I did not call him Master Miles to them until they asked me some impudent questions about how much wine my lord usually drank at dinner. I can't bear that Mr. Plimpton. Excuse me, Master Hyland, I know he is your cousin, but that is not your fault. Well, they did not get any satisfaction here, so they went to Mr. Brentam. Why, they asked me what clothes my lord took away with him! And, would you believe it? they stopped on their way back from Mr. Brentam's to ask if my lord took his evening dress with him! You know, Master Hyland, I always pack your trunks when you leave home, and I always take a list of your things. So I just gave Mr. Plimpton the list of things in my lord's trunk. That little red-eyed ferret wished to take the list away with him, but I refused, so he asked for paper and copied it. I like his impudence! But Mr. Plimpton said it was all right."

She paused in her narration to watch the Hindoo. There were several portraits on the walls of the library, where the trio sat. Hyland sought this room after dinner, because it was the customary smoking-place at Hawkley. Zeba, candle in hand, was going the rounds, gravely studying the various portraits. He paused before one at length, and after intent scrutiny of the handsome face on the canvas, turned to Hyland.

"Picture of sahib's brother?" he asked.

"No; it is like him, though. There is no picture of my brother." Zeba replaced the candle and resumed his seat.

"If you have that list, Mrs. Hicks," said Hyland, as he threw away the fragment of his cheroot, "I should like to see it too."

"Certainly, Master Hyland. Excuse me a minute, and I'll fetch it."

While she was gone, Hyland pointed out the portraits to the Indian.

"Those are all my ancestors, Zeba. The portrait you selected is my father. This, my mother. My brother is like both. He has the eyes of the lady, but otherwise resembles my father."

"Sahib has eyes of his father, and all the rest like lady."

"Perhaps. I think you have hit the mark exactly. But we have another picture of both father and mother together. Ah, here is the list! Mrs. Hicks, can you find the photograph in the morocco case?"

Mrs. Hicks pointed to the list in his hand. He read as follows:
"In my lord's satchel :

"One box cigars.

"One small dressing-case."

"So long as Miles had his smoke, and his shaving appliances, he was equipped for a journey," observed Hyland. "But I see he was more elaborately furnished in his trunk."

There was a long list of clothing, with some peculiar memoranda which Mrs. Hicks added for her own guidance. Hyland read the list attentively, with some vague idea of Siberian weather on his mind. And he found sundry articles of winter apparel enumerated. The catalogue concluded with—

"Three boxes cigars.

"One writing-desk.

"The Clifton picture, in morocco case."

"I cannot show you the picture I spoke of, Zeba," said Hyland, returning the list to the housekeeper. "To-morrow I will call on Mr. Brentam, and then we will go to London."

"Miss Carey went to London this morning," said Mrs. Hicks, "and Mr. Brentam is going to-morrow."

CHAPTER XX.

THE SEARCH BEGUN.

MRS. HICKS looked out from her chamber window the next morning, and admired the beauties of Hawkley Park by sunrise. She saw Lord Rayneford's dog-cart, driven by Hyland, disappearing at the turn in the avenue. He was taking time by the forelock and seeking Mr. Brentam. On the lawn she beheld the Hindoo, kneeling on the grass, his face towards the sun, and evidently engaged in his private devotions.

"Pious, anyway !" she thought, as Zeba bowed his head twice, until his turban touched the ground; "what in the world will Master Hyland do with this one-armed blackamoor !"

While she watched him, Zeba arose and drew his tulwar, flourished it around his head, cut upward, downward, crosswise, tossed it whirling in the air, caught it by the hilt as it fell, cut right and left, cast it upward again, causing it to describe a glittering arc, and leaping forward caught it again, and, holding it at arm's length, pointed it motionless at the orb of day. Taking a cord from his pocket, he suspended the weapon from the bough of a tree, where it slowly gyrated as he marched around it.

The housekeeper was thoroughly mystified, and withal fascinated. There was something portentous in the aspect of the grim Hindoo. "One eye like a fire-coal," she thought, while he circled more and more slowly round. Presently the sword was still, and the Indian knelt again and carefully sighted along the blade. Apparently satisfied, he then unfastened the cord, slipped the tulwar into the scabbard, and paced soberly towards the house.

In his attendance upon Hyland, the quick-witted native had picked up a fund of practical knowledge. Hyland frequently found him more prompt and efficient in his surveys than his educated European assistants. He seemed to divine the use of the engineer's scientific implements by an instinct; and on several occasions he had astonished Rayneford by producing the right thing at the right time before it was named.

When Hyland returned from his morning call upon Mr. Brentam, he found the Indian squatted on the grass, under the tree upon which he had suspended the tulwar at sunrise. He had a small compass, a part of his surveyor's outfit, and a map of England, which he had taken from the library wall. He was absorbed.

"What are you studying, Zeba?" said Hyland, relinquishing the reins to the groom, as he descended from his perch.

"Salaam, sahib!" replied the Hindoo. "I am looking for the north."

"Indeed!" said Hyland. "Well, the second window there is about due north."

Zeba pointed to the compass.

"What! you want an accurate survey?"

"See, sahib!" said the Indian, thrusting a cane in the sod, and then walking rapidly to a lilac-bush, twenty or thirty yards distant, stuck up a second cane near the root. "Will sahib survey?"

"Northwest and by west."

Zeba spread the map out on the grass.

"Will sahib draw the line on the map?" said the Hindoo. "Here, Taunton. Here, Hawkley?"

"No. A little more north. Here is Hawkley." And he made a spot with his pencil to indicate the locality.

"Now, sahib, draw the line northwest and by west."

8

Hyland laid a scale on the map and drew his pencil lightly across it.

"Your line runs all in the water, Zeba," observed Hyland; "out Bristol Channel, touches Milford, crosses St. George's Channel, and strikes Ireland somewhere about Cork, I fancy." Zeba listened with profound attention.

"All water! No English land?" said the Hindoo.

"None. Except the twenty miles between Hawkley and the channel. Then open water—here is a little spot of an island—then all water to Ireland. Come into the library. I have a larger map there, with Hawkley on it."

The large chart was the record or result of certain geological surveys of England and Wales, and the names of many insignificant localities were given that could not be found on any ordinary geographical maps. Hyland's more careful examination of this revealed a few unimportant villages under the northwest and by west line.

"Here are the villages, Zeba," he said; "Handon, Skarr, Lakly, and Dimmot. Then the channel. All water to Milford Haven. Then this last little spot, what is it? Linton Sands. Then all sea again to the Irish coast. What the deuce are you hunting?"

"Don't know, sahib," replied the Hindoo, gravely, while his single eye glowed with smothered fire. "Tulwar point so! In seven days can try again."

"Suppose you try again now?" said Hyland.

"Can't ask tulwar twice!" replied the Indian. "Handon, Skarr, Lakly, Dimmot. All the rest jungle?"

"No. We have very little jungle in England. These are farm lands and gentlemen's parks. The villages are small. We came through Skarr yesterday. Where we changed horses."

"Any forts, barracks, bungalows, prisons?"

"Nothing of the kind. All peaceful country. And, I may add, the sweetest country in the world. Suppose you explore it, Zeba?"

"Yes, sahib."

"Well, I go to London this afternoon. You can amuse yourself in that way until I return. Mrs. Hicks will take care of you. You shall have a horse——"

"Don't want horse. Walk," said Zeba. "Sahib write names. Handon, Skarr, Lakly, Dimmot, water, Linton Sands."

Hyland tore a leaf from his pocketbook and wrote the names.

"Money?" he said, as he handed the slip to the Indian.

"Plenty money. Thanks!"

After breakfast the Hindoo disappeared. Hyland made a record in his diary.

"The Indian," he wrote, "has another attack of superstition. He has been practising the black art with his tulwar again, and has gone in obedience to its directions on the hunt of Miles. There is something sublime in his unquestioning reliance upon his mummery. It is unspeakably absurd in this age of the world, and would have been absurd two thousand years ago. Yet this man of keen intellect follows a delusion that could not deceive an English child, with unflinching faith, and his failure will not shake his faith. And the most curious thing to note is its effect upon me. I cannot shake off the influence of Zeba's manner. I have not seen his later incantations, but Mrs. Hicks described his methods to me, which were quite similar to his practice at sea.

"He comes of the Hindoo race, of course. What have been the characteristics of this race, so far as history reveals them? Is it also my race? Is Zeba Turanian or Aryan? Comes he from Ham or Japhet?

"What is the difference? Cultivated Turanians have had a habit of deifying insensate matter. They worshipped heroes. And I have read somewhere that they invested their weapons with some occult intelligence.

"Pooh! Why should I pore over these musty figments! It has not been long since Christian duellists sought the church's blessing upon their swords!

"Suppose I state the case here for future reference.

"I go to London to-day. I will get what information I can at the club, and from Plimpton. Then I start to find Miles. I shall hunt all over England first. I expect to employ no agency, except common sense and vigilance. I know the country. I know the probabilities. I can read the papers every day, and can utilize any hint that may point to Miles.

"Zeba has started, with a list of villages and—his tulwar. He knows literally nothing. A stranger in a strange land. Yet he starts with calm confidence, and I start with many misgivings and the heartache!

"Conclusion: The more a man certainly knows, the more does he distrust his knowledge. The more he learns of invariable law, the more does he look for variations. I shall meet Professor Schmiser at the club to-night, and if I have opportunity I will ask his opinion."

While Mr. Rayneford was gliding over the iron road that afternoon, his face turned Londonward, Zeba was marching across hills and valleys in precisely the opposite direction. He had laid aside his turban and his red coat, assuming ordinary English attire, excepting the tulwar, buckled close to his side, the end of the scabbard protruding below his coat. The few people he met in traversing lanes and by-ways—for he kept a tolerably direct course—generally glanced at him with slumberous curiosity as he strode by. Children, playing at cottage-doors, usually shrank into shelter as he approached. Once or twice he was accosted by parish officials, and required to produce his credentials. On these occasions he promptly presented the document he had received in Calcutta, setting forth the main facts in his history. "He had been loyal and valiant in the army, a sergeant in a native regiment, had been maimed in the discharge of his duty, and was honourably dismissed with a pension." His solitary eye blazed with sleepless vigilance, scrutinizing every face he encountered. His manner was always dignified and courteous, but there was an air of relentless determination about him that had its effect upon all he met. Once, a rural policeman, after reading his discharge, asked why he wore his sword. Zeba pointed his slender finger at the official document, and answered, "Officer!" and the guardian of the peace was silenced. So he kept his pilgrimage unmolested, sleeping at country inns at night, and living frugally upon one meal a day of animal food, and content with a crust and a mug of beer at morning and night.

When Hyland left England he was closely shaven, and he had never begun the cultivation of hirsute adornments until he went to the cinchona plantations. Persuaded by his new friend, the American doctor, he had there abandoned his razor, and returned to his native land bearded like the pard. It was so effectual a disguise, that Mr. Plimpton did not recognise him. Hyland had left his card at that gentleman's residence, with a pencilled note, saying he would dine at the club. Here he found Professor Schmiser, an old, spectacled savant, with whom Hyland was a favourite at college, and as the professor lived mainly upon the fumes of tobacco, they got a quiet corner in the smoking-room, where Rayneford recounted the story of Zeba and his superstition. He had already told him all he knew of Miles.

"About twenty-five?" said the professor. "Not'ing to do? Coming to London twice a month, and den pack to his pooks? Sound mental force? Engleesh? Mine friend, your brother is after a womans!"

"A woman!" said Hyland, horrified.

"Yah! Ter Engleesh is ter tuyfel! Mebbe your brother run avay *from* a womans. Mebbe a womans gourt him, und he didn't want to be gourted, but wanted some other. He read much pooks, und shmoke only leetle. Dere must pe a womans!"

"My dear professor," said Hyland, "you are certainly mistaken. I have a letter from Miles, in which he expressly says the contrary."

"Ah, dat makes no difference!" responded the professor; "ven he runs avay, he don't know ter womans drives. He tell ter troot, but he has a hallucination. No matter. I'll dink some more und write you word."

To Hyland's great astonishment the professor did not exterminate Zeba and his superstition with a word, as he had expected.

"We think a great deal of our learning," said Mr. Schmiser; "but do you know these Indians were scholars when we were savages? Their civilization antedates ours by centuries. And there are men among the Brahmins to-day who know more about magnetism, I mean magnetic psychology, than we do. I cannot understand, from your description, where science ends and where mummery begins, but I can easily believe there is a scientific foundation for all that seems to be folly to you. And the employment of the steel blade is especially significant."

He was talking in his native tongue now, and his words flowed more rapidly and smoothly.

"Science habitually frowns upon all inscrutable phenomena. It is not the province of science to analyse the occult. Her efforts tend to expose a fraud or a delusion, but never to formulate non-provable systems. Therefore her deliverances upon the topic of Animal Magnetism have been very cautious or very rude. I can illustrate my thought thus: two men assert, separately, that they have seen a ghost. The scientific world meets the assertion with disdain, and rejects this double testimony upon scientific hypotheses, well established. First, there is no proof that can be subjected to analytical tests that the vision was not a mere delusion. Second, it is a maxim in science that disembodied spirits cannot be visible to the physical organism. Third, there is no evidence, satisfactory to science, that man has any existence outside of his material organism. It does not assert the opposite doctrine, but it declines to discuss the proposition. Indeed, it is asserted that there is no entity that is not material, and I cannot controvert that point. At least, not yet. It is asserted that thought is only phosphorus. I do not know.

" But I do know that in any civilized jurisprudence the testimony of these two eye-witnesses would be more weighty than all the books of all the philosophers, always provided that they testified of facts of ordinary occurrence.

" If I had to deal with your Hindoo, I should follow him so long as he would lead. I should distinguish between a mere mountebank and a sincere believer in his art; and I should investigate each step in his progress."

" I am entirely bewildered," replied Hyland. " You seem to be reviving all the abominable humbug of the Middle Ages!"

" Engleesh!" quoth the professor. " Ah, well! Here is Mr. Plimpton looking for you."

Hyland and Mr. Plimpton withdrew to another corner, leaving the savant to his pipe and his meditations.

" There are two Englishmen," thought the professor, " who think wisdom will die with them. You could not knock a philosophical idea into their heads with a sledge-hammer!"

" There goes an obstinate young cub!" thought Mr. Plimpton, when Hyland left him. " He rejects the aid of Dancer with haughty persistence. He will find his brother by what he calls common-sense methods. Meantime, I intend to keep Dancer on the track."

" There are two maniacs," said Hyland, as his cab rolled on to Charing Cross Hotel; " one offering to find Miles by setting a thief-catcher on his track; the other advocating magnetism, necromancy, humbug! Plimpton, a remarkably sensible man on most subjects, but entirely insane in his admiration of his detective, because he once unravelled a complicated fraud. Schmiser, a square-headed thinker, who put me through Kant only two years ago, now swallowed up in mesmerism! And here am I, the one sane man of the trio, about to search England over without the slightest clue. I will go to Bath to-morrow, consult Colonel Mordaunt, and then start out on my search. And I will explore every nook of this island."

CHAPTER XXI.

A New Enterprise.

COLONEL MORDAUNT and his daughter had left Bath a week before Mr. Rayneford arrived. Mr. Daltman was with them. The latter was about to start on a cruise in his yacht, now at Milford. The colonel would be at Clifton in a few days. The arrival of the "Bengal" had been announced, and he had probably gone to London, as he expected Mr. Rayneford in that vessel, and was doubtless watching the marine intelligence in the papers.

Thus said Cabbil, Colonel Mordaunt's valet. He knew Hyland, and was sure the colonel would expect him to remain at his house in Bath until he returned. They had frequently spoken of Mr. Rayneford on the voyage. The "Lord Clive" had made a splendid run from the Cape. The ladies were quite well. Miss Juliet had not been comfortable at sea, but was well now. The colonel was going about the country with Dr. Leigh, and was improving. If Mr. Rayneford would not stop, would he please leave his address? Charing Cross Hotel, London. Thank'ee, sir.

Then Hyland prowled over the old city. He was forming his plans and did not want advice or assistance. He was just going to hunt for Miles. He was not much disturbed in mind, but there was constant occupation before him, and he would use his reason, and perhaps he could accomplish as much as Zeba and the detective together.

Presently he found himself in the country. He had strolled along paying slight attention to the direction he took, constructing hypotheses and then demolishing them.

"Will you ride, sir?"

The speaker was driving a nondescript vehicle on four wheels. The seat had a gig-top, now thrown back and resting upon the hinder part of the wagon, which was a sort of box covered in. An inscription on the panels read, "Timothy Holly, Photographer. Stereoscopic Views." The driver was a ruddy-faced man with a pleasant smile. A plump pony was drawing the vehicle at a very moderate trot, the reins being twisted round the whip standing in its socket. While Hyland hesitated the driver halted.

"Ho, Tommy! Stop! The gentleman is going to ride a bit. There is the step, sir, just before the wheel. Going far, sir? I am very glad to get your company! I was almost asleep. Bath is a fine place to sleep! Been there four days. Had splendid weather, and got a lot of new views. Can't say much in favour of Bath as a market for views. Have only sold three dozen in the four days! Go on, Tommy!"

"This is very comfortable," said Hyland, as the pony resumed his trot; "I did not know that I was fatigued. How far are we from Bath?"

"Four miles. You walked out? Ah, well! I think it is far pleasanter to ride. Tommy don't bother, you see. He turns out of the road as the law directs when he meets a trap. If you go to sleep, he just jogs on till he comes to some place where oats are kept. Then he stops, does Tommy."

"I suppose you inform him at starting what road you will take?" said Hyland, amused.

"Sometimes, sir. Roads are all alike to us. If we come across any good views, we just stop and take 'em. Which way are you bound, sir?"

"Really, I have not decided. I am just looking about—for views."

"Can you photograph?" said the driver.

"Yes. I have done a little in that way. But I am not very skilful."

"All depends on the focus," said the other, confidentially; "of course you must have your chemicals all right. I learned on cards, in Bristol, yonder. But now I only take views. Don't object to figgers in the views, if they're still. I thought of turning off here, to take Carsel Dane. It is a bit of a ruin with some splendid trees in the background. Would you mind?"

"Certainly not," replied Hyland. "I have heard of Castle Dane, and should like to see it. Also to take some lessons from you in your art. That is—if you do not object."

"Delighted, I'm sure, sir," said the artist, cheerfully; "Hi! Tommy! Turn to the right. Right! That's it! You see, sir, Tommy knows English. That is the wisest little lump of a horse I ever saw. He can pretty near talk. When I get out, if there is a bit of grass on the roadside, I just loosen his check-rein and leave him. I am fond of Tommy, and I don't like the thought of losing him."

He spoke as if the calamity was impending, letting off a cheerful sigh.

"Lose him?" said Hyland.

"Yes, sir. I think I must sell out. Forty pound offered for the whole rig. There is Carsel Dane. You can see the tower through the trees. Good day for views. Sun not too bright. No breeze to speak of. I know a gent as will take a dozen views of Carsel Dane. In Bristol. He wants some views of Clifton Downs, too. How much do you know of the art, sir? Armachure, I suppose?"

"Yes. No. Not exactly. I have been doing some surveying, and had to take some photographs to illustrate my reports. But I am quite clumsy."

"Easy as winkin', sir," said **Mr. Holly.** "It wouldn't do to say that either, to everybody. My customers think Timothy Holly can bang the world on views! But it is all in focus, and good chemicals. Stop, Tommy! I must open the gate." And he slid down from his perch, opened a gate on the roadside, and held it while the pony walked soberly into the lane. Refastening the gate, he resumed his seat, and Tommy resumed his jog-trot.

"It is a fine old park," observed Mr. Holly; "but a good bit run down. It has been let for a long time, twenty years or more. But the owner is back now, and it will be put in order, I fancy. Belongs to Colonel Mordaunt. Old house over there on the right. I know every inch of this ground! Used to be a grand place, but there were some family troubles—let me see: it was in 1840. Nigh twenty-five years ago. My father was steward of this estate, and I was born close by the park gates. Not where we came in. It is on the other road. If you like, I can tell you the story."

"No family secrets, I suppose?" said Hyland, doubtfully.

"Bless you, no! That is, not exactly secrets. Of course my father knew a lot of things, being steward, that everybody did not know. But there was no bloody murders or anything. The Mordaunts were always a stuck-up——"

"I know Colonel Mordaunt," said Hyland, interrupting him, "and he is my friend."

"And a first-class, A one, gent!" continued the artist. "I meant no offence. The Mordaunts were always proud and rather haughty, as they had the right to be. And the family trouble began——"

"Ah, here is the ruin!" said Hyland; "Tommy has stopped without orders. I suppose he knows when he reaches the proper locality for views?"

"He knows when he gets to good grass," said the other. "I'll let him pick a bit here in the lane. There is a gap in the hedge just beyond. I'll get out the camera. Here is the tripod, under the seat."

"Give me that and the camera," said Hyland. "I'll take them in while you prepare the plate."

"All right, sir. I'll follow you in a minute. There, Tommy, nip away."

In the course of the next hour Hyland had taken several views of Castle Dane, moving the tripod from place to place, and exhibiting so much judgment in his selection of sides and angles, that Mr. Holly was profuse in his praises.

"You don't need any lessons from me, sir," said he, as he examined the last view; "leastways not in this part of the work. You have got the best positions every time, and the negatives are perfect. You know how to manage the bath——"

"Yes, I think I do. If you will allow me, I will finish these, and then I will buy a dozen or two."

"Wish you would buy the lot!" said the artist, earnestly. "My stars! what a lucky day it would be for me and Nanny if you would."

"Nanny?"

"Yes, sir. That is my wife. When I left her this morning, she said, 'Tim, if you meet a customer for your whole rig, don't higgle over a pound or two,' said Nanny, 'because,' said she, 'a week is worth more than a five-pun' note,' says Nanny."

"I do not understand why you wish to sell," said Hyland, cautiously, "and I do not see what I could do with your rig if I bought it. And if I coveted this exact rig, I could not consent to buy it from you when you are pressed to sell. I could not speculate upon your necessities."

"You are going to smoke, sir," replied Mr. Holly. "Sit down here in the shade. Thank you, sir! This is a queer cigar, cut off at both ends. Which end must I light? Either? Well, that's jolly! Cheroot you call it. Prime!"

"Now, sir, I'll tell you my necessities, as you call 'em. Nanny is an orphan, and she has a twin brother. They were never separated until we were married, and then John had a good offer in Australia. So he sailed a year ago, and he keeps writing, does John, to Nan about the climate and the kangaroos, and telling her to bring me out there, until the poor girl is pining to go! I suppose twin children are fonder of each other than common children.

"So I have been looking about for a chance to sell. A chap in Glo'ster offered me forty pound last week, and Nan thinks I ought to take it. But Tommy is worth nigh forty pound himself. Not a blemish, sir! If I could sell out, Nan and I would be on the water in a week. A regular liner sails next Saturday. Bless you, Nan keeps a watch on the Australian lines! John says I can make money taking views, or I can be foreman on a sheep-farm at good wages, and have my own horse. That is the whole story of my necessities.

"I am sure I can't say why you should buy me out! Except that you are a gentleman, and perhaps have plenty of money. You couldn't smoke this kind of double-enders if you hadn't! And then, if you want to roam about the country, promiscuous, why, here you are! You can take views anywhere you like. I have a license——"

"But I cannot buy *your* license."

"No," said Mr. Holly, meditating. "But," he continued, brightening up, "I can tell you what you can do. You can take pictures under my license. Timothy Holly will employ you—say for a year. No gentleman could stick longer than that. And you shall have for wages all you can make on the pictures."

"What is the value of your 'rig,' my friend?" said Hyland.

"Sixty pound. And I'll take anything over forty. You can have the run of the British Isles. And Tommy will take to you just like a dog. My stars! If I was a single gentleman, with enough money to buy bread and cheese, and such an eye for views as you have, sir——"

"When do you desire to sell?" said Hyland, quietly. He had made up his mind.

"This minute," replied Mr. Timothy Holly, starting up and stamping on the sod. Hyland took out his pocket-book and counted twelve five-pound notes into the hand of his interlocutor.

"Now, Mr. Holly," said Hyland, "you have writing materials there in your box. Make out the necessary papers. Endorse on your license authority for me to show if I am questioned."

"What name, sir, please?" said Mr. Holly, after some laborious scratching with his pen. The poor fellow was half crazed with joy.

"Name? Certainly. Jack Robinson. You had better write it John."

"Never found it so hard to write in my life," said Mr. Holly, signing his name with a flourish. "There you are, sir, Mr. John Robinson, with my compliments, and wishing you the best of luck. My stars! How can I tell Nan! She will hardly believe me.

Sixty pound! Full value, and no heart-burnings. I don't know what game you are up to, sir, but I do know you are a true-grit English gentleman. If you are just idling about the country to kill time, you could not have a pleasanter lay than this. When it rains you can put up the gig top and unroll the apron, and there you are —water-proof. The box is water-tight too."

"Well," said Mr. John Robinson, when the other paused to take breath, "I am sole proprietor of this extensive establishment. My friend, I had no thought of buying five minutes ago."

"Very likely, sir. I've seen many a gent go off sudden-like before to-day. Nan will be sorry to part with Tommy, but Tommy could not take her to her brother."

"Perhaps he will take me to mine," said Hyland, thoughtfully. "Who knows?"

"Tommy is used to a good rubbing down, sir," said Mr. Holly, "and of course you can't do that. But wherever you put up you can give the 'ostler a sixpence, and tell him to spread it all over Tommy in an extra rub. And when you are alone on the road you can talk to Tommy—anything you like—and he'll never tell your secrets. Bless you! he understands all you say, though. I suppose you'll hardly believe it, sir, but when I came out of the stable this morning I just said, 'Tommy, we are going to Bristol to-day.' And I never touched the reins! He just turned off to the left and trotted up this road."

"I will cultivate Tommy's friendship," said Mr. Robinson, "and will adhere to your method of driving. Unfortunately, I cannot announce my intentions so decidedly, as I do not know where I am going."

"Leave it to Tommy, then," replied the other, confidently; "he will take you right. There's always good luck in trusting him. Did he not bring me to you this blessed day? Go on to Bristol, sir. There is a lot of views there. And to Clifton. No end of views there. My stars! Isn't it odd now, sir, that you should have taken these views of Carsel Dane, right here on the Mordaunt lands?"

"I don't understand you," said Hyland, bewildered.

"Why, these views, and what we were saying awhile ago about the Mordaunts. My stars! I *must* tell you that story." And he sat down again, while Hyland lighted a fresh cheroot.

"What story?"

"About the Mordaunts and their Clifton picture."

CHAPTER XXII.

THE MORDAUNTS.

"WHEN I was a mere kid, sir," began Mr. Holly, "I lived over there, about a mile beyond the fir plantation at the park gates. There were three Mordaunts in the big house: two brothers and a sister. They were all stately kind of people, but as kind to the poor as could be. My father was steward, and knew all about the estate, just as well as the lawyers. The estate is named Carsledane, after this old ruin, I suppose, and was left by will to the 'two brothers or the survivor of them,' with a charge upon the estate equal to one-third of its revenues in favour of Miss Mordaunt. My father knew all this, because he had to distribute the revenues under the will.

"The elder brother, Mr. Horace Mordaunt, was a very quiet gentleman, and lived among his books. The other, Mr. Dane Mordaunt, was a fiery young fellow, always getting into scrapes, but always coming out of them heads up. I think they would have quarrelled, being so different, only they both doted on their sister. They had their own friends, of course; Mr. Horace taking to book-men, who could spend a week with him in the big library, and Mr. Dane taking to army-officers, or men who knew horses and dogs, and could follow him across country without stopping for fences. Miss Mordaunt was gracious to both sets of visitors, showing no preferences, but giving each brother's friends share and share alike of her attentions, as mistress of the house. I can just remember her. I know I used to think she was exactly like the angels, only wanting wings. I remember Mr. Dane, too, who used to come tearing down the drive on his iron-grey horse every day, worrying the old porter's life out, as he had to get the gates open in time, lest Mr. Dane should leap his horse over them! I was most afraid of Mr. Horace though, for all he was so quiet. Somehow I got the idea that he would be a terrible man if his temper could be roused.

"There were two visitors who kept about even with both brothers. I mean they did not take to one and leave the other. The oldest was a rich manufacturer, who was full of knowledge about machinery and chemicals, and mines, and everything else. His name was Mr. Brentam. The other was just a plain country gentleman, who knew everything there was in books, and also everything about politics all

over the world. His name was Mr. Dale. They were both from
Somerset, neighbors and friends. Mr. Dale knew next to nothing
about business matters. He had a moderate estate, spent his money
freely, but not recklessly, and always had the same cheerful smile
for everybody. Mr. Brentam knew everything about money matters, and though he was wonderfully liberal in providing for the
comfort of his tenants and workmen, he got richer every year.

"It soon got to be known that these Somerset gentlemen were
rivals. They both wanted Miss Mordaunt. That much was certain.
But nobody could say which one pleased the lady best, or indeed
whether she would take either of them. It also got to be known
that Mr. Horace favoured Mr. Dale, while Mr. Dane was anxious to
give his sister to the manufacturer. He was at least ten years older
than the other, was a widower, was not very handsome or stylish,
but he had the tin.

"There was an artist at Clifton, name of Morrow, who was getting celebrated. He was the first man in these parts to take stereoscopic views. Twenty years ago they were not so common as they
are now, but were a real curiosity. People used to ride miles on
miles just to visit Morrow's gallery, and my father was lucky enough
to get me apprenticed to Mr. Morrow, having a good word from
Mr. Horace, and also from Miss Mordaunt. And it was in my first
year there, only a kid, when Mr. Dale and Miss Mordaunt came one
day together to have pictures taken. They did not want paper, they
wanted the old-fashioned metal. In lockets, too. Mr. Morrow was
very polite and attentive, because these locket pictures were a pound
a piece, besides the locket. When they had selected the cases, they
decided to have the pictures taken out on the Downs. Miss Mordaunt objected at first, but Mr. Dale said ' he must have the Observatory in the background,' and at last the lady consented. It
was quite early in the day and very few people were out. I carried
the tripod, and the two likenesses were soon taken. Mr. Dale gave
me half a crown. He was remarkably jolly. The lady was very
quiet, but she gave me half a crown too. The tripod was heavy,
and I was only a kid.

"I saw the pictures the next day, after they were fitted in the
lockets. Each one was full length, with the Observatory in the
background. Miss Mordaunt had taken off her hat, after many
denials, and her picture was just prime. Mr. Dale's was good-look-
ing enough, too. But old Morrow said he hated to part with the
lady's, as it was the loveliest he had ever taken. It sounds curious

now, but he did not know in them days that he could have made as many copies as he pleased from the original picture.

"Mr. Dale came the next day for the lockets. Mr. Brentam was with him. And I remember that Mr. Dale borrowed ten pound from him to pay for them, and that Mr. Brentam wrote the amount down on a scrap of paper, and got Mr. Dale to sign it. He slipped the lady's picture in his pocket, and showed only his own to Mr. Brentam. Kid as I was, I understood.

"I was at home on the next Sunday, and my father asked me a lot of questions about the likenesses, but did not tell me then what had happened. He never mentioned family matters to anybody while he was steward of Carsledane. But he told me the story afterwards, when everybody was gone and Carsledane let to strangers, and my father was living in Bristol and done with the estate.

"There had been a devil of a quarrel between the brothers. Mr. Dale had asked Horace for his sister's hand. Mr. Brentam had asked Mr. Dane the same day. The brothers had asked Miss Mordaunt to decide between the gentlemen, and she said she had already accepted Mr. Dale.

"Then Mr. Dane flew into no end of a rage, and asked her if they had really exchanged lockets, and said the 'poor beggar had borrowed the money from Brentam to pay for the pictures.' Miss Mordaunt said nothing, but she enclosed ten pound in a little note to Mr. Brentam that same evening, and said in the note that she would be pleased to cancel any other obligations of Mr. Dale's that he might hold. You see the gentlemen had both quit Carsledane, and were over there at Bristol, waiting to hear from the Mordaunts.

"That little note made matters worse. Mr. Brentam was insulted; and withdrew his suit. Mr. Dane bought a commission in a regiment that sailed for India in a week, and went off in a rage. Mr. Horace stayed long enough to see his sister married, and then he bought a commission also, and got exchanged into an Indian regiment. Mr. and Mrs. Dale stayed here a few months, and then sailed for America, and nobody has ever heard from them since. Mr. Dale was so much in debt that Dale's Manor had to be sold, and Mr. Brentam bought it. It was dreadfully mixed up, but there was some story about Mr. Brentam calling on Mr. Dale just before the sale, and offering to give him Dale's Manor free for that Clifton picture. All this was because Mrs. Dale had stung him to the quick by sending the ten-pound note.

" You see how it is, sir.   Mr. Brentam was rolling in riches, and he thought he could take any lady he might pick out.   He had been very friendly with Mr. Dale, and had lent him lots of money, but he always had little slips of paper with acknowledgments signed by Mr. Dale.   Mr. Dale said he had paid these sums all back, but was careless or ignorant, and had not taken back his acknowledgments. Mr. Brentam only pointed to the——"

" If you will excuse me, Mr. Holly," said Mr. Jack Robinson, " I will venture to interrupt your story.   I know Colonel Horace Mordaunt, and I am ashamed of myself for listening so long to these revelations of his private history.   I also know Mr. Brentam, and I do not believe one word against his honour.   I do not know Mr. Dale, but I have no doubt he was unjust and cruel to suggest such infamous——"

" Whew !" said Mr. Holly, with a long whistle, " I beg your pardon, sir, but I was only telling the story as I heard it, partly from my father, when I was only a kid.   I did not intend to say as much as I did, but the story of the picture came to my mind because I was thinking of old Morrow's saying."

" Did it relate to the Mordaunts ?"

" Oh, no, sir !   It was only a queer notion.   You see, sir, Morrow was an old bachelor, and he hated women like snakes, though he was polite as a dancing-master to his customers.   But he says to me, ' Tim,' says Morrow, ' you notice, whenever a cove has a woman took with the Observatory for a background,' says Morrow, ' then you notice, there'll be the devil to pay !' "

" Observatory for a background !" said Hyland, starting ; " what did he mean ?"

" Why, he meant marriage, sir !   ' I've took more than a hundred,' says old Morrow, ' and every one of 'em was a regular gone case !   Never knew a man to have the picture of a woman with the Observatory in the background,' says Morrow, ' that failed to be a gone goose, sooner or later !' "

" It's very odd," said Hyland, " but I happen to know of a picture of a gentleman and lady, taken less than thirty years ago, with that very Observatory——"

" Married, sir ?"

" Yes, certainly."

" That's just it !" ejaculated Mr. Holly ; " old Morrow was right, you see.   No doubt he took that very picture !   And when he took Miss Annot——"

" Miss Annot?'"

" Yes, sir. That was Miss Mordaunt's name. 'Tim,' says he, 'mark my words! Here's another gone goose!' meaning Mr. Dale, 'he's as good as married!' says Morrow. So if you take any pictures on Clifton Downs, sir, be very careful about the Observatory! Ha! ha! It won't hurt *you*, sir, unless you keep the picture yourself. It never hurt old Morrow, for he died single."

" Now, by this light!" said Mr. Robinson, " I'll put this to the proof! I will take the first woman I find between me and the Observatory, if she will be still long enough! And I will put her in a locket and wear her if she should be ugly as Hecate! If she can make me marry her, I will——"

" Will what, sir?"

" I will sell my books, will go to India, turn fakir, and sit in the sun until I am broiled. Philosophy will have become a delusion. Common sense will be midsummer madness, and human speech will be no wiser than the chattering of monkeys."

" All right, sir!" said Mr. Holly, cheerfully. " It is all foolishness, of course. But when I first set up, I used to prowl about on the Downs taking groups and the like. One morning a lot of girls got together and bargained for a picture. Ten shillings for a single head, with five duplicates. Half a crown each for groups of six, with five duplicates. They got me down to two shillings apiece, and then took their positions. Would you believe it, sir! when I squinted through the camera one girl was in the field, a little apart, and I just took her first. Then I changed the negative and took the group. After I had finished up the pictures and got my twelve shillings, I took the first plate out and made a separate picture, and there was the Observatory in the background!"

" Well?"

" You see I had moved the tripod when I took the group, and the Observatory was two hundred yards off. So an inch to the right or left threw it out of the field."

" Well," said Mr. Robinson, impatiently, " what of the single picture?"

Mr. Holly took out his pocket-book, unwrapped a carte, enveloped in tissue-paper, and handed it to the other.

" A fine, honest, English face," said Mr. Robinson. " So you kept the carte?"

" Yes, sir," replied Mr. Holly, replacing the picture, "and I mean to keep it while I live. That is my Nan, sir."

"What!" said Hyland, starting to his feet. "Do you mean to tell me that you married that girl?"

"Indeed I do," answered Holly, with a complacent grin. "Of course, the Observatory had nothing to do with it; but I just kept that picture in my pocket wherever I went. I never saw any one of the girls before that morning. I never saw any one of them since, except Nan, and I stumbled on her, promiscuous-like, down there in Bath. I had just bought Tommy, and had put him in the stable, and was on my way to my lodgings, about sundown. I saw a half-drunken fellow annoying a girl, who was trying to get away from him, and I persuaded him to leave her alone, and then I took her home. She was apprenticed to Madame Nash, the milliner. I was took up the next morning for assault—you see I had to tap the brute on the nose to get the girl away—and Madame Nash got me out of limbo. It was six months after that when I showed Nan that picture."

"Mr. Holly," said Hyland, "I will amend my resolution in one respect. If the first woman should happen to be particularly hideous, I will allow her to escape. And now, shall I drive you back to Bath?"

"Which way are *you* going, sir?" said Mr. Holly.

"I am going to Clifton. I have a curiosity to see that Observatory."

"Well, sir," said Mr. Holly, "if you will drop me at Ganton, I will take the train down. It is on your road, and I will get to Bath sooner than Tommy would take me. Shall we start now? Ho! Tommy! You have a new master now, old fellow, and I'll go bail for him."

When Mr. Holly slid down at Ganton he shook hands with the new proprietor at parting.

"It has plagued me a little, sir," he said, with a film over his cheerful eyes, "to think you maybe bought my kit because you wished to help a fellow. No? Well, it was a great kindness, anyway, and my Nan will pray for you every day of her life. I wrote my brother-in-law's address on the back of that certificate, and if you would just drop me a line out there, and say how you get along, and how Tommy is, I will be grateful. And when you go to Clifton, if you don't want to stop at the big hotels, I can recommend Mrs. Noils. She is a widow, and has a spare room to let, just across the high bridge. Tommy will take you straight to her gate."

"Many thanks, Mr. Holly," said Hyland. "Do not be concerned

about Tommy. I will be his friend. I will go to Mrs. Noils's as you suggest."

"And, sir—there comes the train! I've only a minute left. But when you do write—Timothy Holly, in care of John Brand, Murrigattee, Adelaide—would you mind telling me what comes of it?"

"Comes of what?"

"Why—hi! here's the train! Good-bye, sir! the best of luck! I mean what comes of your Clifton picture?"

CHAPTER XXIII.

Courting.

A WEEK after the battle at Long Meadow, Dale's Manor was depopulated. There were some domestic animals left, including a dozen venerable hens, but all the chickens that had cracked their shells in the previous spring-time had become fries, broils, and pies, and had nourished the fast recovering invalids. On the train for Charleston were Mr. and Miss Dale, Mr. Miles and Mr. Boston. The latter had discovered Miles's devotion, and beguiled Mr. Dale into the smoking-car, leaving Annot and Miles to their meditations. There had been very little private conference between them since the interview recorded in a previous chapter. The lady had been constantly occupied making preparations for the journey, and all that Miles had been able to get during the busy days was an occasional interchange of glances; his full of adoration, and hers shy and demure as possible.

"I have been trying to hope, Miss Dale," he said, as her father left the car, "and have watched for one encouraging look from you. I don't think I got it."

"You did not answer my last remark, Mr.—my lord."

"We were interrupted," he answered. "You say 'my lord.' If I might call you 'my lady,' I would be willing to relinquish all my possessions for the privilege. Will you please let me be plain Miles to you?"

"You are Lord Rayneford," she said, "are you not?"

"My name is Miles."

"Father told me that dreadful day, when you had gone to Long Meadow, that you were one of the Rayncfords of Hawkley. He knew you by a dozen proofs. He said you had a brother, who had inherited the title probably, and you, being a younger son, had changed your name when you undertook your present adventure. He knew the late Lord Rayneford, and to-day he said he could see a striking resemblance to him in you. When you told me the other day that your brother was the younger, I knew you were the present Lord Rayneford."

"I am under a promise to remain Mr. Miles until I return to England. I will not contradict you, however. Indeed, I should have told you all my history, because no promise could bind me to keep a secret from you. When I made the compact, it was stipulated that the woman I asked to be my wife should be informed of all I might desire to tell her. We have known each other but a few days, and yet, events have happened in this short acquaintance that make up for longer intercourse. It seems to me that I know you more intimately than I know any one else in the world, except Hyland. I am sure I shall never love any woman but you. If you can say I may continue loving you, I will not ask any more, until you know me better."

She looked away from his glowing eyes, which were giving the lie to his moderate speech all the time. The bright country swept back as the train sped onward, and all the face of nature looked more beautiful to her eyes than ever before. It was not so much the consciousness of owning a devoted lover that added the bloom to her cheek, as the growing consciousness that she was being owned by him. She was not the least bit dazzled by his title. On the contrary, she was sorely disappointed when the truth flashed upon her mind, three days ago.

"If you had only been plain Mr. Rayneford," she murmured, turning to him, at last, "then I might have——"

"What, Annot?"

"I would have promised never to marry any other, perhaps."

"And would that promise be made because you could love plain Mr. Rayneford?"

"I don't know. You had made me like you so well, that I could not love any other. Never!"

"And you cannot like Lord Rayneford?"

"Oh, yes. But it does not seem proper—please don't look at me that way—it does not seem proper for me to—to take you at dis-

advantage. You are away from friends and kindred, and the swift
rush of events you just referred to has carried you away from your
ordinary prudence and sense of propriety. You have fought for
me. You cherished pity for me, thinking I had my life desolated
by the death of Captain Stanly. You are so kind and unselfish
that you suffered great pain in thinking of the terrible pain your
message from the dying man would inflict upon me. Please look
out the other window. I cannot talk while you glare at me."

"I cannot! Do you remember what Toby said yesterday when
you gave him that enormous chicken-pie, and bade him be careful
of his steps?"

"No."

"He said, 'Miss Annie, my eyes done sot!' Please go on."

"Every person in the car can tell what you are saying——"

"I am saying nothing. There are only two old ladies behind us,
and they are four seats distant. The persons in front of us cannot
see out of their back hair. I *must* look at you! If I close my eyes,
I still see you. Even when I sleep, you are present in my dreams;
and when I waken, though surrounded by the blackness of darkness, the same vision of loveliness illuminates my chamber. I hear
your voice in the wind or the rainfall, and if all is still around me,
I still hear you in the throbbings of my heart, where you live."

She listened, entranced. The warm blood spread over her pleasant
countenance while he spoke, and she glanced timidly at his honest
eyes, which were endorsing his words with emphasis.

"I am so ignorant of the forms of courtship," he continued, "that
I make no progress. I do not know what to say, except that you
are all my life. If I cannot win you, I know perfectly well that I
shall walk apart while my life is prolonged, trying to perform my
duty as becomes a man, but with no sunshine upon my path. If I
can win you, it seems to me that there are no impossibilities in my
future. If this eager desire to possess you is merely selfish, I mistake my own feelings. On the contrary, it seems to be the single
desire of my heart to make you happy. I can imagine no self-denial
in this either, because I could know no happiness that failed to give
you pleasure. I could find no gratification in pursuits where your
sympathies were wanting."

She made no reply, but listened with downcast eyes. She could
not venture to meet his eyes now. She wondered if the music of
"Annie Laurie" seemed as sweet to him as his calm accents seemed
to her.

"I do not answer your remark about friends and kindred. I am my own master, and need ask no one. But if I had to please others by my choice, there is no woman in the world who would rival you! My brother has been nearer to me than all the world besides until now. And you have supplanted him. When I tell you I love you more than I love Hyland, I have said more than I ever said before. But, Annot, this is not like other loves. I cannot think of you as having any separate interests from mine. In spite of your cold-ness——"

She just shot one look at him. It struck him between the eyes and went whirling through his brain like a rifle-ball.

"I was saying," he stammered, "that—that you could not appreciate my feeling of identity—unless you loved me. And I could not expect you to love me, at least not in the degree that is requisite, until I learn to court you less clumsily. I have thought, indeed, if I could marry you at once, to-day, that the remainder of my life would only be one unceasing courtship. Because I long for such a wealth of love from you! If I had known you a long time, and if there were no shyness, and no feeling of strangeness separating us, I should still see that nothing but an entire life of devotion could earn from you the love I covet so hungrily."

It is highly probable that Annot would have remained silent if the train had jumped the track and gone ploughing through the pine forest. Her feelings were not dissimilar from those of the man who has taken too much champagne for the first time. There is a novel exhilaration, with a faint suspicion of coming inebriety, and a vague dread of impropriety—a vague distrust of one's tongue, inducing the conclusion that, on the whole, silence is golden. But with this there is a warm glow over the entire organism, mental and physical, that breeds contentment. It is not easy to describe, but you probably understand.

"I retort your suggestion," said Miles, "that I have mistaken ordinary or even extraordinary sympathy for warmer emotions. You, having a high-bred, generous nature, feel excessive gratitude for such service as you say I have rendered. Therefore you are reluctant to appear ungracious, and so you listen with patient courtesy to me."

Another shot from slightly humid eyes made his heart bound.

"Because," he continued, "there was really nothing in my acts beyond those that the ordinary instincts of manhood would prompt. I did no good. Probably I incensed the villains by my assault, and made them ruder in their treatment of you. I cannot plead anything that I have done. I can only say I love you, and ask you to love me in requital."

"Listen!" she said, turning suddenly to him: "I have not the courage to assume the position you offer me. I am not accomplished enough for Lady Rayneford. I do not like fashionable life. I have always belonged to my father, and cannot belong to another. All my tastes and habits are homely, and I could not bear to see you ashamed of me! I should die! If you had been plain Mr. Rayneford——"

" I listen," he said, as she paused.

" Even then I should have doubted. Because your brother would have been Lord Rayneford, and you might have to apologise to him for my lack of culture. I cannot be so deceitful as to profess indifference to you, and I do not think these exciting experiences you speak of have anything to do with my—my regard for you; except so far as they served to reveal your nobleness of character. My lord, I am sensible of the honour you offer me. I am proud of your friendship. If you had been only what you seemed, I—perhaps I should have been proud of your love! That is," she added, hurriedly, "after a time."

"There are certain obstacles in the way," said Miles; " I was so unlucky as to be born two years before Hyland, and the laws of England compel me to take my rank. But you are the daughter of Windham Dale of Dale's Manor. Do you know the Dales were English gentry when the Raynefords obtained their title? Do you know that the Mordaunts of Castle Dane, to whom your mother belonged, were the proudest race in the south of England? Your objection to my rank is idle, Annot. The title has been in my family only two or three generations. Do you not know that every motion of your hand, every intonation in your speech, every sentiment you utter bespeaks your gentle breeding? I don't think I could be attracted by the loveliest woman that poets have ever dreamed of if she were not a lady. I would freely venture you in the company of the haughtiest women of England, who are the haughtiest women in the world, and I should dread no comparison that might be instituted, leaving you to your native instincts. If I were the proudest duke in England, I should feel honoured in making you my duchess."

She had gone off in a trance again. No man had ever talked to her in this fashion. It was not like the frivolous compliments, half jest and half earnest, that she had received from quondam admirers. It was not like Stanly's courtship, which had been far more aggressive than that of Miles, and would easily have become impassioned if her cold exterior had not kept him in a state of perpetual snub. But this man talked with courtly grace, in dead earnest all the time, and yet refraining from vows and protestations, while he said such astounding things to her. He put aside her most formidable objections with a few plain words in even tones. And the utter sincerity of all his prettiest speeches was constantly apparent as he battered down her feeble defences.

"You spoke of Hyland," said he, after a brief silence. "Shall I tell you about Hyland?"

"Yes," she whispered. She was oppressed by the conviction that her voice was not to be trusted.

"I am thankful that you did not know Hyland first!" said Miles, fervently, "because you would never have listened to me. When I was dismissed by Mr. Plimpton, my guardian, I found I had about a thousand pounds a year. My estate had been encumbered so seriously that only retrenchment and economy could save it, and during my minority Mr. Plimpton had wisely managed my affairs. Hyland inherited two thousand a year from my mother, which came to him two years after my majority. His first act was to apply to Mr. Plimpton, who is our family solicitor, to transfer his inheritance to me, to aid in freeing Hawkley from mortgages. His argument was this: a foolish old grandfather had no right to tie up a fortune for him that righfully belonged to Lord Rayneford. When he found that this would not be allowed, he went to India 'to better his fortunes,' he said, but really to earn enough to free Hawkley for me —for me! The boy has no selfish desire or purpose in his organism. Ah, if the woman I love so tenderly could only love me as tenderly as Hyland does!"

"Belton Junction!" bawled the conductor. "Passengers for Charleston change cars! Refreshments at the depot! Express train down in forty minutes!"

She took his offered arm as they moved down the aisle, though she had not heard a word the conductor said, and as they came out in the sunlight she dropped her veil over her face. They walked silently along the platform, meeting her father and Mr. Boston, bond-slaves to smoke.

"Go into the ladies' room, Annot," said Mr. Dale; "we will come for you when the train arrives. Come, Mr. Miles—smoke!"

"Thank you, no," replied Miles; "I will watch over Miss Dale."

"Ah, but you cannot enter there," said Mr. Dale. "Don't you see the prohibition over the door? 'Gentlemen will please take the other room.' Come, we have forty minutes to wait."

"This train will be off in two minutes," quoth Mr. Boston. "In two more minutes the station will be empty, as we are the only passengers for Charleston. In two more minutes that dusky damsel, keeping guard over the ladies' room, will be asleep. Meantime, my friend, you can converse with Miss Dale through the window. Mr. Dale and I will take our unwholesome fumigations into the 'other room.' Come on, Mr. Dale."

While the long, black trail of smoke from the departing train was floating out of sight in the pine woods, the "dusky damsel," a fat negress of fifty summers, waddled out with pitcher in hand.

"Gwine to de spring, sah," she said. "Back directly."

Miles peeped in the open door. Annot was standing at the opposite window. She had thrown her veil back, and as he crept towards her, she turned her burning face to him. He held out his hand, half delirious, as he read her countenance; and she offered no resistance when he took hers and covered it with kisses.

"Oh, Annot!" he said, "I almost think you love me!"

"I am afraid I do," she murmured; "and I am afraid you love your brother more than me!"

When the black damsel returned, she nearly turned white with horror at the sight of a great man not only in the ladies' apartment, but actually kissing the lady with astounding industry. As Miles sneaked out, guilty and abashed, he dropped a coin into the hand of the indignant negress.

"Golly!" she muttered. "Dis beats de old scratch heself!"

CHAPTER XXIV.

HARDY'S STORY.

THE train stopped twenty miles or more west of Charleston, and Mr. Boston, ever restless, stepped out upon the platform. The little village had been transformed into a military station, and a sentry was marching up and down in front of the ticket-office. As Mr. Boston passed him, the soldier stopped and presented arms.

"Mighty glad to see you, sir!" said the soldier. "Hardy is down with the fever, and he has been asking for you every time he come to."

"Hardy?" replied the other—"where is he?"

"In hospital, sir. There behind the baggage-wagons."

"But I have resigned, my friend," said Mr. Boston, irresolutely; "besides, I should miss the train."

"All aboard!" shouted the conductor.

"Yes, sir," said the sentry, "if you go to Hardy, I reckon you will have to give up this train. He is pooty bad, and I s'pose it's no use, anyhow."

"Mr. Dale," said Boston, "please hand my portmanteau out of the window. It is on the seat beside you. Ah! thank you! I will be in Charleston as soon as may be. Good-bye!"

"Where shall I find you?" said Mr. Dale, as the train moved away.

"At the Mills House. *Au revoir!*"

The hospital was a Methodist meeting-house. The long benches had been utilized by turning them face to face and covering the double seats with straw mattresses. There were a dozen soldiers in the building in various stages of convalescence, nearly all of them suffering from gunshot wounds. Hardy was in a corner, remote from the rest, and Mr. Boston noticed the gleam of satisfaction that spread over his face as he approached him.

"Powerful glad to see you!" said the sick man, with a feeble voice. "I told the boys to keep their eyes skun, and they mought see you. All up with me, Mr. Boston!"

"I hope not, Hardy," replied his visitor, cheerfully. "What is the matter?"

"Fever! Not a scratch on me. Been in ten battles, and not a dogon'd scratch. Don't like dying here, like a sick chicken! But I knowed my time was up when Jim Stanly got his billet! You see, me and Jim was raised together. My father was overseer on his father's plantation."

"Fever is not necessarily fatal, Hardy," said Mr. Boston, regarding the soldier attentively. "What does the doctor say?"

"He don't say anything. He just feels my pulse, and goes on to the other boys. They've all been hurted. Got no k'neen."

"No what?"

"K'neen. Fever stuff. I reckon a bully dose of that would bring me through."

"I will see the doctor about you."

"No use, sir! I'm a gone 'coon!" replied the soldier, hopelessly. "But I wanted to see you—I thought maybe you wouldn't mind seeing the old woman——"

"Do you mean your mother?" said Mr. Boston.

"No. My wife. She lives in Raleigh. You can go there any day from Charleston.".

"I will go if need be. You must give me the exact address."

"You won't know Polly in any kind o' dress, for that matter," said Hardy. "She lives with her folks. Ask at the Yarboro' House. That's the hotel. You can tell Polly I fit my best, and got caught out with fever at last."

"Hardy, I don't believe you are seriously ill," said his visitor. "You seem to be charged with last messages, though; so fire away! I have had forty last messages entrusted to me that the senders corrected when they recovered."

"I wanted to tell you about them Yanks," said Hardy, after a little pause. "I reckon I'd die easier."

"What Yanks?"

"Them three devils we gobbled up at old man Dale's."

"The robbers?"

"Exactly," said Hardy, excitedly. "Please set a little closer. You see, them fellows weren't regular prisoners. There was a lot of prisoners that the cavalry took off with them. But the general told me and Sam Goby to take them three to Haytown and deliver them up to the jail thar. So we started on our tramp through the woods.

"Sam Goby was Stanly's brother-in-law. He used to be well off, but he was the devil on whiskey. I reckon he drunk her to death. He joined the army, of course, and he mought have been an officer, but he could never pass a whiskey jug. So he was always a high private. He was in the guard-house twenty times, but Stanly always begged him off.

"It was nigh sundown when we started from old man Dale's. Haytown is fifteen mile, good. So we had to camp out one night. We had tied the three Yanks together, and made them march ahead of us, and we did not have much chaince to talk till camp-time. We knew all about Haytown. Sam had been in the jail, and knew that them Yanks could break out easy the next night, and we didn't like the idea of their prowling around the country. You see thar are no men about thar but old men and niggers. We thought it was a shame to waste them thieves when we had 'em all secure.

"While you were up-stairs at old man Dale's the officers were out on the front porch, and Sam was with them. You see they were off duty like, and he knew the most of 'em at home. Thar were just twelve of 'em, counting Sam. The general was up-stairs. Them twelve formed themselves into a jury, and sot on the three robbers. And as they had all the facts right before their eyes, they found all three guilty in about three minutes. We have a law in the army that says any soger that ill treats a woman must die, and if the general had been a mile or two off them three murderers would have been hung in half an hour. Sam told me all this that night, when we were smoking our corncob pipes. After they had sot on the case, Captain Green drew up a paper, and they all signed it, Sam Goby and all.

"The paper said these three men had been captured in the act of robbing a house. They had shot an old man, who had no arms. They had ill treated a lady, tearing off her watch and ear-rings. They had also shot a young man, but he was fighting them, and they did not count that. And the verdict was unanimous to hang all three. They were not prisoners of war, but were captured loaded with the plunder taken from a defenceless house. And the paper charged Sam Goby to see the sentence executed. Before we started, Captain Green called Sam and me to his bridle, and whispered his parting orders. 'Men,' says he, 'if there is any chaince for them scoundrels to git clear, see that you lose them in the woods.' And his face was stern as death.

"'Now, Bill,' says Sam, 'thar's nobody in Haytown to do this business. That jail wouldn't hold a good-sized rooster, if he wanted to scratch himself out. The orders is clear. We must lose these devils to-night.'

"I did not feel quite clear about that. I was quite willing to shoot all three when we had 'em at old man Dale's, because my blood was up. So to gain time I proposed to examine the no-account sucker who swore he hadn't shot anybody in the house. Sam agreed, and we strolled over to his tree. You see we had tied each one to a different tree, so that they could not contrive any deviltry without talking loud enough for us to hear.

"'Say, Yank,' says I, 'you said you had not shot anybody. How came one chamber of your pistol empty?'

"'I shot that on the hill,' says he.

"'What did you shoot at?' says I.

"'I shot a fellow that came loping up to my gun,' says he.

" ' What was he riding?' says I.

" ' A big roan horse,' says he; 'and I tumbled him out of the saddle.'

" That was Jim Stanly. Nobody else had a roan horse.

" We went back to our log and sot there, smoking. I was thinking of Jim when he was a boy. Sam was thinking of Jim's sister, I reckon.

" When our pipes were out, Sam asked me if it was all right. I said 'yes.' Then he went round to the three trees and told the robbers that the night air was deadly about thar, and they had better pray a little if they knew how. He told them we gave them an hour, as near as we could measure the time. Sam had brought old man Dale's clothes-line with him, and when the moon was well overhead we—lost all three of 'em, and marched ten miles east, and crawled into a cotton-gin and went to sleep.

" Sam Goby got a quart the next day and got raving drunk. We had to cross the river, but I was took down with this fever. So Sam started alone, and missed the ford, and was drownded. And nobody knows anything about them three but you and me. I reckon I have killed a dozen men since this war begun. But they were always doing their level best to kill me! And since we lost them three devils this fever has been on me. Sam is gone, and I have to go, too!"

The arrival of the doctor stopped the flow of Mr. Hardy's grewsome narrative. After going the rounds the surgeon stopped a few minutes at Hardy's side, asked a question or two, felt his pulses. Mr. Boston followed him out.

" What ails Hardy, doctor?" he asked, when they reached the open air.

" There is some sort of mania—I am perplexed about the case. He grows visibly worse day by day—says he is dying, which is an unfavourable symptom. He has intermittent fever and nothing else that I can discover. We are out of quinine."

" But I am not!" said Mr. Boston. " I have a supply in my portmanteau."

" It is worth its weight in gold," said the doctor.

" Well, I don't want any gold," replied the other. " Here, take my stock. I can replenish in Charleston if I need it."

" Two-grain pills," said the surgeon, examining the box. " Now, Mr. Boston, if you will give Hardy ten of these, and quiet his mind, he ought to get well."

"Suppose you give him a certificate, and let him go home for a month?"

"Certainly. I will explain to the major, and he will grant the furlough, without doubt."

"May I tell him so?" asked Mr. Boston, as the surgeon left him.

"I will send the paper in ten minutes. The major is quartered in the nearest house there."

The perspiration on the sick man's forehead betokened the absence of fever, and the ex-hospital steward administered the prescribed remedy.

"K'neen! by thunder!" said Hardy, as he choked and spluttered.

"It is quinine, my friend," said Mr. Boston, "and the doctor says you will be all sound again. Pluck up your courage, and dismiss your forebodings. I have a plan."

"Ah," said Hardy, drawing his rough hand over his eyes, "you are a true-grit gentleman! Excuse me, but was you born a Yank?"

"A Yank!" exclaimed the other.

"Yes, sir. There are plenty of Yanks in our army that were raised among us. They are nigh as good as our own people."

"I am an Englishman, Mr. Hardy," said Mr. Boston, with a certain air of dignity.

"English! Well, well! What in thunder have you been plodding about with us for? English! Well, sir, a man can't choose where he'll be born! Everybody couldn't be born in North Kalliney, Hoopsy! But that k'neen is infernal bitter! No use, though! Only wasted on me. Sam is gone, and I must go too!"

"Go where?"

"After them lost fellows. The trifling rascals!"

A soldier came in, marched up to Mr. Boston, handed him a folded paper, touched his cap, wheeled and marched out.

"Now, Hardy, this is my plan," said Mr. Boston, after glancing at the paper: "you are demoralized. The affair out there in the Tennessee woods weighs upon your mind. And I must admit that the story is horrible enough. But you will not misunderstand me when I say there are extenuating circumstances. You have a judge here in America who sometimes improves upon your ordinary laws. You call him—Judge Lynch."

"Yes, sir. I knowed him in Californy."

"I think he presided at the jury trial you mentioned, on Mr. Dale's verandah."

"There was twelve of 'em," said Hardy, "counting Sam Goby."

" Yes. And when you and Goby—lost the marauders, you executed their verdict?"

Hardy fumbled in his pocket and drew out a paper.

" Here is the verdict, sir. I thought I would keep it. I took it from Sam when he got tight. All their names are to it."

" Well, keep it still. You may need it some day. Now, to-morrow you will be well enough to go out. Suppose you go to Raleigh?"

" Home!" said the soldier, starting up.

" Yes. Here is your furlough. One month."

" Hooray!" said Hardy, with a feeble shout, " I'm well enough now! Oh, Mr. Boston, I'm so sorry you're a Britisher! You ought to been born in North Kalliney! Heavenly Marster! If I could only wipe them three devils out of my mind I would die happy!"

" Listen!" said the Englishman: " Judge Lynch is known all over this land as the one judge who knows no mercy. Those who come before his dread tribunal bid adieu to hope. He has only one penalty for all offences. In my country we have many cases of murder, but we have no Judge Lynch. Heaven grant that he may never set his foot on English soil!

" It may be that he is a necessity here. I dare not utter a sweeping condemnation, because he may be a necessary evil, permitted to exercise spasmodic authority here by a wise Providence. But I should rather be his victim than his executioner!

" However, there is another Judge, who rules in all lands. And all cases come before His tribunal, sooner or later. And none of the sons of men are pure enough to endure the scrutiny at that bar. But the sentence of that final court may be evaded, because this just Judge is merciful, and He has provided an advocate for all the wrong-doers of earth. Do you understand?"

" Yes, sir," answered Hardy, submissively.

" Then tell your story to this Advocate. And tell all the other stories of evil deeds you have committed. You may get the entire record erased at once! You will be well enough to travel to-morrow. I am going to leave your country very soon, and I have a supply of your excellent currency that will not circulate beyond your borders. Oblige me by spending it for me." And he put a roll of notes on the mattress, shook hands with his interlocutor, and passed out of Hardy's sight, now blurred with moisture—forever.

CHAPTER XXV.

FIXING THE DAY.

MR. DALE discarded the noxious weed when abandoned by Mr. Boston, and passed into the other car. Miles arose and offered his seat by Annot's side; but her father waved him back, and dropped into the seat behind them. There was a cloud of decided sheepishness upon the young couple. Annot endeavoured to look dignified. Miles tried to look stern.

"Been quarrelling," thought Mr. Dale; "it was very thoughtless in me to leave them together. This fiery youngster has offended Annot by some war talk. She looks as cross as she can, and he is evidently foaming with rage."

There had been an accession to the passenger list at the last station, and the car was tolerably well filled. The enraged couple could not talk and listen as they had done before, and they were very cautious about even the exchange of glances. Every man and woman in the car seemed to have eight eyes and sixteen ears. Whenever a masculine passenger looked towards Annot, Miles turned over in his mind various pretexts that might justify him in cutting the onlooker's throat. Gentle Annot, catching the infection, and knowing by magnetism what Miles thought, felt prepared to assume the *rôle* of the fish in "Cock Robin," and to hold the "little dish" to catch his blood. Neither looked strikingly amiable.

"Suppose we reverse your seat, Annot?" said Mr. Dale; "we can converse much more pleasantly."

The young lady and Miles moved out into the aisle, and Mr. Dale turned the back of the seat. Then it was highly important that Annot should not ride backwards. So she took the window-seat next her father. Miles sat opposite, piling up sachels in the unoccupied seat, while the train sped on.

"Mr. Boston left us unexpectedly at the last station," observed Mr. Dale. "He is an extraordinary man; has travelled all over the world. He was a member of the Antarctic Expedition under Spencer."

"Was he?" said Annot, stealing a look at her *vis-à-vis*, who was scowling.

"Is he still at it?" muttered Miles. This question referred to a spruce young gentleman three or four seats off, who had been stealing furtive glances at the lovely woman.

"Occasionally," she replied.

"Suppose you put your veil down?" said Miles, spitefully. And the sun went behind a cloud. The spruce young gentleman looked back once more, and finding the grenadine barrier impenetrable betook himself to the smoking-car. Miles did not kick him as he passed, and therefore mentally scored down one good action for that day's record.

"I think he was in the Crimean War," continued Mr. Dale, somewhat bewildered by this by-play.

"Pity he didn't lose a leg!" murmured Miles. "I beg your pardon, Mr. Dale, of whom were you speaking?"

"Of Mr. Boston."

"Oh!" And he twisted his neck round and surveyed the passengers' backs. They all seemed to be minding their own business.

"Miss Dale," said Miles, politely, "don't you find your veil oppressive?"

"Dusty," she answered. She could see him through the veil.

Miles swept the satchels from the seat, and made room for her by moving away from the window.

"Do you object to riding backwards? Suppose you try? The dust will not annoy you then."

"He is getting in a better humour," thought Mr. Dale, as Annot changed her seat; "or maybe it is only politeness." Annot threw back her veil, exposing her rosy face. Miles glared at it as if he had not seen it for a month.

"Mr. Boston is from Devon. But he knows all our county also. We had quite a discussion as to the relative beauties of Somerset and Devon. Annot, you look very warm! Where is your fan?"

Miles took up the fan, gave it a preliminary flirt, and she quietly took it out of his fingers.

"Cross!" thought Mr. Dale.

"Do you see that deceitful wretch?" whispered Miles; "over there, three seats down. He is pretending to read; but he peeps over his book at you every other minute. I'll spoil *his* game anyhow!"

So saying, he whisked out of his seat and took that beside Mr. Dale, thus putting his broad shoulders between the book-man's eyes and Annot. The book-man gave it up.

"Twelve more miles," said Mr. Dale; "that is a half-hour. I can get one more cigar before we reach the city. Come, Mr. Miles."

"Excuse me, sir," answered Miles; "but take one of my cigars. Partagas."

10

"Ah, Mr. Boston filled my case with pressed Cabañas," said Mr. Dale. "You have not smoked to-day. Come!"

"I could not endure a cigar to-day. My head, you know."

"They will fight again," said Mr. Dale, as he left the car; "but they may as well have it out. Annot looks cross and he looks sheepish. I never knew the child to manifest so much temper! Would not let him fan her!"

"Come over here, you darling!" said Miles; "turn your back upon that wretched inebriate, gazing at you over his book. Come!"

"You are behaving horribly, Mr.—my lord!" said Annot, as she complied.

"My name is Miles Rayneford. Say Miles!"

"Mr. Miles."

"Not Mr. Miles. That is what my old housekeeper calls me. *Your* housekeeper too, Annot!"

They were very circumspect, as they had near neighbours, whose attention had been attracted by their various changes in position. It was not decorous to whisper constantly, yet it was extremely difficult to remain silent. The things Miles wished to say were of the last importance, and he was by no means certain "they would keep" until the train reached the city. Besides, Mr. Dale was happily absent, and in Charleston it would not be easy to find opportunities for private conference.

"Annot!" he said at last, desperately, "may I call you Annot?"

"Yes. That is, if I may call you my lord."

"But you may not! Who ever heard of a lord running block-ades? When we reach England you may."

"Then you are Mr. Miles. Do you suppose I am going to call you plain 'Miles'? Never!"

"I must tell Mr. Dale my true name. But we cannot be married under false names, Annot. I shall have to tell the clergyman too. Do you happen to know a discreet clergyman in Charleston?"

She looked curiously at his sober visage without replying. He had been talking of a speedy return to England only an hour ago.

"And the British consul too!" ejaculated Miles. "The fact is, Annot, a fellow is never safe when sailing under false colours. It was just a fit of squeamish folly and pride that made me drop my true name. Why should I conceal my name? Yet I promised to keep it secret as far as possible until my return. I did not know— that is—I did not—or rather, had not formed any matrimonial plans when I made that engagement."

She still kept silence, waiting for a more explicit statement.

"I have it! by Jove!" said Miles; "we will be married on board my ship, just as we leave. I can arrange it all. How stupid I was!"

"When do you think of sailing?" said Annot, demurely.

"Soon, soon! Ah! trust me to hasten matters. In two or three weeks, my own darling!"

"Don't you think you might find a clergyman on the train?" she said, with superb composure, "or a chaplain, or magistrate, or something?"

"Heh?" said Miles, startled.

"I think you are very remiss not to provide an official of some sort," she continued; "it has been several hours since you—since we stopped at the station where—where you were so rude."

"I beg your pardon!" said Miles, hopelessly bewildered.

"Do you not understand? It is very simple. One can never tell when one may meet a lady, engage in conversation, grow sentimental—propose! Then the next thing, of course, is the clergyman!"

"I see I have played the—mischief—somehow," said Miles, humbly. "Pray forgive me, and enlighten me. I thought you loved me. I know I love *you*. How have I offended you?"

"By talking so composedly of clergymen and consuls, and all that other nonsensical stuff!" she answered, resentfully. "How dare you! Why, I have only known you a week!"

"Yet all my life is compressed into that week!" whispered Miles, mournfully.

Annot did not reply. She was struggling to keep back the tears that were trying to come on several accounts. First, his voice was sad, and her swift sympathy called for tears. Sympathy is always inclined to be lachrymose, whether it be joyful or sad. Second, there was an instant response to the last sentiment he had uttered. All *her* life seemed to be in that same short week, and she repented her slight reference to that eventful epoch. Third, there was a kind-faced old lady on the opposite side of the car, who was looking at her, and if a single tear-drop should come, she felt sure that old lady would offer assistance or condolence. Of course, that reflection made the tear more eager to come! She kept it back, however, by resolute effort.

What a tiger this man was! He had courted her most aggressively from the first, and in an unguarded moment had forced her to acknowledge her interest in him, and then took her in his strong arms and kissed her! No circumspect approaches, but a direct, open assault; so sudden that she just began to be conscious of the outrage! How handsome he was!

"Do you know, Annot," he said, composedly, "that I am still stunned when I think of your affection for me? You say you have only known me a week. It seems to me that I have known you all my life. I cannot recall a time in the past when I have not longed for you! Because you only, of all the women I have ever known, could awaken in me the love I must feel for the woman I marry. How false my life has been hitherto! I thought of marriage very much as I thought of freeing Hawkley from mortgage. Hawkley ought to be free from debt, and Hawkley ought to have a Lady Rayneford! And now—now—I would be entirely happy if I owned yonder hut, and I would rejoice in daily labour if I could go home to you at the close of the day. I do not value Hawkley, except for your sake. I do not care for gentle breeding, except that it admits me to your society. And if you should propose that I relinquish my English home and English name to marry you, my consent would be instant and joyful."

She had no thought of interrupting this fine flow. It was novel, certainly, but not unpleasant.

"It is not at all strange that you should like me a little," he continued, "because I love you so entirely. Of course you can never love a great, rough fellow with equal affection. That is not to be expected."

"What a blind donkey the man is!" thought Annot.

"Now about this matter of clergymen and consuls," he proceeded cautiously, "let me explain. I have been very much of a book-man, and am ignorant of customs. Now, I recall the fact, that fellows who have married, among my friends, seemed to take weeks and months of preparation! I remember Sir Lionel Forbes, who told me in September that he would be married in January. I remember Mr. Compton, who married Lady Agnes Minor; he told me at the club, in June, that he would marry some time in the winter. But I never thought of such a thing as love, and I suppose they did not either. Suppose you were to tell *me* that *we* should be married next winter!"

"I have no such intention!" said Annot, indignantly.

"Heaven forbid!" ejaculated Miles, piously. "Next winter! If my vital energy should be equal to the strain—and there *have* been men who lived in dungeons for a longer period—you would take a shattered wreck of a man after such probation. Next winter! Why, I shudder at the thought of waiting until next week!"

"Lord Rayneford," said Annot, impressively, "it seems ludicrous to answer you seriously. But you talk so seriously that I am forced to believe you are expressing your real sentiments."

"You will never hear from me anything else than my real sentiments, Annot."

"Well—I also am somewhat ignorant of such matters. But I am sure there is no case in civilized lands where—where a lady married a gentleman upon one week's acquaintance!"

"At it again!" said Mr. Dale, suddenly appearing in the aisle, and then dropping into the seat opposite the disputants. "Well, you cannot quarrel much longer. We are at Charleston. Come, now! What in the world are you arguing about?"

"Miss Dale has been reading Sir Charles Lyell's book," said Miles, "in which he demonstrates that the work of creation, instead of taking six days, really required six thousand million ages!"

"Ah!" said Mr. Dale, "there is an excellent book by Hugh Miller. I saw an extract from it recently, in a newspaper. It is the 'Testimony of the Rocks.' But, really, it is not wise to get into such a heat over discussions of this sort! Annot, you look as stern as if the Thirty-nine Articles were in jeopardy."

"You shall have your own way, Miss Dale," said Miles. "Shake hands!"

Annot put her little hand in his, and he crushed her delicate fingers repentingly.

"Gather up your *impedimenta*," said Mr. Dale. "We are nearing the station. Take charge of Annot, please. I will get a carriage. Mills House, of course?"

"I have rooms there," answered Miles. "We will follow you. Allow me to assist you, Miss Dale. Better put your veil down. That jackanapes is gaping at you again!"

Mr. Miles had a parlour. Certain luxurious habits clung to him, and he had taken rooms *en suite*, as a matter of course, when he landed. The trio were conducted into his parlour, and Mr. Dale descended to the office to select rooms for himself and daughter, and once more Annot and Miles were alone.

"Are we friends again?" he said, holding out his arms.

She allowed him to hold her a moment, and then extricating herself, sat down on the sofa, motioning him to a seat beside her.

"Now listen!" she said. "First of all, we must tell father."

"Shall I go for him?"

"He is coming. Second, you may kiss me once a day—only once!"

"I will take to-day's now," said Miles, and he did.

"Third, you must not speak of marriage until—here is father!"

Mr. Dale entered the room. Miles had his arm around her waist, and he did not withdraw it.

"This is Lord Rayneford, father," said Annot, simply; "and he has asked me to become Lady Rayneford."

"Heh! Why, Annot! So sudden! You were quarrelling like Kilkenny cats half an hour ago!"

"But he asked me three days ago, sir. And I have referred him to you. And if you say I must, I am willing to marry him. In about five years."

CHAPTER XXVI.

FIXED.

THE "Nellie" took in her return cargo with rapidity, after the return of Mr. Miles to Charleston. The original plan was to wait for the new crop of cotton, as Mr. Brentam's experience led him to expect lower prices in the early autumn. But Miles was strongly advised by his factors to load his vessel with the old crop, and get to sea as early as possible. The chief argument in favour of prompt action was the increasing rigour of the blockade. Two vessels had been recently captured off the harbour. One, outward-bound, laden with turpentine; the other, a swift English steamer, with a valuable cargo of arms, had been caught almost over the bar by the cruisers outside. This disaster affected the market perceptibly, and Miles bought the cotton that was destined for the unlucky ship last mentioned at a marked reduction.

Miles laid all the facts before the captain of the "Nellie," and asked for his advice as to the matter of sailing. The "Nellie" was a fast sailer, and neither captain nor supercargo had any fears of a chase, if she could only get fairly out to sea. But there were six steamers reported constantly off the bar, and three others were cruising along the coast between Cape Fear and Savannah. The blockade-runners knew the names of them all, the number of guns each carried, and the relative speed of each. They knew when one or two of the squadron would be relieved by the coasting vessels, and generally knew what ports along the coast were being watched with special vigilance. There were four other blockade-runners at the wharves in Charleston, all eager to get out, yet all so demoralised by the recent reverses that the date of their departure was indefinitely postponed.

" My rule, Mr. Miles," said the captain, " is to obey my owners' orders, and not to put in any of my jaw."

" But I want your advice, captain," replied the supercargo.

" Can't give advice," said the captain, shaking his head. " You will have six hundred bales of cotton on board, and the ' Nellie' is worth thirty thousand dollars if empty. That makes pooty nigh two hundred thousand dollars, or forty thousand pounds in your outlandish money."

" It is a large sum," answered Miles.

" Yaas. And if the ' Nellie' should be captivated by them half-dozen blowers outside, I haven't enough money about my clothes to pay for her. Don't want to risk another man's money on my advice."

" But you can indicate what you would do if you owned vessel and cargo."

" It would depend on circumstances," replied the captain. " If the blockade was going to be kept up as strictly as at present, I should most likely try the run when the weather suited. Then the price of cotton in Liverpool would make me more active if it was high, and more lazy if it was low."

" When will you be able to sail ?"

" In five days, if need be."

The supercargo went back to his hotel undecided. Clearly, he must take advice from Mr. Dale, Miss Dale, and Mr. Boston. The latter had spent one day in Charleston, but was absent again, bearing some last words to a soldier's widow in the interior of the State.

The relations subsisting between Rayneford and the Dales were pleasant enough to satisfy a far more unreasonable lover than Miles. Mr. Dale had given instant approval to the engagement of his daughter, merely remarking that he would have been better satisfied if his original supposition had proved correct, and Miles had been only Mr. Rayneford. The suitor himself had reflected upon the matter, and decided that his eager courtship was not entirely decorous ; therefore, since their arrival at Charleston, he had uttered no hint about marriage, except in a few words to Annot.

"I wish to apologise, Annot," he said that afternoon, seizing a moment when Mr. Dale was out of earshot. "I think it was indecorous to press my suit so vehemently to-day. Attribute it to my ignorance, and forgive me. I am too happy in knowing that I need dread no rival to annoy you with aggressive courtship."

There was policy in this as well as delicacy. They were both much more at their ease, and each discovered new traits in the other worthy of admiration as the days passed. At the end of the second week they were more intimately "acquainted" than they could possibly have been in a month of fervent love-making. They fell easily into the habit of referring to their future lives at Hawkley, while Mr. Dale joined in the discussion of their plans. If Miles had only known it, he would have been enraptured at his progress. He was approaching matrimony at a tremendous pace.

"We were waiting for you," said Mr. Dale, when Miles returned from his interview with the skipper. "We have decided."

"What is the decision?" answered Rayneford, retaining Annot's plump hand, as he took the seat at her side.

"To sail with you."

"Impossible! Blockade-runners do not carry lady passengers."

"And why not?" said Annot.

"Because they are not so safe as regular steamers. Mr. Boston said you could easily get through the lines, being British subjects. I wish I could go with you! But I am bound to stick by my ship. Once under the Federal flag, you can reach New York in a day or two. And you can reach England within a fortnight thereafter."

"Mr. Boston is mistaken," replied Mr. Dale, "or, rather, the difficulties are greater than he supposes. There have been some cases of very rough treatment recently. A party tried to get through under a flag of truce last week, but they were promptly sent back, and they have now gone to Kentucky, hoping to reach the Ohio River and get across. We thought of that route, too."

"It is the better way," said Miles. "I wish I might be your escort. But the 'Nellie' will be ready for sea in a few days."

"Suppose you send another supercargo?" said Miss Dale, in a whisper.

"If I were sole owner I would gladly do so," replied Rayneford: "but it is impossible. My partner entrusts his interests to me, and I cannot transfer the responsibility to another. Besides, it is not so easy to get out. There are six cruisers constantly off the bar. I cannot put the risk I dislike myself on another."

" And you are resolved to go in the 'Nellie'?" asked Annot, as her father moved over to the window. The old gentleman had a secret idea that it would be better policy to leave the discussion in Annot's hands. So he betook himself out of earshot.

" *Noblesse oblige,* my darling," answered Miles; " I need not discuss that point with you."

" Suppose," said Annot, shyly—" suppose you had been a long time here, and that we had—married? Would you leave me and take your ship?"

" I would take both! Leave you, my wife! Never! Because I would then belong to you. Because you would risk capture, or the sinking of the vessel, rather than let me go without you! Because I could never allow my wife to travel through this war-torn country without me."

" Suppose," continued Annot, " that father and I both prefer the risk of capture, or—worse, rather than—than incur the risks of the land journey?"

" Then," said Miles, gravely, " my duty is plain. I must show you how much more promising the land route is. I must tell you that I am bound to carry the 'Nellie' past the guns of the Federal ships! And the gunners will not refuse to sink the 'Nellie' because she has a lady passenger."

" You would have a lady passenger if—if my first supposition were true."

" Yes, Annot," answered Miles; " but all the world and my own conscience would acquit me then. But I should feel very guilty if I were to allow a young lady, not Mrs. Supercargo Miles, to run into unnecessary danger. Do you not see the difference? Since I have known you I have learned much about matrimony and its obligations. A wife is so much a part of her husband that she braves death rather than separation. And a husband is so identical with his wife that death does not appal him when it threatens both together! But it is far different with Miss Dale. I should not dream of killing you if I knew I would die to-night."

"That is what father would call 'astounding rubbish,'" said Miss Dale; " and I don't think I could contradict him. Suppose the 'Nellie' captured, what would the captors do? I mean with supercargo and passengers."

" I suppose they would send them all to New York. They would confiscate all the property of the supercargo. Perhaps the passengers—if British subjects—could obtain their freedom by application to Her Majesty's representative. But the blockade-runner is a law-breaker, or rather a law-defier. They would probably put him in a fort until the war ends. You see, he would be a prisoner of war."

"If you sail without us—father and me—would you surrender the 'Nellie' when they began to shoot——"

"How can I tell?"

"Answer me, please! Would you still endeavor to escape?"

"I think I might take a shot or two before I yielded up forty thousand pounds! I cannot shoot back, you know! If the 'Nellie' were armed, she would be called a pirate. But I think I should continue to run so long as her machinery would work."

"And you would be out of personal danger—I mean down in the hold, or whatever it is? Out of the reach of shot?"

"Heh?"

"Oh, what demons men are!" said Annot, in a rage. "Don't I know how you rode up to the very cannon's mouths at Long Meadow? While I was kneeling by my window trying to pray for your safety, and while every boom of the dreadful guns seemed to shake the life out of my body, you—*you* were braving a thousand deaths—for nothing!"

"Were you praying for me then, Annot?" said Miles, tenderly. "Well, I was riding by the side of the man I thought *you* loved—for *your* sake. Do not say—for nothing. If I had not loved you then, I should not have faced those bullets. I had some such thought as this: 'She will ask me how Stanly bore himself, and I must watch him that I may tell her.' Because I thought he would surely be slain. Ah, it was beautiful in all its horrors to see that dauntless warrior!"

"And he, filled with the rage of battle, was excusable; but you——"

"I was filled with something better than battle-rage," replied Miles. "I was filled with pure, unselfish love. For I had no more thought of winning you then than I had of conquering the country. For, look you, if you had loved him, I should never have spoken of love to you, though he were twenty times dead. You would have been his widow, and sacred in my eyes."

"It seems that your theory is one-sided," observed Annot. "I think you told me that you had—had made certain proposals before you left England——"

"But I did not tell you I ever loved another woman," interrupted Miles. "I was ignorant of the very existence of the sentiments I now cherish. I thought of the other as the mistress of my house. I think of you only as part of my own life, and I could not bear to think you had ever given your love to any other. I do not offer you the poor remnants of a broken heart. You have the very first earnest pulsations my heart has ever known."

"If you were to sail on this dangerous voyage," said Annot, after a pause, "and leave me here——"

"My darling!" whispered Miles, "solve the problem. It is in your own power."

"What do you mean?"

"Marry me! No obligation could tear me away from my wife! Why should you delay? Is it because you do not know me well enough? Ah, no! You know everything when you believe the depth and sincerity of my affection. Is it because others might say there was unseemly haste? Why, nobody knows that we were not lovers in our childhood. You come from my birthplace——"

"I was born here."

"Yes. But your father is my near neighbour. The lands of Hawkley are divided from Dale's Manor by a hedge."

"What have you said to Mr. Boston about me?" said Annot, suddenly.

"Not one word. Why do you ask?"

"Because he—he talked to me the other day. After you left us to go to your ship. He said—it was marvellous how cruel gentle women could be! He said I was your Annie Laurie! How did he know anything about Annie Laurie, sir?"

"I don't know," answered Miles. "He meant you were all the world to me."

"Who told him?"

"Not I!" answered Miles, stoutly.

"Well! He said you would certainly never take me on the 'Nellie' as a passenger! And he emphasized the words. And then he took father off for a walk, and when they returned——"

"Well, what then?"

"Both he and father said precisely what you have said." She looked round for Mr. Dale, but he had disappeared. "They said— Mrs. Miles and her father could go with propriety in the 'Nellie,' while Miss Dale and her father could not."

"Go on, my darling!" said Miles.

"I cannot go on, sir!" replied Annot, hiding her face on his shoulder. "You do not give me any choice. You tell me you will leave me to encounter unknown dangers on the sea. I will not be left, sir! A hyena would not be so cruel as you are!"

"Will you go with me, Annot?"

"Why don't you ask father?" she answered, as she tore herself away from his encircling arms, just as Mr. Dale, treading softly, re-entered the room. There was a pleasant smile on the paternal face as she whisked out of it with a parting shot.

"If I live to reach England," and she held up a warning finger, "I will make you both repent your scheming!"

"That means consent, my boy," said Mr. Dale. "It does seem a little hasty, but the circumstances are peculiar. And I can entrust my child's happiness to your father's son. When will you sail?"

"On Tuesday of next week, if no unforeseen obstacle arises."

"And on Tuesday morning we will have a wedding. There are two officers of Her Majesty's army here. Mr. Boston will be here. The British consul will be present also. And we will put them all upon honour when Annot becomes Lady Rayneford."

"Ah, Mr. Dale!" said Miles, "I begin to dread the sea now."

"Do you?" replied Mr. Dale. "Well, that is a good omen. Ha, ha!"

CHAPTER XXVII.

MR. BOSTON.

IT was a very select, but also a very merry party that met at the wedding breakfast, in a private parlor in the Mills House, Charleston. Lord and Lady Rayneford, forming "the handsomest couple he had ever married," were explaining to the Reverend Rector of St. Stephen's Church the urgent need for maintaining their in-cognito until after the "Nellie" crossed the bar. Captains Delancy and Saybrooke were explaining to Mr. Dale how they had obtained furloughs from the Governor-General of Canada, in order to take part in the American war. Mr. Boston was exhibiting certain docu-ments to the commercial representative of Her Majesty, in order to establish his identity.

"As we are all friends and countrymen," said Mr. Boston, when the servants had retired, "we can talk with perfect freedom. I am sorry to say that this happy marriage has been brought about by a

deliberate conspiracy! And as I am the most guilty of the con-
spirators, I beg attention to my penitent confession."

"Hear, hear!" said the company.

"First, then," said the orator, "I knew Lord Rayneford when I
first met him. He called himself by another name, and therefore I
could not reveal my knowledge even to himself. He was pointed
out to me two years ago, in London, at one of the clubs, by Mr.
Plimpton, who is his kinsman. Two or three weeks ago a blockade-
runner brought an English mail into Savannah, and there was a
letter from Mr. Plimpton to me announcing Lord Rayneford's
mysterious disappearance."

"Hear, hear!"

"In the second place, my friend, Mr. Dale, discovering that I was
a barrister, revealed to me certain fragments of legal history, and
quite incidentally referred to my lord as his neighbour in Somerset.
He was strongly attracted, of course, and in the course of conversation (in the smoking-car, Mr. Dale!) he lamented that his daughter,
now Lady Rayneford, had so positive a repugnance to my lord that
she could not refrain from constant quarrelling. As I have had
some experience in a similar direction, I knew there could be no
quarrelling between our excellent friends without some foundation
in previous liking. I had overheard some remarks from Rayneford, when he was delirious from fever, that revealed his interest in
Miss Dale. It was clearly my duty, therefore, to get them married,
so that they might quarrel in peace!"

"Hear, hear!"

"There was, of course, the grand obstacle which senseless custom
has erected for the special torture of humanity. I mean the necessity
for a prolonged engagement and courtship, and the difficulty of ob-
taining dresses from New York or London, the labour of keeping
my lord's courage up, and others which will suggest themselves.
They were originally agreed upon an impossible plan, namely: to
take Mr. and Miss Dale as passengers in Lord Rayneford's ship.
But I managed to drop a hint in his lordship's ear to the effect that
blockaders were very apt to shoot at blockade-runners. This suggestion changed his plans. He must take his ship home. He would
never consent to take a lady passenger. My lady would not consent
to his departure on this journey, whose dangers, I confess, I somewhat magnified. But if married, he thought he might risk his wife,
though he could not honourably risk a passenger in whom he had no
vested interests."

" Hear, hear !"

" I happen also to know that the return of the entire party to England is not at all difficult, by way of New York. I thought it could be done under a flag of truce, but there are doubts and difficulties in the way of this arrangement. However, I know of a sure route by which they can reach Federal soil, through West Virginia."

" And the ship ?" said Lord Rayneford.

" Ah !" replied Mr. Boston, " there is the most brilliant stroke of genius. Now consider the case. If you could get your ship into Federal waters, and get a legal clearance, you would be sure of the value of ship and cargo, always allowing for the dangers of navigation."

" Exactly."

" Well, I have arranged that also. You shall take the ' Nellie' to New York and thence to Liverpool—or her equivalent in money."

" Equivalent ?" said Rayneford.

" Yes. The blockade is so rigid, that she is not saleable as she stands. But I know an Englishman who will buy ship and cargo at your valuation, who will give you a few hundred pounds in Bank of England notes, and drafts upon his London bankers duly authenticated by their Charleston correspondents, for the remainder."

" And the blockade ?" said Lord Rayneford—" does he know there are six cruisers off the harbour ?"

" Oh, yes," replied the other, indifferently, " I fancy he knows all about the blockade. But he is partial to blockaders, and is quite eager to undertake the adventure."

" May I ask his name ?" said Rayneford.

" His name," answered the other, slowly—" is—stay ! I have his card." And he took it from his pocket-book, and gave it, with a bow, to Lady Rayneford. It passed from hand to hand around the table, until it reached Mr. Dale, who read the name aloud..

> " Mr. Lacy Barston,
>   " Oakland,
>   " Lavington,
>   " Devon."

" I know him !" said Captain Delancy, excitedly, " Barston ! Certainly. Just like him ! Never expect Barston to do what other men do. Been all over the world. Half doctor, half lawyer, half parson—and like those Kentucky fellows—half horse and half alligator! Was in the Crimea with our fellows. Rides like a centaur. Fights like the devil! Beg pardon, your ladyship! I was only quoting!"

"There must be some mistake," said Mr. Boston.

"No mistake, I assure you! My brother-in-law was with him at Balaklava. Lacy Barston! Certainly. I have heard a hundred stories about him. Plenty of tin, too! He could buy a dozen of your ships, my lord! Well, well! In Charleston! I will certainly find him to-morrow. I'd give ten pounds just to see him!"

"Ah, he is a friend of yours?" said Mr. Boston.

"Yes! That is, I never saw him, but he is a friend of Tom's—my brother-in-law, you know. By Jove! I should say he *was* a friend of mine! What is he doing here?"

"He has been looking for sugar," replied Mr. Boston, coolly. "He wishes to get a special kind of sugar, and has been on the Louisiana plantations, and now intends to examine the plantations at Porto Rico. He intends to go out in the 'Nellie,' if Lord Rayneford should consent to sell her. Now, gentlemen, you have seen the result of all my plans. Come, Mr. Dale. While my lord and your daughter arrange their first matrimonial quarrel, let us go to the bankers' and investigate this Mr. Barston. Mr. Cardon will go with us."

"With pleasure," said the consul, "and I think you will find his record quite satisfactory. Good morning, your ladyship! Good morning, my lord! Ah, Captain Delaney, I know some of Mr. Barston's tricks that you never heard of! I will tell you another time. Good morning!"

The rector, the captains, and the consul departed, and Mr. Boston, following, was detained by a touch on his arm. It was Annot. She drew him back into the room and led him to the sofa, seating him between herself and Miles.

"Now, sir," she said, "please explain. Begin!"

"Begin?" said the other, sheepishly. "Explain what?"

"Your interest in sugar," she answered, severely.

"My interest—Mr. Barston really desires——"

"Speak in the first person, if you please. Oh, Mr. Barston! If your scheme were possible I could find no words to express my joy and gratitude."

"Fiddle-de-dee!" And he turned his great blue eyes, full of kind sympathy, from Rayneford to Annot. "Listen, then. It is

simple truth I told you.   I want sugar.   And, by the Three Kings
of Cologne! I am going to get it!

"The world is full of frauds.   I have sought in vain for pure
sugar in England.   I am going to Porto Rico.   I intend to see it
made, granulated, packed, and shipped to Oakland.   My friend
Rayneford, you cannot take this little lady out in the 'Nellie.'   My
child, you are a little heroine, but you cannot brave the dangers of
this trip.   I want your vessel, Rayneford.   Will you sell?"

"You do not need the 'Nellie' to get your sugar," said Rayneford.

"But I do.   I am going to buy a blockade-runner and cargo.
And I like yours best.   I have been all through all of them."

"Why do you want mine?"

"Because she is called 'Nellie.'   The darling!   Name your price,
man."

"I am at a loss to decide this matter," said Rayneford, thoughtfully.   "If my partner could be consulted, I think he would advise
me to sell; but he expected me to bring a return cargo.   When I
came in there were only four ships guarding this port.   Now there
are eight.   Compared with the risk of capture, your proposal, Mr.
Boston—Barston, I mean——"

"The soldiers changed my name," interrupted Mr. Barston.   "I
never gave the matter much attention until one of them recently
asked me if I was born in Boston.   I have a commission somewhere,
regularly appointing Lacy Barston as hospital steward, with permission to change from one army corps to another at pleasure.   How
did you identify me so speedily, madame?"

"By your manner when you said you knew an Englishman who
would purchase the vessel.   By Captain Delancy's description—half
doctor, half lawyer, half parson.   I have known you in all char-
acters."

"And the rest," said Barston, laughing—"half horse, half alligator?"

"Accurate enough," replied Annot.   "But I discovered two
weeks ago that with your numerous halves you were also whole
gentleman."

"I thank you, my lady.   Now, Rayneford, hear my proposal.
I will pay you the cost of your vessel and the cost of cargo, adding
the additional value in Liverpool by the latest advices; we will have
the transfer made by your factor, and settle through your bankers
here.   I can give you some money for your present needs, and here

is my circular credit authorising drafts up to one hundred thousand pounds, on **Smiths, Payne & Smith, London.** Come with me and Mr. Dale to the bankers', and see this document verified. You, my lady, will please have all your luggage ready—the less the better— and prepare to start this afternoon for the bleak North. You must go to Charlotte, North Carolina, thence to Lynchburg, Virginia, and then you will have some tiresome stage travel until you are through the lines. The party starts at four o'clock. In four days you will be in New York, and one week from to-morrow you may embark for Liverpool."

"What shall I do, Annot?" said Lord Rayneford.

"Obey Mr. Barston implicitly," replied Annot.

"That is my verdict also," said Mr. Dale, who had been a silent listener to the foregoing colloquy. "Come on, gentlemen. You have so decided, Rayneford, have you not?"

"I am hesitating only because——"

"What is it?" said Barston. "Out with it!"

"Because," said Miles, gravely, "it is not just. You, full of kindness, and careless about money gains or losses, propose a wild bargain. No other man in Charleston or elsewhere would buy the ship under present circumstances! Her escape is nearly impossible!"

"Indeed!" replied Barston. "Well, I can remove your anxiety. First, there is an easterly storm in progress, and it is increasing. By nightfall it will be furious. This is the judgment of your captain, who is an old salt. It is my judgment also, and I am an old salt. When the storm is at its worst, I intend to steam right out and over the bar, and strike down the coast. The cruisers will not dare to follow, even if they see us. The ship is cleared for Nassau and a market. I can go where I please! I do not dread the risk. As for the price, I confidently expect to make at least five thousand pounds by the advance in the price of cotton. It is my first commercial adventure, and I am willing to promise that I will hold ship and cargo until I can get five thousand pounds profit! I am positively certain that it is only a question of time. Because this vigilant blockade tends to this precise result. When you are gliding over the rails this afternoon, the blockaders will be steaming off the coast. I shall escape them, I tell you! Come away! Farewell, my lady! In the dear Land beyond the sea we shall meet again. And," here his handsome face flushed a little, "I hope to introduce to you a darling little lady, some day——"

11

"Her name?" said Annot. "I wish to put it in my prayers, when I am praying for your safety and success."

"Her name?" said the other, doubtfully. "Well, there are two!"

"Two!" said Annot, horror-stricken.

"Yes, two! One is named Nellie. Pray for her, and—and her kindred, and you will include the other! Come! Time is galloping away!"

In two hours more the transfers were all effected. The bankers pronounced Mr. Barston's drafts entirely satisfactory. Mr. Cardon, the consul, knew Mr. Barston, and had known him from boyhood. His brother was a surgeon in London, and had been Barston's preceptor. This was communicated privately to Mr. Dale. Lord Rayneford had caught the infection from Annot, and was quite ready to take Barston's naked word for everything. He received minute directions as to the route to the North, and at four o'clock they exchanged adieux at the station, while the rain was lashing the roof.

"You will reach Columbia by midnight," said Barston, as they parted, "and then will take the Charlotte train. You must travel steadily three or four days. If no misadventure befall you, you may go to church in New York on the next Sunday. Think of me then as in the tropics. Health and high fortune attend you, dear friends!"

"And you!" said they all, shaking hands with him. "You have inspired us with your confidence. We shall meet again."

Mr. Barston walked soberly down to the wharf. He had sent his trunk on board the "Nellie," and went immediately on board, and into the narrow cabin. The captain watched him with absorbed attention while he took off the water-proof coat he wore, drew off his wet boots, and replaced them with slippers.

"Now, captain," said he, stretching himself out at full length on the settee, "I don't think we shall have a more promising night than this. All your stores are aboard?"

"Everything."

"It is all agreed, then, as you said. Steam out whenever darkness comes, and waken me when we cross the bar. I just want forty winks."

And he was sound asleep in two minutes.

CHAPTER XXVIII.

THE CHASE.

THE easterly storm predicted by Mr. Barston was punctual in appearance. When the "Nellie" steamed slowly past Fort Sumter, the waves were dashing at its foundations with a constantly-increasing roar. The captain was carefully watching the progress of the vessel, his design being to cross the bar at the top of the tide. It was near midnight when the regular, long swell of the sea lifted the bows of the steamer, and wakened the sleeper in the cabin.

"Off soundings, by the Three Kings!" said he, broad awake on the instant. "There can be no mistake about that swell. Now, captain, I've had my nap. If you will turn in, I will take the deck."

"Rainin' like blazes!" responded the captain. "You must have navigated some, Mr. Barston, to tell the jerk of the ship so soon."

"Yes; I have been on many seas. How delightful the odour of salt water! I will put on my overcoat and try the deck. See! I am water-proof now—oilskin cap and rubber boots. I paid four hundred dollars for those boots."

"Four hundred—what?" said the captain.

"Dollars—Confederate dollars. I bought them from a soldier I was nursing. The poor fellow had been badly hurt, and both legs were amputated. The boots were much smaller than his feet. I measured them after we—that is—the doctor had taken the legs off. I am afraid he did not get those boots honestly. They were quite new."

"How d'you s'pose he got 'em?"

"There had been a raid into Lexington, but the Confederates were driven out by a superior force. They only had the town about an hour, but my patient had probably visited a boot-store. He made the most of his opportunities. The boots were dangling at his belt when he was knocked over. Hist! there goes a gun! and another!"

"Them blowers are signalling," said the captain, composedly, as he followed the other up the cabin stair. "Whereaway was the shootin', Bill?"

"Fust shot on the port bow," answered the sailor; "second, dead ahead. There they go ag'in! Two shots on the port bow."

"Blank!" said the captain; "they can't see us. That's certain!

They are only signallin'! Watch out ahead, Bill, for the answer. Boom! There it is! No lights on the ship, Bill?"

"Not a spark, sir, 'cept the binnacle."

"That ship to the norrard," observed the captain, "ain't more'n a mile off. Keep quiet, everybody, and listen!"

The patter of the rain on the deck; the whistle of the wind in the rigging; the surge of the sea as the vessel sped onward; the subdued rumble of the engines, deep down in the ship; the wash and rattle of the screw as she rose and fell on the long waves—these were the sounds that the watchers heard and distinguished. Then a clear, metallic tingle, like the rattle of a sixpence on a sheet of glass.

"Eight bells," muttered the captain, "and close by! Hard a port! Put her nose a point east of south. Must allow su'thin' for leeway. Mr. Barston, we must run as nigh south as we can till daylight. Them blowers are as nigh the coast as they dare to be. We must go a little nigher."

"How much offing do you estimate, captain?" enquired the other.

"Eight mile good. It was six bells when we struck open water. My notion is this: them blowers are jest strung out along the coast. If we run straight out they will see us by daylight, and we are too deep to make speed. If we run down the coast we can put into harbour, mebbe, if they get too thick. They know we want to make Nassau just as well as we do! And they know the 'Nellie' is spunky, and I shouldn't wonder if they knew when we cast off at Charleston wharf. Dern 'em, they know everything!"

"This promises to be an interesting little adventure," observed Mr. Barston. "I would give half a crown now for a smoke! But it would not be judicious."

"Can smoke in the cabin," said the captain.

"Cabin! 'Cabined, cribbed, confined!' Not I! While you walk this deck I am with you. Hark! I hear a fog-whistle!"

"Blower ahead!" said the captain. "Hard-a-port! So. Steady! I'll run till I can hear the breakers. There was only seven of 'em yesterday. Now there must be a dozen!"

"A dozen what?"

"Blowers! Quiet now and listen."

Through the slowly-moving hours the "Nellie" ploughed her way onward in the thick darkness. The captain watched the compass with sleepless vigilance, altering her course once or twice, but driven inshore each time by the proximity of a vessel of the blockading squadron. Once he was near enough to catch the glimmer of a light on the war-ship. When the dawn appeared at last, all eyes were intently scanning the waste of waters, but, still shut in by a wall of rain-drops, nothing was visible.

"Breakers on the starboard bow!" sung out the sailor in the fore-top, at a moment when there was a slight lull in the storm.

"Aye, aye, sir!" responded the captain. "Bear a hand there with the lead! Ready?"

"Aye, aye, sir!"

"Then heave!"

There was a short interval of silence, except the crisp rattle of the breakers, now audible to leeward.

"Over!" said the leadsman.

"Heave again! Keep the lead going! Look alive there!"

The captain consulted the compass, listened intently to the song of the breakers, while he waited for the leadsman's report. It came at last.

"Seven!"

"All right! Starboard! Steady! Keep her so, mate. Heave, Tom!"

"Over!" said the leadsman.

"Thought so! Come down, Mr. Barston, and git a cup of coffee. I've smelt it nigh an hour. Call me, mate, if anything turns up."

The two men, erect and vigourous, despite their anxious vigils, ate like famished wolves. Barston's long nap had prepared him for the subsequent wakefulness, and the captain appeared to be indifferent to sleep. Hot coffee, about a gill in each pint cup, washing from side to side as the ship rolled, ham and eggs, the latter delightfully fresh, as they were only one day out, and corn bread walled in by ship's biscuit.

"Appetite all the better for bad weather," said the captain, with his mouth full. "You git ginuwine milk to-day, Mr. Barston. Another cup of coffee?"

"I think I shall want six more, at least, captain," replied Barston. "I have been nibbling at corn bread for six months, but have not yet detected the difference between that and sawdust pudding. I'll trouble you for a biscuit."

"Corn bread is first-class!" said the sailor; "but I remember thinking blubber delightful eating when I was a whaler."

"Yes," replied the other. "Blubber is very fair diet when cooked. I subsisted on it one dark winter."

"You! Then you have been in high latitudes?" said the captain, curiously.

"Somewhere in the seventies."

"I was caught one winter in the pack," said the captain, "and we had scurvy bad. When the seals came and we got blubber, the scurvy left us. That was in Smith's Sound."

"My adventures were on the opposite side of—— Hark!"

The report of a gun, and then a snappish report, as if from their own deck. Both men scrambled up the stair in hot haste.

"Shell, by the Three Kings!" muttered Barston. "No mistake about that snap!"

A large ship on the weather quarter bearing down on them, the black smoke from her funnel extending towards the "Nellie" like a long finger, pointing her out as predestined prey. Another puff and roar, and the crackle of another shell exploding between the vessels.

"Hoop!" said the captain, as he gained the deck, glancing at the compass as he passed the binnacle. "Sou'east and by south! She'll bear another point or two. Port a leetle! So! Now keep her there. All hands make sail! Mr. Barston, you know a rope when you see it—give us a lift, please! Cast the brails loose, there! Are your fingers all thumbs? Now, then, heave, yo! A leetle more sheet, mate; so! belay. And now for the foresail. Bear a hand, boys! Lively!"

A round shot now, striking the sea ahead, bounding upward in a long curve and then plunging in the water.

"That means heave to!" observed the captain. "Thank'ee! but we haven't time! Shake out the jib, mate. It will keep her steady if it don't help much. Dern the blower! He's shootin' again!"

This time it was a shell, bursting a quarter of a mile short of the chase. Mr. Barston sat on the cabin skylight, and, striking a Vesuvius, lighted a cigar.

"No objection to smoking now, captain," he said, apologetically. "Those fellows can see us anyhow, whether we smoke or not. Come, take one."

"Thank'ee!" said the skipper. "Bimeby I'll take one. Can't cuss with a cigar in my mouth! And I may have to do some fancy cussin' before we git outen this mess. Ease the foresheet a trifle, mate. Let's have all the wind we can get. Does he gain on us?"

"Not an inch."

"That's bully! Hoop! That's another shell! Dern him! He

is gittin' the range! That was closer! Say, Mr. Barston, you're
no good up here; s'pose you go down in the cabin? Some of them
bits of old iron might kinder scratch you."

"I'll follow you, captain."

"Foller! But I can't go down jest yet. Do you understand the
game? It's all plain now. That blower chased us from Nassau to
Charleston, and blazed away at me jest as we hit the bar, goin' in.
I know him! And he has been steaming down the coast all night,
because he know'd I'd come out, and he thought he'd have me dead
sure. And he won't fire solid shot at us because he don't want to
sink us. He wants the cotton. He has been shellin' Sumter for a
week, jest to get his hand in. Hoop! Look at that!" he continued,
as a fragment of shell fell on the deck. "Now I call that pooty
good shootin'! Don't you want to go down?"

"After you."

"Well, as I was sayin', my idee is that this blower intends to
have the 'Nellie' without hurtin' her. He don't mind shellin' *us*,
dern him! He will keep us in sight if he can. If we have the best
legs, and git away, he'll make for Nassau. Then if he gits in range,
he'll sink us if he can."

"Suppose we surrender, captain?"

"Surrender! Forty thousand pound!"

"Forty-three thousand four hundred and eighty pounds, exactly,"
replied Barston, consulting his pocket-book. "You may call it
forty-five thousand, as I intend to distribute the fifteen hundred and
twenty pounds among the officers and crew when the 'Nellie' reaches
Liverpool; that is, if she ever gets there."

"I guess our old supercargo is a kinder relation of yourn?" said
the captain, eyeing Barston curiously. "I mean Mr. Miles."

"No. He is a gallant gentleman, but not related to me."

"Well," said the captain, "he has the same sort of grit in him.
The rule is for supercargoes to keep outen danger, and I told him
so. But when we came in we had a little shootin', and he jest
loafed about the deck as if they was shootin' pop-guns! Guess I'll
take that cigar now. Thank'ee! Hoop! it's a buster!"

"Cabaña."

"Aye, aye! Well! The supercargo come aboard three days ago,
and had his state-room scraped from truck to keel. Brought a lot of
new curtains and gimcracks. New carpet for the floor. Then he
told me that we should have a lady passenger. My stars! I was
nigh choked, holdin' in the cussin'. Wimmen on a blockade-run-

ner! So he told me it would be his wife. That laid me out, clean! But I met him next day on Meeting street, and he had her with him. A stunner! They was jest skimmin' along under easy sail when I bore down on 'em. I s'pose he told her I was the skipper, for she held out her little hand to me, sayin', 'Captain, I will be a good sailor.' It was a gone case! He came aboard in the afternoon, and I told him we could not make any fight with wimmen aboard. He said, 'If it comes to surrender or sink, I'll surrender. But if a man's pluck will pull us through, the pluck will not be wanting in the lady.' And he looked jest as cool as a cucumber. Say! when he signed his papers he didn't write his name!"

"Yes. I think he did."

"No! He didn't put any given name at all! It was just 'Ringford,' or su'thin' of that sort."

"He signed his patronymic. That is legal."

"Aye, aye!" said the captain, dubiously. "It's all right. The counsel said so, and put the seal on. You English are a quare set, anyway! It's my belief that the young wild-cat jest came out here after that gal! And it's my belief that you had no idee of buyin' this ship two days ago! You jest saw she was tidy, and walked off singin'."

"My dear captain," replied the other, "I resolved to buy this ship as soon as you told me her name. I suggested the propriety of surrendering because these men are exposed to danger and death. Do you suppose I would kill a man for a few thousand pounds?"

"Say, mate!" said the captain, "call all hands aft. Every lubber! I have a word or two to say. Now, men! this gentleman here is owner and supercargo. You see that fellow shootin' off here to windward? Well, Mr. Barston feels uneasy like. He don't want to expose your precious lives. So he says let's heave to and give up. What do you say?"

The men looked from the captain to the placid countenance of Mr. Barston, who was blowing little smoke-rings to leeward.

"Why don't you speak? Pat Rielly! You gin'rally have your jawin' tacks aboard. Speak out!"

"Sure, cap'n," said Mr. Rielly, "we might as well wait till somebody is hurted! An' we might put a little more stame on——"

"What do you know about steam, you lubber?" said the captain.

"The 'Nellie' is not doin' her best licks, sir!"

" Well, Mr. Barston says if we *do* git clear of these blowers, and land in Liverpool, he has fifteen hundred pounds to divide up among you——"

A cheer that drowned the roar of the frigate's gun interrupted him.

" Git out, you noisy hounds !" said the captain. " I guess we'll run a spell longer. Tumble forrard there ! You see how it is, Mr. Barston. That Irish whelp was quite c'rect. The ' Nellie' *ain't* doin' nigh her best ! I am keepin' her jest this far off until dark, and have got all sails set, jest to fool them fellows ! As soon as it is dark, I intend to put on speed and steam straight out across that frigate's bows ! And I intend to give Nassau a wide berth, and try for Kingston, Jamaiky. We can git coals and clearance there. What do you say, sir ?"

" Your plan has my hearty approval, captain," replied the owner ; " but can't you widen the distance a little before dark ?"

" Wouldn't be safe ! Daren't make a knot more than we're doin'. If the frigate found we were slipping away, we should have solid shot cavortin' round here quite lively. Bless you ! she has rifled cannon; and would knock us into a wreck in an hour. *Now*, she wants to capture, and don't want to sink us. And by this time to-morrow she'll be cussin' herself outen her boots because she didn't sink us to-day ! Bim ! That shell busted a quarter of a mile off ! Mate ! slow her down a bit more. Port a little ! So. steady ! You see I'm runnin' inshore. The wind is falling, mebbe we may git a fog before night ! Let's take a look at the barometer. Mate ! set the lead agoin' again ! We are crawlin' in on the coast."

The captain's hope was fulfilled within an hour. The frigate melted out of sight in the fog that settled down upon the sea. At the first announcement of soundings from the leadsman the steamer's prow was once more turned to the east, the sails all furled, and under a full head of steam she ploughed her way over the billows.

On the following day the sun dispelled the mist, and the " Nellie" had a perfectly clear horizon. One day later, she was within the tropics. On Sunday morning Mr. Barston presented his papers to the official in the harbour of Kingston. All risks were now over, except the " dangers of the seas." A new supply of coals was taken aboard, and the captain informed Mr. Barston of his readiness to sail at noon on Monday.

" Then I bid you '*bon voyage*,' captain," said Mr. Barston. " Here are your papers. The ship is consigned to Herrick and Co., Liverpool, who are instructed to disburse the fifteen hundred and twenty pounds as you may advise, in such proportions——"

"Share and share alike!" said the captain, promptly. "There was fifteen shells shot at us. That's a hundred pound a shell, and every man took his share of the splinters."

"You are right!" replied Mr. Barston, admiringly. "I am going to Porto Rico and then to Havana, and then to England. Good-bye!"

With which salutation this gentleman retires from the present narrative. The reader will regret this the less, as his story is told elsewhere.

CHAPTER XXIX.

ACROSS CHANNEL.

ZEBA marched steadfastly onward, his face turned to the setting sun. At one of the villages through which he passed he invested fifteen shillings in a second-hand camlet cloak, that was about fifty years behind the fashion and six months ahead of the season. But he missed the sun of India, and the cloak concealed his tulwar, which attracted attention wherever he went.

There was something sublime about the patient confidence of the man. He was searching for Sahib Rayneford, with no clue except the point of his sword. He knew nothing about the appearance of the missing man, except the vague ideas gathered from the picture of the late Lady Rayneford; yet he studied the visages of the men he met in his wanderings with untiring vigilance. He listened to all the conversations in tap-rooms, and at other places where he rested and took his frugal meals, expecting to catch some hint that would reveal to him the possible whereabouts of the lost noble. He asked no questions, relying with unflinching faith upon the revelations of his weapon. He felt no disappointment or impatience, as day after day passed, bringing no tokens of success, until his progress was arrested by the waters of Bristol Channel.

It was at the town of Ilfracombe, and the dim, blue line of the Welsh coast was visible across the water. Zeba spent a day here, stalking through the town, and furtively scrutinising the faces he encountered. He had been deflected from his rigid course by the curves in the road, and by the crests of high hills, and had travelled rather more towards the south than he desired or intended. But he consulted his map, and found that he had omitted no village or town between Hawkley and his present resting-place. He had kept the line of march with commendable accuracy, and as there was no limit indicated, he had only to pursue the same inflexible line until some insurmountable obstacle opposed his progress. At present there was nothing in the way except the salt waves of the Channel.

While he meditated in a corner of the travellers'-room at the Anchor Inn, his attention was attracted by some words spoken at a table near his own.

"Milford Haven. Going in an hour. Only waiting for the tide."

The speaker was a seafaring man, evidently. A coat made of yellow canvas, oiled and water-proof, a sou'wester hat of the same material, the long flap hanging down his back. There had been a little shower, and these garments, being wet, looked as though they had been newly varnished. A long black beard, slightly grizzled, covered his mouth and chin, and was at this moment flecked with foam caught from the pewter mug in his horny hand. Zeba saw all this at his first glance, which confirmed his recognition of the deaf mate of the "Bengal," Mr. Jones. The gruff tones of his voice had already revealed his identity to the watchful Hindoo.

The other man was busily writing on Mr. Jones's slate. He was a wiry-looking fellow, with scanty red hair, red eyes, restless and suspicious, darting sharp glances all around the room. He pushed the slate across the little table when he finished his inscription. The sailor read it rapidly.

"Heard there was a tidy fishing-boat here, and came over to buy her. Came in a tug, bound for Bristol. Now I am going back in my own boat. Bought her. But she is in the mud at high-water mark. Am waiting for the tide to lift her." And he brushed his wet sleeve over the slate, pushed it back to his companion, and put some more froth on his beard. The red-haired man wrote a line or two, and again presented the slate.

"Manage the boat easy enough. Jib-sheets trailed aft. D'ye want to cross? Will take you over in two or three hours. Good moon and wind stiddy."

The red-eyed man shuddered visibly at the suggestion. Evidently he did not take kindly to the sea. He wrote again, after glancing restlessly around, and gave back the slate. The mate read and pondered, while he erased the writing as before.

"Don't know what business that is of yours," he growled, at last. "I may know a Mr. Rayneford and I may not. Don't know any hereaway."

Zeba pulled the cape of his cloak over his face, and, supporting his head with his hand, fell into profound slumber. His table was near that of the sailor, and he could hear the grating of the pencil in his dreams as the red-eyed man wrote. Presently Mr. Jones spoke again.

"Seems to me," he said, slowly, "I have heard the name. Can't remember whether it was in England or in some furrin port. Let me see! Didn't he live over here in Somerset? Aye, aye! Thought so! What do you want?"

Another scratch on the slate.

"Aye, aye! Something to his advantage. Well, the Rayneford I know is A one, full-rigged and copper-fastened! Hails from Somerset. Does that fill your bill? Well, I might have seen him a week ago—say ten days ago. That was off Eddystone Light. Heard from him since. He was at Taunton then. That's all I know. Here, Mary, my dear! bring us another mug. What is the advantage? Fortin' left him?"

Zeba dreamed he heard the bar-maid's skirts rustle as she whisked by him, and the clank of the mug which she placed before Mr. Jones. Mingled with these sounds there was the scratching of the pencil.

"Coaster?" grunted the sailor. "Well, you may call it a coaster if you like! It coasted from the Cape of Good Hope to London! Mr. Rayneford was a passenger, and he left the ship at Plymouth. He went to Taunton. What for? Dunno, unless it was for rum! I know he got some rum there! And that's *all* I know. Mary, my dear! Here is my shilling. Fourpence change? Keep it, my dear. I'll take another turn in your long street. Tide must be nigh flood by this time."

The banging of the fly-door as the sailor rolled out aroused the slumbering Hindoo, who arose, and, walking lightly as a cat, also passed out. The man with ferret eyes was busily jotting in his memorandum-book the valuable information obtained from Mr. Jones.

There is a half-mile of pier at Ilfracombe. The yellow coat and sou'wester made the sailor conspicuous, as he tramped along the street and out on the long pier. The dark cloak and noiseless step of Zeba made him look like a shadow flitting behind him. Half-way out, the mate scrambled down on the shingle, meeting a man

who arose from the bows of a large fishing-boat as he approached.
The stern of the boat was rising and falling as the tide rolled in.
Zeba squatted down on the edge of the pier and watched.

"Aye, aye!" said Mr. Jones, "almost afloat. Can push her off in
ten minutes more. Here is your 'arf-crown. Don't want you any
longer. I can h'ist the sail here in the lee of the pier. Good night!"

The man walked along the white shingle, the moon painting out
his black shadow as he crept onward towards the town. The mate
took the seat he had vacated, and lighted his pipe. Zeba, crouching
on the pier above, patiently waited.

Knocking the ashes out of his pipe, Mr. Jones got into the boat
and hoisted the sail. The pier broke the force of the southeast
wind, and the sail swayed gently back and forth, the boom playing
over the gunwales. Mr. Jones fumbled with the sheet, but at last
got it secured. He shipped the tiller, drawing the larboard sheet
taut, and securing it with two half-hitches over a cleat in the stern.
When he stepped out on the shingle, prepared to push the boat off,
Zeba stood by his side.

"Salaam, sahib!" bawled the Hindoo.

"Hillo!" responded the mate, startled. "Where the devil did
you come from?"

"Taunton," said Zeba, giving the name of the largest town he
had seen on English soil. The mate held out his slate, and Zeba
wrote the name with his left hand.

"Aye, aye! And whither bound, shipmate?"

"Milford. Sahib take me in his little ship?" This in a scream.

"Hum! S'pose I am going up channel?"

"But sahib said he was going to Milford," screamed the Indian;
"don't know up channel. Can put up sail, put down sail. Whatever sahib say."

"Get aboard!" said Mr. Jones, after a moment's reflection. "Take
the tiller, and when I push off put it hard a-port. D'ye understand?"

"Yes, sahib," answered Zeba, promptly; "learned all that at
Cape. Need not push off. If sahib come astern, ship float off."
He wrote the last words on the sailor's slate.

"Good, hard sense in the nigger's head," muttered Mr. Jones.
"I'll see what he can do. Take the main-sheet, blackie," he continued, aloud, "and let us see how you manœuvre the barky. Not
much risk in the lee of the pier, anyway."

In addition to the two mugs which Zeba had seen the sailor imbibe, he had taken sundry mugs during the afternoon, and while he was perfectly able to navigate, he was still in a muddled condition. The boat floated off according to Zeba's prediction, and deftly passing the main-sheet around his knee, he seized the tiller and steered boldly out from the pier. The mate watched him closely.

"Pretty well for a man with one arm!" he ejaculated. "If he don't lose his head when we strike open water, I'm blest if I don't take a nap!"

The boat glided onward, sheltered by the pier, in comparatively smooth water. As she emerged from this covering the sail swelled out, the little vessel bent gently over, and the tug of the sheet on Zeba's knee was tremendous. Slipping forward in his seat, he placed his back against the head of the tiller, and then, with his liberated hand, he loosened the sheet, letting the sail swing freely out, clutching the helm again as soon as this was accomplished. The boat raced out into the Channel with accelerated speed.

"Good again!" said Mr. Jones. "Sails like a witch! Wind stiddy. D'ye see those two stars, blackie?"

Zeba nodded.

"Can you steer right between them?"

Zeba drew the tiller to windward, the boat fell off a point or two, then settled down to the course indicated.

"You'll get promoted mate!" said Mr. Jones. "I name you able seaman now. Keep them stars where they are, and wake me when you see the light. Or if anything goes wrong, shake me up. Roll over against me, kick, tramp on my feet, anything! D'ye understand?"

Zeba nodded.

"Only want five minutes," observed the sailor, apologetically; "must have eaten some stuff that disagrees with me!"

The five minutes grew into an hour, the boat bounding over the short waves of the Channel. The breathing of the sailor deepened into a pronounced snore. Zeba, keeping vigilant watch upon the stars, chanted a Hindoo war-song, with a monotonous wail for the refrain, which was really a glorification of the invincible tulwar. In the midst of one of these quavering stanzas he put the helm down, bringing the boat head to wind, to wait for the passage of a schooner passing down Channel. The altered motion of the boat wakened Mr. Jones. Zeba was informing the mermaids of the Channel that the warrior's tulwar was like the resistless flow of the Ganges, in tones loud enough to be heard by them forty fathoms below the surface. Mr. Jones was rubbing his eyes as the schooner glided by; and the Hindoo's last words were echoed from the stern of the vessel with startling accuracy, and in a key a full octave above his own voice. At the same instant the transoms in the schooner's stern closed with a clash.

"Running a little too close, mate!" said Mr. Jones, taking the tiller and drawing in the main-sheet. The boat fell off, pointing once more to the double stars. "Now if it had not been bright moonlight that fellow might have run us down. He is going his best. Both taw'sails, jib and flying-jib. How long have we been running? Nigh an hour, I fancy. If that isn't Nord's Head I'm a Dutchman! Milford Haven five miles off, right under the lee-bow. Well steered, mate!"

Zeba relinquished the helm and coiled himself up between thwarts, staring at the departing schooner as the boom lifted with the roll of the boat. All was quiet on board, and nothing visible except the twinkling light at the head of the foremast. The keen vision of the Hindoo availed nothing, and the schooner gradually melted out of sight to seaward.

Mr. Jones very soon recovered the full use of his faculties, and the "Ripple" bounced over the waves in gallant style under his guidance. When they doubled the point at the entrance of the harbour a steamer passed them, and her passengers were going ashore as the "Ripple" glided into the narrow dock above the landing. The sailor lowered the jib and mainsail, securing them with skilful fingers, while Zeba stood on the dock watching him.

"All snug alow and aloft," said the mate, as he stepped ashore with the anchor-chain in his hand. He passed the end of the chain through an iron ring on the dock, drew the links together, fastened them with a padlock, and dropped the key into the pocket of his oilskin coat.

He stood regarding the Indian a few moments, as if in doubt about the relations subsisting between them. Zeba endured the scrutiny with stoical patience.

"Know anybody in Milford?" he asked, at length. Zeba shook his head. There were two or three boys on the dock, conversing in the language of the bards, and the Hindoo listened with wonder at the unwonted sounds.

"Better come with me," said Mr. Jones. "I can give you a shake-down to-night, and to-morrow we'll go fishing."

As they moved up the pier they passed the covered entrance to the steamboat landing. The few passengers were straggling out of the building, and Zeba touched the arm of his companion and pointed out one of the new-comers a few steps in advance of them. The sailor looked in the indicated direction and caught a furtive glance out of ferret eyes thrown back at them and instantly averted.

"Aye, aye!" said Mr. Jones, in a hoarse whisper, "he is looking after me. I don't owe him anything, as I knows on. Anyway, we'll fool him a bit. Keep close and follow me."

Down through a blind alley, which the mate traversed rapidly, knowing every inch of the way; then emerging in a lighted street, and pausing at a shop window; then back again, through the alley, to the pier, and to the dock where the "Ripple" was secured. The boys were still there, and Mr. Jones addressed them in Welsh, advising them to retire to their respective couches, as the night waned. Zeba drew the corner of his cloak over his face to avert the storm of objurgation which he supposed the unknown accents conveyed. As the juveniles withdrew the sailor seated himself on a beam, drew forth his pipe and indulged in a quiet smoke. All this time the red-eyed man kept them in view, dodging into the shadow whenever possible, and keeping a respectful distance. When the pipe was out Mr. Jones arose, and, taking Zeba's arm, walked soberly into a public house at the town-end of the pier. It was a house frequented exclusively by natives, and the harsh intonations of the Anglo-Saxon tongue were apparently unknown within its walls. The mate ordered bread and cheese, while he watched the efforts of his quondam companion at Ilfracombe to make his wants known. At last the red-eyed man departed in disgust, and after one moderate libation, and one immoderate fit of laughter, the sailor and his guest departed also. The coast was clear, and a short walk brought the two to Mr. Jones's lodgings.

"To-morrow," said the host, as Zeba stretched himself on a cot that stood in a corner—"to-morrow, if wind and weather serve, we'll try the fish. You're welcome! Good night!"

Kicking off his boots, divesting himself of oilskin coat and hat, he rolled himself into a similar cot, laughing solus at the memory of the discomfited ferret, who was at the same moment noting down the number of his house and the name of the street by the waning moonlight.

CHAPTER XXX.

FISHING.

MR. JONES occupied a modest cottage near the pier. He had a tenant on the second floor, who engaged to keep a general supervision over the premises in consideration of a moderate rent, and who was expected to see the outer doors locked at night, in case the landlord should not be in condition himself to attend to that duty. On the morning after the cruise of the "Ripple," the ex-mate slept late, and the tenant, Mr. Flillen, was the sole witness of Zeba's extraordinary antics in the back yard.

There was something unusual in the ceremony on this occasion. The Hindoo was without clothing excepting a pair of short drawers, covering his brown body from the waist to his hips. He was dancing around a stunted tree that stood in the middle of the narrow yard, whirling his tulwar in all directions, tossing and catching it as it descended, sometimes on one side of the tree and sometimes on the other. At last he suspended the blade from a branch by a cord, twirling it violently as he quitted the hilt.

"Beébe!" he said, squatting on his haunches, while the sword gyrated, sparkling in the morning sun.

When the revolutions ceased, he took a boat-hook that stood in a corner of the enclosure and stuck it in the ground, after sighting along the blade. The point of the weapon was towards the west, and the Indian spread his chart out on the ground, beside the compass. Apparently satisfied with his test, he took the blade from the tree, and carefully wiped it with a handful of leaves. He held it up, pointing to the sun, and chanted the ode of the previous night, apparently assuring the great luminary that the tulwar in the hand of its lord was like the rush of waters in the great cataract of the sacred river. Then he cast the sword upward, caught it in descent, hung it on the branch again, and caused it to gyrate as before.

"Sahib!"

The motion ceased at last, the sword pointing a little south of east. Once more the Hindoo ascertained the direction, sighting along the blade, then removing the boat-hook, which he stuck up behind the hilt, and again consulted his chart and compass. Mr. Jones touched him on the shoulder, curiously inspecting the stump of his lost arm while he was thus engaged. Zeba arose and bowed courteously to his host. Then, with his slender finger, he pointed

12

to a spot on the chart. The sailor glanced at it, his practised eye recognising the coast lines on the instant.

"Linton Sands," said Mr. Jones. "There is where we will fish to-day."

"Ready," wrote Zeba, on the deaf man's slate.

"Better get some toggery on first," observed his host; "people will think I have caught a one-armed gorilla if I take you through the streets in that fashion. Besides, we want grub. Come in the house and we will get up some breakfast."

The "Ripple" danced out of her miniature dock at nine o'clock. Mr. Jones skipper, Zeba crew. A trim schooner lay in the stream, just off the entrance to the dock. As they passed under her stern Zeba read the name, "Juliet." Mr. Jones ran a critical eye over vessel and rigging.

"Some swell's yacht," he said. "About eighty tons, I fancy. Very good little craft for smooth waters. Masts rake too much, and too lofty for the hull. Well found, no doubt, in gimcracks. No better than the 'Ripple' in a gale! Came down from Cardiff yesterday, ready for a cruise. Wanted me to sail her. Dock-master asked me yesterday. But I am too old to be swore at by a land-lubber! Rather go fishing with you, blackie!"

Out past the light-house, and on the open Channel. The weather was fine, but the long swell coming in from the Atlantic tossed the fishing-boat about rather more than Zeba approved. He crouched down in the stern sheets, while the skipper "manoovered" the vessel, examining his compass occasionally, and keeping his sharp eye on a spot of white water dead ahead. Beyond this, the top of a light-house stood out against the clear sky.

"Yonder is Linton Sands," observed Mr. Jones; "it was a bad bit of navigation in my young days. But government has built the light-house since I went to Calcutta, and now it is safe enough. It is only the craft from Bristol that need the light. I know all the ins and outs of them sands. Good anchorage in forty places, and good fishing. We must keep a good south offing until the light-house lines with the mountain there on the mainland. Then run in."

A stone building of one story connected with the tower, standing on a ridge of rocks not much above the surface. Then little sand islands, a score of them, spreading out towards the Welsh coast, the waves breaking over the most of them, and thus making thousands of acres of white water. No signs of vegetation anywhere. Close by the light-house, a rocky island of small extent, and a narrow channel of still water. Into this channel the " Ripple" glided, and, obedient to a sign from the skipper, Zeba dropped the anchor. The sails were furled, and the two were speedily endeavouring to entice the fish to nibble at the bait. A man came out of the tower, letting himself down by an iron ladder bolted to the structure, and walked down to the verge of the rock.

" Hillo, dad !" said the man.

" Hillo, Tom !" answered Mr. Jones.

" What have you got aboard, dad ?" bawled the other.

" Injin. Passenger in the ' Bengal.' Found him last night at Ilfracombe. How do you like the barky ?"

" She'll do. Mast stepped too much forward. Can't bawl. Come ashore when you're ready."

" Aye, aye !" responded the elder; " got a bite now." The son, who carried an oil-can, disappeared in the low building, and presently returned and reclimbed into the tower, having replenished his can. In a few minutes his head was projected over the grating that surrounded the lantern.

" Dad !" he screamed, drowning the rush of the breakers that washed the base of the tower—" dad ! did you see a yacht at Milford ?"

" Aye, aye !" replied Mr. Jones—" an eighty tonner; schooner rigged; masts rake like blazes."

" Good !" said the younger, withdrawing his head.

Zeba had taken in all the surroundings by this time. The low ledge of rocks that lay south of the light-house served as a breakwater. No storm that came from the west or south would be likely to damage the building. On the north and east the sandy islets afforded similar protection. There were times when all the area of Linton Sands was covered with foaming breakers. In such a time, the one secure anchorage was the very spot where the " Ripple" now rode on the gentle swell; and even there, no craft whose hull rose above the rocky barriers on either side could live a moment. On the northwest the building stood on the edge of the rock, presenting only blank walls of cemented stone, and the storms of four or five winters had beaten against this wall, producing no impression. The water was shoal all around the light-house, and at low tide the sea broke three or four hundred yards to the westward. At present it was high water, and the waves foamed and frothed at the foundations of the round tower.

Zeba had taken in all this. He had also taken in an accurate estimate of the character of Tom Jones, Junior, and his estimate was not flattering. Something in the tones of his voice; something in the sharp, suspicious glance of his eye; something in the furtive scrutiny of the Indian's placid face; something in his slouching gait as he passed from tower to house and back again—all of these tokens Zeba rapidly translated into choice Hindoostanee, and the phrase they made was equivalent to "rascal" in English.

When the son came back to the water-side he beckoned his father ashore. The elder tossed a line to his son, who drew the stern of the "Ripple" near enough for his progenitor to step on the rock. The boat swung back again with Zeba still aboard, and father and son entered the low building. Zeba continued his piscatorial occupation.

Sitting in the bow of the "Ripple," the Hindoo had a view of the dwelling. There were three windows and a door. The window next the tower was curtained, but both sashes—for all the windows were furnished with double sashes—were up. The curtain waved in the breeze, giving occasional glimpses of the interior. The restless eye of the Indian moved over the entire building. While he watched, a woman came out, went to a water-cask that was bolted down to the rock, and filled a pitcher with water. Presently Zeba heard the clink of glasses, and he inferred that father and son were indulging in a libation. Then the curtain blew aside under a puff of wind a little stronger than usual, and he saw the head and shoulders of a woman, apparently reclining on a couch near the window. Then he began to chant in Hindoostanee. The reader will probably prefer an English version of his poem.

> " Let the lips of Beébe be sealed !
> One watches and sleeps not.
> The bite of the cobra is death ;
> But the stroke of the tulwar is swift,
> And the Lord of the tulwar——"

"Hillo, blackie !" said Mr. Jones, issuing from the door, followed by his son. "What are you howling about ?"

"Don't want any more of that infernal gibberish !" added the younger Jones.

Zeba half rose and bowed.

"Singing to the fishes, sahib," he said, deprecatingly.

"Never mind the fishes !" growled Jones, Junior. "Time you were going, dad, if you want this tide." This sentence was a howl that shamed Zeba's efforts.

"Going to try the South Sands," answered his father; "always had luck there. Give us the boat-hook, blackie. So! Hold on, Tom, till I get aboard. Wind sou'east. We will pole through this channel, mate, and up sail when clear of the sands. Up anchor! By-bye, Tom!"

As the boat glided away from the rock, Zeba caught a glimpse of the face at the window through a rift in the curtain. He threw back the cloak from his shoulder and tapped the hilt of his weapon, and the face disappeared. The bulky body of the ex-mate was between Zeba and his son, and this bit of pantomime was invisible to both of them.

"Not many men would venture through this channel," said Mr. Jones, as he poled the boat along; "but it is safe enough at high water. All these bits of rock are old landmarks for me. I've known—that is—I've heard of smugglers running their kegs through this channel, when the coast-guard boats were rocking on the sea beyond the big ledge yonder. That was before the light-house was built. They call this 'Brandy Channel,' because so many kegs have gone through it. Out there by the double rocks—they're called The Twins—there was a big ship wrecked, twenty years ago. She was a West Injy liner bound for Bristol, and got blowed up here on the sands. All hands lost. It was a big storm. Some of us got a cask or two of rum when she broke up. That was the first time I learnt what real Jamaiky was! And your gov'nor sent me some prime stuff from Taunton t'other day! Keep to starboard now, till you are clear of white water. Once get The Twins fairly astern and we will get the sail up. S'pose you put that oar out on the port bow? Can you pull with one arm?"

Zeba answered by thrusting the oar out and rowing against the larboard stay.

"Aye, aye!" said Mr. Jones. "You manoover pretty well! I'll steer against you a minute or two and then get up the jib. Don't you see the line of deep water in our wake? In two hours it will be all breakers. That is the reason we—I mean the smugglers— could run in a cargo under the noses of the coast-guard. They did not think of looking in Linton Sands, where a dozen boats could ride safely in good weather, and when the tide was young ebb they could slip through Brandy Channel and make shoal water on the coast. Now come aft and take the tiller, and we will get up some canvas."

The "Ripple" had to tack once and again before she could get a "straight slant" for harbour, and it was high noon when Mr. Jones made fast at the dock in Milford. There were sundry casks and bales on the pier, and Zeba's watchful eye caught sight of the red-eyed man, who was peering at them from behind a pile of bales. He announced his discovery to the ex-mate, writing on his slate:

"Red-eye peep from water-side."

Mr. Jones carried the product of his morning's sport, which consisted of two soles. He walked soberly away from the dock, meditating. When he turned the corner he growled out a hoarse whisper.

"Lubber hove in sight?"

Zeba glanced backward. The coast was clear. Another turn brought them to Mr. Jones's residence, and they entered unseen.

"Now, then!" said the host, hanging his yellow coat and hat on pegs behind the door; "some deviltry is afoot, blackie? What's to be done?"

Zeba took the pencil and wrote:

"Red-eye watch us. I go watch red-eye."

"Good!" ejaculated Mr. Jones. "I'll cook the fish. If you can worrit the lubber, all right. If you can make excuse, punch his head. Blast his eyes!"

Zeba adjusted his cloak, and, after a cautious scrutiny of the street, left the hospitable mansion of Mr. Jones, who was already preparing the fish for the frying-pan. The Hindoo went quickly back to the dock, walked around and among the packages of merchandise, but the watcher had disappeared. He walked up the pier, and reaching the landing-place of a steamer, saw the object of his search on board the vessel, intently studying a paper which he held close to his purblind eyes.

"Where ship go?" said the Indian, addressing a sailor, who was tugging at the gang-plank.

"Bristol," was the reply; "get aboard if you're going. Cast hoff!"

And one minute later Zeba was steaming down the harbour. He obtained a second-class ticket, and finding a sunny spot in the fore-castle, coiled himself up behind the windlass and went to sleep.

He was shaken up once by the official who was collecting fares and tickets, but like a true philosopher went to sleep again immediately. He had no definite plan, but the tulwar had indicated this exact direction in his morning incantations, and he was content to pursue it. On the vessel nothing could be done, so he slept on until he was wakened by the stopping of the machinery.

" What town?" he asked.

" Camford, stoopid!" answered the same sailor he had accosted at starting. " You don't seem to know where you are going. Forriner, belike? Aye, aye! Well, this is six miles from Clifton. We wait here an hour for the tide. If you choose you can take the rail here, and you will beat us into Bristol about two hours. There goes a cove ashore now."

It was the red-eyed man. Zeba followed, keeping him in view, until he disappeared in a second-class railway carriage. The Hindoo bought a third-class ticket for Clifton, and took his seat in the same train.

Meantime, Mr. Jones fried the soles. Zeba did not return, so the mariner ate them both. And as the day waned and the Indian still tarried, Mr. Jones sought consolation in the demijohn of " first-class rum from Taunton."

CHAPTER XXXI.

AT BATH.

THIS veracious history began by recounting in the initial chapter certain adventures of a strolling photographer, who had taken a picture, witnessed an abduction, and then suddenly retired from the scene with no satisfactory explanation. He obtained a cab, was driven to Bristol, and taking the train there, arrived in Bath quite early in the evening.

He pulled his felt hat down upon his brows, and stood a moment at the station watching the passengers. One of them is a lady, wearing a straw hat adorned with a scarlet flower on one side. A gentleman meets her, and greets her with eager questions. The photographer is near enough to hear her murmur in musical accents:

" All successful. How came you here?"

Then they pass out of the station, and he follows. Down George street to the corner. The lady enters the corner house. The gentleman goes hastily back to the station. So the picture-maker follows him, and sees him enter an up-train, after getting a ticket for Bristol. Presently the train moves out, and the photographer runs against an unoffending citizen, because his head is turned towards the departing train, while his feet are walking the other way. He apologises promptly.

"Why, Mr. Robinson!" said the citizen.

"Mr. Holly!"

"De-lighted to see you again, sir! This is prime luck! I know you'll be kind and come with me. Nanny is just dying to see you."

"Really, Mr. Holly, I——"

"Now don't say another word, sir. It's only a step, and I won't detain you a minute. We've talked about nothing else but you, sir, since I got home last night. I s'pose you haven't taken that picture yet——"

"By this light I have, though!" said the other, startled. "Do you know I had entirely forgotten your warning until this moment? And I have the picture in my pocket. Come, I will go with you and show it. I took two or three more from the same negative, and have left them at Clifton. Tommy took me directly to Mrs. Noils's, and he is there now. Is this your house?"

A comely young woman, with a wholesome English face, opened the door, and Mr. Holly kissed her without asking leave.

"This is him, Nanny," he said, ungrammatically; "stumbled against him at the station, and he was good enough to come with me. Mr. Robinson, Nan; my wife, sir. Come in, sir. Take this chair. Tommy is all right, Nan. He has got the best master in England."

"I said to Tim to-day, sir," said Mrs. Holly, shaking Mr. Robinson's offered hand warmly, "that I never could leave England without seeing you, and thanking you. But I did not think I should have the pleasure so soon. How kind of you, sir!"

"Pure selfishness, Mrs. Holly," answered the other, "if you refer to my purchase of Mr. Holly's outfit. It was exactly what I wanted. I have to roam about England in odd nooks and corners, and could not do it more pleasantly than with Tommy's aid. Do you think your husband made a good bargain? Well, I would not sell Tommy alone for fifty pounds. In fact, I shall never sell him. Here is the picture, Mr. Holly."

The ex-artist got a magnifying-glass, and, drawing the lamp to his side of the table, examined the picture with absorbed interest.

"*You* will not drive about the country long, sir?" observed Mrs. Holly. "Anybody can see you are not accustomed to that sort of work."

"Why not?" said the visitor, amused.

"Because you are a gentleman."

"And he has taken the picture of a lady!" broke in her husband.
"A real, no-mistake lady. With the Observatory background, Nan.
Lovely! lovely!"

"You excite my curiosity, Mr. Holly," said Mr. Robinson.
"Allow me to look at the picture. I have not had a good view of
it since it was finished."

He took the glass, and drawing the lamp nearer, studied the picture with critical scrutiny. "Three-quarter face," he said; "the
background is perfect. You can see the stones in the Observatory,
and the branches on the trees beyond. The hat is well taken, and
the curls below the rim. The eyes——"

He ceased his audible comments, but continued, mentally:

"The eyes! What glorious eyes! They are not eyes, they are
stars! What a paragon of loveliness is this! I remember noting
her grey eyes. They look darker, but the same expression is here.
By this light! I seem to see the girl again in bodily presence. How
could I be so dull when near her? She seemed a mere child there,
and here, she is a matured woman. Fearless and true, if eyes ever
tell the truth. Surely I have never seen her before to-day, yet those
eyes seem to awaken a thousand memories! If I ever saw that face
before, could I possibly forget it? Positively, there is an air of
queenly dignity in the face! The mouth and chin are entirely faultless, and the poise of the head is simply magnificent. If I were ten
years younger, I could fall madly in love with such a face as this!"

"Mr. Holly," he said, aloud, "I took this picture by accident. I
had the Observatory in focus, and the lady just stepped in and got
taken."

"Exactly!" replied Mr. Holly.

"Well, I never saw this lady—that is—I think I never saw her.
It may be that I knew her when a child, because she seems to remind
me of some one. And I shall never see her again——"

"Ho, ho!" said Mr. Holly.

"What do you mean by that?" said his guest, nettled. "Do you
doubt my word?"

"Oh, no, sir! Excuse me. But you are bound to see her again!
I only wish I was as sure of a hundred pound."

"I have a great mind to promise you a hundred pounds, to be paid
when I see the original of this picture."

"I'll let you off easier!" replied Mr. Holly. "I'll be satisfied
with the hundred pounds when you marry her! For you are bound
to marry her, you know!"

"Indeed I don't know. Come! I bet you a hundred pounds against a shilling that I don't marry her."

"Done away with you, sir! Hooray, Nan! We're a hundred pound richer, or my name's not Tim Holly! Why, Mr. Robinson, if you didn't marry this lady, with the Observatory in the background, it would be flyin' in the face of Providence! Do you remember what I told you about old Morrow's saying? The man who carries the picture of a woman, with Clifton Observatory in the background, is a gone goose! Excuse me, sir! That's what Morrow always said. And I'll swear it always came true as far as I know!"

"Is there no way of escape for me?" said the other, derisively, even while he felt his heart beating rather faster than usual.

"Oh, yes, sir!" replied Holly. "Sell the picture—destroy the other copies and break the negative."

"Will it answer as well if I destroy all the pictures? I am not likely to find a purchaser, you know."

"Just as well, sir." And after a moment's pause, he continued, suddenly, "Excuse me, sir! Will you take five pounds for this picture, and promise to destroy the rest and the negative?"

"Ha!" said the other, the blood rushing to his honest face. "I understand you, my friend. You would not give five shillings for the picture."

"I am certain you would not sell it for a hundred pounds!" said Holly.

"This is too absurd!" said Mr. Robinson, in hot indignation. "Look you! I am not in immediate want of money, and therefore I should not sell the picture at all. It is a curiosity. It has no intrinsic value. It——"

"It is a capital likeness of Mrs. Robinson as is to be!" retorted Holly. "And you are not apt to sell your wife's picture promiscuous!"

"Suppose the lady should happen to be married?" said the other, desperately.

"You would just have to wait for t'other fellow to die, and give her a year for mourning," was the cool rejoinder.

"You are incorrigible!" said Mr. Robinson, after a burst of uncontrollable mirth. "I must leave you now."

"Wait a minute, sir, please. Nan is making a cup of tea. You will do us the honour to take a cup of tea? Besides, I have something to show you."

While his wife spread a snowy cloth on the table, and arranged
cups and saucers, Mr. Holly rummaged in a bureau drawer, and
came presently with a handful of photographs.

"These are some of old Morrow's duplicates," he said, as he looked
through them; "and I saw one yesterday which I'd like you to see.
Ah, here it is! Look through the glass again, sir."

The Observatory again. No mistake about that. And a lady
looking out of the picture directly at you. Totally unlike in dress,
expression, attitude, yet startlingly like! Was there some devilish
enchantment about this Observatory? Or was the last photographer
going mad? He laid the two pictures side by side on the table, and
studied them with absorbed attention. The old one, somewhat faded
and blurred, was still highly attractive. Certain faults in the exe-
cution, which later photographic art had removed, did not destroy
the accuracy of the likeness, and it was the likeness of a woman of
great beauty. The new one, all fresh and perfect as it was, owed its
excellence to the singular sweetness of expression in the countenance,
and the brave eyes which were so brave because the heart was so
guileless. The old one had an expression of hard common sense
and unflinching firmness. The new one had an indescribable air of
romance mingling with its utter perfect truthfulness.

"How old is this picture, Mr. Holly?" asked Mr. Robinson, at
last.

"Twenty-five year, sir."

"What! Do you know the exact age?"

"Oh, yes, sir! The date is on the back. But I'd know *that*
picture, anyway."

"Do you know the lady?"

"Oh, yes, sir! Take a cup of tea, sir. Sugar? Yes, Nan.
These are some of Nan's muffins, sir. When we get out in the
Bush we'll astonish them heathens with Nan's muffins."

When Mrs. Holly removed the cloth the visitor prepared for his
departure. He indulged in another long look at the old photograph,
and fancied he detected more and more points of resemblance to his
own.

"You did not tell me the name of this lady," he said.

"I told you about that picture yesterday. That is Miss Annot."

"Miss Annot? Ha! I remember! This is Colonel Mordaunt's
sister, who was married to Mr. Dale?"

"Yes."

"Can I purchase this from you, Mr. Holly?"

"No, sir! It is not for sale. But I'll give it with all the pleasure in life. It belongs to you by rights, anyway. You bought my kit, and all these pictures belong to it. Take it and welcome, sir. Good night, and good-bye, sir! We shall be on the sea in two days. Don't forget that hundred-pound bet. I'm sure of it, sooner or later. Let me put some tissue-paper around the pictures. There is a likeness between them, by jingo! It is all in the way they hold their heads! Don't you see? They seem to *own* everything they look at!"

Mr. Robinson walked down the street under the mellow light of the moon. Arriving at the corner, where the lady of the scarlet flower had entered, he knocked, and was speedily admitted.

"If Miss Carey is disengaged," he said, giving a card to the servant, "say I ask for a few minutes' conversation."

The footman glanced at the dress of the visitor. They observe the proprieties at Bath. Mr. Robinson's attire was faultless—for morning promenades, but not suitable for evening visits. Still, the footman ushered him into the drawing-room with sober politeness.

"Some beggin' gent," muttered the servant, as he retired, "or, mayhap, a literary gent, wot don't care for looks. His clothes is clean, anyway. Miss Carey can say not at home if it ain't all right."

But Miss Carey was at home. She sent the footman back on the instant.

"Tell Mr. Rayneford I will be down immediately."

"Rayneford!" said her companion, starting to his feet. "Hyland! Stop, Blain, I will go down." And he skipped down, two steps at a time.

"Hyland, my dear fellow, welcome!"

"Glendare! This is an unexpected pleasure!"

"I should not have known you, Hyland," said Glendare, "bearded like the pard, and looking so robust. My last sight of you was when you crawled out of your bungalow, gaunt and feeble. You came by the 'Bengal'? And Zeba also. Where have you been? Where are you going? To Scotland with me? Why, man, I am a landed proprietor. Laird of Glendare, with an actual rent-roll!"

"I congratulate you, Hamish," replied Hyland. "I was wishing for you when you burst in at the door. Are you living here?"

"No. I called to see Mildred. I am at the George Hotel. What do you want? How can I serve you?"

"Let me answer when I have seen Miss Carey. I hardly know yet what I want. I—ah, here she comes!"

Mildred entered with stately grace. A little more colour in her cheek than usual, but otherwise unchanged. She welcomed her visitor with genuine pleasure, and seated herself by his side.

"I heard you had called," she said. "Mr. Brentam told me. We thought we should meet you in London. But you only remained one day. Mr. Plimpton saw uncle on Monday. No tidings of your brother?"

"None," answered Hyland, looking with great curiosity into her placid eyes. "I thought you might give me some hint, perhaps, that would aid me."

"Alas, no!" she replied, with a deeper tint in her cheek. "My lord gave me no clue to his intentions. Where are you going, Hamish?"

"To the hotel. Good-bye. Hyland, you will come, presently? I have a letter to write, which will occupy me half an hour."

"I will be with you when you affix your signature," said Hyland.

When Glendare departed, Hyland walked across the room once and again, Mildred watching him in silent wonder. At last he drew up a chair and sat opposite, regarding her with a troubled expression of countenance.

"We were children together, Mildred," he began.

"Yes," she answered, startled by the sound of her name on his lips.

"I have something to say to you. And I do not know how to begin. I am in great distress. I saw you to-day on Clifton Downs."

CHAPTER XXXII.

THE PICTURE.

HYLAND found Mr. Glendare waiting for him an hour later, at the George Hotel. The night was fine, the moon nearly full, and they took their chairs out on the balcony of the billiard-room, where smoking was lawful and conversation easy.

"First of all," said Hyland, "tell me about your voyage. Where is the colonel? Where are the ladies?"

"The colonel is here, in Bath. Miss Juliet also. Dr. Leigh and Haidee went to Clifton to-day. The others will follow to-morrow. Where have you been?"

"I came from Clifton this evening," answered Hyland.

" Ah! Then you saw Haidee?"

" No."

" But you would not know the child," continued Glendare; " it is another Haidee. Imagine a robust young woman, steeped to the lips in romance, yet full of excellent sense. A reader of heavy philosophy; learned in no end of Hindoo lore; able to translate with amazing accuracy their misty dreams into sober English. Instead of crawling about with muffled cheeks and dreading each zephyr, facing a marine storm with eager delight when stout-hearted men were filled with dread. Instead of the pale and fragile slip of a girl, imagine a pretty—nay, the prettiest woman you ever saw. That letter of yours about your favourite drug did the business."

" But you wrote me she would none of my drugs."

" Exactly! That is, Leigh pooh-poohed your remedies, and hunted up some more powerful agent, and cured her. She has had no neuralgia since, except some slight spasms, which she cures without difficulty."

" And her sister?" said Hyland. " I left Frank devoted to Miss Juliet."

" Yes. He remained constant until we left the Cape."

" And then?"

" And then his affections waned," said Mr. Glendare. " Or rather, he transferred them to the younger, and no wonder!"

" The wretch!" said Hyland, laughing; " he had expressly stipulated that I should court Miss Haidee, and leave him a clear field."

" But you did not."

" No. I am under very peculiar entanglements. Fate has bound me for life to one young woman whom I have never seen, except for a brief instant. And I am trying to perfect a plan to deliver another young woman, whom I have never seen at all—yes! I did see her boot! And there is a third young woman——"

" Well?" said Glendare.

" We will say nothing about the third," said Hyland, cautiously, "especially as two are more than enough. Hamish, my friend, answer me candidly! Have you ever detected in me any tendency to—insanity?"

" What rubbish! Certainly not!" said Glendare, indignant.

" Well, then," continued Hyland, earnestly, " have you ever seen a disposition towards the supernatural: a readiness to swallow superstitious theories?"

" I have seen in you," said Mr. Glendare, with crisp exactness, " a profound belief in any delusion of the devil that came to you in either of two forms. First, any metaphysical absurdity that was endorsed by some High Dutch authority, provided the sum of his philosophy was the annihilation of Deity. Second, any form of pantheistic materialism that has been plucked up by the roots and killed two or three thousand years. Beyond these, I have never found in you a tendency to believe anything."

" Thank you !" said Hyland, much relieved. " Now, then, hear my confession ! All the way from Calcutta to England I was under a devilish spell ! Zeba, who came with me, performed a lot of absurd antics, under solemn forms, every week. And when his manipulations were over, he would come to me with grave politeness and announce that ' Sahib's brother was well, and was over there,' always pointing westwardly."

" What do you mean by absurd antics?" said Glendare, much interested.

" He began by sweeping his tulwar about his head like a stream of light, then threw it whirling in the air, catching it always by the hilt as it fell, then suspended it by the main rigging, and watched its gyrations until it became stationary. Then he got the exact direction by the compass and noted the result. After we rounded the Cape, he would bring me the responses he obtained from his oracle, and they varied very slightly from week to week. As we came north the point of the weapon deflected more and more, and his latest revelation, which he obtained at the mouth of the Channel, indicated a locality considerably south of west.

" I had some books with me, of course. I read Kant and Locke and Leibnitz every day. I would reach the sure conclusion that Zeba and his incantations had not the poor merit of being devilish. They were simply absurd. And then, I waited with feverish impatience for his next announcement, hoping it would contradict the previous record. But there was no such contradiction. Look you ! The Hindoo could not possibly construct a string with the precise twist that would bring the sword suspended by it to repose with its point *always* to the west ! Once I asked him what force controlled the weapon, and he replied, with magnificent confidence, ' Sahib is Lord of the tulwar. Tulwar *must* serve sahib !'

" When we landed at Plymouth we went directly to Hawkley. His mummery was re-enacted on the lawn, and Zeba marched nearly due west in search of Miles, with no more apparent doubt as to the direction than I had as to the direction of London.   I have not seen him since.

"Confession first: Zeba's atrocious tomfoolery has bewitched me to such an extent that I cannot get up enough steam to search for Miles in any other direction than westward.

"However, I bought a horse and conveyance, intending to travel over the entire island, by cross-roads and lanes, any way, every way, and hunt for traces of Miles. The trap I purchased is a photographer's trap. You know I can take pictures. When I parted from the seller he gave me a word of caution. 'If you take a view of Clifton Observatory,' he said, 'be sure there is no woman in the picture! Because, if you take such a picture, and keep it, that woman will own you, sooner or later!' Did you ever hear such rubbish?

"Of course not! Very well! I went to Clifton. I went to the Observatory. I arranged my apparatus, and just as I was ready to take the Observatory a woman stepped in between it and the camera, stood stock still, and was taken! What the deuce are you laughing at? I feel more like weeping or swearing!

"Mark! I had forgotten that foolish caution. It had gone clean from my memory until an hour ago, when I accidentally met the man from whom I bought the trap. His first question was about the picture. I declare to you, Hamish, I felt my heart bound as his warning came back to my mind; and now that I am recounting all this to you so composedly, I am labouring under strong excitement.

"I know very well all you are going to say. You will prate about remarkable coincidences. You will quote a dozen cases where similar unaccountable events occurred. But you do not thereby deliver me from the appalling weight of the delusion! It fills my mind!

"I hardly know whether to tell you any more or not."

"Go on, my dear Hyland," said Glendare. "I am enormously interested."

"Well," said Hyland, slowly, "I happened to have the picture in my pocket, and Holly—that is—my ex-photographer, produced a magnifying-glass, and I have studied the picture very carefully. And positively! the mere picture has taken such possession of me, that I would follow blindly to the gates of death wherever that face might lead! Feel my pulses! Try me on some complicated problem in Euclid. Ask for a lucid synopsis of the Cartesian philosophy. Put me to any test, and you will find me sane. And yet this bondage is so real, that material chains on my limbs would not bind me more effectually!"

"Let us discuss the points separately," said Glendare, gently. "About Zeba first. Do you doubt the Hindoo's sincerity?"

" Not at all."

"These high-caste Indians are peculiar people. They are delicately organized. They are marvellously acute reasoners. Yet I have found several mesmerisers among them, and I am bound to admit that I could not account for their sublime confidence in their occult powers. Now, all these manipulations of the tulwar accord with one of their theories, which invests steel with unusual properties. 'One old Brahmin in Calcutta, who is an accomplished magnetiser, has a steel baton covered with curious hieroglyphics, which he habitually uses at his séances. Remember that science does not say much about magnetism. It does not know much. It has recorded a mass of phenomena, but it makes no dogmatic laws. You can place me on a stool with glass feet, and charge me with something which you call electricity. Then, if I put my finger on a third person he feels an electric shock. Now suppose I have within my organism something analogous to the Voltaic battery. Suppose this force latent, and suppose I discover a method whereby it can be vitalised at will. In such a case you do not need the isolated stool or the mechanical battery.

"I believe Zeba magnetises *you*, Master Hyland!

"Next, about the picture. Are you sure, quite sure you did not remember the artist's prediction when you took it?"

"Positively sure!" answered Hyland. "I was trying to get the Observatory into focus. The girl annoyed me by darting in my way once and again. I did not notice her, except as an obstruction. At last, when I was all ready, had the plate in, and was about to remove the covering, she stepped in again, and, with her face half turned to me, stood still as a rock. It was a momentary impulse that led me to remove the velvet and allow the sun to take her. I expected her to fidget about and spoil the picture. But she was a statue. I saw her on the bridge a little later, and then for the first time I noticed her fine eyes. And after I had obtained two or three proofs in the afternoon I mounted one, only because time hung heavy on my hands and I wanted occupation. And I did not look at the picture until Holly accosted me, two hours ago, here in Bath."

"What brought you here?"

"Heh? I—I was going—I was looking for——"

"No matter," said Glendare. "Pardon me; my question was indiscreet and not pertinent at all. May I see the picture?"

"Certainly! When we finish our cheroots we will go in and you shall examine it."

"Meanwhile," said Mr. Glendare, "I will tell you a bit of personal history. I came home with the Mordaunts because Leigh said the summer would kill me if I remained. I was very eager to come. But my missionary work was encouraging, and I was reluctant to leave it, and nothing short of positive orders from Leigh would have brought me. When we reached London I took the first train for the North, and was in Glendare, my native village, the next morning.

"A life-long enemy of my house, the hereditary enemy of my clan, was owner of Glendare. You do not know anything of Highland enmities! However, I had no personal enmity towards this old solitary man, though he had injured me to the extent of his power in my youth. He was dying, Hyland, and the local minister, an excellent Presbyterian gentleman, was in Edinburgh. The old laird heard of my arrival and sent for me, saying he was dying. I went and remained until he breathed his last, having assured him of my full forgiveness and received his blessing. I attended his funeral, wearing my native tartans as the only representative of the old clan. And when his will was opened I found myself·his sole heir.

"Now for the superstition. A week before I landed he had sent for his lawyer and executed that will. He had an old servant, Strachan, who had been a playmate of my grandfather's, and Strachan has fits of second sight. And in one of his recent visions he had seen Hamish Glendare somewhere off the Canaries, with his face towards bonnie Scotland. Hence the will. The old laird was waiting for me when I arrived."

"Mr. Glendare?" said a servant, stepping out upon the balcony.

"I am Mr. Glendare."

"Beg pardon, sir, a telegraph. Boy waitin' for answer."

Mr. Glendare threw away his cigar and entered the billiard-room, followed by Hyland. He read the despatch, handed it to his friend, while he wrote a reply. Hyland read:

"From Dr. Leigh, Clifton, Bristol, to Hamish Glendare, George Hotel, Bath. Haidee cannot be found. Have not seen her since arrival. Am still searching. Tell the colonel. She may have met some acquaintance here, and is perhaps in some private house. Am searching systematically through the town."

"This is most extraordinary," said Glendare. "They were at some little town on the Welsh border, and were to come to Clifton this morning, and to Bath to-morrow."

"Does he mean Miss Mordaunt?" said Hyland, a thousand thoughts rushing through his mind, some wise, some grotesque, and all maddening. "Can he possibly mean Miss Mordaunt?"

"Undoubtedly."

"Come!" said Hyland, impetuously. "How can we get there? That poor child! Oh, matchless scoundrel!"

"There is no train to-night," said Glendare, astonished at Hyland's vehemence. "Where are you going?"

"To Clifton."

"What can you do, Hyland? What do you know?"

"Everything! Nothing! But I will find out, and find her."

"Sit down a moment," said Glendare, "and answer me a few questions. You know something or suspect something. Did you see or hear anything to-day at Clifton about Haidee?"

"Nothing. That is, I am not certain. But delay will drive me mad! Let us go to the station, and find when a train will go."

"What is that in your hand?" said Glendare, still detaining him.

"Ah! this is the Clifton picture! It has lost its influence already! Take it, and come away."

Glendare unwrapped the picture and held it up to the gaslight. As he looked, he uttered an exclamation of wonder.

"Whose face is this, Rayneford?" he said, watching Hyland's countenance with earnest scrutiny.

"I do not know! I do not care! Come!"

"One minute. Have you never seen this woman?"

"Never, except for one short minute. Why do you ask? Why do you gaze at me in that fashion?"

"Because this is Haidee Mordaunt, beyond the possibility of doubt!"

CHAPTER XXXIII.

Sista.

SISTA, Haidee's ayah, had two distinguishing habits. These *differentia* separated her from European ladies of an uncertain age, rather than from her own countrywomen. The first was her custom to fall asleep upon all occasions. She was more somnolent than the fat boy immortalized by Dickens, but her slumbers were so light that she generally knew all that was proceeding around her. Her second specialty was a habit of confiscating any sort of intoxicating liquid that came within reach of her slender fingers. She was omnibibulous. Pale ale, sherry, brandy, or gin never came amiss. Everything alcoholic was grist to her mill. In India, the Mordaunts, who knew her peculiarities, locked up their liquids much more diligently than their plate. Sista was unswervingly honest about all other descriptions of property, but the appropriation of loose drinks was to her an act without a moral quality. She had been nurse to Haidee from the infancy of the latter, had taught her two or three dialects of Hindoostanee, including the Pracrit. The use "Beébe" made of her lingual accomplishments was to scold Sista in various dialects whenever she violated her temperance pledges, which was about three times a week. The old woman sustained such a relation to her charge that she was dominant as nurse and submissive as servant. When neuralgia dulled Beébe's acute faculties, Sista got drunk.

On the voyage from Calcutta the ayah had few opportunities. Her young mistress was in excellent health, and provided one bottle of pale ale per diem for Sista. This quantity, albeit received with profuse outward gratitude, was always imbibed by Sista with an inward sniff of disdain. It was equal to a quart of water poured upon a sand-heap occupying a cubic yard of space.

No one knew by what subtle processes Sista obtained her drinks. She waited upon Haidee at meal-time, and utilized all the dregs of beer, brandy, or wine in any of the glasses on the table. She had a remarkably happy faculty of slipping a half-emptied tumbler from the side of any unobservant diner, tossing the contents into her stomach, and deftly substituting a clean glass. If "Beébe" turned her reproachful eyes towards her ayah on such occasions, the latter incontinently fell into innocent slumber.

One day, after leaving the Cape, Daltman found a shady spot to windward of the funnel. He was seated on a coil of rope, regaling upon hardtack and beer, an hour after regular luncheon-time. Sista was near him, waiting to remove his plate and glass. As he caught her wistful glance, he beckoned her to him.

"Here, Sista," he said, pouring the remains of his bottle into the tumbler; "toss it off, old woman. I have had enough."

"Ram, ram, sahib!" said Sista, obeying on the instant.

"I say, Sista," said Daltman, cautiously, "how long have you been in the colonel's service?"

"When Madame Sahib die I take Beébe."

"You mean Miss Haidee?" said Daltman, eagerly. Sista nodded.

"Where was that, Sista? In Calcutta?"

"No, sahib. In Punjaub."

"Did Mrs. Mordaunt die there?"

"Yes, sahib; when Beébe born."

"And Miss Haidee was her only child?" said Daltman, eagerly.

"Yes, sahib. Did not know Colonel Sahib. Zeba bring me and Beébe many days through jungle. Zeba no sleep. When get to Lucknow, find Colonel Sahib. Hab Beébe Juliet. Much fight in Lucknow. Much fight Lahore."

"I have heard," said Daltman, watching the sharp black eyes of his interlocutor, "that Colonel Mordaunt adopted Miss Juliet, the daughter of a brother officer, who was killed during the mutiny."

"Yes, sahib," answered Sista; "brudder hab Beébe too. Brudder get kill in fight. Colonel Sahib make Beébe same as other Beébe."

"You mean Miss Juliet?" said Daltman, somewhat confused by the defective English.

"Yes, sahib."

"That is—Miss Haidee is the colonel's real daughter?"

"Yes, sahib."

Daltman allowed the nurse to depart. Here was a piece of valuable information. He knew of a certain estate in England, somewhat dilapidated now, but of great value doubtless. Mr. Brentam had told him about it. The colonel was the last of the Mordaunts, and Castledane would certainly be inherited by Haidee. He had neglected the child too much hitherto. He would be more attentive henceforth. He had asked Glendare and Dr. Leigh the same questions, but neither of them could furnish the required information. He had it now from the best source, and he would keep his knowledge to himself. He was not impecunious, by any means, but he had a hankering after Castledane. "Frank Daltman of Castledane" was far better than plain Frank Daltman. He would certainly cultivate Haidee.

There she sat under a strip of awning with her everlasting book. Juliet was walking with Dr. Leigh. Frank had always been rather patronising in his intercourse with the slender girl, but she was quite a robust young woman now. She had suddenly emerged from misshood under his very eyes, and he had not noted it. No sea-sickness; no neuralgia, and with eyes that were positively lovely! If Hyland had not been such a chucklehead he might have gotten this prize for the asking!

He strolled across the deck and sat down on one of Haidee's numerous cushions.

"Pardon me, Miss Haidee," he said, "but I saw you so absorbed in your book, that I could not restrain my curiosity. May I ask what you are reading?"

"'Ivanhoe,'" answered Haidee, politely closing the book.

"Ah, yes! I remember. All about knights and warriors and lovers."

"Not much about lovers," replied Haidee. "I was just reading about DeBracy and his courtship of Rowena. He wanted an estate."

"Mercenary!" ejaculated Daltman, while he winced under the grey eyes. "Still, I suppose he had the requisite amount of affection for the lady. I forget. Did he get her at last?"

"Certainly not!" replied Haidee. "Sir Walter could not make such a mistake as that! I really think the Templar far more respectable."

"The Templar? Oh, yes! He was the fellow that carried off the Jewess. What stunning horses they must have had in those days! You see the Templar had half a ton of old iron on his body. You have read the story?"

"Six times."

"By Jove!" said Daltman, involuntarily, "I've heard of a fellow that kept sane when in a dungeon by losing six pins and then hunting for them in the dark! But to read one of those books six times! Whew!"

"What sort of books do *you* read, Mr. Daltman?" asked Haidee, demurely.

"I? Oh, I have to read up all sorts of things. Chiefly scientific books. Those that relate to my profession, of course. You know we subalterns have a lot of engineering to do. Then we have to study histories of wars. But Sir Walter always seemed dry sort

of reading to me. Anyhow, you have read enough for to-day.
Allow me to escort you from the after hatch to the foremast and
back. You should take more exercise. The doctor says so. See!
he is giving your sister a regular constitutional. Let us take the
other side of the deck."

Haidee took his offered arm, wondering what this unwonted politeness meant. He had been very devoted to Juliet hitherto, and
this was a sudden attack of courtesy. It indicated something, and
Haidee with keen vision sought out the motive.

"Why don't you read poetry sometimes, Miss Haidee?" said
Daltman, as they began the promenade.

"I do. I read the 'Lay of the Last Minstrel' yesterday."

"Scott again. He must be your favourite author."

"I have not read much poetry. I mean rhymes. I have read
'Paradise Lost.' Also 'Pollok's Course of Time.' It is dreadful!"

"Which?" said Daltman, smiling.

"The 'Course of Time,'" answered she, with a shudder. "But I
have read *Maha Nataka.* It is in the Pracrit, and is very pretty.
Zeba taught me more than anybody else. Poor Zeba!"

"What ails Zeba?" said Daltman, a little roughly. He was
jealous of Zeba.

"He lost his arm, you know," said Haidee, simply, "and his eye.
There was more poetry in Zeba's attitude when he faced the tiger
than I ever found in books. He is a noble, you know. He taught
me a Pracrit song—the 'Song of the Tulwar'—while he was getting
cured of his wounds."

"It was quite plucky, no doubt," observed Daltman, "but he
probably thought he had killed the brute instead of only wounding
him."

"I fancy not," replied Haidee, quietly; "he only stood there because we were in danger. He says he knew his shot had missed."

"Well," said her companion, "Zeba was a soldier. He was
brave. He risked his life, of course, but all soldiers do that. There
is poetry in all battle-fields, only a fellow don't have time to pick it
out. Any soldier would have done the same that Zeba did."

"Mr. Rayneford did more," said Haidee—"he killed the tiger.
And he is not a soldier either."

"Ah, well!" answered Daltman, "I see that tiger fight made a
great impression upon you. I have killed a dozen tigers, and never
found much fun in the sport."

"When one is on an elephant, with plenty of guns, and with

plenty of armed companions, it is not so exciting as when one stands alone with nothing but a tulwar and a dauntless heart."

"Really!" said Daltman, laughing, "you should write that down! It sounds like a passage from a romance. But I am not going to make game of your heroes. If you had passed through rough scenes, and escaped from more frightful perils, you would not invest that encounter with such romantic interest. By-the-bye, Rayneford prefers the more peaceful pursuits. He refused to join us, because he was cultivating some horrid vegetable drug!"

"And Zeba?" said Haidee.

"Oh, Zeba was just mysterious and obstinate. He pretended, or perhaps believed, that his tulwar announced Hyland's return to Calcutta. Of course, *we* knew better."

"*I* don't," murmured Haidee.

"Why, Zeba would have detained the ship if he could!" said Daltman.

"And as he could not he—waited."

Mr. Daltman was growing weary of the discussion. But Haidee went on.

"When I was too young to know anything, Zeba brought me and Sista through a howling wilderness to papa. Sometimes we were surrounded by enemies, and had to hide for days in the thickest jungle. The Sepoys were chopping up little children wherever they found them, only because they were white. If he had given me up he could have gone with safety from Lahore to Lucknow. There was no risk. Papa did not dream that I was living until Zeba placed me in his arms at Lucknow."

"I shall remember Zeba with gratitude hereafter," said Daltman, fervently.

"It was because Zeba was a gentleman," continued Haidee; "that is all. Papa sent him to Lahore without any positive orders. Certainly not to bring *me* back. For he did not know that I lived. He knew my mamma was dead, but did not know that I was born. And Zeba was only instructed to get all the information he could obtain and some jewels of value that my mamma owned."

"Did he get them?" said Daltman, much interested.

"Oh, yes! Heigho! I don't like to think of that horrible time. I have learned all I know about it since I have grown up. How nice it is to have all the sails spread! The captain says we shall be in England in two weeks."

"And you have never seen England?"

"No. But I know Castledane. Papa has told me so often about it. And Clifton Downs! I am more eager to see Clifton than any other place."

"There are hundreds of places in England far more attractive," answered Daltman. "I hope to show you all the Court beauties during the summer. When the colonel is well enough, he is going to take a cruise in the 'Juliet.'"

"But I am going to explore them by land," said Haidee. "I have had enough of the sea."

"Do not traduce the sea, Miss Haidee! It has planted a large crop of roses in your cheeks. I look back with amazement to the time, only a few months ago, when you were a confirmed invalid. You are not the same little Haidee of the hill country. The sea has transformed you."

"With the aid of—quinia," thought Haidee. "And now," she continued, aloud, "I will go back to 'Ivanhoe,' if you please."

Mr. Daltman had full occupation for his wits during the remainder of the voyage. He had been quite pronounced in his attentions to Juliet hitherto, and it was no easy task to reduce the devotion by degrees, while he made regular approaches in a different direction. He was, happily, so completely satisfied with himself, that he had no doubts of the result, when he decided which lady to take. Castledane with either, and neither without Castledane. He was by no means a "bad fellow," only supremely selfish, and consequently totally incapable of the sort of affection that would attract Haidee. If he could have seen into her mind, and detected how accurately she had weighed him, he would have abandoned all hope of winning her. The conceit that blinds its victim is a beneficent infliction after all. It prevented Daltman's discovery of the humiliating fact that Colonel Mordaunt would promptly decline the honour of his alliance; that Juliet thought him a terrible bore, and that Haidee would far prefer her old neuralgia to him for a life-long companion.

He had repeated short colloquys with Sista. The ayah had discovered that it was important for Sahib Colonel to be Haidee's progenitor. She got more beer for any little additional knowledge she could impart, and when her memory was defective or her knowledge limited, her imagination was active. Daltman became possessed of sundry scraps of personal history concerning the Mordaunts which certainly could not have been found in their diaries, if they kept them. Sista was acute enough to know she incurred no risk in making these liberal revelations. It was a secret investigation, and she knew it.

Once Daltman ventured a hint to Dr. Leigh.

"Doctor," he said, "do you think there is a more decided likeness between Miss Juliet and the colonel than between the two ladies?"

"Hum!" said the doctor, "did you ever notice the colonel's nose?"

"Not particularly."

"Well, there it is! Take a look."

The colonel was in his hammock, ten yards distant. His profile stood out against the horizon. It was a well-cut nose, with thin nostrils. The ladies were promenading the other side of the deck, to windward, as they did not like smoke. Daltman examined the fair faces, as they passed near him, in their walk.

"I think they all look alike," said Frank, at last. "They all have noses and I cannot detect the least difference. Miss Haidee is singing some gibberish——"

"Gibberish! That is the 'Song of the Tulwar.'"

"But the noses, doctor?" said Daltman.

"Well! They all have noses, as you have said, and so they resemble one another. But the girls have very defective noses. Don't you see? They don't like the odour of our cheroots."

CHAPTER XXXIV.

DISINTERESTED AFFECTIONS.

"UNCLE," said Mr. Daltman, three weeks after the discussion of noses, "please tell me what you know of Castledane and its owner."

Mr. Brentam started. They were seated at dinner, Miss Carey and Frank on opposite sides of the table, and Mr. Brentam at the head.

"Castledane?" said the latter, deliberately. "That is the name of an old ruin not far from Bath. The estate belongs to the Mordaunts."

"Exactly!" responded Frank. "And I am curious to know to which of them."

"Which of the Mordaunts?" said his uncle. "So far as I know, there is only one of them left—Colonel Mordaunt, who came with you from India."

"And the estate is his?"

"I suppose so. I remember there was a joint ownership, twenty-odd years ago. Two brothers, Horace and Dane, inherited jointly. There was some sort of encumbrance upon the estate, in the form of an annuity, I think; but it probably ceased at the death of the annuitant. It is a very pretty property. Horace, the colonel, is sole heir, no doubt."

"He was married in India, I suppose?"

"Yes. So I have heard. He is a widower, I believe, with two daughters."

"Only one."

"You certainly wrote about two," said Mildred—"Juliet and Haidee."

"One is adopted," said Daltman. "At least that is the rumour. No one seems to know which of the ladies is the colonel's daughter."

"You might detect a family resemblance, certainly," observed Mildred.

"Well! I spent two weeks on that special investigation," replied Daltman, discontentedly, "but I could reach no certain conclusion. At one time I would fancy I had detected a distinguishing trait of character, or tone of voice, or peculiarity of feature, and the next day I would be sure to find these very marks more decidedly manifested by the other."

His uncle and cousin laughed immoderately at this speech. Frank was nettled.

"A fellow would like to know positively, you know," he said. "But there is no way to find out. One cannot ask the question, of course. It would be a pretty mess—no end of a sell—for a fellow to propose to the wrong one!"

"You can afford to take your choice, Frank," said Mr. Brentam. "Give me a drop of Burgundy. Plenty, thank you! Your fortune is large enough now for either of the ladies."

"Yes. But Castledane?"

"Pooh!" said his uncle. "What of Castledane? If you get the wrong one you can probably buy Castledane of the other. Anyhow, the estate belongs to the colonel. He can leave it to either."

"Ah!" answered Frank, "that is precisely what he cannot do. The estate is tied up by stringent provisions."

"How did you learn that?" asked Mr. Brentam, incredulously.

"Oh!" replied Daltman, with charming frankness, "I investigated that point since I landed. Castledane is certainly Colonel

Mordaunt's property now, but he cannot bequeath it at all. It is entailed. The future owner may be the child of either one of the joint heirs, and there were three—Horace, Dane, and Annot. But no one of their children can inherit except by the concurrent conveyance of the others. Horace still lives, and is present owner. We have to find proof of the death of the others, without issue, before Colonel Mordaunt's daughter can perfect her title."

"A little more Burgundy, Frank," said Mr. Brentam. "Dane went to India before his brother. He may have married there, and there may be a dozen heirs."

"No, sir," replied Daltman. "I think—that is—I have heard the colonel has his brother's will. He died very soon after his arrival, or very soon after the colonel arrived. The difficulty is about the other."

"What other?"

"Annot."

There was a pause in the conversation. Mildred arose and passed out to the drawing-room. The gentlemen cracked walnuts and sipped wine in solemn silence. Mr. Brentam appeared to be meditating over by-gone days. Mr. Daltman was recalling his talks with Sista. While they were smoking, each waited for the other to renew the conversation.

"Annot Mordaunt married a Mr. Dale," said the other. "It is twenty-five years, I think, this summer. They went to America. Mr. Dale once owned land here——"

"Dale's Manor?" said Daltman.

"Yes. Twenty years ago I wanted his signature, and I sent a trusty man to hunt him. He was gone six months. America is a large country, and he could not find Mr. Dale. But he found a cemetery and a tombstone in it, bearing the name of Annot Mordaunt Dale, and the age recorded was twenty-eight years. I have no doubt this was the colonel's sister."

"And her heirs?" said Daltman, eagerly. "Did she leave children?"

"I cannot tell. No traces could be found. My agent advertised in all the large papers, offering a reward for intelligence of Mr. Dale. It was in Charleston, South Carolina. So I have concluded to wait patiently for some claimant to demand the signature of Mr. Dale, to perfect my title. It is not probable that the property will be offered for sale, so it makes little difference."

"It borders on Hawkley, if I remember," observed Daltman.

"Are you going in, sir? Thank you! I have had plenty. Mildred will give us some tea."

They gathered around the whist-table after the conventional cup of tea, Mr. Brentam taking the dummy.

"By-the-bye, uncle," said Frank, "talking of Hawkley, what has become of Lord Rayneford?"

"That question has been propounded a hundred times since the spring, but I have not been able to give a very satisfactory answer. The general impression is that he has left England."

"His bankers ought to know," said Daltman.

"They have not heard one word from him since his disappearance," replied his uncle.

"If anything should happen to him Hyland would be in luck. That is, if Hawkley is not weighted down too heavily. He would have the title anyhow. And he is such a skinflint that he is safe to die rich."

"Skinflint!" said Mildred. "That must be a slander, Frank!"

"Well, I did not mean skinflint. I should have said prudent or economical. He would not participate in any expensive amusements in Calcutta. He said 'he was after rupees.' He told me so. He wanted a lac. Now if he meant silver rupees only, you can judge how long he would have to scrape and save to make ten thousand pounds!"

"Is he in Calcutta?" asked Mr. Brentam. "Diamonds, Mildred! You are certainly not going to revoke, with the trump turned up at your elbow?"

"Excuse me, uncle. Play, Frank!"

"Calcutta?" said Daltman. "Oh, no! He is up in the mountains. Got a fine post. Getting double pay. He has made friends with the chief, and gets no end of praise. He is engineer, photographer, and arboriculturist. We wrote, inviting him to join our party and visit England. But he was too busy to answer."

"Perhaps your invitations did not reach him," said Miss Carey.

"But they did!" replied Frank. "Glendare got some missionary news from the same station a day before we sailed. This was in response to enquiries that went with our invitations. Why, I asked him to join me in a cruise in my yacht! By-the-bye, uncle, I shall be ready for sea in a week or two. Will you go?"

"Not I!"

"It will be jolly!" said Daltman. "I am going to sail right down Bristol Channel, and then circumnavigate the island! We will stop where we please, and as long as we please, and when you get enough of the sea, you can always get to a railway——"

"Provided you are not wrecked!" said the elder. "I am grateful for your invitation, but beg to decline. I can get quite as much sea as I want in crossing from Dover."

"Mr. Plimpton says," continued Frank, "that Lord Rayneford is somewhere in England. He is entirely satisfied about that. He has some detective fellow prowling all over the island. But I forgot! that is a secret. I played the king, sir. Three honours in my own hand. That is game."

"Well," said Mr. Brentam, rising, "I am going into the library, if you will excuse me. You and Mildred can play cribbage."

But the younger gentleman preferred a cheroot out on the lawn, and Miss Carey was kind enough to accompany him, and endure the detestable odour. There were sundry matters relating to his Indian experience that interested her. When they were comfortably seated, Frank being to leeward, she adroitly drew out the information she sought.

"You wrote me that you and your friend had drawn lots for the ladies," she began, "and I think you said you won the elder?"

"Ya-as!" drawled her cousin, "that is very true, Milly. But Rayneford is a flirt! No constancy about the fellow!"

"Oh, then! he began with attentions."

"No," interrupted Frank, "not that exactly, either. He did not draw lots. But I made him choose between Juliet and Haidee before we had seen them. I can't say he selected Haidee; he only rejected t'other angel. At that time I thought Juliet as the elder would be most likely to inherit Castledane. I don't mind telling *you*, Milly, that my heart has been set on Castledane for ever so long. I went all over the property ten years ago. And when I met the colonel in Calcutta, I thought it was quite providential." And he blew away a cloud of smoke and fell into pious meditation. Mildred waited.

"Rayneford is a sort of woman-hater!" he continued; "that is, he has a lot of romantic ideas about the sacredness of marriage, the necessity for undying mutual attachment, the meanness of taking a young woman who happens to be encumbered with tin."

"Tin?"

"Yes. Tin, loot, money," explained Daltman. "Hamish and he read me an awful moral lecture on the subject. They were thick

as thieves, inseparable in fact, and I did not see as much of Rayneford after we went to the hills."

"But you did not go," said Miss Carey; "you wrote uncle an
account of Mr. Rayneford's departure, and said something about his
wound healing. What wound?"

"He got a scratch in a tussle with a tiger," answered Frank;
"we were all in the mess, Glendare and I, but Rayneford was armed
and we were not. The brute leaped at him, and as he was not
accustomed to the use of weapons, he was clumsy, and got a bad
scratch."

If it had happened that Mr. Daltman encountered that tiger
instead of Hyland, it is not at all probable that he would have
recounted the adventure in after-life. Some such thought occurred
to him.

"But I must say," he went on, "Rayneford showed no end of
pluck! He stood his ground, and killed the beast. And it was a
royal man-eater, too!

"I tell you, Milly!" he continued, after a pause, "that adventure was unlucky for me! The girls were present, and Rayneford
has been a kind of demigod in their eyes ever since. Haidee especially holds him in reverence! I should not care if the fellow had
any heart. But he is callous as a stone! It would be an immola-
tion for a sensible girl like Haidee Mordaunt to be married to
a cold-blooded fellow like Rayneford! It makes me shudder to
think of it!"

"But you are surely needlessly distressed," said Mildred. "You
say he cares for no woman. Miss Mordaunt will hardly marry him
against his will."

"He has never seen her," said Daltman; "I mean since she has
come out. She used to go about the bungalow with her head tied
up in a sack. After he went to the mountains she was cured of her
neuralgia, and she suddenly bloomed into a beautiful woman. I did
not notice her particularly until we were at sea. She is always
swallowed up in some infernal romance, and Miss Mordaunt was
rather exacting, and—and, I did not dream that Haidee would
inherit Castledane until recently."

Mildred laughed at this last sally, blurted out with rare honesty.

"Your disinterested attachment—to Castledane, is quite touching,
Frank! But I am still at a loss to account for your disquietude.
Your formidable rival is at the other side of the world——"

"Ah, but I don't know that!" said Frank. "Another ship was

to follow the ' Lord Clive' in a few days, and it is possible that Hyland may come in her. In fact, both Haidee and Juliet expect him."

" Why should he decline your company, and then come at last ?"

" Just like him !" ejaculated Frank. " It does not seem reasonable to expect him, yet he may come."

" And if he does ?"

" Then he will see Haidee ! And then—good-bye to Castledane !"

" Really, Frank," said Miss Carey, with some asperity, " you are an enigma! You have everything in your favour. You are upon terms of particular intimacy with the lady. You have a hundred opportunities. You are far more eligible——"

" Ah, Milly ! will you help me ? I need your woman's wit."

" How much money is Castledane worth ?" said Mildred, mischievously.

" Castledane be blowed ! I tell you I could get spoony about that girl in a week. Now hear the whole truth. If I knew Haidee Mordaunt had not a shilling in the world, I should court her with all my powers. She has laid a spell upon me. And the devil has made her prefer Rayneford. I cannot tell you how I know that, but I *do* know it. Will you help me ?"

" Yes."

" It is a compact, then," said Frank, " and now I will tell you my plan. She is full of romance. Any fellow who would put on a lot of armour, and go gallopping over the country, and run his head into danger on her account could get her. I am going to rescue her, by Jove !"

" From what ?"

" I don't know yet. I must think about it. I will——"

" Frank," said Mr. Brentam, from the library window, " have you seen the paper ?"

" No, sir."

" Well, here is a bit of news. The ' Congo' arrived yesterday, bringing late news from the Cape. The ' Bengal,' from Calcutta, sailed on the 10th, with one passenger, Mr. Hyland Rayneford. She will arrive within a week. Better come in. It is damp out there."

" Did I not tell you ?" said Frank, as they went in. " My prophetic soul warned me ! What next, Milly ?"

" Wait," she answered ; " the ' Bengal' has not arrived yet."

CHAPTER XXXV.

THE START.

VERY soon after the mysterious disappearance of Lord Rayneford, his kinsman, Mr. Plimpton, decided to employ the detective, Mr. Dancer, who had distinguished himself several times in the service of Mr. Plimpton's legal firm. He had unearthed two or three frauds of large proportions in a celebrated will case; had recovered certain stolen documents that were hopelessly lost, and virtually gained the case for the clients of Plimpton and Plunger. It was not strange, therefore, that the senior partner had great confidence in Mr. Dancer's abilities. And as he was at this time on a cold scent, hunting an absconding cashier whose testimony was all-important to the firm, Mr. Plimpton added the search of Rayneford on his private account.

The effect of this double commission was to keep Mr. Dancer in perpetual motion. When in York, for example, and quite warm on the track of Mr. Nokes, the missing cashier, the detective would suddenly obtain some scrap of information that seemed to promise the recovery of the missing nobleman. And, travelling all night, he would take breakfast at the Queen Hotel, in Belfast, the next morning. After running this clue to earth, and, as the reader knows, without result, he would start for Plymouth on an errand similarly fruitless. The travelling expenses of Mr. Dancer, which were paid by Plimpton and Plunger, kept the head clerk of the firm in a half-frantic state of mind, as he was obliged to analyse the account of outlays and distribute the expense among the clients "in interest."

It was some stray scrap of information from Ilfracombe, about a half-drunken mariner who had spoken of "Rayneford," that took Mr. Dancer to that village. It happened that he encountered Mr. Jones, as already recorded in a previous chapter, and the mysterious obstinacy of the sailor, and his sudden departure in the "Ripple," convinced Mr. Dancer that he was at last on the right track. His course was plain enough now. He had only to keep the ex-mate in sight and wait developments. So he telegraphed Mr. Plimpton that he had a promising clue, and announced his intention to remain a few days at Milford. He was very much discomfited the next day by the receipt of a despatch from Mr. Plimpton, requesting his immediate presence at Clifton on urgent business.

He found the lawyer at one of the hotels, in company with Dr.

14

Leigh. The urgent business was the recovery of a lost young lady, who had disappeared unaccountably the previous day. She was a stranger in England, having very few acquaintances in the country, and there was no conceivable motive to induce her voluntary disappearance. Her father, his client, Colonel Mordaunt, had just arrived with his family from India, and he was the only person who knew her that had not been consulted about her. The colonel was an invalid, and the fact of her disappearance was concealed from him by the doctor's advice.

Mr. Dancer listened to this account without winking his ferret eyes, and noted in his memorandum-book the chief points in the story.

"Now, gents," said Mr. Dancer, "please answer one or two questions. How old is the lady?"

"Twenty."

"Where was she positively seen last?"

"I left her at the door of this hotel," answered the doctor, "and I saw her turn the corner and walk towards the Observatory on the Downs. Then I went in, examined rooms, ordered dinner, drove to Bristol in a cab, and returned before dark. She had not been here at all."

"Did anybody else see her?" said Mr. Dancer.

"The porter who took our luggage in saw her a few minutes after she went on the Downs. She was near the Observatory."

"Was anybody else there? Was she talking to any one?"

"No. Nobody was on the Downs except a travelling photographer, who was taking views."

"Who is he? What does he say?"

"He is gone. Probably driving about the surrounding country taking pictures."

"Have you looked for him?" enquired Mr. Dancer.

"Not specially."

"All right, gents; I'll report to you in the morning." And Mr. Dancer bobbed his red head, winked his red eyes, and departed.

Out on the broad Downs, prowling around the Observatory, peering into the eyes of every person he met. An old woman seated on a stool, having a rough table covered with a newspaper, and exposing bits of polished stone for sale. Geological specimens from St. Vincent Rocks, in the shape of paper-weights, worth about a penny a bushel, and selling at a shilling each. It is a fine evening, but yonder is a man with a cloak on his shoulders. Hi! It is the very foreign savage he saw at Ilfracombe, going out into the Channel with the gruff old sailor. What is he up to? He just slouches about, looking at the people. He don't notice women or children, but watches all the men. By-the-bye, he does not seem to see Mr. Dancer. Can hardly call that slouching, either. His step is even, and rather stately. His head erect, and his body straight as a pole. Now he steps aside in the damp grass, to allow a little party of children passage on the path. The heathen bows like a courtier.

There comes the moon, and the sun has just disappeared behind the western hills. And here comes the foreign gent, marching straight down the path, and facing the moon. His eye—he has only one eye—fixed in steadfast scrutiny upon the ferret eyes of Mr. Dancer. It is rather jolly now. Here is a savage that the detective has been shadowing in desultory fashion for a day or two, and the swift conviction flashes upon the mind of Mr. Dancer that the heathen is perhaps shadowing *him*. Better accost him.

"Fine night," said Mr. Dancer, as the Indian reached him. "It will be cooler in an hour."

"Sahib Rayneford?" answered the Hindoo, cautiously. "You look for Sahib Rayneford. Find him?"

"Oh, ah!" said Mr. Dancer, cautiously; "you are looking for Lord Rayneford, are you? When did you see him last?"

"You look last night," replied Zeba; "look in ale house; look on pier when boat sail away; look on pier at Milford; look up two streets; look behind bales and casks. What want?"

"Suppose we go down this court?" said Mr. Dancer. "There is good beer in a house I know. I'll stand a pot."

"Thanks, sahib," said Zeba; "no want beer. Promenade down river. Promenade across bridge. Sahib go get beer and come back."

"This looks like business," thought Mr. Dancer; "he wants to get rid of me. No harm in killing two birds with one stone. I'll work up this case a bit. When did you come here, friend?"

"Came with sahib in train."

"And Jones?" said Mr. Dancer, suddenly. "What have you done with Mr. Jones?"

"Ah! sahib know Jones? Jones much drink rum. Too much drunk. Jones in Milford." And, with a bow of dismissal, Zeba turned away, catching the arm of a new-comer who brushed by them, and putting an interval of ten yards between Mr. Dancer and himself before the detective recovered from his surprise.

"Salaam, sahib!" whispered Zeba; "thief behind. Look for Lord Hyland. Ask me much question."

"Zeba!" said Hyland, astonished. "How did you find me?"

"With tulwar," answered Zeba, simply. "Find Beébe with tulwar. Safe. Lord Hyland come get Beébe? Out on the sea."

"What!" said Hyland, clutching his arm, "do you mean the lady Haidee?"

"Yes. Beébe Haidee out on the sea! Tulwar find her. Come!"

Crossing the high bridge with such enormous strides that Mr. Dancer, trotting behind them, was quite blown, they paused at a cottage door. There were tall trees along the roadside, shading the path and hiding him, and when the door was opened, he was near enough to hear the voice of the old woman who opened at their knock—"Mr. Robinson!"

"It is I, Mrs. Noils," said Hyland. "I want Tommy."

"He is in the stable, sir. Walk in, and I'll fetch the key."

"Stable?" said Zeba, in a whisper, "horse? Too slow! Sahib take train on river-bank. Catch steamship at Mendon, where river grow large. Steamship get Milford when moon high in sky. Get Beébe before sun come back. Come!"

While Mr. Dancer crouched down on the roadside in the shadow, the two men came racing out from the cottage, and passed him. The heathen's cloak blew aside, and the detective saw the long sword strapped up to his left breast, his hand resting on the hilt.

"Desperate burglars, murderers, and savages!" said Mr. Dancer, rising, and watching them as they sped across the bridge; "but I'll know 'em. And now to see what is in the house." So saying, he entered the enclosure, and knocked at the door just closed. A placid-faced old woman opened, holding up a lamp, and peering at him through her spectacles.

"Sorry to disturb you again, Mrs. Noils," said he, "but Mr. Robinson left a paper, and sent me back for it."

"Walk in, sir!" replied the landlady; "he was only at the door. Did he drop it?"

"Oh, no!" answered Mr. Dancer, readily; "it is somewhere about his room. Lend me your lamp, please. I can find it." And he passed in with easy confidence.

Meantime, Hyland and Zeba descended the bank to the railway station. Zeba had gained accurate information about trains and connections. The train about to start would reach Mendon as soon as the Milford steamer, which had left Bristol two hours earlier.

They obtained tickets for Milford, and entered the first little tunnel, while Mr. Dancer was industriously searching for the lost "paper."

Hyland had spent the entire day in seeking some information about the "Ariadne." He had witnessed the abduction of Haidee, and had seen the name of the schooner, as she passed down the river on the previous day. He had a vague idea that some villainy was afoot, but was perplexed when he discovered that Miss Carey was an apparent party to the abduction. The object of his visit to Bath was to see Colonel Mordaunt and tell him the whole story, little dreaming that Haidee was enwrapped in the bundle of shawls he had seen on the deck of the "Ariadne." His subsequent discoveries came in rapid succession. First, the arrival of Mildred at Bath in his own train. Second, the information he gained at his interview with her. Third, the fact that Haidee Mordaunt had disappeared, and the swift conclusion that she had been carried off by the schooner; and last, the identity of Haidee with the maiden whose picture he had in his breast.

Then came the prompt impulse to find and rescue her, and he and Glendare had gathered all that could be learned about the schooner at the Bristol docks, and this was very meagre information. A stupid clerk at a shipping office only knew she had sailed for Cork. She had brought a cargo to Bristol from some Spanish port, and she went to Cork in ballast. He parted from Glendare at the hotel in Clifton, and encountered Zeba a few minutes later, on the Downs.

He had eaten nothing during the day, and when the little steamer left the dock at Mendon, he and Zeba obtained a substantial supper in the dining-saloon. With the after-supper cheroot, Hyland's faculties recovered their normal tone, and as he and the Indian paced the narrow forecastle, Hyland began to be conscious that he was being led by the most absurd of superstition or humbug, and to doubt his own sanity.

"Tell me, Zeba," he said, leaning against the capstan, and looking steadily at the sober face of the Hindoo, "how did you happen to find Beébe?"

"Not happen," replied the Indian, composedly. "Hunting sahib's brother. Ask tulwar. Tulwar say to Milford go. Find Jones at Ilfracombe, and sail in his little ship to Milford. Jones sleep and I sing. The song of tulwar sing. Big ship sail past while I sing, and Beébe sing back to me. Nobody know song of tulwar but Beébe and warrior. Ask tulwar next day, when sun come. Tulwar say to Linton Sands go. Find light-house there, and sing again. Sing

not same song; but sing Beébe wait till Lord of tulwar come. That
Sahib Hyland. Then to Clifton go. Ask tulwar where Sahib Hyland find? Tulwar say, Clifton. Jones want drunk. Go Clifton
and find sahib. That all."

"But you were not hunting Beébe," said Hyland.

"No!" answered Zeba, thoughtfully. "I go Milford to find
sahib's brother. But tulwar know Beébe on ship. Tulwar must
serve Lord of tulwar."

"I do not understand you."

"No. Myself not understand. Sahib Lord of tulwar. Sahib
must be Lord of Beébe too!"

Hyland felt the warm blood rushing to his forehead. Despising
himself for the weakness, he was still conscious of a thrill that shook
his frame, and seemed to shake the solid capstan. With a shame-
facedness that he could neither justify nor resist, he changed the topic.

"And when will you find my brother?"

"Tulwar will show," answered Zeba, tapping the hilt; "get Beébe
first, then sahib's brother find."

It was near midnight when Mr. Flellen, who occupied the upper
floor of the ex-mate's domicile, admitted Hyland and Zeba. They
found Mr. Jones spread out upon the cot in a state of happy uncon-
sciousness. There was a fine aroma in the room, compounded of
Jamaica rum and tobacco-smoke. He was deaf when awake and
sober. He was totally oblivious when asleep and drunk.

"Good drunk!" said Zeba, after a vain effort to arouse the sleeper.
"Not wake till sun come. Sahib take boat and get Beébe."

"This is madness!" said Hyland. "Who can guide us to the
light-house?"

"Zeba," answered the Indian. "Sahib not fear! Come!" And
he took down the key from the wall. "Unlock boat. Sail put up.
Know all the way. Come! Sahib put on Jones's coat and hat.
Jones's son have light-house. Maybe get Beébe without kill. Son
think Jones come back. If he find sahib not father——" He drew
the tulwar out a few inches and drove it back into the scabbard with
an ominous click.

The moon was directly overhead as the "Ripple" glided out of
the narrow dock. Hyland sat on the after-thwart, holding the sheet,
while Zeba steered. They had to tack once to pass a yacht anchored
in the stream. As the "Ripple" luffed up, almost under her bows,
Hyland heard the clank of the capstan bars as the anchor was hoisted
in, and saw jib and mainsail rise in the bright moonlight.

"Boat ahoy!" came the hail from the yacht. There was no response, and the little fishing-boat slipped away as the larger vessel slowly moved in the light breeze.

"No use to hail," said a voice from the waist of the yacht. "It is old Jones. Deef as a log! Belay there and up with the foresail! Never heed Jones. He will keep out of our way. He can see prime if he is deef."

CHAPTER XXXVI.

A PROPOSAL.

COLONEL MORDAUNT found Castledane in a dilapidated condition. The great park had been neglected for twenty years. The mansion had been rented to a succession of tenants, who had not improved the appearance of the property. The agent made no repairs that could be avoided, the owner was at the antipodes, and one tenant after another vacated the house, which was in charge of a keeper when the family arrived in England. The young ladies were charmed with the natural beauties of the grounds, and especially delighted with the ivy-grown ruin that gave the name to the estate. That was to remain in its rugged wildness, but extensive inroads upon the colonel's stock of rupees had been projected at their first hasty visit.

The day following Mr. Daltman's confessions to his cousin found that gentleman at Bath. The colonel and his daughters had driven over to Castle Dane with an architect from London. Mr. Daltman, if he arrived, was to follow, and join the party at luncheon *al fresco* at the ruin.

He found the party exploring the mansion, which was quite ancient, though more recent than Castle Dane. It had been erected in the days of the Virgin Queen, when the Mordaunts were prosperous courtiers, but had suffered at the hands of the soldiers of the Commonwealth. From that time to the beginning of the present century the Mordaunts had been poor and proud, and the first representative of the line who might be called rich was the present owner, who had held lucrative offices in India, and was entirely able to restore the ancient inheritance to its original grandeur. And as Daltman, following them from room to room, overheard the discussions between the colonel and the architect, he gradually reached the conclusion that his host had "lacs, no end." His own inheritance, with its late addition, made him quite eligible, however, and the uppermost thought in his beneficent mind was, that he had better secure one of the two ladies for himself before some enterprising countryman should also learn the financial dimensions of his proposed father-in-law. He observed that the colonel always paid special attention to any suggestion from Haidee touching the projected improvements. This confirmed his conclusion that Haidee was the true heiress of Castle Dane.

The park in the neighbourhood of the ruined castle had been severely left to nature, and was consequently "lovely," as the ladies asserted. After luncheon, when the rest of the party returned to the grounds near the mansion to inspect the stables and coach-houses, Mr. Daltman begged Haidee to remain and explore the surroundings, offering to forego his cigar. The quick-witted maiden had divined his purpose to make serious proposals to herself, and quietly consented. They had taken their mid-day repast under a giant oak, which was reproduced in Mr. Robinson's first photograph a day or two later, and they were seated upon very old-fashioned chairs, which had been brought from the dining-room at the mansion for this special occasion.

"I am not going into the park, please," said Haidee; "it is too pleasant here. The view is beautiful, and these old chairs are far nicer than bits of stone and roots of trees."

"But I want to see the wood," expostulated Daltman.

"Ah! Well, I will wait for you. I have been all through it once."

"But I don't want to see it without—that is, alone," said Daltman. "I cannot tell what should be admired. You see, I have been in the jungle of late years."

"It is not as pretty as the jungle," said Haidee.

"So you keep up your attachment to India?" said Daltman. "You surely would not go back?"

"Yes. If papa and Juliet went."

"But Castledane?" said Daltman. "Do you feel no attachment to Castledane?"

"Yes. I should like to live here always. It is more beautiful than I expected to find it. I am quite impatient to see it in winter."

"I have almost decided not to go back," said Daltman, after a pause. "I have a little place in Essex, and I think of settling down, and quitting the army."

"And go into Parliament?" said Haidee.

"Perhaps. But I must relinquish my bachelorhood. A fellow is nothing in Parliament without a wife. And I feel"—putting as much pathos into his tones as he could command—"quite lonely. A fellow's life is wasted so long as he is single."

Haidee did not reply. She had eaten a liberal supply of salad, and had imbibed some beer, and was drowsy.

"Perhaps you—perhaps I had better stick to the army?" said Daltman, after some reflection. "You would think so, I suppose, as the colonel——"

"Army?" said Haidee, rousing herself. "Oh, no! I am going to make papa retire on half-pay."

"Ah, then!" said Daltman, eagerly, "we are agreed thus far. Now about matrimony. Don't you think I might venture to marry?"

"Certainly."

"You know I am not at all exacting," continued Daltman, trying to recall some of Glendare's postulates. "Marriage is a very serious business."

"Yes," said Haidee, nodding, partly in acquiescence and partly from somnolency.

"Very serious! No fellow should marry until he—until he has fully weighed the responsibilities. Should he make a mistake, and get the wrong young woman, there would be no end of a mess, you know."

"You might take a middle-aged lady," observed Haidee, who had actually caught a dozen winks, and had heard the last remark imperfectly.

"I wish you would tell me what *you* think about love and matrimony, Miss Haidee. You know you have read such a lot of books about that business, and I am entirely green. I only know there is a depth of devotion, and all that sort of thing. Of course! Very proper! I am sure I am capable of undying devotion, if encouraged. There is no fellow in England more easily satisfied than I would be. All I would ask would be a—a sympathising heart, you know. My estate is quite respectable, and no doubt I could take my pick of—that is—I mean I would not be rejected as ineligible. But the heart! the heart! Ah! one may control everything else, but his affections once fixed on the beloved object! If his hopes are wrecked, it is—a dreadful sell! Will you please give me your opinion?"

"My opinion?" replied Haidee. "I have not formed one, Mr. Daltman."

"Oh, yes! Excuse me, but you must have some theory about love——"

"Yes," answered Haidee, coolly; "but you would not understand it, Mr. Daltman. Let us go see how they will remodel the stables."

"Pardon me," said Daltman, "and hear me out. I am safe to make a mess, I know, but you will forgive me. If I had only read up a little more on this subject! But I can learn. Miss Haidee, if you could only give me the least bit of encouragement, I would kneel at your feet——"

"Pray don't!" said Haidee, rising. "John spilled some oil there when he was dressing the salad." She moved away, and he caught her hand and detained her. She looked round at him composedly, but with a little more colour in her cheek than usual.

"Pardon me again," he said, humbly; "my awkwardness is shameful, I know. But I am in dead earnest, Miss Haidee. I will do anything you wish. I will wait as long as you say. I will never oppose your preferences, and I will swear to make no complaints. Do not say no without reflection. You think I will be exacting and capricious and unreasonable. I swear to you——"

"Pray don't swear at all, Mr. Daltman," said she, withdrawing her hand; "I am quite flattered by all you say, but I'd rather go look at the stables."

"What the devil ought a fellow do?" said Daltman, despairingly. "I am quite ready to prove my sincerity, if you will only say the word. I have set my heart upon this—upon you, and you throw me over without mercy. Will you marry me—upon any terms you like? Settle your property—every penny of it upon yourself—yes —and mine too! every penny of it! Only say I may hope!"

"Mr. Daltman," said Haidee, slowly and with stately dignity, "I am very sorry I allowed you to say all this. Forget it, and I will forget it, and no one in the world will know. You seem to be so earnest that I cannot believe you are not sincere. But there is no possibility——"

"Please don't, Haidee!" said he, eagerly—"please don't say the final word yet! Please wait until to-morrow—next week! Only wait! Something may turn up. I may have the chance to prove my devotion. Grant me only this. I will not ask for anything but delay. Heavens! How can you be so cruel as to tear a fellow's heart up into bits and then trample on it?"

" It is not probable that I shall ever marry," said Haidee, as they walked away. " I *could* not marry unless the man I called lord were nobler than any ideal I have formed. I have never read in books any description of the man I could marry——"

" Is there no such man on the earth?" said Daltman, jealously.

" I do not know," she answered, with perfect composure; " but I am certain he is not among my acquaintances. All you have said about hearts broken and trodden down I have read. It is quite pretty, but—excuse me—it is your word, you know—bosh!"

He staggered as if hit by a bullet.

" I am quite willing to believe you are disappointed. Nay, I am willing to believe you prefer me to any other woman you know——"

" That is true as gospel!" he said.

" Well, I thank you for the compliment then. And show the sincerity of your attachment by granting my request."

" Any request of yours is law to me," he said.

" Then let this be our last conversation upon this subject. You need never refer to it to me or to others. I certainly shall not remind you of it. We have been very good friends. Let us fall back into our old relations."

" You seem ten years older," said Daltman, " since I began this talk, and ten years wiser, and ten thousand times more attractive. I have been a rash fool, and destroyed my chances by my unseemly haste. If I had known you better, I should have been more circumspect. I should have made my approaches in more courtly fashion. But I was afraid some other fellow would see you, and win you before I had spoken, and so I rushed headlong to my own destruction."

" Do not think so, Mr. Daltman," said Haidee, as they drew near the stables. " It would not have been more impossible to marry you, if I had been already married, or already buried! Excuse me, please! I say this to relieve your mind. You have thrown away no chance. Do not think so. You never had the ghost of a chance to throw away. Your mode of address made no sort of difference. If you were king of England it would not alter the case. Excuse me again!" And she stopped in the path and faced him, with fearless grey eyes, full of truth and gentleness. " You have laboured to convince me that you would be entirely satisfied with me, and would not exact too much. But it has not occurred to you to enquire whether *I* might not exact more than you could render! With all your excellent qualities—and doubtless you have many—you have one fatal fault. You are selfish!"

"I suppose so," said Daltman, gloomily; "all men are selfish."

"Then I shall never marry," answered Haidee; "and let that content you. I do not even say you are more selfish than other men, or more selfish than all humanity. But I shall never marry a selfish man!"

"If the old times would come back again!" said Daltman, speaking through his teeth, "when deeds of valour counted, when patient endurance found a reward, when long exile awakened pity——"

"Bosh again!" said Haidee; "excuse me! But don't you see that your persistence is the proof of all I have said? Knightly valour counted for nothing unless the valour was beneficent! Patient endurance never found a reward when the reward was payment for the endurance."

"It seems to me," said Daltman, sullenly, "that you are full of romantic notions that every day's experience should dispel. Do you suppose any man in the world would seek to marry any woman in the world merely for *her* sake? It is *because* you are necessary to my happiness that I sought you! Why should I attempt to deceive you by so shallow a pretense as an unselfish affection. There is no such thing on earth. It is a contradiction in terms. You have heard the absurd stuff that Glendare and Rayneford used to formulate last year! It is the same idle dream, of unselfish devotion!"

Ah, Mr. Daltman! That was a very unfortunate speech! While Haidee turns that pleasant smile upon you, it is not *you* she smiles at.

"Come, Mr. Daltman," she said, "let us go in. I hear papa's voice. "But do not delude yourself by supposing I have learned my theories from Mr. Glendare or any one else. I never heard a word spoken on the subject by any one. I never read it in foolish romances. All that I think on the subject of marriage I have gotten from one Book—the Holy Scriptures!"

"Why!" said Daltman, startled, "that is precisely what those fellows said last summer!"

Oh, blockhead!

"Haidee!" said Colonel Mordaunt's voice, "are you there?"

"Yes, papa."

"You must have been asleep! Come round to the door."

"I think I have been asleep once or twice. It was the salad."

"Asleep!" murmured Daltman, lighting his cigar, and walking away. "Asleep! Well, that is positive mendacity! I wonder if she learned that in the Bible, too! What a beautiful little devil she is! I'll not relinquish her, by Jove!"

CHAPTER XXXVII.

The Abduction.

HAIDEE was impatient to see Clifton Downs. Dr. Leigh was going to Mendon by the Bristol steamer, and coming back by rail, and would spend a day or two in Clifton. So a letter was sent to St. Vincent's Hotel to secure rooms. In due time they reached Clifton, and after climbing the Zigzag, the doctor proceeded to the hotel, charged with the bestowal of the luggage, and with an order for dinner at six, at which time Haidee promised to present herself. Then she walked out upon the wide Downs.

The Observatory first. She was going to inspect it carefully, and then cross the bridge. There was a photographer near the Observatory, crawling around his tripod half asleep. His wagon, drawn by a glossy pony, was rather in the way, but she walked by. The pony looked good-natured and winked lazily at her, and she put out her hand and patted his neck. Then she peeped over his back to see if the owner had noticed her. But he had buried his head in a yard of black velvet and was adjusting his camera. So she passed on and surveyed the structure with great deliberation. The photographer was still "under a cloud," jerking the tripod about, and turning screws back and forward in a half-somnolent fashion. How tiresome the man was! Then she saw a placard announcing a grand display of fireworks at "the Gardens" at nine o'clock sharp. She would make Dr. Leigh take her, and she carefully read the list of attractions, standing still as the Observatory behind her. A few seconds were enough, and in those few seconds the artist had withdrawn the slide, uncovered the camera, counted fifty, and thrown the velvet cloth over the instrument. While he was fumbling about the tripod, she turned away, repassed the pony, who remembered her and winked again, and who received another gentle pat. Then she strayed on to the bridge, and leaning on the parapet, looked down the Avon, admiring the hills on either side.

Here comes the photographer. He is lolling indolently on the seat, not driving at all! The pony is master of the situation. The reins are twisted around the whip, and the driver is asleep and smoking. Look at the smoke coming through his thick beard! No! he is not asleep! He straightens his body up—he looks like a gentleman—he lifts his hat as he passes her with a courtly bow.

Sir Hyland! All bearded and bronzed, but undoubtedly Sir

Hyland. And he does not know her. He never looks back—not once!

She walks back to the Downs, recklessly sacrificing the sixpence she had paid to "cross the bridge and return." Why did he not recognise her? When she saw him last he was thin and feeble, wearing a well-trimmed moustache. Now, his face is covered with a lovely beard, and he looks strong enough to lift the Observatory. He does not know that he cured her neuralgia. Some day she will tell him in strict confidence.

Three o'clock. Plenty of time to spare. She will go down the river and see the Carpen Rocks. Mr. Glendare mentioned them as curious geological formations. And Mr. Daltman was quite eloquent about them yesterday. By-the-bye, Mr. Daltman had entirely recovered from his late attack of tenderness. The Rocks were a short mile from the Observatory. She can see them already.

What a pretty river! Here comes a schooner down, passing under the bridge. She will reach the Carpen Rocks before it is abreast. There are two men on the bank, with a quantity of shawls on their arms. One of them has tied his handkerchief to his cane and waves it high above his head. She had better go back, as there are no people about here. Yes! there is a lady at the base of the Rocks. It would be absurd to go back without seeing them. The two men are going—no, they are coming. And the lady is beyond them. Here they come. Honest-looking men.

"Beg pardon, miss!" said the foremost, touching his cap. "Miss Mordaunt?"

"Yes." The lady is approaching with rapid steps.

"Then it's all right, miss!" said the man. "The colonel is aboard the schooner, and sent us for you. See! the boat is coming ashore."

"The colonel!" said Haidee, drawing back. "There is some mistake."

"No mistake, miss!" replied the man, shaking out a shawl and throwing it suddenly over her head. "Don't be alarmed, miss. Nothing will harm you. Only we *must* take you aboard! Put another shawl on, Bill! She may squeal! Hurry, stoopid!"

Almost smothered and entirely helpless, the shawls bound over her arms, she feels the men lift her from the ground and bear her swiftly away. And while bewildered and half unconscious from fright, she still knows she is on the boat, is lifted up on the vessel, and laid upon the deck. She makes one struggle to free herself, but is picked up again and carried a few steps down into the cabin.

Then she hears the hatch close with a snap, and the click of the capstan as the anchor is raised.

"Now, miss," said a voice near her, "if you will promise to make no noise, I'll take off the shawls and trust you. Please hold up your hand if you promise and mean fair."

She held her hand up promptly, and in a moment was freed from the smothering wrappings. She took in the surroundings rapidly. A small cabin, with a mattress on a long locker. Two windows in the stern. A small table in the centre, bolted to the floor. The man was standing at the stairway waiting for her to speak.

"What does this mean?" she said. "Is it money you want? How much?"

He shook his head. "It is nothing, miss! Only be patient a little while. No harm is intended. We would not have touched you if you had come along."

"Where am I going?"

"Only down the river a bit. Cawn't tell exactly how far. But you'll be taken home as soon as possible. I am ordered to tell you this."

"Ordered by whom?" said Haidee.

"Ah! that I cawn't tell you, you know! No use to ask that! Nobody knows but me, and fire wouldn't burn it out of me! I must go on deck now, miss. If you want anything just knock on the table, please."

"Before you go answer me one question. Will you put me ashore for money? A hundred pounds. A thousand pounds."

"I dasn't listen to you, miss!" said the man, ascending the stairs. "Please don't worrit yourself. It'll all come right. I swear it, by gum!" And he departed, closing the cabin hatch behind him.

What can it all mean? Apart from the outrageous seizure of her body she had been treated with the greatest deference. The man who had just left her stood with cap in hand while he talked with her. There was certainly no cause for present alarm. She had a vague knowledge of the geography of the east coast, but could not remember how far Clifton was from the sea. She had promised to make no outcry, and no help was near, let her cry never so loudly. She climbed up on the after locker and examined the fastenings of the stern transoms. They were secured by bolts, and she found she could slide the sash back, which she did. The cool breeze from the water revived her, and she actually found herself admiring the scenery upon either bank of the widening river as the schooner glided onward. By-and-bye she remembered that she had ordered dinner in Clifton, and she had eaten no luncheon. She descended from her perch and knocked on the table. The hatch opened on the instant, and her captor appeared.

"I want some tea!" she said.

"Coming, miss!" he replied. "Almost ready. Bear a hand there, Bill!"

In five minutes he descended the stairs, bearing a tray. There was a pot of tea, a sugar dish, six large buns, a plate of cold roast beef, and a salt-cellar. He placed the tray on the table, touched his cap, and scrambled up the stairway.

"I cannot eat anything," she murmured; "but perhaps I can drink some tea." And when she mounted the locker again there was one bun left and almost all the salt. The sun was down, the river was still wider, and the vessel rose and fell upon a very perceptible swell. In spite of her indignation and excitement the monotony told upon her, and she leaned her head upon the window and fell asleep.

Two or three hours of dreamless slumber, and then she was in India again. Some incidents of her early life came to mind, and she dreamed she was pursued by rebellious Sepoys. Her only hope was in Zeba, who was hidden in the jungle. He was to announce his proximity by singing a Pracrit war-song, which her enemies could not understand. And while she slowly awakened, and confusedly mingled the realities around her—the lapping of the water against the hull, the creak of the yards on deck, and the flap of the sail—with the fading fragments of her dream, the song came, clear and distinct, from the moonlit river:

> "The Ganga is born in the high hills
> Where the frost god chains the streams;
> But it leaps from the rocky prison
> Tearing its path to the plain.
> So is the sweep of the tulwar
> In the hand of the tulwar's lord."

It was the Pracrit song. She leaned out, and anticipating the singer, who should have repeated the last two lines, she sang:

> "So is the sweep of the tulwar
> In the hand of the tulwar's lord."

"Beg pardon, miss," said a voice at her elbow, "but this is against contract! Orders is to close the transoms." And he shut the sashes and secured them.

"I insist upon an explanation of this outrage," she said, facing the man with haughty vehemence. "I recall any promise I have made. I will scream for help as long as I can raise my voice."

"What will you have, miss?" said the man, submissively. "Don't make a row, and I'll do whatever you bid me."

"Put me ashore instantly," she answered. "That is all I ask."

"We are a good bit away from the shore, miss. If you promise to keep quiet, I'll take you on deck and let you see for yourself."

"I promise," she answered, eagerly. "Where am I?"

"Honor bright," said the man. "You won't cut up rough, nor flop down in a fit nor nothin' if I take you up?"

"I will not."

He went up the stairway, and held his hand out to assist her, as she gained the deck. A wide expanse of water, the moon gilding leagues of wavelets in the wake of the vessel, and nothing in sight except a cockleshell of a sailboat far astern.

"Now, miss," said the man, with contrite accents, "I am sick of this business! If you want to stay aboard, and go to—to Glasgow —all right! If you want to be landed, I'll put you ashore. I swear it, by gum!"

"Where can you land me?" she said. "And when?"

"Look forrard, miss," replied he. "D'ye see that red light just off the starboard bow?"

"Yes. What is it?"

"That is Linton light, miss. There is shoal water all round this end, but we can heave to, and land you there. The light-house keeper will take good care of you, and you can get to Milford to-morrow. There is a steamer running from Milford to Clifton."

"How soon can I land?" she asked, all other considerations sinking out of sight. Once on terra firma, she would be safe.

"In thirty minutes, miss. Will you go?"

"Go! Certainly. I have very little money with me, but I will pay you any sum you demand after I get home."

"Don't want no money, miss," said the man, sighing. "thank you all the same. Only want to get my conscience clear of this here business." And he smote his breast with his fist. "You see I'm under orders, miss, and I should be broke if I disobeyed. But I'm going to land you, by gum! And if you could only forgive me for my part of this here outrage, I'd die happy."

15

"Only put me on land, and I will forgive you all you have done."

"Thank'ee, miss. It takes a load off my mind. Would you mind signing a bit of paper, just to show in case I get nabbed? I'll write it, if you'll be so kind. Here, Bill, bring me that lantern. Set down here, miss. Bill, spread a cloth there on the hatchway." And taking the lantern, he dived down into the cabin.

"What is the name of this vessel?" said Haidee to the attendant.

"The 'Swaller,' miss," said Bill, promptly.

"And the name of—the gentleman who just went down?"

"Captain Scroggs, miss," replied William.

These two lies slipped from his tongue so readily that he rose largely in his own estimation. Somehow, Haidee knew he was lying, and propounded no more questions. Captain Scroggs reappeared in a few minutes with a slip of paper and pen.

"I'll read it, miss," he said, putting the lantern on the hatchway. "This certifies that John Scroggs has landed me at Linton light, without reward, and at my own request."

Haidee read the paper, and affixed her signature, notwithstanding the defective orthography. He had spelt the final word "rekwest."

Her attention was next attracted to the movement of the vessel, which turned towards the light-house, now plainly visible, and quite near. She could hear the breakers and see the line of white water. The boat was lowered, and she was carefully assisted over the side and seated in the stern sheets. Captain Scroggs and Bill dropped aboard, put out the oars, and pulled straight for the light. Presently the boat grated against the landing, and she was assisted again as she stepped out upon the flat rock at the base of the tower. To her joy, she was met by a woman, whose arm she grasped, while she tried to gather some meaning from the strange language the woman used to welcome her. A man was standing at the door of the tower with a pipe in his mouth.

"What is all this?" said he.

"Lady. Seasick. Take her to Milford in the morning. You'll be well paid." This came from the boat, already backing away from the landing.

"Aye, aye! Walk in, mum. She'll show the way. Pity she can't talk to you, mum. Leastways not in Hinglish. She don't know a word of any lingo but Welsh. Walk in, mum."

CHAPTER XXXVIII.

THE RESCUE.

HAIDEE MORDAUNT could never give a coherent account of the events of the next twenty-four hours. She knew she slept fitfully through the night, and that the next morning she explored the narrow, rocky ledge upon which the light-house stood. She heard the Pracrit war-song again in the morning, and saw Zeba through the window, which was securely fastened. She saw an old sailor in an oilskin coat, and saw the sail of the "Ripple." She snatched up her hat to rush out, but her door was locked on the outside! And while she debated the question as to whether she should scream for help, she saw the "Ripple" glide away. She had heard the warning song of Zeba, enjoining silence, and suddenly concluded that Sir Hyland was busy planning her rescue! She repeated this to herself a thousand times, and therefore did not go mad as the hours wore on. The wife of the light-house keeper could not make her understand a solitary word, and the man kept out of her sight except during the few minutes before the "Ripple" sailed away.

On the second night, about an hour after midnight, she was startled by the sound of the Pracrit song, and, rushing to the window, she saw the "Ripple" coming through the narrow channel in the sands. While she watched with absorbed attention the boat touched the landing, and a man leaped ashore. It was the old mariner of the previous day, in his oilskin coat and hat. He came to the window and endeavoured to open the sash, which was secured and bolted, and of course immovable. After a momentary hesitation he returned to the landing and took an axe from the boat, while Zeba, for it was he beyond doubt, secured the vessel to the rocky pier. The old sailor wedged the axe in the outer sash, and with a wrench tore it from its fastenings. Two quick blows demolished the inner sash, and Zeba put his hand through the opening, while the sailor cleared away the fragments that prevented her egress.

"Beébe, come quickly!" said Zeba. She stepped upon the sill, and, supported by the two men, reached the boat as the door of the dwelling opened and the light-house keeper appeared.

"Hillo!" he shouted, "what the devil are you up to, dad?" His voice was husky and his step uncertain as he stumbled down to the pier.

"Gov'ment property, old man!" he roared. "What d'ye mean

by smashing winders this time o' night? What are you doin' with the girl? You are ruining everything! Come back, bless your eyes!"

Zeba faced the drunken keeper, disdaining to draw his weapon, while the old man drew the boat near the rock. At the moment, a boat containing half a dozen men glided up to the mimic pier, and a gentleman sprang ashore. The moon was full and the sky cloudless. The tall masts of a yacht, just off the shore, drew graceful curves against the sky as the vessel rocked on the waves.

"Oh, Mr. Daltman!" said Haidee, springing to the side of the new-comer, "take me away from this dreadful place!"

"That is just what I came to do," said Daltman; "what devil's work is this! Who has dared——"

"No matter now!" said she; "take me away!"

Zeba glanced at the old man in the oilskin garments, and then silently drew his tulwar. But his companion caught his arm, and whispering a word in his ear, stepped aboard the "Ripple," followed by the reluctant Hindoo. As the boat drifted away, Daltman called out—

"Stop that boat! Cockswain! stop them! I want to investigate them a little."

A boat-hook was thrust over the side of the yawl, and catching the "Ripple" by the mainstay, drew her back to the landing. Mr. Daltman stepped aboard. The oilskin coat was in the stern, quiet and peaceful.

"Tumble up here!" said Daltman, imperatively. "Let us see what you are like."

"Deef!" said the keeper, with drunken gravity—"deef and drunk! smashed the gov'ment winder! Here's a go!"

"Come out, I say!" said Daltman, in a louder tone. The oilskin arose, stumbled over the after-thwart, caught Mr. Daltman's legs as he recovered, and with the strength of a giant, raised him up bodily, and tossed him over the gunwale, into five feet of water. The tulwar flashed in the moonlight, and descended upon the boat-hook, cutting it in twain, and the "Ripple" once more drifted into the smugglers' channel. And when the cockswain had drawn his dripping commander ashore, the "Ripple" was forty yards off.

"Follow them!" said Daltman, savagely. "Capture or kill! Follow!"

"Aye, aye!" said the cockswain, "but that is old Jones, and he has his sail up, and he knows every foot of the channel! You will have

to give him up to-night, captain. We can get him when you want
him, at Milford."

Zeba sat in the stern of the flying "Ripple," steering through the
channel with rare dexterity. He looked anxiously into the sober
face of his companion, who sat opposite, holding the sheet, but remained silent until they had passed The Twins, and were clear of the
sands.

"Where go, sahib?" said the Hindoo, as the boat danced over
the waves, beyond the line of white water.

"Back to Milford."

"With tulwar and axe could make good fight," observed Zeba,
his nostrils dilating; "but sahib like not fight. Beébe go in ship."

"Mr. Daltman will take her home," said Hyland, composedly;
"did you not hear her? She called for him."

"Beébe know not Lord Hyland," replied the Indian, "yellow
coat and hat. Sahib not speak."

"But she knew Mr. Daltman!" said Hyland, with a jealous pang;
"she flew to his side as soon as he appeared."

"Sahib Daltman dressed. Good coat. Good hat."

"I am afraid they got wet!" muttered Hyland, "but I could not
help it! It was bad enough to be too late. It would have been
worse if they knew it! You and I will keep the secret of this
adventure, Zeba."

When Mr. Daltman planned this rescue, he arranged to take
Haidee on a little longer cruise. He had prepared a lot of answers
to account for the delay, such as tides and currents and adverse
winds. But he had not made provision for the effect of salt water
on his habiliments, and no amount of romance could atone for
trousers that exposed his stockings, and a coat whose cuffs drew up
to his elbows. He found when he had dried his garments at the
galley stove, that he was not at all well gotten up, and he had no
change of raiment on board the yacht. It was absolutely imperative
to return to Milford, where he had left his luggage, and repair
damages. He gave up the luxurious cabin to Haidee, informing her
that they would reach Milford in an hour or two. Before they left
the light-house, while he was assisting Haidee into the yawl, Mr.
Jones, Junior, staggered up and touched his wet shoulder.

"Bad business, gov'nor!" he said. "Gov'ment property. A
matter of two pound smashed. Have to get a man from Milford.
Another pound!"

"Here is a five-pound note," answered Daltman. "It is rather

damp. You will have to dry it. I shall be back here, and will see
that you are satisfied. Did you know the men who left the lady
here?"

"Perfect strangers!" replied Mr. Jones. "I say, gov'nor, how
the devil did the old 'un—I mean dad—you know—him that tossed
you over—how did he get mixed up in this here——"

"How do I know!" said Daltman, angrily. "Cast off there!
Give way, men, and get the lady on board the yacht."

It was three o'clock when Haidee landed at Milford. No cabs in
attendance at that hour, so Daltman escorted her to the hotel. She
clung to him, the heroism that had sustained her so many weary
hours deserting her now that she was in positive safety. She was
filled with a nameless dread, and Daltman seemed like a guardian
angel. The tide would not serve for six hours, and the yacht could
not enter the Avon. So he assured her, and she reluctantly consented to go to her chamber and wait for daylight. The sleepy
chambermaid gladly accepted her proposal to lock the doors and to
sleep in the anteroom within call. And the worn-out maiden obtained three or four hours' sleep, waking with the dawn, restored to
her ordinary vigour. She dressed rapidly and then wakened her
attendant.

"What is your name?" she asked, while the girl bored her eyes
out with her knuckles.

"Lucy, miss."

"Lucy, are you awake?"

"Yes, miss."

"Well, I want some tea and toast. How soon can I get them?"

"In five minutes, miss. I'll go order them."

"Go, then, and return immediately. And bring me a time-table."

"Beg pardon, miss—what kind o' table?"

"The book that tells about trains and steamboats. I wish to find
out how I can get to Clifton."

"Oh! Don't want a book, miss. My mother lives in Clifton,
and I know all about it. The boat leaves for Mendon at a quarter
after seven. There it sometimes waits for the tide. But there is a
train for Clifton that leaves Mendon as soon as the boat gets there,
miss."

"Then we can go!" said Haidee, joyfully; "you can go with me?"

"Don't know, miss. I'll ask the master."

"Send him to me. Run! It is seven o'clock now! Never
mind the tea."

A sovereign in addition to the charge for lodging bought Lucy's attendance for the day, and when Mr. Daltman was leisurely dressing for breakfast, the " Prince of Wales", was steaming out the harbour with Haidee and her new maid on board. Mr. Daltman sent his card to Miss Mordaunt's room, and received in exchange the following little note:

" DEAR MR. DALTMAN—I have just learned that the ' Prince of Wales' will sail for Mendon in fifteen minutes. As she is a steamer, she will go so much faster than your yacht, and I can get to Clifton by rail. I know the route, and have engaged a maid to accompany me. I can take luncheon with papa to-day! I am quite well and filled with joy, thanks to your kind attention.

" HAIDEE MORDAUNT.

" P. S.—I hope you did not take cold."

The remarks that fell from Mr. Daltman's lips when he mastered the contents of this epistle made the attentive waiter's flesh creep. He mentioned the " Prince of Wales," the hotel, the yacht, the tide, and various other objects with an objurgatory prefix, and with heartfelt emphasis. Then he ordered breakfast.

His cockswain waited upon him at eight o'clock by appointment. There was some solace in the thought that Mr. Jones was within reach. He would at least give the old wretch full payment for his assault of the previous night. The cockswain led the way to the Jones mansion, near the pier. They were admitted by Mr. Flellen, the second-story lodger, who informed the sailor that his landlord had passed a terrible night. They found Mr. Jones upon his cot, with a medical man in attendance.

" What ails the old marauder?" said Daltman, rudely, after a glance at the sick man.

" Threatened with mania-a-potu," answered the doctor.

" When did it begin to threaten?" said Daltman, sarcastically, while the cockswain examined the oilskin coat and hat, hanging against the wall.

" I was called at midnight exactly," answered the doctor. " Flellen came for me, saying the old man was mad. I found him in a very precarious condition demanding prompt treatment. I have been exhibiting *spiritus Mindererus* with very satisfactory results! He is mending. I do not apprehend another paroxysm. Probably I shall administer some stimulant later in the day."

"Why, I saw this man sailing out into the channel at midnight!" said Daltman.

"And I saw him, too!" added the cockswain. The doctor shook his head with an incredulous smile.

"Sorry to contradict you, gentlemen," said he, "but you are certainly mistaken. Here, Flellen! What time was it when I came last night?"

"Twelve!" answered the other, in good Welsh.

"And I have not been out of this room since," said the doctor.

"And did he have this coat and hat on?" asked the cockswain, derisively, touching the yellow garments.

"No. Those belong to a sailor friend, I suppose. He came in between two and three o'clock, and hung the coat on that hook. I saw him do it! There can be no mistake about it," he continued, with professional dignity. "The man left a sovereign with me, and here it is! It was to pay me for medical attendance."

"There is some mystery about this business, Blain," said Mr. Daltman, as he and the cockswain walked down the pier. "Do you think that doctor fellow was lying?"

"It is Doctor Rice," said the cockswain; "I cannot think he would be up to any trick."

"It was that coat that threw me overboard!" said Daltman. "Who the devil is the sailor friend? Where is he?"

The sailor friend was seated in the forecastle of the "Prince of Wales" at that precise moment, watching Haidee Mordaunt promenading the deck, leaning on the arm of her maid.

A one-armed Hindoo was coiled up on the deck at his feet, fast asleep.

CHAPTER XXXIX.

The Arrest.

MR. HYLAND RAYNEFORD sat in moody silence on the forward deck of the "Prince of Wales," his broad-brimmed felt hat pulled down over his brow. Haidee was in sight, on the after part of the vessel, sometimes promenading the deck, and sometimes seated on the long bench against the bulwarks, but always closely attended by her maid. Zeba had drawn his cloak over his head and shoulders as soon as he saw Haidee on board, and, dropping down on the deck, propped himself against the capstan and fell asleep. He and Hyland had watched the hotel at Milford during the time that Haidee slept, walking along the solitary street and subsisting upon the fumes of cheroots. As soon as daylight returned, and the streets became populated, Zeba mounted guard opposite the main entrance while Hyland obtained his breakfast. Then Hyland took his place, having ordered chops and tea for the Hindoo. They were close behind Haidee and her maid when they boarded the steamer, and, finding Daltman did not appear, Mr. Rayneford betook himself to the forecastle, where smoke was legal.

While he sat there he reviewed the course of events, and once he half started to accost the maiden when she came up the stairs from the dining-cabin. But Haidee had clutched the arm of her maid and withdrawn from the little group of passengers, and a fit of shyness came over Rayneford, and he resumed his seat. It was not at all necessary to offer assistance or escort, and the offer would have a second-hand appearance. Why did Daltman send her without him? Why did she fly to Daltman last night when *he* had broken her prison open? Common sense answered. Daltman had a sea-going vessel, with all appliances of comfort and safety, while he had only an old fishing-boat. And she did not know him. Ah! when he took her hand in his and led her down to the boat he was dumb! If he had spoken—— Well—she would still have gone with Daltman! This was his conclusion.

At the same instant Haidee was reviewing. How did Daltman find out her hiding-place? And Zeba? Zeba must have told Daltman. But Zeba came to England with the Lord of the tulwar. Surely he did not give that title to Daltman! Did Sir Hyland send Zeba with that old sailor? It must have been, because Daltman assaulted them and was thrown into the sea by the sailor. She saw that. Where was Sir Hyland? Perhaps on Clifton Downs, and she was going there! What had become of Zeba? She saw his lithe figure in the stern of the boat as it drifted away, while the old sailor was fumbling with the mainsheet amidships; and she had previously seen the sweep of Zeba's sword as it cut through the staff of the boat-hook. It was very mysterious!

By-the-bye! It could not have been an accidental encounter out on the river when she was wakened by Zeba's song! Zeba must have known she was there! Therefore Zeba must have had some part in the outrageous abduction! Now whom did he serve? Sir Hyland, of course! Would he be guilty of such a crime! Never! Never!

"Talk to me, Lucy," she said, desperately, "or I shall go mad! Tell me about Clifton—your mother, where does she live? Have you any sisters or brothers?"

This opened the sluice-gates, and a torrent flowed. Lucy did not pause, except to draw breath, until the "Prince of Wales" reached Mendon.

At Mendon, Hyland watched as she went ashore, saw her pause at the telegraph-office, rush in and write a message, pay a shilling; heard the operator read the message aloud: "From Haidee Mordaunt to Doctor Leigh, St. Vincent's Hotel, Clifton, Bristol. Safe and well. Will reach Clifton at eleven o'clock." Then he drew back against the wall as she passed out and entered the station. Saw her get into a railway carriage with Lucy. So he and Zeba took seats in the next carriage, and the train started for Clifton.

Along the river-bank, sometimes through tunnels, sometimes skimming over long stretches of coast, river on the right and rocks on the left, until they passed the spot where the "Ariadne" had anchored. The high bridge was in sight now, then the dark tunnel, and then slowing down as the train slipped into the Clifton station, and the guard unlocked the doors.

Doctor Leigh and Glendare catching Haidee's hands as she descended. A torrent of questions, of course, and a torrent of tears for answer. Then the two men take her between them and start for the Zigzag, Lucy meekly following. And Hyland and Zeba crawl out of their carriage and turn their backs on the party. Safe now, certainly. No further need for watching.

There is a rude stairway nearer the bridge, partly cut in the cliff and partly builded of timbers, and Hyland and the Hindoo climb that. A few steps to the Downs; they pass the Observatory, and sit down under a tree.

"Zeba, my friend," said Hyland, "we have not yet found my brother."

"Sahib's brother west," replied the Hindoo, sweeping his arm in that direction.

"How long shall we look in that quarter?" asked Hyland, incredulously.

"Until find," answered Zeba, steadily. "Ask tulwar at Calcutta. Ask tulwar on the sea. Ask tulwar at sahib's bungalow. Ask

tulwar at Milford. Tulwar say west, west, west, west! Four times
tulwar answer."

"Suppose it had happened to change——"

"No happen!" interrupted the Hindoo, with dignity. "Sahib
know law of happen! If happen two times, then tulwar kill thirty-
one other happens. If happen three times, then tulwar kill many
thousand other happens. If happen four times, then tulwar kill
more other happens than all the stars in the sky—all the drops of
water in the sea."

Hyland was stunned by this unexpected rejoinder. He had, in
previous intercourse with Zeba, been frequently astonished by the
display of unusual mathematical knowledge, sometimes by the native's rapid mental solution of abstruse problems, which solution he
afterwards verified by elaborate processes. Given, the accuracy
of the tulwar's responses—Hyland felt that Zeba's argument was
unanswerable on any scientific hypothesis.

"Tulwar find Beébe," continued Zeba.

"Yes," muttered Hyland, discontentedly; "and a devil of a mess
it made of it!"

"When tulwar chop enemy down," continued the Hindoo, "enemy
live two, three hours. Tulwar only chop once. But not *done* till
enemy die."

Hyland felt his heart bound at this suggestion, but remained
silent.

"Beébe safe," said Zeba, meditatively; "but end not yet! Tulwar
find Beébe because Lord Hyland look for her. Tulwar find Beébe
eleven o'clock two nights gone. When did sahib first want find?"

Stunned again! Hyland remembered that it was eleven o'clock
when he discovered Haidee's identity with the maiden on Clifton
Downs, in the billiard-room at Bath.

"By this light!" said Hyland, "this beats ordinary necromancy.
Tell me, Zeba, has the tulwar ever revealed other things to you?"

"Many times," replied Zeba, readily. "Tulwar tell sahib coming
from the frost-hills. So Zeba wait. Not sail with Colonel Sahib.
Tulwar tell sahib at Clifton, two days ago. Not point west then."

"I'll hear no more of this awful rubbish!" said Hyland, in a rage.
"My friend, I will follow you! The west is as full of promise as
any other direction. I will humour you and go."

"Sahib always wise!" answered Zeba, courteously.

"Now to go to Doctor Leigh. Learn what you can. Miss Mordaunt saw you, and knew you. She will ask you many questions.

It is not necessary to tell her who was with you. Probably she will not enquire."

"Zeba has no tongue."

"I do not mean that exactly," said Hyland, "and I put no restrictions upon you. You are wise enough to answer discreetly. Anyhow, it is great folly to be sensitive because I attempted to rescue her and—failed."

"Sahib not failed. Enemy struck. Not yet dead. Only dying!"

Once more Hyland noted the bound of his heart, which he sternly repressed on the instant. At the same time he was touched by the evident devotion of the Hindoo.

"Give me your hand, Zeba," he said, stretching out his own; "you are a brave gentleman, and I am proud to call you friend. It may be that we can discover the actors in this outrage. If we do, let us be discreet."

"Sahib want? Tulwar find," said Zeba, as he left.

Hyland arose, and passing the Observatory, crossed the bridge, and reached the cottage of Mrs. Noils. His first visit was to Tommy, who was sleek and comfortable. Then he entered the house, and after a luxurious bath, dressed with more care than usual. His luggage had been sent from London during his absence, and he had a choice of habiliments. It was possible that Zeba might bring a message from—Dr. Leigh or Mr. Glendare, that would make it proper for him to call on them. He was hungering for some slight intercourse with his Indian friends. He would give fifty pounds just to hear Haidee talk. Then he went into his dark closet to inspect his pictures. He missed some of them.

"Mrs. Noils," he said, coming into his sitting-room, "somebody has removed some pictures from the bath. I left them last night."

"Nobody has been there," said Mrs. Noils, "except the gentleman you sent back. He went in there for the paper you left."

"Ah!" replied Hyland. "When did he come?"

"As soon as you went away last night, sir. He said you had sent him back for a paper, and he took my lamp and hunted around this room, your bedroom and the closet. He was here about ten minutes."

"Indeed!" said Hyland. "What was he like?"

"An ugly little man, sir, with red eyes. There he is! That is the same man out there under the tree."

Hyland looked through the window and investigated Mr. Dancer. Although not very attractive in appearance, Hyland desired a closer view; so he put on his hat and walked out and across the road, where the detective was standing.

"Mrs. Noils tells me," he said, with cold composure, "that you searched my apartments last night. Who sent you, and for what?"

"Oh!" said Mr. Dancer, politely, "excuse me, sir. Mr. Robinson?"

"What did you seek in my rooms?" said Hyland, sternly.

"Beg pardon, sir," replied Mr. Dancer, "but you had better come up on the path. Cab coming. Hi, Tom! Stop!"

The cab stopped, and a man who was seated by the driver slid down from his perch.

"All right, Tom!" said Mr. Dancer, "this is the gent! Now, Mr. Robinson, if *you* please, I want you."

"What do you mean, you insolent scoundrel?" replied Hyland.

"Better go slow," said the detective, menacingly. "Of course you cawn't understand! Not much! But I want you all the same. I have a warrant for you. D'ye want to see it? *Of* course! Well, I'm an officer of the law, and I want you on two or three accounts. Do you happen to know Lord Rayneford? Ah!"

"What of him? Speak, man! Has anything happened——"

"Better go dark now, young man," said the detective, impressively. "Don't be fool enough to criminate yourself. You're wanted; that's enough. You never saw Miss Haidee Mordaunt, I s'pose? Ah! troubled again! Now, take your choice"—and he exhibited a pair of handcuffs—"have these on, and walk in town with me, or get into the cab with me and Tom, and we can ride in."

Hyland reflected a moment.

"Suppose this is an absurd mistake of yours?" he said, coolly. "I am not going to resist lawful authority, but what redress should I have if you have blundered in this matter?"

"Here is the warrant," replied the officer, exhibiting the paper. "It orders me to take the body of John Robinson, Photographer."

"And suppose I am not John Robinson, but a gentleman——"

"I'll have to take the risk," said Mr. Dancer, a little staggered. "Mayhap it's a blunder, as you call it. If you are not a gentleman you are a cool hand. But appearances are against you. Get in the cab. Help him in, Tom."

"I require no assistance, thank you," said Hyland. "Do not touch me, if you please. There! You and your friend will please occupy the front seat."

As the cab rolled across the bridge, Hyland decided upon his course.

"There are two questions which you may answer," said he. "First: about Lord Rayneford. Do you *know* of any harm that has befallen him? Do not hesitate, man! I know he has been missing, and Mr. Plimpton told me he had set you on his track. Have you any information about him?"

"I fancy I don't know any more than *you* know," replied Mr. Dancer, with a grin. "I found a pockmantle in your room marked 'Rayneford.'"

"Ah! Then that is all?"

"That is all I have to say," replied the officer.

"Question second. Was the paper you sought in my rooms—a picture, for instance?"

"I found a picture or two," replied Mr. Dancer.

"Then will you have the kindness to preserve them carefully? I shall want them. That is all. Where are we going?"

"To the lock-up at the Town Hall."

"I suppose I can have a room—for a price—until the authorities discover your mistake?"

"Oh, certainly!" said Mr. Dancer, airily. "Hope you won't get tired waiting for that. Well, you are a cool hand, and no mistake! I've made many a haul where coves carried a high hand, but you bang them all. It is good as a book to listen to you. If I didn't know better, I'd think you was His Royal Highness. But then I've seen His Royal Highness, and you ar'n't a bit like him. What are you laughing at?"

"What an enormous ass you are, Mr. Dancer!" replied the prisoner. "I am laughing to think how Mr. Plimpton will look when I tell him——"

"Well," said the detective, "that's lucky! Mr. Plimpton is in Clifton now."

CHAPTER XL.

CROSS-EXAMINED.

ZEBA entered the spacious hall of St. Vincent's Hotel, arrested a flying waiter, and asked for Glendare.

"Gone to Bath. Will be back to-night," said the servant.

"Doctor Leigh?"

"Gone to Bristol."

"Missee Mordaunt?" persisted the Hindoo.

"Ah! Cawn't see her. She is very tired, and is in her room."

"Take name. Zeba. I wait."

The attendant hesitated, glancing doubtfully at the foreigner. Zeba's make-up was not artistic. The old camlet cloak was weather-stained and faded. His shoes were dusty. His one eye had a ferocious gleam, though his manner was highly polished.

"Better take name!" he said. "Write on card Zeba. I wait."

The waiter departed, and in two minutes came down the stairway three steps at a time.

"Walk up, sir, please!" he said. "Miss Mordaunt will see you immediately. I'll show you her parlour. This way, sir."

A volley of Hindoostanee came through the doorway when Lucy opened at the modest knock of the servant. Haidee was reclining on a sofa near the window.

"Salaam, Beébe!" said Zeba.

"Come here, Zeba!" replied Haidee, relapsing into English. "Shake hands and sit down there," pointing to a stool at the foot of the sofa.

"Zeba stand!" said Zeba, touching her extended hand, bowing profoundly.

"Sit down!" stormed Haidee, going back to Hindoostanee, "and tell me everything that has happened since we left you in Calcutta."

The hotel-waiter retired stunned. The horrible gibberish sounded more horrible by reason of the musical voice of the speaker. Lucy returned to her seat equally astounded. Zeba dropped his camlet and hat on the floor, tucked his long sword under his arm, and obediently squatted on the low stool indicated.

"My lady asks too many questions at once," said the Hindoo, in his native language. "I waited in Calcutta for the Lord Hyland. Then we sailed many days on the sea. When we landed I began to look for Lord Hyland's brother. Found him not. But found my little lady."

"And you told Mr. Daltman?" said Haidee.

"No. I have not spoken to Sahib Daltman since he left Calcutta."

"Did you know I had been seized and carried away?"

"No. Tulwar knew. I did not know my little lady was in the ship. But tulwar bade me sing when the ship passed. And my little lady answered. Then I knew."

"And do you not know who carried me away?" said Haidee, watching him keenly.

The Hindoo deliberated. "Will find, and tell another day," he said.

"Do you not know now?"

There was another pause. "Little lady will wait," he said. "I do not know. I only think. When I know I will tell."

"And how did you find me?"

"Tulwar said, Go to Linton Sands," replied Zeba.

"But it could not say Linton Sands!" said Haidee, positively. Zeba drew a map from his pouch and spread it open on his knee.

"Here is Lord Hyland's bungalow," he said, putting his finger on the locality. "I asked tulwar there. When the answer came, I drew this line. It goes through Milford to Linton Sands, and the sea is beyond. When at Milford I had heard Beébe sing back to me, and I asked again. It said Linton Sands. Then I saw Beébe through the window. Could not kill light-house man Jones, because his father fed me. Could not get Beébe without killing Jones. Then went back for—my friend."

"Well?" said Haidee, with glowing eyes.

"Find friend," said Zeba, in English, and choosing his words carefully. "He was not home, and had wait. When find, night come. Tell friend I had Beébe in prison, and want help."

"And your friend's name? What is he called? Where does he live?"

"Name?" answered the Hindoo. "Is called Mr. Robinson. Live? Anywhere! He sometimes here, sometimes there. Find him with tulwar."

"Go on."

"Friend go with me. Get boat, get axe. To Linton Sands sail. Break down window. Get Bebée, and——"

"What next?" said Haidee, impatiently, as the Hindoo hesitated.

"Sahib Daltman come. I tell Sahib Robinson take axe. I take tulwar and we take Beébe. But Beébe call Sahib Daltman, and friend say, 'Come away. Beébe safe.' Then Sahib Daltman come in boat. Friend put him in sea. I cut hook, and boat sail home."

"Home?" said Haidee. "Do you mean Clifton?"

"No. Milford. Sailor man Jones come in 'Bengal' ship. Good friend, too. Live in Milford. Borrow Jones boat. Borrow yellow coat. Take boat back, and watch for Sahib Daltman ship. When ship come, see Beébe go in house. Watch house all night. See Beébe get on ship. Get on, too. See Beébe on train. Get on, too. See Beébe with Doctor Sahib. Then done. That all!"

"And you left your friend at Milford?" said Haidee, very carelessly.

"No. Friend come too."

"Ah! He lives here, then?"

"Live anywhere, everywhere. Have horse. Drive about country."

"Bring him here!" said Haidee. "I wish to thank him."

"Not come!" answered Zeba: "going away."

Haidee mused, while Zeba waited. Then she took out her purse, ostentatiously.

"Beébe not pay rupee," said Zeba, rising. "She take magic from tulwar!"

"But it is not for you," she answered. "Sit down!" And she took out some coins.

"Beébe not *send* money!" said Zeba. "A thousand lacs too little!"

"The money is for my maid," said Haidee. "Here, Lucy. I may forget it when Sista comes. This is for yourself." Then turning suddenly upon Zeba, she opened the cross-examination in Hindoostanee.

"How did the tulwar find me, when you were looking for Lord Rayneford?"

"Little lady will not understand Indian magic," replied Zeba, evasively.

"Yes. And I know the Indian noble speaks always truth in Hindoostanee. Answer!"

"Tulwar in magic must serve Lord of tulwar. When Beébe was near, tulwar made me sing. I did not think of Beébe."

"Then it told you, because you were its lord?"

Zeba glanced at her, uneasily. She was propped up with pillows

16

in a corner of the sofa. Her eyes were half closed, and she looked so innocent that Zeba was reassured.

"Tulwar serve tulwar's lord," began Zeba in fair English.

"Hindoostance!" said Haidee, opening her eyes, and glancing at Lucy.

"The tulwar has no lord until warrior gains the lordship!" continued Zeba in his own language. "I have fought with it in many battles, and have killed many times."

"And so became Lord of the tulwar?" observed Haidee, when he paused.

"The lordship cannot be gained in battles," said Zeba; "too many helpers. It must be won with naked hand, without defensive armour, and the blood of the lord must mingle with the blood of his foe on the blade. No other hand must help. He who would rule the tulwar must stand alone and defy death! If his breast is iron, he will win. If he tremble once, he is lost! No man can try twice."

"And you won the lordship in single combat?" asked Haidee, quietly.

"I fought three times in single fight. Once at Lahore, but my enemy was shot before I conquered. Then in the jungle, when I carried Beébe to Colonel Sahib, I killed Sepoy scout. But I had not a scratch on my body. Then at Cattaghur, I met rebel chief on horseback. He gave me this"—and he showed a deep scar on his neck—"and I killed him. When he fell from his horse, I found a bullet in his side. Some stray shot had struck him, and the victory was not all mine."

"Then I understand!" said Haidee: "you must kill a man in his full power, without aid?"

"Man or——" He hesitated.

"I wait," said Haidee, patiently.

"Man or man-eater!" answered Zeba, sullenly.

"And have you killed a man-eater?" persisted his tormentor.

"No, Hyland Sahib took the lordship! I wear the tulwar, but Hyland Sahib is Lord of the tulwar. Lord of Zeba, too! If I ask tulwar to serve me, it answers not. If I ask for Lord Hyland, it answers always!"

There was a silence of several minutes. Zeba was wondering if Beébe had gained any information. Haidee was wondering how she could draw more information from the reluctant Hindoo.

"Did Mr. Rayneford come with you from Calcutta?" she asked; "I mean in the same ship?"

"Yes."

"Did you go with him to his bungalow?"

"Yes."

"And left him there?"

"No. Hyland Sahib went to London. I went to Linton Sands."

"At Linton Sands you found me," said Haidee, reflecting; "how many days have you been in England?"

"Twelve."

"How many times at Clifton?"

"Only once before. Came here for friend, two nights ago."

"What does your friend—Mr. Robinson, you called him—what does he drive about the country for?"

"He make pictures with the sun."

"Who told you he was at Clifton?" said Haidee, suddenly.

"Tulwar!"

"Zeba, you are not trying to enlighten me!" she said, severely. "You said but now the tulwar would not answer you!"

She thought this was a shot between the eyes. But Zeba answered composedly.

"I asked for Hyland Sahib. I knew Hyland Sahib had stood between Beébe and the man-eater. I knew he would take her from Linton Sands, if he had to swim over the sea; and tulwar must serve sahib. So tulwar brought me to—Robinson."

"And Mr. Robinson does not desire any thanks?" said Haidee, with flushed cheeks. "I should not have known he sought me but for you."

"Robinson say he do nothing," responded Zeba, in English; in which tongue he always took refuge when driven into a corner.

"Speak in Hindoostanee," said Haidee. "Did Mr. Robinson know Mr. Daltman?"

"Beébe called out Daltman Sahib," replied the Indian. "Then he know."

The flush deepened. While she revolved this answer, there was a knock at the door, and a card presented.

"Mr. Plimpton!" said she. "Request Mr. Plimpton to walk up." Zeba threw his cloak over his shoulders, and prepared to retire.

"Please wait, Zeba," said Haidee; "I will not detain you long." And Zeba walked over to the projecting window, and studied the scenery on the other side of the Avon. Mr. Plimpton, rubbing his hands and chuckling audibly, came in.

"My dear Miss Haidee!" he said, shaking hands, "welcome back. I have good news for you. We've got him!"

"Got whom, Mr. Plimpton? Sit down."

"No time! Dancer has caught your abductor! Got him safe at the Town Hall. He is a swell, and is ensconced in a private room. And the rascal had the impudence to send for me!"

"Have you seen him?" said Haidee.

"Not yet. Thought I would take you down to identify him. Put on your hat; it is a short distance, and I have a cab. Where is Leigh?"

"In Bristol."

"And Glendare?"

"In Bath. He went to tell papa. He will return this evening."

"Well, come along. I'll bring you back."

"Really, Mr. Plimpton, I am not well enough to go out to-day. I have been so excited, and have passed through such strange adventures, and am so wearied, that Doctor Leigh says I must keep quiet until to-morrow."

"But I want you to identify the rascal."

"Which I cannot do. I do not remember what the man was like. He is a sailor, and called himself Captain Scroggs."

"Oh, yes! he has a dozen aliases, no doubt. At present he calls himself Robinson, and is a peripatetic photographer. What's that?"

It was the click of the tulwar. Zeba had drawn it a little way out of the scabbard, and suffered it to fall back, as he whisked through the open door and disappeared.

"What the devil—excuse me! What was that?" said Mr. Plimpton.

"That is Zeba—a soldier in papa's regiment. I think I will go with you. Can Lucy go also—my maid?"

"Certainly; cab carries four. Come on! I am curious to see this fellow! To think of his impudence! His compliments to Mr. Plimpton! Are you ready?"

"Quite ready," said Haidee. "I feel some curiosity also. Come, Lucy!"

CHAPTER XLI.

MR. PLIMPTON.

THE cab drew up at the Town Hall, and Mr. Dancer and his friend alighted, followed by Mr. Robinson. There was an old man at a grated wicket, who inspected a paper presented by Mr. Dancer with great deliberation, then unlocked the wicket and admitted the party.

" Back or up?" said the aged warden.

" Oh, this gent wants a private room," answered Mr. Dancer. " Regular swell, you know."

" Five shillin's a day, in advance," said the old man, after a glance at the prisoner. Mr. Robinson paid the money, and was ushered up-stairs.

" S'pose I ought to search you," said Mr. Dancer, who followed him into the room; " but don't want to be troublesome. Got any pistols or things?"

" I have no weapon more formidable than my pocket-knife," answered Hyland; " do you want that?"

" It's no consequence, I fancy," said the detective, somewhat subdued in manner. " Do you want to send for anybody?"

" Certainly! My compliments to Mr. Plimpton, and say he will please come soon as possible. Here is money for the messenger. Half a crown is enough. Stay! It is possible that a friend of mine may come. He is a Hindoo with one arm. Admit him, if you please."

" All right, governor!" said Mr. Dancer. " We will entertain him too, blast his black skin! I want him. Don't say nothing to me. Needn't criminate yourself!"

" Get out, then," answered Hyland, " and find Mr. Plimpton. I must leave Clifton to-night."

Mr. Dancer withdrew and locked the door on the outside; then, holding the key in his hand, he addressed some remarks to it, in a low tone.

" If you get a cucumber," he said, " and freeze it in four foot of ice all round, and throw a peck o' salt on the ice, it's my opinion the cucumber won't be as cool as yon chap! Smash me, if he don't take the conceit all out of *me!*" The key made no reply, and Mr. Dancer walked down-stairs, depositing the key with the warden. He thought he might as well earn that half-crown himself; so, leaving directions to admit Zeba if he appeared, he started off in a brisk canter for Mr. Plimpton.

Hyland looked around his five-shilling apartment. There were two windows looking out on the courtyard. No door except that by which he had entered. The windows were grated, and the door was substantial. There was a notice on the wall: "Smoking positively prohibited." So Hyland lighted a cigar, drew one of the two chairs to the window, took a picture from his breast-pocket and studied it with patient scrutiny.

"It is an eminently wise face," he murmured, "and full of candour. It is strange how it fascinates me. I wonder how it looks when lit up by smiles? I never saw the child smile. Out yonder, it was always muffled up, and I never saw anything but those wonderful eyes. Poor little martyr, how I pitied her! I used to think what a crowning mercy it would be if the child would only die. And now she has emerged from martyrdom and childhood at one bound. What a beautiful face! You can see truth and brave confidence in every line of it. That detective ass carried off the other copy, which I left in the bath. And the negative is spoiled by my clumsiness, and this is therefore the only copy extant. By this light! there is not enough money in England to buy it!

"It is strange, too, that the prediction of my mad friend, Holly, should have faded clean away when I took this picture. If I had been weak enough to attach importance to his foolish prophecy, I could not have selected a better fate than this. The woman does not live who could buy this bit of cardboard, with herself and her fortune. If I could ever entertain matrimonial intentions at all, how easily could this girl take me captive! Glendare says no man can lawfully marry until he has found the only woman in the world whom he could love. There is but one, he says, and when she is found, the orderly march of nature's laws and the stately march of Providence will do the rest!

"Which better endures the test of logic? Glendare's philosophy or Holly's superstition?"

Steps on the stair, and then along the corridor. The key rattling in the lock. He returns the picture to his pocket, and facing around, meets Zeba, who bows profoundly.

"Salaam, sahib!"

"Smoking!" said the turnkey, sniffing the polluted air; "werry well! That's two shillin' more. That's not rent, it's a fine!"

" Here is the florin, friend," said Hyland ; " now get out, if you
please !"

While the old man was shuffling down-stairs, Zeba walked around
the room and examined the walls. Then he drew his sword.

" Will sahib take tulwar," he said, politely, " or Zeba cut down
door ?"

" Neither, my friend," answered Hyland, laughing ; " it would be
a difficult task, and would do no good if successful. But we shall
get out anon without fighting. How did you find me ?"

" Sahib never fight more ?" said Zeba, enquiringly. " Sahib
prisoner, lock up, and fight not? Sahib travel all night to find
Beébe, and sleep not, and then to prison come, because he steal
Beébe! And no fight! Is sahib sick ?"

" Pretty well, thank you," replied Hyland, " but fighting is not
the wise thing to do now. A foolish man with red eyes thought I
was the criminal, and he obtained legal authority to arrest me. If
I had killed him, all the world would pronounce me guilty. If I
wait a short time, I shall be set at liberty by lawful process, and all
the world will know I am innocent."

Zeba struck his weapon into the scabbard by a dexterous motion,
sending it home with a crash. Evidently, he considered England a
semi-barbarous country.

" Man came see Beébe, said have Robinson in Town Hall. Then
I came, ask two men where Town Hall. Man unlock door and let
me in. Ask for Sahib Robinson. Say, all right. Lock me in too!"

" How is—Miss Mordaunt ?" said Hyland.

" Little sick. Lie down. Ask who in boat with me. Say friend.
Not let me talk English. Say Hindoo noble no lie in Hindoostance!
Ask where Sahib Hyland go? I say, London. Ask who took
Beébe away ?"

" Well ?" said Hyland, as Zeba paused.

" Not know. Only think. No tell her my think. Here come
men on the steps."

The door opened, and Mr. Plimpton, followed by the detective,
entered. Hyland sat with his back to the door, his elbow on the
window-sill, blowing smoke through the grating.

" Upon my word !" observed Mr. Plimpton, " you are right,
Dancer. This gentleman is particularly cool !"

" Rather warm day, though," replied Hyland, turning. " Take a
chair, Mr. Plimpton, and fix the bail matter. I must get away from
Clifton to-night."

"Hyland!" said Mr. Plimpton, in blank astonishment. "What the devil are you doing here?"

"Waiting for you. This enterprising friend of yours was quite pressing, and I concluded to come. Your absurd laws make no provisions for fool-killing. Hence he walks over England in safety."

"Where is this Robinson?" said Mr. Plimpton, bewildered, turning to Dancer. The detective pointed doggedly at Hyland.

"This gentleman!" said the lawyer, white with rage. "You miserable blockhead! This is Mr. Hyland Rayneford! Lord Rayneford, for aught I know! Do you go prowling over the country arresting British noblemen, you unmitigated ass? Come in, Miss Haidee. Get out, you red-eyed scarecrow, and undo this mischief as far as you can! Confound you!"

Hyland rose, threw his cigar through the grating, shook Haidee's offered hand, and gave her his chair. Dancer looked from one to the other, blinking his red eyes, while the old turnkey peered through the half-open door in stupid wonder.

"Will you please listen to me, sir?" said Dancer. "I found this gent was the last man that had seen the lady. I found out his lodgings, where his name is Robinson."

Mr. Plimpton looked at Hyland, who nodded his head in confirmation.

"When Mr. Robinson stepped out, I stepped in. I looked about the room a bit, and found this in a basin of water." And he unrolled a picture, handing it to Mr. Plimpton. The lawyer put up his eye-glass, examined the photograph, and handed it to Haidee.

"Oh, Mr. Rayneford!" she said, astonished, "how did you get this?"

"I was about to take the Observatory, the other day," he answered, "you stepped in just on the instant, and—that is the result. I need not say I did not know you. I went to Bath the same evening, met Glendare there, and he told me you were missing and that was your picture. Then I endeavoured to find you."

She took the picture nearer the window and studied it more carefully. Then she offered it to him.

"It is yours," she said, shyly. "I had almost asked if I might keep it."

"Keep it?" said Hyland, promptly. "Undoubtedly you may. I will get a cardboard and finish it."

"It is better as it is," she replied, "if I may have it? You can make others?"

" I can take you again," said Hyland ; " that is, if you desire
more. I was so unlucky as to spoil the plate after taking that.
Nay ! keep it, Miss Haidee. May I enquire, Mr. Dancer, when I
shall have the pleasure——"

Dancer jerked his thumb over his shoulder at the turnkey, who
was in hot debate with Mr. Plimpton.

" Don't know nothin' about any Lord Rayneford," said the turnkey, obstinately. " I only know this man coomed in here with a
warrant, and he cawn't get out until you bring the dockyments !"

" *Habeas corpus !*" said Mr. Plimpton, dancing around the narrow
room in a towering passion. " All the newspapers will have a full
and true account—oh, you blundering donkey !" turning upon the
unfortunate Dancer. " How the devil can you undo this mess ?"

" I can go to the magistrate who issued the warrant," said Mr.
Dancer, " and get it countersigned and cancelled. Say, Sammy,
come down-stairs !"

" Don't stop for a fi'-pound note or so, confound you !" whispered
Mr. Plimpton. " Persuade that old dunderhead to let us out, and
fix the paper afterwards. I would not have this story get out for a
hundred pounds ! What the devil do *you* want ?" turning fiercely
upon Zeba, who had touched his shoulder. The Hindoo bowed,
threw back his cloak, and tapped the hilt of his tulwar.

" Will cut off red head," he whispered, " if sahib say so."

" Who is this, Hyland ?" said Mr. Plimpton, despairingly. " I
vow I cannot decide whether I am awake or suffering under some
infernal nightmare !"

" This is Zeba," said Hyland, " sometime sergeant in Her Majesty's
army ; now honourably discharged with a pension. Colonel Mordaunt will endorse him, no doubt."

The red head was thrust in, and the door thrown open.

" You can all walk out, gents," he said, civilly. " I am sorry if I
have made a mistake in this here business. But I'll swear I was
actin' under orders. And I can show 'em in black and white, too.
And it's a clean loss of five pounds to me——"

" Get out !" said Mr. Plimpton ; " put it in your bill. Come,
Haidee. What are you up to now, Dancer ?"

" Want the nigger with the sword," whispered Mr. Dancer.

" Nigger with sword ! You thick-skulled vagabond ! He is an
officer in Her Majesty's army ! You'd better retire into private
life, Mr. Dancer. At least until you get sober. I'm blest if I don't
believe you'll want to arrest me next !"

The cab took Haidee and her maid, escorted by Mr. Plimpton, to St. Vincent's Hotel. Hyland and Zeba took another cab and drove into Bristol. When the sun went down, Dr. Leigh and Mr. Glendare appeared with Sista, and Haidee's *ad interim* maid was sent to her mother's house, happy in the anticipation of a permanent home at Castle Dane under Haidee's domination, at the end of the month.

"I wonder where Rayneford has gone?" said Mr. Plimpton, when dinner was announced. "I asked him to dine here this evening."

"I saw him in Bristol," said the doctor. "He and the Hindoo were just starting for Cork by the steamer. I did not know the fellow. He is sunburnt and robust, and has a great beard all over his face. He used to be so handsome, too! Poor fellow! He is a perfect scarecrow now!"

"Did he say he was going to Cork?" said Plimpton.

"Yes. By-the-bye, that reminds me. He requested me to present his compliments to you, and he begs you will telegraph any secret agents you may have in Cork, or any other part of Ireland, to let Zeba go free."

"Ah!" stammered Mr. Plimpton. "Yes, certainly. You see one of my men is down here, and the Indian looked so outlandish that he wished to arrest him. No danger in Ireland though. Come, don't let the dinner spoil. Glendare, take Miss Mordaunt. Come on, doctor."

While Hyland was tranquilly sleeping midway the channel, Haidee was examining the Clifton picture in her chamber.

"He did not want it, evidently," she murmured, "and he has destroyed the negative. And he went away from that horrid prison without a word. It is my fault! Oh, yes! He must hate even to think of me. But he never asked for Juliet!

"What in the world has he gone to Cork for? Oh, yes! I know! Isn't it in the paper to-day? Steeple-chase!

"What in the world made him throw Mr. Daltman in the water? Ah! if I could only get Zeba ten minutes!"

CHAPTER XLII.

THE MEETING.

CORK harbour is probably the most beautiful harbour on the Irish coast. The town is not specially attractive in appearance, though there are many points of interest in the neighbourhood. On the morning of Hyland's arrival the town was agog, because of the hurdle races announced for the day, and the hotels were all full. But Mr. Rayneford did not appear to be concerned about lodgings, as he and Zeba went prowling along the docks as soon as they landed from the Bristol steamer. It was high noon when they stepped aboard a schooner, fully a mile from the steamer landing.

"Is the captain on board?" asked Hyland, as a sailor approached.

"In the cabin, sir. Walk aft, please."

"What is his name?" said Hyland.

"Cap'n Scroggs, sir," answered the sailor. "Cap'n! here is a gintleman that would spake wid ye!"

Hyland descended the stairs, leaving Zeba seated on the cabin hatch. The captain was at the little table, copying invoices. Hyland took a seat under the transom, and steadily investigated the skipper.

"So!" he said, at last, "your name is Scroggs, now? It was something else in Calcutta. Captain Scroggs of the 'Ariadne,' now. Then it was Corporal Logan of Her Majesty's twenty-ninth foot."

"I don't remember you, sir," said the other, uneasily; "did I know you in India?"

"Probably not," replied Hyland, coolly, "but I knew you. I saw you when you were taken from the barracks. You remember? Do not be disturbed. I only want some information concerning your later exploits. I know all about your Calcutta history, but that need not be brought to the surface. Please inform me what devil instigated your latest crime? Who employed you to carry the lady off from Clifton Downs?"

"Excuse me a moment, sir," said the captain, rising, "I'll get the papers. They are in my coat-pocket, on deck." And he slipped up the stairs, drew the sliding hatch tight, and was securing the fastening, when he was interrupted by a peculiar sensation in his shoulder.

It was the point of a tulwar that had passed through his shirt-sleeve, and was entering his flesh as he fell back. A capstan bar was leaning against the hatch, and this the captain seized with both hands and raised over his head, as Zeba rose and confronted him.

"Salaam, sahib!" said Zeba.

"What the devil do you want?" said the captain, savagely, poising the bar.

"Open door!" answered Zeba, politely.

The captain glanced around. The Irish sailor was coiling a rope at the foot of the foremast. Nobody else in sight. It was the dinner hour, and the dock was deserted, so Captain Scroggs concluded the time propitious, and aimed a blow at the Hindoo that would have killed an ox. It missed, however, as Zeba leaped aside, and made a deep indentation on the hatch. Before he could heave it up again the keen weapon arose and fell, and the bar was in two pieces, and the point of the tulwar at his throat.

"Open door!" said Zeba, his single eye blazing with ferocity. The captain recoiled a step, and Zeba pushed the hatch open with his foot.

"Sahib, come up!" said Zeba.

"On the contrary," replied Hyland, "the captain will please come down."

There was no escape for him. Throwing the stump of the bar on the deck, he descended into the cabin. Zeba seated himself on the top of the hatch. The Irish sailor, who had raised his head at the moment of the encounter, returned to his rope-coiling when the captain disappeared.

"May I use this paper?" said Hyland, courteously, drawing some loose sheets across the table. "I shall want your signature presently."

"Help yourself!" replied the captain, with surly resignation. "I s'pose you're a bobby?"

"Well," answered Mr. Rayneford, "I flattered myself that I might pass for a gentleman."

"Pooh!" said the captain, disgusted, "you detective swells can pass for anything, by gum! What do you want of me?"

"The lady. Miss Mordaunt."

"No lady aboard."

"But she was aboard on Tuesday night. You arrived here on Wednesday night. And she was not on your schooner. I can have you imprisoned without bail in ten minutes on that simple statement. Who can say you did not murder her?"

"If that is all," said the sailor, "I am all right." And he produced a slip of paper. "Please read that, Mr. Officer!"

"Hum!" said Hyland, copying the paper rapidly. "This will do, though defective in orthography. The signature is probably genuine. Here is your acknowledgment. You will need it, I suppose, to get your reward. Where were you going—I mean if I had not found you? What port?"

"Ostend."

"And when did you expect to sail?"

"To-night, with young ebb. Cargo aboard."

"And you expect to meet your employer at Ostend? Ah, yes! I understand now. Very well! I am disposed to be lenient. Answer my questions truthfully, and I will not interfere with you. What amount did your employer promise for this service?"

"Fifty pound. Twenty down, and thirty more when I produce this receipt."

"Then Linton Sands was already selected as Miss Mordaunt's landing-place?"

"Yes. I'm obliged to split on this here business, by gum! That is, if you mean fair. You won't ask for any names, governor?"

"No names at present," replied Hyland, writing his answer. "Come, man! Tell your story in your own fashion. Tell the truth, or as near the truth as you can. I will not use your confession against you. Zeba!"

"Sahib?" answered the Hindoo, from the hatch.

"Chant a line or two of the Song of the Tulwar."

The captain looked in blank dismay at the inquisitor, while the strange gibberish rolled from Zeba's throat. When the song ceased, Hyland again addressed him.

"Have you heard that before? Passing Milford, for instance?"

"Yes!" said the captain, bewildered.

"Well," said Hyland, dipping his pen in the ink, "begin your story. I will not interrupt you. Go on!"

"He came on board at Bristol, and called me Logan. Never had that name except in Calcutta. Then I knowed as he knowed—what you know. So he told me to keep shady, and earn fifty pounds. Said it was a bet, and no harm would come. I was to go to Clifton Downs with one man to help. I was to take a lot of shawls which he would send. I was to hang around a pile of rocks opposite Hasper Head. At four o'clock there would be a lady walking there. I was to ask her if she was Miss Mordaunt. If she said no, I was to leave her alone. If she said yes, I was to take her aboard any way I could get her. Better tell her the colonel was aboard and wanted her. If she refused—to wrap her up in the shawls and take her, but to treat her gently as possible. Then I was to land her with Tom Jones— I mean at Linton light. He had arranged with Tom. And I must have the schooner off Hasper Head in time. It all happened right. I spoke to the wrong lady first. She was at the rocks, drawing. I asked her if she was Miss Mordaunt, and she said no! So I backed out and left her. She followed us down to the boat, after we had wrapped the right one up, and asked me about five hundred questions. She asked me if this here schooner was a yacht. I told her yes, because it wasn't, you know. Then she asked if Mr. ——, my employer, was aboard? And I told her yes again, because he wasn't. Then she said this was a horrible outrage, and she would scream for help if I did not release the lady. So I got aboard as fast as I could, and she waved her handkerchief at me, by gum ! as we got anchor up. I suppose she put *you* on my track ! Of course she did. No one else knew. But how the devil she got that blacky up there, to overhaul me off Milford—cuss me if I know ! Would you mind telling me *that*, just to relieve my mind ?"

"She never saw him," answered Hyland, quietly; "he got his information from another source. Go on."

"There is not much more. I worried the lady until she insisted on going ashore, and I took her receipt when I landed her. Tom had a room all fixed up at the light-house, and she was going to be took off the same night. Mr.—my employer—was going to get Tom's father for his sailing-master, and he knew all the shallows on Linton Sands."

"And did he appoint Ostend——"

"Yes. He was going to cruise up channel a bit, round by the Orkneys, and then down on the other side. That gave me time to take in my cargo here."

Hyland had written all this account verbatim, question and answer. Then he read it aloud to the captain, who pronounced the record correct.

"Now," said Hyland, "please tell me who else is implicated. I do not mean your employer. But what aid had you ?"

"Only my mate. He is not aboard. I let him go to the races."

"Why did you consent to commit this felony? You certainly knew it was a crime, and a very serious crime. Do not fear to answer. I shall not use this to harm you. Probably I shall not

harm any one; but I must have an honest statement from you. If
Colonel Mordaunt can get his hands on you—well, I suppose he
will hang you! But I prefer hanging the instigator, by this light!"
He wrote down the question as he spoke.

"Well, sir," said Logan, submissively, "it looks like giving him
away; but I am in a cussed hole! You see, he knew all about—that
Calcutta business. And he said he would keep dark about that if
I served him well in this. I am going from Ostend to Havre, and
have a cargo engaged there for New York. And I thought if I
could give him this lift and make fifty pounds, and then get clear
off to the States, it would be a good job. But I made him swear on
the Bible that he meant no harm to the lady! And, by gum!—I
may as well tell it—he swore he was going to marry her before he
took her home!"

"Only one more word," said Hyland, "and I will tear myself
away from your agreeable society. Now I write—look or listen:
'My employer came from Calcutta in the steamship "Lord Clive,"
a few weeks ago, and is an officer in Her Majesty's army.' If that
is not true, write 'No' under it. If it is true, just oblige me with
your signature. I do not ask for any *names*, but I want the truth."
And he handed the pen to the captain, and pushed the paper over to
his side of the table. The sailor held the pen irresolutely a moment.

"Is this all?" he said.

"All."

The other wrote, in a bold hand, "John Scroggs" at the bottom
of the sheet.

"I will have to trouble you to add one of your other names," observed Hyland, courteously. "Suppose you add there, 'otherwise'
—your last Calcutta name?"

The sailor growled some inarticulate reply, which did not sound
like a pious ejaculation, and added "William Logan."

"Farewell, captain!" said Hyland, rising. "It is not probable
that we shall meet again. May I advise you to keep on the sunny
side of the law hereafter? I am not very old, but I have yet to find
a solitary man who prospered in dishonesty. That is a poor argument, I know. But if you will try some of the legitimate pursuits
for which you are qualified you will probably be surprised to find
how pleasant your life will be. Why, man, you may obliterate your
evil record—I mean so far as this life is concerned. And if you
take any interest in another life—I suppose—you had better consult
a clergyman!"

"I flatter myself," said Hyland, as he walked ashore, "that I delivered a very passable moral lecture, though the conclusion was rather lame. Zeba, where shall we go?"

"Has sahib got all he want from captain?" said the Hindoo.

"All! And now I want Miles! Miles! my brother!"

Zeba drew forth his weapon, circled it around his head, tossed it, flashing, up in the air, caught it by the narrow hilt as it descended, threw a cord over a projecting yard of the "Ariadne," and set the tulwar whirling at the end of the string.

"Tulwar alive to-day!" observed the Hindoo. "Have little fight!"

It ceased its revolutions, the point steadily turned down the bay, the direction not changing with the slight vibrations of the schooner.

"Must go back!" said Zeba, with unflinching gravity.

"Back?" said Hyland.

"Yes. Take first boat. No matter where go! Here boat! Much people go on board. Sahib, come!"

It was a small steamer, just casting off from the dock adjoining the berth of the "Ariadne." Hyland, followed by Zeba, leaped on board as the wheels began to revolve.

"Liverpool, sir?" said an official with a gold band around his cap.

"Yes," replied Hyland, somewhat bewildered.

"Get tickets, sir, at this window. Cannot promise a berth. The 'China' is unusually full. You will have to arrange with the purser."

Hyland hardly noticed his surroundings until they passed out at the mouth of the harbour. A black-hulled steamer, with red funnel, sea-stained. A gangway passed from the wheel-house of the small vessel, and a stream of people passing over it to the steamer. Gazing curiously at the strange faces on board, he is caught by the shoulder and waist.

"Hyland! Can it be you?" said a familiar voice.

"Miles!" And the two stalwart men turned their faces to seaward to hide the moisture that welled up from full hearts and showed in their eyes.

CHAPTER XLIII.

A CHALLENGE.

CASTLEDANE was inhabited. The "improvements," which is the name given to the unspeakable horror of house repairs in civilized society, were postponed until later in the autumn. The colonel was regaining health rapidly. Miss Juliet had gone to London to inspect a house recently purchased, and which was also open to improvements. It had been agreed that Juliet should regulate the repairs to the town house, and Haidee should have full sway at Castledane. To cut a doorway through solid stone walls; to fill up a window with masonry, and strew the grounds near the house with rubbish; to make the atmosphere reek with odours of paint, while an army of workmen in soiled apparel infested every quiet nook—these were the pleasant dreams of the gentle improvers.

The party at Castledane was composed of Mr. Glendare and Doctor Leigh; Mr. Plimpton and Mr. Daltman. Haidee was hostess, and on hospitable cares intent. Mr. Daltman, who was assiduous in his attentions, was constantly baffled by incursions of domestics requiring Miss Mordaunt's instructions. He had relinquished his cruise, or rather had postponed it, until he could make up his party. The yacht was in dock at Bristol.

A little time after breakfast, Mr. Daltman was on a camp-stool, under the library window, and he overheard a conversation between Colonel Mordaunt and the lawyer. They were evidently discussing a will, and the listener was stricken dumb by a few words from the colonel, distinctly spoken.

"But Haidee must be specially provided for!" Then the voices sunk into lower tones, and Mr. Daltman lost several sentences. Presently the colonel's voice was raised a little, and the listener caught another announcement.

"But Haidee inherits nothing from me, I tell you! You know she is not my daughter!"

This was the intelligence that confounded Mr. Daltman. And while still bewildered there came a final shot.

"No use to talk about Castledane," said the colonel, positively, "let the law settle that. I have no power to disturb the title, if I would. Give Haidee *all* the consols."

As Haidee happened to approach at this juncture, Mr. Daltman

17

thought it politic to move. He threw away his cigar, and met her on the lawn, and out of earshot of the library. The charming young lady looked smaller and more childlike to Daltman. Heretofore when he looked at her she represented five hundred acres of park and the bulky ruin of Castle Dane, to say nothing of the mansion, which held twenty guests without crowding. Now she had shrunken into the compass of an ordinary school-girl, without even a definite amount in the three per cents. Nothing of her own—and the colonel positively growing younger every day! It was beneficial on the whole, as he could now show disinterested affection. His own fortune was big enough. It was hard though—deuced hard—to think of Juliet taking some chucklehead who should be lord of Castledane!

"I am glad to see the colonel improving so rapidly," said Daltman, as he joined her; "he looks ten years younger already."

"Yes. He shall not go back to India," replied Haidee; "he has promised me that. Just now he is very full of my adventures. He is going to discover the 'marauder,' he says."

"Has he any suspicions?" asked her companion.

"I think not. He sent the detective to Linton Sands yesterday. That dreadful man there drinks, and the detective expects to discover some clue. The vessel went to Cork, and—some one has gone there too."

"What object could your abductor have?" said Daltman, enquiringly.

"Money."

"Has it occurred to you that some one might have seen you, and being carried away by all-controlling passion, ran this desperate risk in the hope of winning you?"

"Oh, no!" answered Haidee, promptly, "that is not a thinkable proposition."

"Thinkable proposition!" muttered Daltman. "Where did you pick up these phrases? You have listened to Glendare and Rayneford, wrangling over some German metaphysics! Anything is thinkable!"

"I suppose," said Haidee, quietly, "that Mr. Scroggs was not a victim to the sudden enchantment you suggest——"

"No. But he may have been employed by another."

"Yes. And the other could not have had very violent attachment to me, or he would not have placed me in custody of Mr. Scroggs! I hope he will not be found! If he is a gentleman, papa will shoot him. If he is not, he will hang him. But Zeba is looking for him, and will be sure to find him. Oh, dear!"

"Zeba!" said Daltman, with a start. "I forgot about Zeba. The black rascal was at the light-house that night! He was with the scoundrel that——"

"Put you in the water?" said Haidee, as he paused.

"I should like to see him," said Daltman, through his set teeth.

"So should I!" This was said in so low a whisper that Daltman only heard a sigh.

"Here comes Glendare," said Daltman, "his eyes blazing through his spectacles. What is up, Hamish?"

Mr. Glendare put a paper in Haidee's hand. "Read!" he said, "here is great news!"

Haidee read aloud: "Liverpool. Hyland Rayneford to Hamish Glendare, George Hotel, Bath. My brother arrived by Cunarder to-day. We go immediately to Hawkley. But shall stop in Bristol to-night. All well."

"Liverpool!" said Haidee. "Why, he went to Cork only two days ago! Does papa know?"

"Yes," said Glendare. "The message was sent out from Bath, and has just arrived. I showed your father, of course, and he sent me for you. This is joyful intelligence, eh, Frank?"

"Um! Ah! Yes, certainly!" said Daltman, looking after Haidee, as she floated over the lawn. "What the devil was she saying about Cork?"

"Oh! You did not know about it?" said Mr. Glendare. "Zeba and Hyland went to Cork to overhaul the vessel that carried Haidee away. 'The Eradne,' or some such name. Hyland found out somehow. He has been prowling about the mouth of the channel with Zeba. The colonel is bloodthirsty. Zeba is a hyena. And Rayneford——"

"What of Rayneford?" said Daltman, with a malignant glare in his eyes.

"Rayneford would not be in Liverpool unless he had finished his search. He probably has the agents of the abductor in prison. From Haidee's account, I judge the man—the miscreant who planned the outrage—must have money. But all the money in England will not buy him off if either one of the three can get at him. And if all three should fail——"

"Well, what then?"

"Then I, Hamish Glendare, will take up the case, and I shall not fail."

Daltman looked with admiration into the eyes of the truculent parson flashing through his spectacles.

"Why, Hamish!" he said, "you look positively bloodthirsty!"

"Consider the provocation!" replied Glendare. "The scoundrel seized and carried away this innocent child, kept her in untold terror two nights and a day——"

"But can you think of no palliation?" said Daltman. "Miss Haidee is no child. She is a most attractive woman. The fellow may be madly in love with her——"

"Love!" said the missionary, indignantly. "Frank, you disgust me! To talk to me of love, when you know this man subjected Haidee to unspeakable horrors. What do you suppose were her thoughts in the thirty hours of captivity? Among rude people, the one woman on the island speaking only an unknown tongue; the man half drunk all the time, and whole drunk generally. The fellow who planned the outrage is no fool, and he must have known all this. Hanging is a mild punishment for him!"

"Mr. Glendare," said Colonel Mordaunt, whose step had been inaudible in the soft grass, "you will go to Bristol to meet the Raynefords?"

"Undoubtedly," answered Mr. Glendare.

"Well! The train is due at six. Bring them directly here. We will wait dinner."

"Dinner at eight," said Haidee, who had followed the colonel. "Take the grey horses. They can do it in seventy minutes."

"And I will go with you!" said Daltman, suddenly. "I want to see about the yacht, anyhow. And, colonel, if the tide serves, I may go down the river. Will you excuse me if I absent myself a few days?"

"Certainly. But you had better wait for a change of wind. Due west now."

"I will decide when I see my sailing-master. I'll get my valise and be ready in five minutes, Hamish."

When the carriage reached Bristol there was an hour to spare. Daltman said he expected to find Mr. Brentam at the hotel. He would look for him and return before six. But he went first to the docks and examined the sailing-master of the "Juliet" respecting tides and winds. The yacht could go out at dusk. Weather good enough. Breeze a little stiffish, but none to hurt. So he left his valise in the cabin. Then he went to find his uncle. Mr. Brentam had just gone to Clifton, and would return to-morrow. Back to the station, which he reached in time to see the colonel's carriage drive away. A gentleman and lady on the back seat. Mr. Glendare and another stranger, an elderly gentleman, on the front seat. Hyland on the box with the driver.

"Clifton, sir? All the way to the Rocks!" It was the driver of the omnibus who spoke. Daltman entered the vehicle and took a seat next a dark-skinned passenger. It was Zeba.

"Hi!" said Daltman. "Is it you, Zeba?"

"Salaam, sahib!"

"Where are you from?" enquired Daltman, scanning the Hindoo's altered appearance curiously. He had his red coat with the sergeant's bands on the sleeve, his white turban, and uniform trousers. The cross straps for bayonet and cartridge-box were wanting, but he wore his tulwar, as of old. "Why, you are in full uniform! Not in the service?"

"Discharged," said Zeba, politely. "But paper say may wear uniform."

"But you cannot wear a sergeant's coat if you are a servant!" said Daltman, rudely. "I suppose you are Mr. Rayneford's servant?"

"No servant!" replied Zeba, gravely. "Sahib Hyland friend, not master!"

Daltman laughed derisively. The omnibus rolled away from the station, following the colonel's carriage. Instead of turning in the direction of Castledane, the carriage took the Clifton road. There were three or four passengers in the omnibus, all of whom got out at the outskirts of Clifton, and Zeba and his ex-officer were the only "insides."

"Have you been to Cork?" said Daltman, when they were alone.

"Yes, sahib. Find Lord Rayneford there."

"Did you find anything else?"

"Sahib Hyland look," replied Zeba, cautiously.

"It was Rayneford who was with you at Linton Sands," said Daltman—"I mean in the yellow coat, the other night?"

"Sahib know him?" enquired the Hindoo.

"Oh, yes! Hi! this is the hotel. Listen! Say to Mr. Hyland Rayneford that I will be at the Observatory, and will wait for him. Do you understand?"

"Yes, sahib. Will tell." And Zeba descended and entered the

hotel, while Mr. Daltman passed on to the Downs. He reached the Observatory, and seating himself on the bench near the building, waited. In a few minutes Hyland turned the corner, walking rapidly, and stopping suddenly before him, bowed.

"What is your pleasure?" said he, coldly.

"Um! That depends. Suppose I say I am your enemy?"

"I hope you are," replied Hyland. "I am certainly yours!"

"Will you fight?" said Daltman, starting up. "Out here by the Rocks, or down in Nightingale Valley. An hour hence. I have pistols in Bristol, and will be punctual."

"I cannot fight *you*, Mr. Daltman," said Hyland, after a pause. "The temptation is very urgent, but I dare not! I should rejoice to kill you, but cannot stain my name. I know everything."

"So much the more reason why I should kill *you!*" retorted the other, savagely, as he raised his clenched hand. "A blow may awaken your courage, curse you!"

Hyland caught his arm as it descended, held him a moment in a grip of such tenacity that he was utterly helpless, then threw him backward upon the bench.

"Heed what I say!" said Hyland, sternly. "You are a base reptile, but your kindred are my friends! To-morrow, if I speak the word, your name will be stricken from the army rolls, and you will be an outcast from all society. I have the written confession of Logan and of Jones, the drunken light-house keeper. I know why you perpetrated this desperate villainy, and—only one other knows, and she has promised to remain silent. Oh, Frank! I am heartbroken about you! I always knew you were horribly selfish and unscrupulous, but you were brave and jolly, and I thought you were a gentleman. I cannot bear to destroy you! God forgive me if I do wrong in this; but I cannot be your executioner. I know the disgrace would kill you. Will you obey me if I show you a way of escape?"

"Yes," said Daltman, with white lips.

"Then take your yacht and disappear! If you cannot cross the ocean in so small a vessel, go to Ostend and join your confederate, Logan. He is going to the States. In a month or two write—to Mildred, and we will send you money."

"And your confessions——" stammered Daltman.

"Shall die with me! I will shield your name for Mildred's sake. Trust me to avert all suspicion from you. I dare not do it if you remain in the country, or in Her Majesty's service."

"Touch my hand once, Hyland. Thank you! I'll obey to the letter. Farewell!"

That night the "Juliet" went to pieces on Linton Sands.

CHAPTER XLIV.

REUNION.

MR. GLENDARE and Zeba were the only occupants of the carriage when it returned to Castledane. The latter received a cordial welcome from the colonel, and an injunction in Pracrit from Haidee to keep within call until she found an opportunity to converse more at length with him. The excuse for the non-appearance of the Raynefords was, first, that Lord Rayneford had his wife and her father in his party; and, second, that Mr. Brentam and his niece were to meet them in Clifton by appointment. It was quite nine o'clock when they left the dinner-table—Haidee to investigate Zeba, on the east terrace, and Mr. Glendare and the colonel to fumigate the library.

"It was a disappointment to miss the Raynefords," observed the colonel; "perhaps we can get them to-morrow. What *is* my lady like?"

"She resembles Haidee somewhat," replied Mr. Glendare, "though rather more robust. She was so shy and reticent that I could not draw her out successfully."

"An American lady, I suppose?" said the colonel. "There must be some romance about this match. Lord Rayneford evidently went to America for her. No other motive can be imagined. Is she thoroughbred?"

"Undoubtedly. Her father is an Englishman beyond doubt, and a gentleman."

"Did you hear his name?" said the colonel, carelessly.

"Yes. Mr. Dale. He is from Somerset, I fancy. What is the matter?"

The colonel had started from the lounge, dropped his cheroot on the floor, and was standing at Glendare's side.

"Did he know you came from Castledane—from me?"

"I think not. I met Hyland first, and he and his brother were busy with luggage. There was a great lot of it. I talked with them while Mr. Dale and his daughter waited on the platform. We drove them over to Clifton, and then came directly back. Nothing was said about Castledane, as I had already received Lord Rayneford's excuses. There was some business with Mr. Brentam that was apparently urgent."

"And you heard no other name but Mr. Dale's?" said the colonel. "Can it be possible——"

"I heard him call Lady Rayneford, Annot." The colonel rang the bell.

"Tell the coachman to—you had the grays, Glendare? Tell him to put his best horse—the dog-cart is best—the dog-cart soon as possible. I am going to Clifton. Make haste!"

"Beg pardon, sir," said the footman, reappearing in a moment. "The dog-cart will be here in a minute. But Sam can drive you to the station in time to catch the up train——"

"Good!" said the colonel. "Haidee, get your hat and shawl—not a minute to spare. And if we catch the train, let Sam drive the carriage to Clifton and bring us back. What hotel, Glendare?"

"St. Vincent's. May I enquire without impropriety what all this means?"

"Keep house for me, my dear fellow, until I return," replied the colonel. "Here is the cart. Up, Haidee! Sixteen minutes, Sam."

"That is three more'n I want, sir," replied Sam. "G'long!"

Zeba crawled in from the terrace, coiled himself up in a corner of the library, and went to sleep. Beébe, who had just begun her investigation when her father's summons called her in, had laid stringent injunctions upon the unhappy Hindoo to wait her return. She had asked him fourteen questions in one sentence, and required categorical answers to each. He had previously been pumped dry by Mr. Glendare during the drive from Clifton. Haidee asked no questions until they were gliding over the iron road on their way to Bristol. They had a carriage to themselves.

"Now, papa," she said, "if you will please tell me where we are going, and what for, I will be very thankful."

"What for, child?" replied the colonel. "Well, first, I am going to look for a niece for myself and a cousin for you. Second, for a brother-in-law for myself and an uncle for you. Lady Rayneford is your cousin, I think—nay, I am sure. It would be cruel indeed if it were not so. Poor child! you have been brought up in ignorance of your only relations. My sister, my only sister, married Mr. Dale. They went to America twenty-five years ago. I went to India soon after, and there was no intercourse between us after our separation. Lord Rayneford found her daughter in America, and has brought her to Clifton, his wife. Glendare only knew she was Miss Dale, and her name was Annot."

"You have never told me about these relations," said Haidee. "I thought we had no kindred in the world."

"And therefore you think of increasing our kindred!" said the colonel, slyly. "You little goose! You thought I would not discover your secret!"

"What *can* you mean, papa?" said Haidee, blushing safely in the dimly-lighted carriage.

"Have you not an admirer, an Indian friend who has developed into a lover? Ah! you don't answer! But I think I have discovered his intentions. In fact, he said to me to-day, in a very sheepish manner, that he thought of marrying!"

"I do not see how that concerns me," replied Haidee, majestically.

"I have no proofs," said the colonel, laughing; "he only said he had an old attachment—there was some obstacle, he said, but he would overcome it in time. But he is too old for you, child! 'I may not win her for some months,' he said, 'but I shall, eventually!'"

"Will he?" said Haidee, in a whisper. "We shall see!"

"He is a good man, Haidee," continued the colonel; "a gentleman of good blood, and with good enough fortune."

"You are very kind, sir," said Haidee, resentfully, "to offer me, especially as he has not asked me——"

"But he has! And you told him your affections were already bestowed——"

"Of whom are you speaking, papa?" said Haidee, in fine wrath. "The wretch! to tell such infamous stories! *My* affections bestowed! Did he enlighten you as to the beloved object, too?"

"Certainly!" replied the colonel, with provoking coolness. "He said it was—but I have no right to betray his confidence. I suppose *you* know?"

"Upon my word!" said Haidee, in white heat by this time. "I don't know, of course, who this well-born gentleman is. But I do know he is a—mendacious coxcomb! *I* tell him my affections were engaged! *I!* Oh, if he will dare to talk such horrid rubbish to me, I'll—make Sista scratch his eyes out!"

"Well, well!" said the colonel, "here is a coil with a vengeance! I only intended to tease you, my dear, and I have raised the devil.

However, be mollified! I promise to give my consent, whichever one you take. What the deuce did he come to me for, confound him! until he had made matters right with you?"

"Please tell me the name of my——"

"I'll tell you nothing!" interrupted the colonel. "Find out for yourself. Here is Bristol. Now for a cab. Come on, you irritable little vixen!"

"I only wished to ask, sir," said Haidee, plaintively, "the name of the gentleman who has won my affections. I don't care about the other."

"Exactly!" responded the colonel. "Now that is the very name I shall not mention. He is a gallant fellow, though, and I believe I like him best. Have your own way, as usual! Here is a cab. Get in! St. Vincent's Hotel, Clifton. How long?"

"Fifteen minutes, y'r honour," said Cabby, as he shut them in.

"Make it twelve, and charge me an extra shilling," said the colonel. "Now, Haidee, if I find my niece,' as I hope, I'll cut you off with a shilling, and that will make two. And then you will have to take my confidant, who has more money than t'other fellow."

"I would not take him if he owned all England!" answered Haidee, hotly.

"My dear, you had better get Leigh to bring back your neuralgia!" said the colonel; "you used to be so sweet-tempered and patient! But since you have been robust your temper has—well—got short!"

"Because I was not beset by fools and story-tellers," said Haidee, promptly. "The Hindoos were not fools, though they could lie quite glibly. But Mr. Daltman——"

"What about Mr. Daltman?" said the colonel, with surprise in his tones.

"Nothing. Except what you have said."

"I've said nothing about Daltman. Good heavens! You did not think I meant Daltman! If he has been courting you—confound him, I'll break his neck!"

"Tell me instantly, sir!—I mean, if you please, who has talked to you about courting me?"

"Well, Glendare! He is Laird of Glendare now, you know."

Haidee sat silent, trying to remember how much wine had been imbibed at dinner. *She* had taken none. Mr. Glendare had taken only one glass of claret. And the venerable colonel had the claret jug at his elbow all the time. But he was drinking beer. He had divided his bottle with her. It could not be intoxication. Then it must be some strange mistake. Glendare! Thirty-five, if he was a day! And he called her "Haidee" and had no more love in his body than a turnip! She would like to laugh out loudly at the mere thought! But—t'other fellow! What wretched inebriate was meant by t'other fellow?

"Clifton!" said the colonel. "Here is the hotel!"

Haidee followed the colonel into the hotel. Then, after a momentary delay, they were ushered up-stairs into a parlour on the second floor. Then the colonel was shaking hands violently with two gentlemen, one fifty years old at least; the other about twenty-five, and like Sir Hyland. Sir Hyland standing apart in the bay-window. Then the colonel embraced a lovely lady, and led her to Haidee, and the lovely lady embraced her vigourously! And everybody was talking and laughing, and weeping a little. And when Haidee recovered consciousness she was seated in the bay-window, with Lady Rayneford's arm still around her.

"Every one of you must go to Castledane!" said the colonel, with the tone of one accustomed to command. "Every one of you, and to-night! Don't speak! I will hear no denial! Dale, there is no roof in England excepting mine that can shelter you. Lord Rayneford, do not deny me, I implore you. Haidee! Why don't you speak?"

"I have cousin Annot here, sir," replied Haidee; "and if she will not go with me, I shall stay here with her."

"But we have a prior engagement," said Lord Rayneford; "I would gladly accept your invitation if I could. But——"

"My carriage will be here in an hour," said the colonel; "we came by train. You certainly have no engagement at this hour. And I will send you back to-morrow. There are only six of us. We will be at Castledane by midnight. You must come!"

Miles looked irresolutely at Annot. Annot looked at Hyland. Hyland was looking at Haidee, who returned his glance with her grand eyes full of imperious authority.

"Why don't you speak, sir?" she said. "I have a quarrel with you, which must be settled at Castledane. Ah! I know some of your exploits!"

"Let us go, Miles," said Hyland, submissively.

"Yes!" said Annot. And Haidee kissed her.

"Make your preparations, then," said Colonel Mordaunt. "The carriage will hold all of us and such traps as you may require. But you will not sleep to-night! I warn you that the whole night will be taken up with questions and answers. Look at the moon, just coming over the tree-tops! The ride to Castledane will be like enchantment!"

"I am a believer in enchantment," said Hyland. "When you have all told your stories I will relate mine. I have stubbornly resisted the occult spell that has led me along until now. And now I lay down my arms and submit. When I go back to India I'll join the fakirs."

"You may safely promise that, Hyland," said his brother. "Colonel, our engagement is with Mr. Brentam, who was to meet us here to-night. But he sent an apology instead, and promises to come to-morrow morning. Some unexpected business took him to Milford this evening."

"Have you seen Frank?" said the colonel to Hyland. "He came here to meet you."

"I saw him only a few minutes," replied Hyland, cautiously. "I think he was going to sea in his yacht. He said so when we parted."

"Did you see him at the station?" enquired the colonel. "Glendare was greatly annoyed because he could not find him."

"No. I met him out on the Downs," said Hyland, avoiding Haidee's big eyes.

"This is a bad night to go out into the channel," observed the colonel. "It is very pleasant on land. But this western breeze is a half hurricane at sea."

"It is possible that he took Mr. Brentam to Milford. Indeed, it is quite probable. His note intimates as much. And if the sea is too rough, they may wait at Milford for better weather."

"Have you any—engagement—for this week?" said Haidee, still watching him.

"None."

"Because I was going to ask you to take your apparatus with you to Castledane. I want three hundred views taken!"

"Ah, if I dared to propose such a thing! But I have all my apparatus in my wagon. And I have a gorgeous pony that knows every foot of the road to Castledane. And the wagon has a great broad seat, cushioned, that will hold three persons comfortably. And the moon is getting higher and brighter every moment. Now, if you two charming ladies would go with me, I would get Tommy ready before the carriage arrives——"

"Done!" said Annot, promptly. "Away with you! We shall be ready!"

" But, Annot!" said Lord Rayneford, " I cannot go in Hyland's trap——"

" No. But you may drive behind us in the carriage."

"Oh, yes!" said Haidee. " Let us go, my lord. It is such a duck of a pony. I know him! Run, Mr. Rayneford, please! We shall be ready."

CHAPTER XLV.

THE PICTURE.

WHEN he parted from Hyland, Mr. Frank Daltman was horribly demoralised. He had been under more or less apprehension for some days previously, but the succinct account which Hyland had announced was far more elaborate than his worst fears. The loss of his status in society, the dishonour that would attach to his name, were formidable dangers, and the only exodus from the impending disaster was just what Rayneford suggested. He must pass away, for a time at least, from the knowledge of all England.

As he turned the corner, coming from the Downs, the omnibus that had brought him from Bristol was just starting on the return trip. He climbed up to the top, and sat in moody silence until he reached Bristol. It was a short distance to the docks. He would go down to the yacht. Entering the handsome cabin, he found his uncle, Mr. Brentam.

"Ah, Frank!" said Mr. Brentam. " I was just writing a note to you. Your man on deck there says you are going to sea to-night."

" I was thinking of it," replied Daltman, irresolutely.

" I have to go to Milford," said Mr. Brentam. " The steamboat has been gone an hour. There is a brig going out presently, in tow of a tug, and the captain says he can land me at Milford, where he drops the brig."

" He can tow the " Juliet" also, no doubt. The wind is against us, but from Milford Haven we have plenty of sea-room. Where is the tug ?"

" The captain is on deck now, at least I left him there a minute ago."

Daltman ascended the stair and found the captain conversing with his own sailing-master. The bargain was quickly concluded, and the delicate masts of the " Juliet" passed under the high bridge while it was still light enough for the Clifton loungers to distinguish her outline. Mr. Brentam was accustomed to a half-hour's nap after dinner, and he betook himself to the starboard state-room, leaving Mr. Daltman in a reverie at the cabin table.

"He will get her, no doubt!" muttered Daltman, "and all my scheming comes to naught. I don't mind Castledane. It is the girl herself I want. If I had taken Milly's advice I should not have been in this mess. Too late! Rayneford would tell the whole story. But he won't get Castledane either. By Jove! I'll write him!"

He drew the writing materials across the table, and dashed off a few lines.

"DEAR RAYNEFORD,—One good turn deserves another. I will give you a bit of information that may be valuable to you. H. cannot inherit the property. She is not the real daughter. I had this from the lips of the colonel himself to-day. You used to hold certain theories about marrying for money. If you still hold them, you can very safely venture to claim the property which you won when we gambled for the two in Calcutta. You remember. You may get plenty of happiness, but very little tin. I tell you this in some small requital for your advice to me when we parted.

"Yours,   FRANK DALTMAN."

He sealed the note and addressed it. When Mr. Brentam's nap was finished, he came into the cabin, and Daltman gave him the letter to mail at Milford.

"Hyland?" said his uncle. "No use to mail it. I shall see him at Clifton to-morrow. I have an appointment with Miles, and Hyland will be with him."

"Very well, uncle," replied Frank. "And please tell Milly I will write her as soon as I land. Do you notice the increased swell? We have gotten well down channel. Milford light must be visible now."

An hour afterwards the tug cast off the brig, and dropping alongside the "Juliet," took Mr. Brentam aboard. There was some bungling over the rope that held the yacht. The brig was getting sails set, and so was the "Juliet," and the two vessels were rubbing their hulls together, and while a lubber on board the yacht was still labouring over the after-line, Frank closed his own cabin hatch and stepped on board the brig. There was no little confusion on both vessels, as the wind was high and the sea rough. The mate of the brig came aft with an axe in his hand and cut the entangled line with one blow. The yacht drifted away, running northwest, while the brig, close-hauled, took a southwest course.

Mr. Daltman sat unnoticed on the quarter-deck another hour. The impulse to leave the "Juliet," without a word of warning, came upon him suddenly. He had a good lot of money in his pocket-book, and could get along several months after he reached America. The brig was bound for New York. What story should he tell?

"Hillo, shipmate!" said a gruff voice at his elbow; "where from, and whither bound?"

"Ah!" answered Daltman, coolly, "where is the captain?"

"Here, at your sarvice!" said the other. "What lark is this?"

"No lark at all, my dear captain. I am Mr. Trelawney, of Brampton, Cornwall. My doctors have sent me to sea. I was going to take a trip in my friend's yacht; but I felt uneasy about her, as she seemed so flimsy when rubbing up against your big ship, that I just scrambled aboard. Left my overcoat and portmanteau, by Jove! In Daltman's cabin, you know. We had been wining just moderately, you know; but my head is not worth a sixpence since I have been ill! It's all right, you know. But lend me an overcoat and tell me how much passage-money you want. By Jove! Cawn't you make this infernal ship stand still a minute?"

"Well, I'm blest!" said the captain, "if this ar'n't a devil of a go! Do you know where we are going?"

"Not in the least, and don't care. You can go to the devil if you like! By Jove! Cawn't you turn the ship around, so the water won't shake her so blasted unpleasantly! Hi! I must get some place to lie down! I say, captain, when will you land?"

"In about twenty-five days, if we're lucky," answered the skipper. "I don't know what to say about this here business. I have no 'commodations for passengers. No stores aboard; no license——"

"Blast the stores and license!" said the passenger, with a hiccough. "Only take me some place where I can lie down! And stop the infernal ship, or the wind. By Jove, what a roll that was! I say, captain, let me have a drop of brandy, will you?"

"Here, mate!" said the captain, "help this gentleman down. Better give him the berth next the china-closet. He has been with another gentleman, and the other one took a little too much wine, and that makes this one sleepy. Mr. Trawny——"

"Trelawney!" shouted the passenger. "Don't call a fellow out of his name!"

"Beg pardon!" said the captain. "Take my arm, sir."

"And here's your passage-money!" continued Mr. Trelawney, presenting a twenty-pound note. "Give me the change when you stop this pitching. By Jove! but that was a jolly good pitch! Where the devil is the bedstead?"

"Step down, sir," said the captain, taking the note. "Notice, mate. He has given me twenty pounds. Get him into his berth. He'll be better to-morrow."

Mr. Brentam was interrupted at his breakfast the next morning by a remark from a gentleman at the adjoining table.

"Storm last night; did you hear the house rattle? Vessel cast away on Linton Sands."

"What sort o' vessel?" said his companion, chipping the end of his egg.

"Yacht."

"Any lives lost?"

"All lost, they say. Found three or four bodies. She must have struck near the light-house."

"Excuse me, gentlemen," said Mr. Brentam, "may I ask what vessel you speak of?"

"Don't know, sir," replied the first speaker; "old Jones came in at daylight. His son keeps the light-house. He has brought some of the stuff that washed ashore."

"Where does he live? Where can I see him?" asked Mr. Brentam. "My nephew went out in his yacht last night, and I am in terrible suspense. Can you direct me to this man?"

"Nothing easier, sir. Tom, show this gentleman the way to the pier. Jones lives near the landing, sir. Any one can point out his house."

The waiter accompanied Mr. Brentam to the door, and pointed out the direction. "Keep down this street, sir," he said, "until you reach the pier. Then turn to the right, and you will see the steamboat dock. Jones lives within a stone's-throw."

Mr. Brentam found the house without difficulty. There was a little crowd about the door, and the men moved aside to give him ingress, and then pressed in after him. Something in his face told them he was interested in the fate of the wrecked vessel, and with that eager appetite for horrors that belongs to rude humanity, they watched for the effect of the story upon him. Jones was relating for the twentieth time his experiences of the past night.

"She was standing no'thwest and by no'th," said the narrator; "too close to the light. I saw her make one tack, but she luffed up too soon. Wind blowing half a gale, and more leeway, because the tide was three-quarters flood. She struck in the worst place she could pick out, on the spit of sand off the light-house. I knew it was all up with her then! You see there are two sets of breakers, part rock and part sand, deep water on both sides, and her masts went at the first knock. The moon was up, and I could see her chopping herself up, but could not get out to her. Nothing could live in that bit of water if the sea had been calm!"

"What was her name?" said Mr. Brentam, pressing nearer. Jones looked up at him, enquiringly, and handed his slate.

"Name of vessel?" wrote Mr. Brentam.

"Name?" replied Jones. "Couldn't see any name. No name on the bits of drift that came ashore. But she looked to me like a craft that was anchored off yonder two or three days ago. Masts too tall and raked too much. Bad rig to claw off a lee shore. I can't say for certain, but it's my belief she was the 'Juliet.'"

"Did nothing come ashore that could be identified?" wrote Mr. Brentam.

"Not much," replied Jones. "A bit of rack with brass hooks washed up, and a coat hanging to one of the hooks. Here it is."

It was a light overcoat made of dark-gray cloth. Mr. Brentam examined it minutely and sank into a chair, pushed forward by a sympathising listener.

"This is my nephew's coat," said Mr. Brentam, in a husky voice. "See, here is his handkerchief, with his initials, 'F. D.' And here is a paper, let us dry it and see. It is a picture. Stop! Don't handle it too roughly; it will unfold when dry. Could not a good swimmer get ashore? Write it on his slate please, one of you."

"Swim ashore!" said Jones, after reading the question. "Not possible! A duck would be killed a thousand times between that spit and the light-house. No man that was on that yacht when she struck was alive ten minutes afterwards! Look at the coat!" and he held up the wet garment and shook out the clinging folds; "it is full of holes and snags, caught as it bounced over the sharp rocks. Remember, the sea was pounding it upon the rocks with rollers ten foot thick! I thought the Atlantic was coming in to drown out the light! The sea washed clean over the top of the tower twice. I saw three or four bodies in the smugglers' channel as I came through this morning, but they were all out of reach. Can get at 'em at half ebb, maybe."

Mr. Brentam went back to the hotel, and telegraphed as follows: "From Brentam, Milford, to Hyland Rayneford, St. Vincent's Hotel, Clifton, Bristol. Come to me immediately. I am in great distress, fearing Frank was wrecked last night on Linton Sands."

During the long hours that must pass before Hyland could reach Milford Mr. Brentam went from the hotel to the pier several times, and at last prevailed upon Mr. Jones to brave the rough sea and look for the bodies of the drowned men. They chartered a tug, as the "Ripple" could not tack in the narrow lane of water, and Jones undertook to steer through the tortuous smugglers' channel. It was in the afternoon when they returned to Milford, with two bodies— all that were left, and both of them identified by a dozen sailors as part of the crew of the "Juliet." Mr. Daltman had hired them a week before, at Milford. The sea refused to give up any more.

Hyland was at the pier when they landed, and met Mr. Brentam, learning from his countenance that he had abandoned hope. They walked silently to the hotel and went up to Mr. Brentam's room. The tattered coat was hanging on a hook, and the picture, nearly dry, was on the bureau.

"Poor Frank!" said his uncle. "By-the-bye, he wrote you just before we parted. Here is the note. Don't mind me! I'll take off my coat and lie down awhile. Sit there at the window, and we will order some dinner presently. That is Frank's coat. It was washed ashore with a fragment of the wreck. When can we go to Clifton?"

"The steamboat will go in an hour," answered Hyland.

"Well, I only want fifteen minutes. Read your note, and see what the poor boy says. I cannot resist this drowsy fit!" And, overcome by fatigue, he was asleep before Hyland mastered the contents of the missive. He read it eagerly first, his heart bounding with delicious joy, then read it slowly and carefully twice more. The fifteen minutes sped away while he sat and pondered, and Mr. Brentam awoke, and resumed his coat.

"We may as well go down," he said; "I will take the coat with me. Nothing in the pockets except his handkerchief. Ah, yes! That paper. Unfold it carefully. Don't tear it."

Hyland handled the paper with great delicacy. It was a picture, and he seemed to recognise it, as he parted the folds. As he spread it out on the bureau, he thought he could feel his pulsations slacken, then stop altogether. The Observatory, a woman's figure in the foreground, with the face upturned. The paper was wrinkled and the picture hopelessly marred, but it was undoubtedly the same that the enterprising Mr. Dancer had stolen from his lodgings.

Mr. Brentam peered over his shoulder, as he gazed silently at the central figure in the photograph.

"Good heavens!" said Mr. Brentam, "can this be possible? It is the Clifton Picture!"

CHAPTER XLVI.

Mr. Dancer.

O N the deck of the "Prince of Wales" the two gentlemen continued their conversation. Hyland had restored the damaged picture as much as possible, and, protected by cardboard, it now reposed beside its duplicate in his breast-pocket. Mr. Brentam was disposed to be communicative, feeling specially attracted to Hyland because of his intimacy with his lost nephew.

"I cannot conceive how Frank obtained that picture," he said. "It was taken when he was a mere infant, and I saw it by—by accident in the hands of the husband of the lady. They were not married then, but very shortly afterwards."

"By this light!" said Hyland, abruptly, "I begin to see through this mystery! Whose picture—who is the lady?"

"She was Miss Mordaunt," replied Mr. Brentam, "the sister of Colonel Mordaunt. She married Windham Dale of Dale's Manor."

Hyland took a parcel from his pocket, carefully enveloped in tissue-paper, which he removed. He handed the enclosure to his companion without speaking.

"Ah, yes!" said Mr. Brentam. "That is she! Annot Mordaunt. Frank's picture is so much soiled that you would scarcely recognise the identity. But I knew it at once."

"This is Annot Mordaunt. Then Annot Dale?" said Hyland, looking curiously at the worn face of Mr. Brentam.

"Yes."

"But the other is not Annot Mordaunt! It is Haidee Mordaunt, the daughter of the colonel."

"Impossible!" said Mr. Brentam. "Colonel Mordaunt has no daughter! Never repeat what I tell you. I *know* he is childless. The two girls are both adopted."

"You know Miles is married?" said Hyland.

"Yes. He wrote me from Queenstown, saying he had brought a Lady Rayneford from America. An English girl, I think he said."

"Her name was Annot Mordaunt Dale," said Hyland. "Her father, Windham Dale, is with her. And Miles has the duplicate of that picture. I have compared them. And she and her father are at Castledane to-day. This other picture I took with these hands, less than ten days ago. It is Haidee Mordaunt. I put that picture in her hands three or four days ago. How Frank got it—— Ah! that is the question! And who can answer it?"

"Poor Frank!" said Mr. Brentam. "You were his friend, and I may tell you. His heart was set on getting Castledane, and I think he cherished a sincere admiration for this young lady. But she could not inherit Castledane! I will tell you another secret. Lady Rayneford is the only woman alive who can inherit that estate. The entail is one of the most curious pieces of legal twisting I ever encountered. But it ends with the present generation. Mordaunt owns it now. But Mordaunt cannot sell a foot of it. I feel impelled to tell you another secret. Some day you may reveal it to Miles. Windham Dale did me a cruel injustice, ignorantly, I believe, but most cruel! I have felt resentful for twenty-five years, but my anger is dead now. I held all the deed he could give to his estate—Dale's Manor. But it was swallowed up in mortgages, and I laboriously strove to clear away the encumbrances from the date of—well, from the day that picture was taken until the day he sailed for America, leaving an insulting message for me. I am not in the habit of parading my motives—you know this. But my sole motive was to perfect his title for—his wife's sake. The foolish man thought I coveted his inheritance. And he was fiery and rash, and Annot was misled by him, and I was too proud to make explanations. Dane Mordaunt knew, but he died in India. I had sworn him to secrecy before I revealed my plans. I had to take possession of Dale's Manor because the claimants, a crew of cormorants, would never come to equitable terms with Dale, a man born to be cheated. It was quite another thing to deal with the owner of Brentam Mills. Remember all this, and do me justice, Hyland, when opportunity serves. Here is the landing. We take the train here."

"Let us go to Castledane, Mr. Brentam," said Hyland, gently. He was deeply moved by the evident distress of his companion, who appeared ten years older since he parted from him in London, only a week or two past.

"Not now," replied Mr. Brentam. "I am going to Somerset tonight. Make my excuses to Miles, and tell him to wait at Castledane for me. And ask Plimpton to follow me to Brentam Villa. I am not equal to any business just now."

Hyland waited upon Mr. Brentam with assiduous attention until his train departed. Returning to the hotel at Clifton, he found Zeba waiting for him, with his photographer's wagon and Tommy. The latter was lazily switching the flies from his flanks, and endeavouring to extract some meaning from Zeba's prolonged discourse, still in his memory. The Hindoo had talked and sung to him all the way from Castledane, and had thoughtlessly confined himself to Hindoostance. Hyland had left Mr. Brentam's despatch for the colonel when he took the train for Milford, and Zeba brought him a reply from Castledane, bidding him bring Mr. Brentam with him, if the latter accompanied him to Clifton.

Going back, sometimes by the highway and sometimes through verdant lanes, Tommy selecting the route, Hyland meditated upon the rapidly moving events of the past two weeks. That picture in Frank's pocket! This was the knotty point, coming back constantly and demanding solution. Did she give Frank the picture? Why not? Frank had rescued her from Linton Sands, and had been in her society ever since. He had been with her on the long voyage from Calcutta. He was a handsome fellow, very brilliant in conversation, and, above all, in the army, though only a subaltern. A man with these advantages and owner of a good estate was entirely eligible anywhere. How could he be in daily intercourse with that lovely girl and fail to love her? Alas! poor Frank did not know what love meant. But Haidee would readily give credence to his professions, and might easily love Frank! "Poor Frank!"

He uttered the last words aloud, and Zeba, who had waited with heroic patience for a word from him, answered:

"Colonel Sahib say Daltman Sahib drown?"

"I fear he was drowned, Zeba," replied Hyland; "indeed, it is nearly certain. His yacht was wrecked, and he was aboard."

"Not drown!" said Zeba, coolly.

"The vessel went to pieces," answered Hyland, looking with surprise in the stolid face of the Hindoo; "and several bodies were found."

"Daltman Sahib not found?"

"No."

"Daltman Sahib not drown," repeated Zeba.

"What do you mean, Zeba?" said Hyland, turning in his seat and facing him.

"Water not drown Daltman Sahib," answered Zeba, sententiously. "If Lord Hyland put him in water, then drown."

"I put him in water? I drown my friend?"

"Not friend! Enemy! Sahib Hyland Lord of tulwar. Tulwar say Daltman not drown. Life belong to Lord Hyland. If he say, Live, Daltman not drown!"

"This is most extraordinary!" muttered Hyland. "Am I never to get rid of that tulwar? Has it told you anything else?"

"Yes," answered the Hindoo, with undisturbed gravity. "Tulwar say sahib lord of Beébe. Sahib want Beébe? Take her!"

"By this light!" said Hyland, the blood rushing to his cheek and brow, "this is perilous talk, Zeba. Have you said this to— any one else?"

"Zeba have no tongue. Sahib call Zeba friend. Friend talk to friend only."

As they rolled along over the smooth road, Tommy putting forth his best efforts, Hyland glanced occasionally at the placid face of his companion. He was eager to ask a dozen questions, but, with the rare delicacy of the thorough gentleman, he shrank from the mention of Haidee's name, since Zeba had so openly coupled it with his own. And Zeba waited with the patience of the true philosopher, knowing that Hyland would renew the conversation, if he gave him time enough.

"The tulwar!" said Hyland, at last. "How does the tulwar tell you—these things? Do you ask?"

"Ask, but not with tongue. Ask with soul," said Zeba in reply. "Tulwar not know language. Not know Pracrit. But know what *mind* say. When mind ask, where Lord Hyland this morning? tulwar say, *Milford.* When mind ask, where Daltman? tulwar say, *out on sea.* Mind know Daltman want fight—want fight Lord Hyland. Mind think Lord Hyland fight *now* when Daltman ask him. Mind know Daltman steal Beébe away. Mind say Lord Hyland kill enemy. Ask tulwar. Tulwar say, *no fight, no kill!*"

Hyland rode silently on, cogitating the metaphysical problem. The acute perceptions of the Hindoo had revealed so many truths to him that it was difficult to think of him as the victim of a superstition so baseless as his faith in the tulwar. It never occurred to Hyland to suspect Zeba's sincerity. And, in fact, sincerity always commands credence. You may doubt the accuracy of statement when you have unswerving faith in the truthfulness of the speaker.

"There are only two entities—matter and force," thought Hyland. "The phenomena of matter are various, but generally scrutable. Force is too vague a term. It may mean the attraction of gravitation. But that may also be a property of matter. It may mean the overbearing power of affection. There is such a thing as mental force. The mind moves the muscles, but the muscles wield the tulwar. Can the mind reach the tulwar without the intermediate agency?"

"When we sail from Calcutta," observed Zeba, as if replying to his thoughts, "the ship go far from land. Cloud hide sun. Cloud hide stars. But ship know how to sail, because little steel tulwar point north. Does captain make tulwar *always* say north?"

"You might as well ask if the miller makes the water run down hill," said Hyland. "Who is this?"

"Red-eye man," answered Zeba.

They were within sight of Castledane, and Tommy, who approved of the stable appliances there, was surpassing himself; nevertheless he stopped when Mr. Dancer stood in the road with his hand up.

"Good evening!" said the detective, with an awkward effort to appear at ease. "I thought I might meet you here, Mr. Rayneford, and I waited."

"Ah!" said Hyland. "I cannot go with you this time. If you have a warrant, produce it, and my friend here will cut off the hand that presents it."

"Pooh!" said Mr. Dancer, as Zeba showed eight or ten inches of steel; "put up your chopper! I have no warrant. And if I had I would serve it all the same, if you had six swords." There was so much genuine pluck in Mr. Dancer's attitude that both Hyland and Zeba were impressed.

"I am willing to own that I made a bad mess of that business," said Mr. Dancer. "But I had three strings in hand at once. I wanted somebody that stole some money. I wanted somebody that stole Lord Rayneford, and I wanted somebody that carried off the lady. I thought you might do for one of the three. But I should not think so now. Cawn't you make some allowance for a fellow who was trying to do his duty?"

"Certainly!" answered Hyland, promptly. "There's my hand! I bear no malice. Will you climb up here and ride? There is room enough."

"Thank you," said Mr. Dancer. "I am going the other way. But if you will get down and walk with me a little way, I'll be obliged."

Hyland threw his leg over the side, stepped upon the wheel, and joined the detective on *terra firma.*

"Go on, Tommy!" he said; "we will follow you. Wait for me at the head of the lane, Zeba."

"I thought I would just tell you, Mr. Rayneford," said Mr. Dancer, snapping his eyes viciously. "You might have played the devil with me about that Clifton thing. But you didn't! Mr. Plimpton is cross as a bear! And I am dead beat anyhow. You swells are a hard lot! May I tell you something in confidence?"

"Yes, if you so desire," answered Hyland; "but I think I prefer——"

"Won't mention names, sir. I thought you had carried off the lady. Now I know you didn't. And I know who did. But he was smart enough to make proof very difficult. I could have got a full confession from Tom Jones, but some cove has been ahead of me, and pumped him dry and then greased him."

"Greased him?" said Hyland.

"Yes. Bribed, or hired, or whatever you please. Any way, I know who did the carrying off, and I suspect somebody else, who has been covering up the tracks. I won't name any names, sir.

"But I've got a bit of news, maybe. And if you say so, I'll tell you and nobody else. It's not against law, for law cawn't reach this case, without extradition papers. And I judge it's a matter for pistols and ten paces, rather than law, any way. The man who stole the lady went down channel last night. I wanted to see where he went, so I turned into a tug-hand. Tug carried an American brig down the channel in the same tow. When I cast off from the brig, I saw a man come out of the cabin of the other vessel, and I watched him. Before the brig got clear of the little schooner that man got aboard the brig. I saw him squat down, while the yacht— I mean the schooner—slipped away. The schooner was wrecked; all hands lost. The brig is south of Ireland now, on the Atlantic, and the lady-stealer is aboard. That's all."

Hyland listened with profound interest. The red eyes snapped once or twice, and then fell into repose.

"Now, Mr. Rayneford, if this news is interesting to you, you're welcome. And we can say quits about that Clifton fizzle. Never did such a Tomfool of a trick since I've been in the force! If you say the word, I'm mum about this business till you tell me to speak."

"My friend," said Hyland, "your discretion charms me. Oblige me by investing this trifle"—and he slipped a twenty-pound note into Mr. Dancer's hand—"in any souvenir you may fancy. And when we meet again, I'll—take your photograph! Good day!"

CHAPTER XLVII.

HYLAND'S PERPLEXITIES.

MRS. HICKS, the housekeeper at Hawkley, had written Lord Rayneford begging him to defer his return a few days, as the "house was upside down." The carpets would be down within a week, and she particularly desired "my lady," to whom she sent her declaration of allegiance, should receive a pleasant impression of Hawkley upon her arrival. There was a postscript, in which she entreated my lord to prevent the return of Master Hyland to India. The letter was delivered to Annot, of course; and Annot—also of course—sought Hyland immediately, and invited his attention to the missive.

He was alone in the library, and Lady Rayneford had a clear field.

"Welcome, sister!" he said, rising and placing her in the luxurious arm-chair he vacated. "Just try this abominable chair! It is a snare of the enemy to put such luxuries in a fellow's way."

"It is quite an innocent luxury," answered Annot. "Bring the other chair; I want some conversation with you. It is a far greater luxury, Hyland, to call you brother! I have longed for a brother all my life!"

There was undoubted pathos in her tone, and Hyland was touched by it.

"My lord longed for you also," she continued. "All the days we were at sea he talked of you, and concocted plans to get you home. How fortunate we are to have you, without the delay of the long voyage! Promise to stay, Hyland. Nothing else will quiet my jealousy! I do not object to the eagerness with which Miles seeks your society so long as I also am within reach."

"Old Miles sent you?" said Hyland, half interrogatively.

"No. We have talked about your return to India, certainly, but there is no conspiracy between us. He says you are talking about the date of your return, and he is greatly troubled."

"Those cinchona plantations!" replied Hyland. "I am enthusiastic about them. Just think of England making her own quinia! And the surveys there are very important. I wrote a paper upon the Himalayan flora while I was at sea, and I got ten pounds for it yesterday. It will be printed next week in the 'Journal of Arboriculture.' You must read it."

"If the cinchona plantations were in England——"

"Would not grow here!" promptly answered Hyland. "You must have suitable climate and soil, and also a special altitude."

"But, if these trees *could* be cultivated here," persisted Annot, "are there other attractions in India for you?"

Hyland sat in silence, meditating, stealing furtive glances at her honest face.

"You wish me to stay," he said, at last, "because Miles wants me. Oh, yes! I know what you would say. You were kind enough to think you would keep me for my own sake. And I don't know how a fellow would feel towards a real sister, but I don't believe I could love a twin sister more than I love you." And he took her hand in his. "And now to show you how sincere my affection is— I am going to tell you the whole truth. I could easily relinquish India. Indeed, the object for which I went out there is already attained. I only wanted enough money to pay Hawkley's debts! Don't you dare tell this! But that was my solitary object. And now Miles has gone and done it for himself! He has made more money by one adventure than I could make in ten years. But I want India now because I have a—an ailment, which won't get well if I stay here. Don't open your eyes in that fashion! It is a mental ailment. I have been reading Kant for two days, and it all seems like rubbish to me! I spent one day over Descartes. It appears to be worse rubbish than Kant's philosophy! Now you know a fellow could not get into that sort of a mess unless there were some serious defect in his mental organism!"

"I am sure I *don't* know!" replied Annot. "I don't know anything about Kant or Descartes. Has any other philosophy attracted you and crowded them out?"

"No!" answered Hyland, with profound disgust. "That is just the trouble! If I had any new theories I should not be disturbed. But I have looked at this thing objectively, and find nothing about it. I try to examine it subjectively, and my mind goes off from the emotional to the objective in spite of my best efforts!"

"If you would only talk English," said Annot, "I might understand you. If what you have just said comes out of Kant or Descartes, I think you exhibit true sanity when you call it—rubbish!"

"By this light!" said Hyland, stunned.

"If you mean to say there is a side of your mental organism that demands other food than pure philosophy—that is sense!"

"Sister," said Hyland, humbly, "you are a stunner!"

"Please tell me what ails you. Perhaps I can aid you. Perhaps I know some things you have never learned."

"Well, then," said Hyland, drawing his chair nearer, "I will unbosom myself. I am bewildered whenever I see Zeba, whose one eye has a glare of fiendish triumph in it whenever I catch his glance. He has done some tricks of legerdemain which defy scrutiny. I am obliged to confess myself floored. Then, a crazy fellow whom I met near this spot a few weeks ago announced a sort of prophecy about the consequences of taking a certain picture. I took that picture, and—the prophecy clings to me like the shirt of Nessus! I firmly resolved to burn the picture two nights in succession—last night and the previous night. But I cannot burn it! And that Mephistopheles of a Hindoo has announced a totally distinct prophecy, which has precisely the same termination. I *know* both prophecies are false; but, by this light! they have taken my soul captive. The only escape for me is India! There, if I get there—if I can tear myself away from you and Miles and—these luxurious chairs —there I should be a man again!"

"Where is the picture?" said Annot. "Can I see it?"

"Heh!" said Hyland, aghast.

"The picture!" said Annot, quietly. "Let me see it, brother."

"That last word does it!" muttered Hyland, fumbling in his breast-pocket and drawing forth the picture. The sunlight coming in through crimson curtains cast quite a glow upon his face as he handed the picture. Annot studied it carefully with undisturbed composure.

"It is very beautiful," she said, at length, "very like, and very innocent. I will keep it, Hyland, and break one of the charms. Or, if you will sell it, I will give you your price for it. Perhaps, if you reduce the affair to a money transaction, it will be still more effective." She laid the picture on the arm of her chair and drew out her purse. Hyland snatched up the photograph and replaced it in his pocket.

"What I tell you now, sister," he said, in husky accents, "comes from the core of my heart! I could love this maiden—oh, how easily!—if I dared. But I dare not, and I must get some thousands of miles of sea between her and me. First, I thought she owned this lovely paradise, and then I found she was not the colonel's real daughter, and thought I might venture to offer myself and my little fortune. Then I found the duplicate of this picture (which I gave her) in another fellow's possession. Then the colonel told me—only to-day—that Glendare—my *friend* Glendare—had hinted his desire to enter the lists—to court Haidee!"

"And have you asked Haidee, or the colonel, or Mr. Glendare, or the other fellow who had the picture?"

"Certainly not! Do you think I am mad? Hush! There is old Miles at the door!"

Annot turned her head and beckoned Lord Rayneford into the room. She took his arm to fulfil an engagement made at breakfast, to walk to the ruin. As she passed Hyland she leaped forward and kissed his burning forehead.

"Oh, you great, overgrown ninny!" she whispered. "Come on, my lord. Good morning, brother!"

"Miles is in no end of a mess!" said Hyland, as the couple sailed out on the lawn. "He has gone and married a regular she-hyena. Poor old Miles! But somehow the little dev—duck, I mean, has comforted me. What the deuce did she call me a ninny for? Who is this?"

Zeba, in white turban and scarlet jacket, marching up from the stables, chanting his favourite ode, and tapping the hilt of the tulwar to emphasize each stanza. Hyland goes out on the lawn to meet him.

"Salaam, sahib!"

"Ram, ram!" answered Hyland. "Where is Daltman?"

Zeba bowed, and waved his hand in the direction of a giant oak that stands upon the wide lawn. Hyland walked down under its shadow, and the Hindoo followed. Beneath the spreading branches Zeba whirled his sword from the scabbard, cutting right, left, upward and downward, and then threw the weapon up, caught it in descent, produced a cord from his pocket, and suspended the sword from an overhanging bough.

"Sahib turn tulwar," said he, with another genuflexion; "sahib think Hindoo play trick. Turn tulwar as sun turn, and ask for Daltman. Not with voice. But ask with mind."

Hyland twisted the weapon from east to west, and as it swung around, Zeba squatted down near the trunk, resuming his chant. Hyland stood by and waited. When the revolutions ceased the Hindoo produced his compass and chart, and spread the latter out upon the grass, beneath the motionless blade. Hyland examined the chart, which was accurately adjusted in accordance with the points of the compass.

"Now supposing all this to be real," muttered Hyland, as he sighted along the blade, "the ship might be at latitude 40, long-itude 20 west. And that is about the locality that was in my mind."

He walked back to the library, and wrote the following note:

"MY DEAR MR. BRENTAM,—I have reason to think your nephew was not on board the yacht at the time of the wreck. We cannot obtain certain information for three or four weeks, but while I do not assert positively that he is alive and well, I have no doubt of the fact myself, and I write this to relieve your mind and to awaken your hope. I am not at liberty to say more, but beg you to trust me, and wait a few weeks for more positive information.

"Very truly yours,   HYLAND RAYNEFORD."

"There!" said Hyland, as he sealed the note, and dropped it in the mail-bag. "This is based upon Mr. Dancer's revelations, of course. Also, upon my knowledge of Frank's character. As for that mummery out under the oak—it was devilish curious, to say the least! What did Annot mean by calling me such opprobrious names? Does she think I should demand categorical explanations from everybody? Why did she offer to buy my picture? There goes Glendare! I'll collar him, by the light!" And he darted out after the ex-missionary.

"My dear Hyland," said Mr. Glendare, "I have been seeking you. Let us walk to the brook. I have something to tell you." And he hooked his arm in Rayneford's.

"Now it is coming!" thought Hyland.

"Hyland," said Mr. Glendare, "I think I shall marry."

"Wish you joy, Hamish," answered his friend.

"But I wish you to follow my example. Give up India and take a wife."

"Well," answered Hyland, "let me see how it agrees with you first. Have you—settled the preliminaries?"

"I decided six years ago," said Mr. Glendare, "but I have been obliged to wait. Now I am a landed proprietor, and am ready to marry. I am building a chapel at Glendare, and shall be Rector as well as Laird. And I look forward to a life of unmixed happiness and increasing usefulness."

"And the lady—whoever she may be? Did she suggest all these plans? It seems to me that I heard you discourse eloquently once about the predestined partner, the one woman in all the world, and so forth. Do you still hold the theory then advanced?"

"Certainly," replied Mr. Glendare, promptly. "There is but one woman in the world that can attract me. If I cannot win her, I shall not try to win another."

"Win?" said Hyland. "Are you not secure? Have you been six years courting without any token of success? What the—deuce do you mean?"

"I am not exactly certain," replied the Scot, "except upon general grounds. I know there is no doubt about my choice being made, or about its finality. And I believe when an honest man reaches this conclusion he assumes a sort of proprietorship over the woman he loves. But she has had a passing fancy for another—and she is just now distressed about Frank, and I cannot be very urgent on these accounts. She was fond of Frank."

"And he was the other fellow?" suggested Hyland.

"No—that is—I think not. I thought it might be Mr. Hyland Rayneford."

"Hamish," said Hyland, reddening, "where did you get that insane idea?"

"I took occasion to tell her that your affections—if you had any —were elsewhere placed——"

"The devil you did! Excuse me, and proceed."

"Oh, I did not violate any confidence. She and I were vying with each other in sounding your praises. I told her some things in your favour which she did not know, and she told me many that I did know. Her chief theme was your unvarying, unselfish kindness. And we agreed that she would be a happy woman who won your love. And at this point I merely suggested that you were, perhaps, nay—probably—about to——"

"Would you mind," said Hyland, white with rage, "would you be so kind as to arrange the matter for me? You know so well all my attachments, preferences, and virtues, that you can manage far better than I could."

Mr. Glendare was near-sighted, and did not discover his friend's heat.

"Arrange for you!" he answered, drawing away his arm indignantly. "Certainly not! If I did not think you were joking, I believe I'd knock you down! You great long-legged ninny! Have you not enough pluck to state your own case? However, I am glad you said it. I'll tell Mildred to-morrow. Every word, you vagabond!"

"Mildred?" said Hyland, confused.

"Yes, Mildred! Ah, here comes Haidee and the colonel! Take Haidee off, there's a good fellow! I must have a private talk with the colonel."

CHAPTER XLVIII.

To Brentam Mills.

"MILDRED CAREY, Brentam Mills, to Hamish Glendare, George Hotel, Bath. Uncle is very ill. He has asked for you and the Raynefords repeatedly. Please come immediately. The carriage will be at station two twenty."

This document, presented to Mr. Glendare by a telegraph messenger, interrupted the party at the moment of the colonel's arrival with Haidee.

"The Raynefords?" said Hyland, when he read the despatch. "That means Miles and me, certainly. Eleven o'clock. I will find Miles. Get ready, Hamish." And he started at a brisk pace for the ruin.

"Better take Annot, too," he thought, as he approached the old castle. "It is highly probable that he will ask for her. Besides, Miles will not willingly leave her. Wonder if we might take Dr. Leigh? Ho, Miles! Where are you?"

"Here!" answered Lord Rayneford, emerging from the great hall, his wife on his arm. "What is up, Hyland?"

"A despatch from Miss Carey, saying Mr. Brentam is seriously ill, and calls for Glendare and us." And he handed the message to Miles.

"The Raynefords?" said Annot. "That includes *me*."

"Undoubtedly," answered Miles. "Two twenty. That is at Taunton. She will send the carriage. We must leave Bath at noon."

"And sister Annot will require three hours——"

"I do not require three minutes, sir!" answered Lady Rayneford, indignantly.

"Take my arm also, sister dear," said Hyland, "and be pacified. My first thought when I read this message was, 'Annot shall go also.' So you will see dear old Hawkley 'upside down' after all. Poor old Miles!"

"What ails him?" said Annot.

"Married!" answered Hyland. "That answer covers everything. No will of his own. No liberty. No remnants of affection for his own kindred. A bond-slave! He has to go plodding through the damp grass just to wait on his wife. Look at his boots!"

"And tied to an obstinate, whimsical brother!" added Annot. "He cannot cast him out of his affections if he would. But he cannot make the least impression upon this brother by precept or—example. Headstrong and wilful!"

"You called me a ninny!" said Hyland, reproachfully.

"I will apologise when you do better. And now excuse me three minutes. My lord, do we return to Castledane?"

"Without doubt!" answered Haidee, suddenly appearing at the window. "How could you ask such a question, Annot? You would not be cruel enough to leave us in this abrupt manner? Lord Rayneford, why don't you answer?"

"Certainly!" said Miles, confusedly. "That is, Annot, Mr. Dale will be here——"

"And I am coming back, if the roads are not impassable," said Hyland.

Zeba stalked majestically up as the carriage approached.

"Will sahib take Zeba?" he said, addressing Hyland.

"No," replied Hyland, in defective Hindoostanee; "abide and guard those I love." And he remembered that Haidee understood the "lingo" as he saw her face disappear from the window. He did not see the warm hue that overspread her countenance, as the wall of the mansion was about two feet thick, and she had withdrawn below the window-sill.

"'Ninny' was the correct word, by this light!" muttered Hyland, as he entered the carriage. "What will she think of that speech? I should apologise, but what could I say? I might tell her I did

not mean her, but that would be uncomplimentary. Moreover, I
fear it would be a lie as well. I cannot get out of this uncomfortable mess any way, except by going to India. I vow, I wish my
leave had expired! And I fear that is mendacious also."

"What are you saying, brother?" asked Annot, politely.

"I? Oh, nothing. Do you see how beautiful that hedge is? I
am going to photograph this view when we return."

When they reached the station a shilling to the guard secured them
a compartment in which there were no other passengers, and they
were duly locked in. As he closed the door the guard whispered
Hyland:

"If the lady don't object, you gents can smoke, if you like. Nobody will disturb you. Taunton, sir? Yes, sir. Two twenty."

"Smoke!" said Hyland. "Of course not! It would be brutal!
Sit here by the window, sister. Get over on the other side, you two.
I have something to say to Lady Rayneford which you should not
hear."

As the train glided along through the beautiful scenery of Somerset,
Annot was busy with questions. The name of each striking object
was recorded in her note-book, the local histories, all familiar to
Hyland, were stored away in her memory, and the first hour of the
journey slipped rapidly away.

"By-the-bye," said Annot, "you said you had some remarks to
make. I am all attention."

"But I meant my remarks to be replies to yours," answered
Hyland, sheepishly. "You terminated our interview this morning
rather abruptly. Can you not resume your discourse where you
left off?"

"What did I say last?"

"Only that I was an overgrown ninny!" said Hyland, with an
injured air.

"Ah! Well, I will amend that," replied Annot. "I should
have said 'milk-sop.' Have you talked with Mr. Glendare?"

"Yes. And he says he is going to marry. He has been meditating the fatal step six years. And now he is ready. All smooth
and methodical. He has talked with the colonel, and with me——
By this light! Maybe it was confidential. I really never thought
of that!"

"Never mind, brother," said Annot, "you are a good boy now.
Do you think Mr. Glendare has proposed and been accepted?"

"What a stunner you are!" answered Hyland. "No. I don't

think he has been accepted. In fact, I think the lady has been
troubled with a—what do you call it? Oh, a prior attachment.
And Glendare thinks I am the favoured Adonis. I happen to know
it is another fellow! In either case I am like the poor little Johnny
in the nursery song, id est, 'out in the cold.' Don't you see how
clear the case is?"

"Yes, I see," answered Annot, quietly. "Pray tell me, how
much do you love Haidee Mordaunt?"

"How much?" said Hyland, his face aflame. " I dare not say
I love her at all! Do you suppose I am going to whine after a
woman who gave that Clifton picture to the other fellow——"

"Gave WHAT!"

"The picture. The Clifton picture! I made it; did I not tell
you? I gave her a copy of that you saw this morning. There
were only two."

"The Clifton picture!" said Annot. "Brother, I am going
to tell you something in strict confidence. Before Miles—spoke
to me—over there in America—he found a picture in the hands
of another gentleman. The only name it ever had was the
Clifton picture. My lord, please lend me the Clifton picture a
moment."

Miles felt in the inner pocket of his waistcoat and drew forth a
locket, secured by a bit of ribbon to his button-hole. His wife took
it, touched a spring, and gave the locket to Hyland, who examined
the portrait with increasing astonishment.

"Miles thought it was mine. So did—the other gentleman. But
the latter took it secretly, and sent it back to me—from the grave!
Sent it by your brother's hand! And he—drew back from me—
just as you do now from Haidee, because he thought I had given
this locket to the other. It is my mother, you know."

"Do you know, Annot," said Hyland, at last, "that you are telling impossible things? If I were to describe such a coincidence as
this, and print the description, the whole civilised world would sneer
at the madness of such an imagination! And to add to the vast
mountain of improbability—see! here is the duplicate of your picture. I obtained this from the lunatic who uttered the prediction
of which I told you. Oh, this is too absurd for discussion! Tell
me the rest of the story."

"There is not much more," answered Annot, blushing. "My
lord was very gentle and sympathising, and somehow—he discovered
that I was not disconsolate—even as you might discover—you poor,

blind mole!—that Haidee is not disconsolate, and then——— That
is all!"

"Ninny, milksop, and mole!" ejaculated Hyland. "Suppose you
were a man, and had a preference—or a growing attachment—or
some humbug of that sort, do you think you would be quite content
to have your beloved object giving her picture to another fellow?"

"I think I should ascertain the facts before I did anything,"
answered Annot.

"How can I ascertain the facts, sister?" said he, plaintively.

"Ask Haidee!"

"Heh! By this light! you cut the Gordian knot with a vengeance! Don't you see how promptly Haidee would recognise my
—my liking for herself? Do you recommend me to go whining
after another fellow's woman? Not I!"

"I have no patience with you!" said Annot, viciously. "Oh, if
a man were to come courting me in that half-hearted fashion, I think
I'd———"

"What?"

"I'd set the dogs at him!"

"I shall ask Miles to tell me, circumstantially, how he courted,"
said Hyland. "It is a grand thing to have the benefit of another
fellow's experience. It cost poor Miles enough, too. Ah! when we
were boys it was said Miles was sedate, demure, proper, placable,
cautious, and good; while Hyland was impulsive, headlong, quar-
relsome, passionate, and utterly reckless. Now behold the contrast!
That quiet-looking fellow over there in the corner just shut his eyes
and plunged headforemost into a sea of trouble. And I am proceeding with careful steps, not only to save myself from disappointment and humiliation, but also to save a darling little woman from
pain, or annoyance at least. I'll ask him how he courted you, by
this light!"

"If you dare!" said Annot, menacingly—"if you dare speak on
the subject, I'll write Haidee this evening!"

"Mum is the word, sister!" said Hyland, horror-stricken. "Mum
on both sides. I won't ask a question; and if Miles should volunteer to tell me, I'll punch his head. It would be an agreeable varia-
tion to him, though, to exchange that terrible tongue for a regular
pounding!"

"What tongue, sir?"

"Glendare's!" answered Hyland, promptly and mendaciously.
"Don't you see how he is talking Miles to death. What a splendid

fellow Miles is, Annot! It is a bad business to destroy the usefulness of a man like Miles! Why, he used to go to London to read
papers on no end of topics, and was an active member of three or
four stunning societies. But now! Othello's occupation's gone!"

"What misfortune has overtaken him?" asked Annot, looking
proudly at her handsome lord; "he looks quite well. If he were
troubled by some unsolved problem affecting his welfare or happiness, it is not probable that *he* would go moonstruck and moaning
to India!"

"Indeed?" said Hyland, with a grim smile. "But notice how
snubbed and subdued he looks. If you had known him in happier
days——"

"Be quiet, sir! You are trying to provoke me, but you fail.
Ah, brother! I am not going to meddle with your affairs at all.
Because I know your excellent sense will deliver you from all perplexity. Just now you are jealous and sensitive, but I am not disquieted. A little time, a favourable opportunity, a word or two of
explanation—— What are you going back to Castledane for?"

"I—I left my things there!" said Hyland, startled by the abrupt
question. "Besides—who said I was going back?"

"You did! You said you would go afoot if necessary. You
can send for 'your things.' I can send for mine. You only had a
portmanteau. Why did you leave it?"

"I have plenty of things at Hawkley," he answered. "What is the
use of encumbering one's self with luggage? But I have my wagon
there, and Tommy, and Zeba."

"Zeba can drive Tommy to Hawkley and Tommy can draw the
wagon. Your excuse is absurd! You are going back to see Haidee!"

"Hush!" said Hyland, anxiously, "those fellows will hear you.
Have your own way! I'll contradict you no more. I'll go back to
Castledane, and if you will write down what you wish me to say—
I'll say it, by this light! You might be satisfied, though, with ruling
Miles with a rod of iron, and let me off! See here, sister. On
honour, now! Do you think if all should turn out right, and I
should get that little angel—do you think she would be as relentless
a tyrant as—as some other married women?"

"How can I tell? I have never known any tyrannical wives!
Hyland! Look at that lovely view——"

"Bother the view!" was the rude rejoinder. "Now talk seriously
a moment. I am willing to admit the spoons——"

"Spoons?"

"I mean the tender emotions, sister. But you seem to think I might properly enter the lists against Glendare. Now suppose I could win in such a contest? Can you counsel me to destroy the happiness of my friend? Could I be happy with her, if I thought Hamish was dying for her?"

"Suppose you were dying for her yourself?"

"Well—suppose I am? All the philosophy I know culminates in one postulate, to wit: he who secures the happiness of another by self-denial gains a great good at a small price. You may prove the postulate by reversing the proposition. Consider how much you could enjoy a blessing gained at the cost of another's misery! You will not find this set down in the books. But I know it is true."

He looked so handsome as he spoke, that Annot gazed with admiration at his animated countenance.

"Here is Taunton!" said Hyland, "and there is John. Hi! John! How is your master?"

"Dead, Mr. Hyland," answered the footman. "Apoplexy, sir."

CHAPTER XLIX.

The Will and Letters.

THE travellers found Mr. Plimpton at Brentam Villa. He had been with Mr. Brentam since his return from Milford, and had drawn his will. The attack was quite sudden, and Mr. Brentam died a few minutes after the arrival of the physician. He had been greatly depressed, though he made no complaints, and his appetite was very good at breakfast. He walked from the table into the library, and there Mr. Plimpton found him speechless. He rallied only once, and asked for "the Raynefords and Hamish." These were the only words he had spoken.

Lady Rayneford suggested the propriety of going immediately to Hawkley, leaving the gentlemen at Brentam Villa, if Miss Carey desired their presence. This proposal was communicated to Mildred, who sent a return message, begging the guests to remain, and requesting Lady Rayneford's presence in her chamber for a short time. Annot went in prompt response to this invitation. Mildred was dressed, and met her visitor at the door, placed her in a luxurious chair near the window, removed her hat and shawl, and took a seat near her.

"It was kind to come," she said, "and I hope you will remain a few days. I have no one to talk to me, and suffer more from loneliness than anything else. Uncle died very suddenly, but he did not seem to be in pain. Apart from the shock, which has unnerved me, I think I could be thankful that he departed so quietly. The doctor says he certainly did not suffer from the first attack."

"If my presence will comfort you, Miss Carey——"

"Please call me Mildred—I seem to know you, and I am sure I desire your friendship. In such a time as this we may dispense with forms. I should like to call you Annot, if I might."

Annot leaned forward, put her plump arm around her neck and kissed her. Mildred hid her face on her new friend's neck a few minutes, and when it reappeared it was quite serene. The two women looked steadily at each other as they talked. Annot knew this was the woman who had first attracted Miles, and Mildred knew the extent of Annot's knowledge. Miles, the outspoken, honest gentleman, would never have proposed to another woman without telling of his previous admiration for her. And with the clairvoyant perception of her sex, she saw the thoughts in Annot's mind.

"Lord Rayneford has been so dear a friend," said Mildred, "that I am more than ready to love you for his sake. We were children together, and he has always seemed like a brother to me. Uncle was very much attached to him also; and since he learned your name, he has charged me more than once to cultivate your friendship when you got settled at Hawkley. I am sure he had a presentiment of approaching death. My cousin Frank—— What is it, Mary?"

"Letter, mum," said the maid. "Mr. Plimpton said you had better open it."

"It is from Bath," said Mildred, "and looks like Mr. Rayneford's hand. I will see if it is important, Mary." She broke the seal, read the note with close attention, and after meditating, dismissed her maid.

"Tell Mr. Plimpton it contains only private matters, and I will keep it." When the girl closed the door, Mildred gave the letter to her companion. It was Hyland's note to Mr. Brentam, asserting his confident belief in Daltman's safety. Annot read and returned it to Mildred.

"What do you think of it?" asked Miss Carey. "It is very strange! I cannot see the possibility of Frank's escape."

"If Hyland says so, it is certainly true!" replied Annot.

Mildred looked at her enquiringly.

"I mean," said Annot, "that Hyland would not say so much—would not speak so confidently, with all his caution, unless he had nearly positive proof. Your cousin is alive."

"You have not known Mr. Rayneford long," observed Mildred, "yet you have exactly described him. I have known him many years, and never knew him to be guilty of even those small deceits that are generally permitted in polite society. The terrible calamity of Frank's death overwhelmed me far more than the later bereavement. I am quite able to go down, I think. I am eager to ask Mr. Rayneford——"

"Come, my dear," said Annot, rising; "they are all in the library."

"Not in the library!" said Mildred. "Do you go down, my lady——"

"I thought we had agreed to be Mildred and Annot——"

"Annot, dear friend, please go down and take them to the drawing-room. I will follow in a moment."

She was met at the foot of the staircase by Glendare and Hyland. They walked in the hall, talking chiefly about Daltman until Lord Rayneford joined them. They met again at dinner, later in the day, and the gloom that overhung the household was perceptibly lessened. Mr. Plimpton announced that special reasons made it proper for them all to remain at Brentam Villa until after the funeral. He telegraphed for Mr. Dale the same evening, and the next day brought that gentleman to Taunton, where the carriage was sent to meet him.

Lady Rayneford thus became known to all the families in the vicinity of Hawkley, who assembled at Brentam Villa on the day of the funeral. The formality of introduction into this society was a very slight ordeal under the circumstances, and the shy young bride was astonished to discover how closely the gentry of Somerset resembled the cultivated people she had known in her birthplace. After the funeral ceremonies were over, the household, with a few near neighbours, were summoned to the library to hear the will of the deceased gentleman.

There was a list of legacies to the servants of the household, to some of the older operatives at the mills, and to one or two personal friends. Then came the first important item, bequeathing to Miles,

Baron Rayneford of Hawkley, the sum of thirty thousand pounds, represented by certain mortgages upon the estate of Hawkley, all of which had become the property of the deceased by purchase from the original holders. The last transfer had been made at Milford only a week before.

Item: To Miles, Baron Rayneford of Hawkley, certain moneys now in his hands, being the undivided proceeds of a joint investment, amounting to forty thousand pounds or more, and which his executors were directed to assess upon the accounting of the said Baron Rayneford of Hawkley.

Item: To Annot Mordaunt Dale Rayneford, Baroness Rayneford of Hawkley, all that parcel of land known as Dale's Manor, adjoining the lands of Brentam Mills on the east, and consisting of sixteen hundred acres, more or less. The possible imperfections in the title to this estate would all be removed by a deed from Windham Dale, Esquire, gentleman.

Item: To Windham Dale, Esquire, gentleman, ten thousand pounds in the three per cent. consols.

Item: To the Honourable Hyland Rayneford of Hawkley, two hundred shares of the capital stock of Brentam Mills, with the request that he would give his personal supervision to the finances of that property so long as he held said stock.

Item: To Mistress Mildred Carey, spinster, presently residing at Brentam Villa, all the residue of his estate, real, personal, and mixed.

Hamish Glendare and Hyland Rayneford were appointed executors.

The effect produced by the reading of this last testament was very curious. Mildred was the only one of the listeners who heard Mr. Plimpton's monotonous sentences with composure. Lord Rayneford was burning with indignation at the thought of having this load of money thrust upon him without his knowledge or consent. His wife, who had a vague idea that Dale's Manor was the rightful inheritance of her father, was indignant at this transfer to her of the very estate he was preparing to take by litigation. Mr. Dale was disquieted because the legacy of ten thousand pounds was appended to the bequest to Annot, as an apparent equivalent for his signature to the imperfect title-deeds. Hyland sat quiet, like a true philosopher, and thus cogitated:

"That lot of tin was intended for Frank. Mr. Brentam left it to me because he thought Frank was drowned. Now, I shall just pass it over to Master Frank as soon as he returns to England, and in the meantime I'll let Hamish do the executor work."

These meditations were interrupted by Mr. Plimpton's announcement that a private letter had been written by the deceased to each of the legatees, and confided to him for distribution. Producing the letters, he folded the will and bowed, dismissing his audience.

"You all know my address in London," he said, "and can apply to me for copies of this will, or for any information relating to the estate. Miss Carey, I must be in London to-morrow. Will you please send me to Taunton at the proper time?"

The shutters were all opened, and the signs of mourning all disappeared, excepting the black habiliments of the mistress of the house. Lord Rayneford and Annot withdrew to the bay-window and read their letters.

"My dear Miles," ran the first epistle, "you would not be surprised at my will if you had known my thoughts since your boyhood. I have watched your career with great interest, and, with Mr. Plimpton's assistance, I have gradually got possession of all the claims upon Hawkley, for the sole purpose of leaving your inheritance clear at my death. If I had announced this to you when you were younger it is possible that you would not have acquired your conservative habits, even if you had been willing to accept the legacy. But you will have no such scruples in taking the gift from me when I am in the church-yard. As for the value of the 'Nellie' and her splendid success, *that* is all due to your discreet management, except the original outlay, which was very moderate. I may add— but you will find that in your wife's letter. I shall not see you again, even to welcome you to English shores, as I cannot mistake the frequent warnings that betoken my approaching death. Take the gifts, my friend, without reluctance, and my blessing with them."

Annot's letter was shorter:

"My dear young lady, you are dear to me for your mother's sake, and also for the sake of your gallant husband. I leave your father's estate to you instead of to him, as I at first purposed, because I bought it for your mother. You will find an old will, cancelled by this last one, in which Dale's Manor is given to Annot Mordaunt Dale. The title is not so clear as it might be, but no one except your father can contest it. I have given Rayneford the proceeds of the sale of his vessel, because his adventurous expedition in the 'Nellie' ended in his marriage with you. There is no man in England to whom I would so gladly give you. There is no woman in the world whom I would so gladly welcome as his wife as Annot Mordaunt Dale."

Mr. Dale's note had neither address nor signature. It was as follows :

" The thousand pounds sent to me by Mrs. Dale on the day of her marriage was in excess of any debts due me from her husband. I did not return it because I could not properly answer the message that came to me with the money. But I invested the sum, and added its accretions year by year, and the ten thousand pounds left by my will to Windham Dale is the same money and its gains."

Hyland's letter was the longest :

" I know very well, Hyland, what your thought will be when my will is read in your presence. You will immediately conclude that you owe this gift to Frank's death. But you are mistaken ; I should have made the same disposition of this stock if Frank had been alive. And now I will give you my reasons, if my strength holds out while I write.

" There are only three hundred and ninety-five shares of the stock, and I retained these two hundred, which is rather more than half, in order to keep control of the property. Two hundred shares elects the managing director, and my earnest desire is to have you in that position. There is no salary and very little responsibility, but there is plenty of occupation. Your duty will be to supervise the financial operations of the corporation. You cannot transfer this duty to another. The managing director is instructed and required to audit all accounts, to authorise all outlays of money, and no indebtedness that binds the property can be incurred without his signature. Your pecuniary rewards must come from the dividends upon the stock.

" I have spent a long life in bringing Brentam Mills to their present condition. And this property has taken the place of kindred in my affections. It would be a sore thought to me if I could imagine these vast interests going to decay or loss through mismanagement, neglect, or dishonesty.

" With the exception of twenty shares, belonging to Mildred, all the rest of this stock is held by people in moderate circumstances. A large part of it is held by widows and minor children ; sometimes five shares, and sometimes only one or two, form the sole source of revenue to helpless families. The charter provides that no share can be sold or transferred except with the consent of the managing director, who always has the right of purchase *first* at the offered

price. I need hardly tell you that I have always bought any stock
that was offered for sale, sometimes with, and sometimes without
competition. But I have never held such purchases a day. Because
I have a list of applications for any of the stock that may be for
sale, and I have selected the new owners from this list according to
my best judgment.

"Hyland, I leave this trust to you. There are sixty-one owners
of the stock—nearly all of them sustained by its dividends alone.
These sixty-one represent fully fifty families—all of them in
Somerset. The chief occupation of my later life has been to conserve their interests. Do you think I could have left this burden
upon poor Frank? And if I had, do you think he could have met
the responsibility?

"The dividends upon this stock have been uniformly twenty
pounds per share per annum, and there is a steadily increasing sur-
plus, which will be divided some day. Your income will therefore
be four thousand pounds, if you keep up the prosperity of the mills.
I would gladly pay you that salary, if I could live and watch your
management. Farewell, Hyland.

"Affectionately yours, H. BRENTAM."

CHAPTER L.

THE OVERCOAT.

MILDRED consented to spare Lady Rayneford two hours the
next morning to drive over to Hawkley, "just to get one
look." Lord Rayneford was obliged to escort her, of course, and Mr.
Dale begged permission to accompany them, to revive the memory
of scenes he had not looked upon for twenty-five years. Glendare
and Hyland, in their official capacity as executors, were to spend the
two hours over the private papers of Mr. Brentam, assisted by Miss
Carey. They had opened the iron safe in the library, and were
seated around the centre-table, deep in the investigation of title-deeds
and certificates, when the carriage bore the others away.

"Hamish," said Miss Carey, "there will perhaps be no more
favourable opportunity than the present to tell you certain things
which you must know."

" Allow me to walk down the garden," said Hyland, rising. " I am hungering for a cheroot."

" On the contrary," said Mildred, "your presence is needed. There are gaps in my story which you must fill. It is about Frank."

" I really know next to nothing——"

" Do not waste valuable time, Mr. Rayneford, please," said she. " You know far more than you will tell. But we three must act in concert, and there should be entire confidence between us." Hyland resumed his seat.

" Hamish, I think Frank undoubtedly carried Miss Mordaunt away in his yacht. I saw the yacht, and saw her taken aboard——"

" No, you didn't !" said Hyland. " Excuse me, but the yacht was at Milford that evening."

" But the man told me it was a yacht——"

" Yes," said Hyland. " And he told me afterwards that he had lied to you."

" I think, Hyland," observed Mr. Glendare, with crisp gentleness, "you had better allow Mildred to tell her story without interruption."

Hyland stammered an apology and subsided.

" Frank told me he was bent upon a desperate venture, and asked for my aid. He would not give me any hint of his purpose, but promised that no harm should befall any one. I consented to meet him on Clifton Downs, where Miss Mordaunt would be found at a certain hour. I had never seen her, and did not know it was she that the men seized until it was all over. One of them asked me if my name was Mordaunt, but this did not occur to me until they were bearing her off. I think I threatened them, but they paid very little attention to me and got away. Then I saw Mr. Rayneford on the opposite bank of the river. I thought it was Frank. I waved my handkerchief to him, but he did not respond. Then, after some hesitation, I walked back to the bridge, crossed, and went to the point where I saw Mr. Rayneford. But he was gone. I took the first train to Bath, intending to find Colonel Mordaunt, and Frank met me at the station as soon as the train arrived, and his first eager question showed me that he had not been to Clifton at all. He took me down to Mrs. Gordon's, where we always stopped when in Bath, and besought me to have patience and keep quiet only two days, when his scheme would be a grand success, and Haidee would be Mrs. Daltman. Then he left me. You came immediately afterwards, and Mr. Rayneford still later.

"When you left us, Mr. Rayneford told me he had witnessed the abduction, and had seen me also. He thought I had assisted in this atrocious act. I could only tell him that Frank had misled me, and that I had his promise, solemnly pledged, that no harm should follow. I did not mention Haidee's name, but he found it somehow. Who told you, Mr. Rayneford?"

Hyland pointed across the table.

"What! Hamish? How could he know?"

"Hyland had a picture," said Mr. Glendare, with precise enunciation, "and at the moment that Leigh's message reached me, telling me Haidee was lost, Hyland was showing the picture to me. He had some confused story about the picture—— Ha! Hyland! Are you ill?"

The question was induced by Mr. Rayneford's contortions of countenance. He was endeavouring to stop the even flow of Mr. Glendare's narrative by making faces at him that would have frightened a timid child into convulsions.

"It is nothing," answered Hyland. "We discovered together, Miss Carey, that Miss Mordaunt had been abducted. We both went to Bristol that night, and after all our investigation we found no certain clue. I did not mention Frank, because—for several reasons." (The chief reason was because he wished to strangle Frank with his own hands.) "Please resume your story."

"I came back here the next day," continued Miss Carey, "and on the second day I received a message from Frank, by telegraph, from Milford. He merely said he had found the lady, and she was safe and on her way to her father. On the next day I received a note from him. He was at Castledane. His note said his scheme was foiled by the officious interference of some sailor, who was assisted by a Hindoo. He was pushed into the sea, and his dress was so utterly ruined that he could not show himself to Haidee. Besides, the Hindoo would go directly to Colonel Mordaunt with the story. So he assumed the *rôle* of rescuer. And now he was courting in orthodox fashion. This was his last message. I could understand his reluctance to appear in soiled garments, as he has been more precise and old-maidish about his attire, all his life, than any woman of my acquaintance. He was a dandy when in short clothes. I never saw him otherwise than scrupulously neat.

"He sold his commission and had the money with him when he

sailed away the other night. He told uncle this on board the yacht. I think he must have had some success with Miss Mordaunt, as her picture was in his possession. Uncle saw it. It was taken on Clifton Downs, near the Observatory."

"Why, Hyland!" said Glendare, "there is some absurd mistake here! Frank certainly could not get *your* picture, and——"

"Bother the picture!" said Hyland, frowning like a thunder-cloud. "I never saw such a fellow! You were quite ready to rebuke me a moment ago for interrupting Miss Carey, and yet you have stopped her a dozen times with some rubbish about a confounded picture! Never mind him, Miss Carey, but proceed."

"I cannot proceed if I set you two to quarrelling," replied Mildred, eyeing the two keenly. "Pray, what is the picture you speak of with such vehemence?"

The two men sat in gloomy silence, glaring at each other across the table.

"Will one of you gentlemen oblige me with an answer?" said Mildred, composedly.

"Pardon me, Miss Carey," said Hyland. "Mr. Glendare meant to say—that there was a certain picture of mine, which he saw—er—which was taken on Clifton Downs, near the Observatory."

"And what has that to do with the picture Frank had?" she asked.

"Nothing. Only—that is—Miss Mordaunt had a copy—a kind of copy——"

"Bosh!" said Glendare. "Hyland, my dear boy, let *me* tell the story."

"Tell, then!" said Hyland, "but try to adhere to the truth!"

"Certainly!" responded Glendare; "nothing but the truth. And not all of that, if you object. It is very simple, Mildred. Mr. Rayneford was photographing the Observatory. Haidee was in the way, and her picture was taken. It was quite accidental. He was not trying to take the lady, but only the structure. It is unfortunately true that the picture of the lady was perfect, and as she was from three to ten feet nearer the camera than the structure was, it was a wonderful accident that made the focus just right. Perhaps Hyland can explain that! I am not a photographer."

"Pish!" said Hyland, impatiently; "what is the use of talking about matters you don't understand? You see, Miss Carey, the focus is changed by a single turn of a screw, and when I saw the lady in the foreground——"

"You just turned the screw?" said Glendare. "I thought so!"

"And this picture Frank had?" asked Mildred.

"Well. You must enquire of Mr. Rayneford," said Glendare, politely. "If he gave the picture to Frank, or to Haidee, he has not got it now, I suppose. If he has it now, I presume he can say so."

Hyland took the soiled picture from his pocket and unwrapped it. Mildred took it and walked to the bay-window, where the light was better.

"What a lovely girl!" she exclaimed. "This is the lady I saw on the Downs. Is it Haidee?"

"Yes," said Glendare. "Is that all, Hyland?"

"All what?"

"All the pictures you took?"

"I only took one picture."

"And this is it?" persisted Glendare.

"Yes. That is—that is taken from the one plate. You can take a hundred copies if you like from the one negative."

"But you took only this one?" said Mr. Glendare, gently.

"I usually take three or four copies. I did not count. I don't remember accurately how many I took. *That* is the picture Frank had, though."

"And the same you showed me at Bath?"

"Now, by this light!" said Hyland. "Excuse me, Miss Carey, but this fellow is like a whole swarm of wasps buzzing around one's ears! What possible difference can it make whether that is the solitary copy or one of a thousand?" And he rewrapped the picture and replaced it in his pocket, while his friend shook with merriment.

"There, old fellow!" he said, when he recovered his voice, "I will ask no more questions. Frank stole the picture, Mildred. I am sure of it. Haidee had it. She would never have given it to Frank, poor child!"

"Why not?" said Hyland, distrustfully; "why should she not? He was with her day after day, and no one to interfere with him. She did not know of his rascality."

"Ask yourself, Hyland!" replied Glendare, his eyes sparkling through his spectacles, as Mildred moved away. "How could a girl —a sweet girl like Haidee, with pure and noble instincts, and with quick perception of character—how could such a girl like *you* and Daltman at the same time?"

" Like me!"

" Yes, you owl! She believes in you to an unlimited extent. Many times in your absence, when Master Frank would insinuate something to your discredit, I have seen her flame up, and while her head was encased in those dismal wrappings, I have known her to fly at him and exterminate him with a sentence."

" How about Mr. Glendare?" said Hyland, with an effort.

" Mr. Glendare? What do you mean? Did I not tell you—— Here! I have not showed you Mr. Brentam's letter to me." And he gave Hyland the note.

" My dear Hamish," it ran, " I have had a long talk with Mildred. She will be your wife in due time. She has promised me. No other man has ever had her real affection. She may have had a passing fancy for another, but I am sure she would rather entrust her happiness in your hands——"

" By this light!" said Hyland, starting from his seat, " I must go! I am in no end of a mess! Do you know anything about trains, Hamish? You jolly old vagabond, let me hug you! I am just dying to go——"

" Go where?" said Mildred, returning. " Anything the matter?"

" Matter?" ejaculated Hyland, taking her hand and kissing it. " Ah, Mildred, I am miserable until—I left my overcoat!"

" Where? We can get you one. Hamish!——"

" Left at Castledane! No other will fit me. Can you let me off, just a few hours—and tell me how to go? I could walk!"

Mildred touched the bell.

" Tell the coachman to saddle Zephyr for Mr. Rayneford immediately." The footman disappeared. " Now, Mr. Rayneford, my mare is suffering for a gallop. She has not been out for six days. Take her to Taunton, and leave her at the King's Arms. It is near the station. Hamish, lend Mr. Rayneford an overcoat."

" With pleasure," said Glendare, rushing up-stairs.

" Dear friend!" said Hyland, " how can I repay you?"

" Bring the overcoat back with you," she answered, laughing, as Glendare came in with the garment on his arm.

" Bother the overcoat!" said Hyland, " but thank you all the same. I am roasting! Nights are cool though, you know! Here is Zephyr, by this light! Tell old Miles, dear friends——"

" If you should happen to see Haidee," said Glendare, while Hyland had his foot in the stirrup, " will you please deliver a message?"

" With pleasure! Fire away, old man! *Tempus fugit!*"

" Please tell her nothing but the want of an overcoat induced you to ride sixteen miles on horseback and far in the night by rail——"

" I'll be guided by circumstances," answered Hyland, mounting. " Miss Carey, I will ride gently. I have at least four hours. King's Arms. I'll not forget. Good-bye!"

There was a sore disappointment in store for Hyland. He reached Taunton in time and caught the last train. But ten miles from Taunton there was a most vexatious breakdown, and he spent several hours watching the repairs that seemed to drag along at snail's pace. The number of cheroots he turned into ashes was enormous. Then he found a passenger whose wife was ill, at the other end of the line, and who was half frantic at the delay. So he put his own disappointment in the background, and strove with earnest zeal to comfort the distressed man. And thus the hours glided by, until the train was once more in motion. It was after midnight. He wound his watch, and propping himself up in his corner he fell asleep, and dreamed of Juno with the great eyes, and called her Haidee.

CHAPTER LI.

TULWAR AND PICTURE.

WHEN Hyland reached Bath the sun was illuminating the house-tops. He obtained a vehicle and was driven out to the gates of Castledane, where he alighted and dismissed the driver. He felt a little shy as he walked up the green lane, as it was still quite early, and the breakfast hour was ten o'clock. If he could only see the housemaid or footman, he might slip quietly into his room and remove the travel-stains from his habiliments, and hunt for his—overcoat after breakfast. He was eager to see how Haidee would receive him. He had not gotten a glimpse of her at parting from these lovely scenes a week ago. Only a week! It seemed like a year to him. There is the mansion, just visible through the trees. There is Haidee's window, the sash open and the muslin curtains floating inward, swayed by the gentle breeze, redolent of sweet odours. " Peaceful be thy slumbers, sweet maiden." He will just walk under the window, with stealthy footstep, and blow a kiss through the curtains.

But there is a man stalking back and forth under the window. As he approached, this man faces him, flashing out his tulwar against the level rays of the sun, and saluting—military fashion.

"Salaam, sahib!" said the Hindoo. "Welcome! Sahib come. Guard relieved."

"Guard?" answered Hyland. "What can you mean, Zeba? Anything the matter? Everybody well?"

"All well," said Zeba. "Sahib say, 'keep guard,' and Zeba watch here every night. Sleep in day, when Beébe wake. When night come, and Beébe put out light, take tulwar and watch."

"This is very extraordinary!" said Hyland, meditating.

"When sahib drive away, say in Hindoostanee, 'Zeba guard all I love.' Then Zeba mount guard here."

"Thanks, friend! All right!" said Hyland, blushing. "I remember. Can I get in without disturbing the household? I mean to my room. See how dusty I am. Have been travelling all night."

"This door," answered Zeba. "Sahib find staircase through passage." And as the two departed the window-curtains were drawn aside and Haidee's glowing face saluted the orb of day.

The morning bell sounded about an hour earlier than usual, and while Hyland still doubted and examined the internal arrangements of his watch, the second bell rang. That meant breakfast. He went down to the drawing-room, meeting the colonel at the door.

"Welcome back, Hyland!" said his host, extending his hand. "Mary just informed me of your arrival. We shall have an earlier breakfast than usual. That restless little Haidee has some expedition on foot, and had me called at eight o'clock. Ah, here she is!"

Haidee, who had been waiting impatiently for Sir Hyland to get down-stairs, walked in, kissing the colonel and holding out her hand to Hyland. Her face had caught the sunlight, but her honest eyes met his bravely.

"I knew you had come," she said, simply, "and I ordered breakfast earlier. I am going to sketch the old castle, and I expect you to escort me, and take some views. Breakfast is served, papa. Come!" And she took Hyland's offered arm composedly, while he gazed around to discover where the flood of sunlight that filled the room came from.

There was a constant flow of conversation, as toast and muffins and chops melted away before Hyland's assaults. He had lived on cheroots since yesterday's luncheon. It was agreed between him and Haidee, who sat by his side, that Tommy should take them to Castle Dane, and with sketch-book under her arm, she took her seat in Timothy Holly's wagon at ten o'clock.

"How did you get away from Brentam Villa?" asked Haidee, as they started. "Annot wrote me yesterday that Miss Carey would not hear any suggestion——"

"I told her—I left my overcoat here," answered Hyland, "and she allowed me to come for it. You have the same dress on that you wore—when I took your picture."

"Yes," she answered. "I wore it on that account. Because you must take another. That one is lost."

"Lost!"

"Lost!" she said, sadly. "I am so sorry! I want another exactly like that."

"How did you lose it?"

"I don't know," she answered, with a troubled expression on her face. "I am not sure, but I think somebody stole it. I saw him with my portfolio——"

"Him?"

"Yes. Don't ask me. He is dead now, and I am trying to forgive him."

Hyland took the picture from his pocket and put it in her hands.

"It came to me from the sea," he said. "I was at Milford when the yacht was wrecked, or the next day, and his coat was found, and this in the pocket. It is not entirely spoiled. I have tried to restore it for you."

"And this is the only one you had?" said Haidee, shyly. "You do not care to keep it? I mean for the Observatory."

"There is one more—Beébe. May I call you Beébe? It means little lady, does it not?"

"Yes. Zeba gave me the name. But over there, at Nuttagur, you called me Haidee. You have never called me Haidee here."

"Tommy has stopped," said Hyland. "Let me help you down. Here is the castle. Haidee! How dare I call you Haidee? Over there you were a mere child, always suffering. I never saw your face but once, and then only your eyes. Poor child! How deeply did I pity you in those days! Let us sit down here."

"Yes. And you sent all the way from the mountains the remedy for my neuralgia. How kind of you!"

"But it did not cure you, Beébe."

"But it did, sir! Doctor Leigh said I should not take it. But I had your written directions. See! here is the paper. And I weighed the quinine myself and took it—and was cured. And I have never told it."

"Took it! Against the doctor's instructions!" said Hyland, aghast.

"Yes. Because Sir Hyland sent it," she answered.

"Sir Hyland?"

"Yes. You have always been Sir Hyland since you killed the tiger. Come! let us sketch that buttress——"

"Wait! Here is the other picture, Haidee. When I took it I did not know you. When I saw you on the bridge afterwards I did not know you. But when I looked at this picture I knew I loved you!——"

"May I keep it?" said Haidee, demurely.

"Keep it? Ah, no! All the wealth of the world could not buy it! When I am absent from you I look at this, and see in those beautiful eyes the calm, clear light of your pure soul. Do you know, Haidee, that those eyes enslaved me the day you bound up my wounded arm over there? Up in the mountains they haunted me by day and by night. And yet I never thought of you as my possible wife, but as the child Haidee, the martyr to an incurable ailment. When Doctor Connor told me of his drug, I was frantic with eagerness until I could convey the good tidings to you."

"And I should have taken it if all the doctors in India forbade me!"

"Then, when I heard you were coming to England, those eyes brought me after you. I was not much disquieted about Miles. But I longed for you! When I came, first, I heard Daltman was your suitor. And the picture was in his pocket!"

"He stole it, the wretch!" said Haidee, and then, remorsefully, "Poor Mr. Daltman!"

"Don't waste pity on the scoundrel!" said Hyland, with savage jealousy. "He is not dead. That sort of rascal don't die! We shall hear from him again."

"Why did you throw him into the sea?" said Haidee, suddenly. "Ah! I did not know you then! I thought you were the drunken old sailor. If you had only spoken then I should have gone with you and Zeba. Brave Zeba! He has been under my window every night—seven nights!"

"He was guarding my love!" said Hyland, kissing her hand.

"I heard you tell him, in Hindoostanee," replied Haidee, slyly, "and I hid. It was very bad Hindoostanee, too! And I heard you

talking with him this morning. I thought you might come, and I
was watching the lane. I saw you, sir!"

"Did you know how I loved you, Haidee?"

"Annot told me. Dear Annot! And you told me."

"When did I tell you?"

"At Clifton. In the Town Hall. Don't you remember?"

"I did not say——"

"Your eyes said everything! Papa told me a few days afterwards
that Mr. Glendare wanted me. It was all a mistake, I knew. So
I did not tell him you had spoken first."

"Oh, Haidee! my own darling——"

"When you killed the tiger—then I belonged to you. I said,
'This is Sir Hyland. My knight!' Juliet laughed at me when I
forgot and called you Sir Hyland. I never told any one—except
Annot. You know she is my own cousin. And she held me in
her arms and told me how you loved me. And she warned me not
to tell you that I should inherit Castledane. She said you Raynefords were prouder than the Mordaunts. I cannot tell you any more,
sir! That is the third time you have kissed me!"

"Forgive me!" said Hyland, penitently. "I did not know—
that is—I did not count. Just one more, and then I will never
offend again, until—oh, Haidee, my love! I am in constant
dread lest I should waken and find all this only a delicious
dream."

"Let us walk here," said Haidee, rising; "we can see Tommy.
May I have Tommy?"

"You own me, Haidee, and all that I own. Ha! I have lost a
hundred pounds, by this light!"

"Where? How? You have not been away from this buttress.
Let us look."

"No use, Beébe. I lost it at Nuttagur; at the base of the Observatory; out on the sea; among the breakers at Linton Sands. I
have not paid it yet. But I'll pay it anon. Before we face the
cold world again strengthen me for the encounter."

"I do not understand," she said, turning her big eyes to his.

"Do you not?" he answered. "Well, I mean let me kiss you
just once, and call me Hyland."

"Just plain Hyland?" she asked, doubtfully, while he took the
first part.

"Yes."

"Hyland! But I shall do it no more. Because you shall go

into Parliament and get your title. I don't want you to be Lord Rayneford. But you must be Sir Hyland. Will you do it?"

" Yes."

" And you give up India?"

" Yes."

" It is dreadful to be telling you all these secrets; but this is the last one, positively. When you went away from Nuttagur, with your arm bound up, you left Zeba. And I watched him while he recovered. He and I could talk Pracrit, and nobody understood that except Sista. And when she was asleep I made Zeba tell me many things about you. He told me how gentle you were, how kind to him. He was only sergeant, and all the white officers were rude to him. But he is a noble, and he is sensitive. He told me you had never wounded him, even by a contemptuous look or gesture. One day we were talking in the shadow of the bungalow, and I told him about knighthood and what I understood to be included in it. And I hinted that you were like the knights of my dreams. 'Beébe,' he said, 'I call these English sahib. They are the lords of the land, whether they are noble or not. There is only one sahib in India! It is Sahib Hyland.' Then he told me about the tulwar, and tried to draw it with his feeble arm. 'Hyland sahib was Lord of the tulwar. So long as the blade was bright Lord Hyland was well.' All foolish superstition, is it not?"

" Yes, darling. Certainly."

" Well, every day, and many times a day, I, poor Haidee, ailing, morose, and stupid, drew out the sword and examined the blade. So long as Zeba was near enough, I consulted the tulwar. And seven times a day in the past seven days I called my bodyguard to me, when no one else was near, and bade him present arms. This morning, when you came under my window, Zeba was only performing his customary duty, when he unsheathed his weapon and presented arms to you. But I did not see the bright blade to-day. I only saw you, my lord! And I knew you had travelled through the long night to come to me."

" Haidee! the devotion of my entire life——"

" Hyland sahib!" she answered; "give me the tulwar, and you may——"

" What, Haidee?"

" You may keep the Clifton picture."

CHAPTER LII.

L'ENVOI.

LETTERS came from Mr. Daltman before the Christmas holidays and while Haidee's honeymoon was still full. He was residing in New York, and gradually withdrawing his capital from consols and from his Essex estate, and was investing in various American enterprises. He wrote only to Miss Carey, but his letters were exhibited to Mrs. Rayneford, and it is highly probable that the Honourable Mr. Rayneford was acquainted with their contents also. There was a full and very truthful account of the abduction, with a confession of his motives and purposes. He intended to take Haidee out to sea, if necessary, and to force a marriage. Castledane was the chief attraction, he acknowledged, but he had also become fascinated more and more each time he encountered Haidee. He spoke in discontented tones of the stringency of English law, and boasted of the superior civilization of America, where such a small personal exploit could be easily rendered legal by the judicious application of money. Divorce laws were plenty, and, of course, there could be no difficulty about establishing a legal marriage. When Haidee read this passage, her teeth clicked together like the snap of a percussion-cap, and she privately meditated upon the propriety of sending Zeba and the tulwar to America to put the laxity of the laws to the proof.

Hyland quit Kant, Spinoza, and Compté, and took a course of reading upon mill management and finance. It was the constant boast of Brentam Mills, that no claim against the corporation that was a week old could be produced in the world. The scrutiny of the complicated accounts, the outlays for supplies, and the income from sales engrossed his attention three days in each month. As managing director he had to be mayor of the village, and being mayor he was commissioned as justice of the peace. Then there came a time when an address to the Crown had to be prepared and presented, and it was part of his official duty to write and present this important document in Downing Street. The consequence was knighthood, which he took from the sword of the prime minister. At this point Lady Rayneford protested against any advance in rank. He was legally Sir Hyland, and this was the summit of her ambition. But he unfortunately got into politics, and was returned to Parliament as member for the borough of which Brentam Mills was a part. And he has never been able to shake off these honours. Twice, and under different cabinets, he has been invited to accept a peerage, and Haidee now shakes her head less resolutely, as she watches the antics of Master Mordaunt Rayneford, aged ten, and reflects that the knightly title does not descend from father to son. She thinks Lord Castledane might still be plain Sir Hyland to *her.*

Juliet, the adopted daughter of Horace Mordaunt, and real daughter of a certain Major Landis, who died in India, inherited the London house under the colonel's will, together with enough rupees in various Indian stocks to make her independent, and also —to make her suspicious of all admirers. She still lives in single-blessedness. But a large part of her mansion is reserved for Sir Hyland and Lady Rayneford's frequent visits, and the amiable spinster is kept in perpetual terror lest the two boys, Mordaunt and Dane, should blow the walls out or the roof off at some unguarded moment.

Brentam Villa is closed during the summer, when Mr. and Mrs. Glendare are in the Highlands. In the winter they return to sweet Somerset, and at Christmas there is the regular reunion at Hawkley. Here Zeba is in his glory, with the boys of the various houses depending upon him for ghastly stories of Indian life, while another Beébe Haidee nestles in his lap, and promises to mature in all the loveliness of the original of the Clifton picture.

THE END.